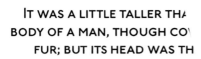

IT WAS A LITTLE TALLER THA
BODY OF A MAN, THOUGH COV
FUR; BUT ITS HEAD WAS TH

It wore armor of bronze and leather, a   ̣ps and discs with curious engravings, and carried a great black spear with a vicious point at each end.

Marish had heard that there were all sorts of strange folk in the world, but he had never seen anything like this.

"May you die with great suffering," the creature said in what seemed to be a calm, friendly tone.

"May you die as soon as may be!" Marish cried, not liking to be threatened.

The creature nodded solemnly. "I am Kadath-Naan of the Empty City," it announced. "I wonder if I might ask your assistance in a small matter."

Marish didn't know what to say to this. The creature waited.

Marish said, "You can ask."

"I must speak with . . ." It frowned. "I am not sure how to put this. I do not wish to offend."

"Then why," Marish asked before he could stop himself, "did you menace me on a painful death?"

"Menace?" the creature said. "I only greeted you."

"You said, 'May you die with great suffering.' That like to be a threat or a curse, and I truly don't thank you for it."

The creature frowned. "No, it is a blessing. Or it is from a blessing: 'May you die with great suffering, and come to know holy dread and divine terror, stripping away your vain thoughts and fancies until you are fit to meet the Bone-White Fathers face to face; and may you be buried in honor and your name sung until it is forgotten.' That is the whole passage."

"Oh," said Marish. "Well, that sound a bit better, I reckon."

—*Benjamin Rosenbaum, "A Siege of Cranes"*

TWENTY EPICS

ALL-STAR STORIES • BERKELEY, CA & BASEL, SWITZERLAND

TWENTY EPICS

edited by
David Moles & Susan Marie Groppi

ALL★STAR STORIES

BERKELEY, CALIFORNIA, USA

BASEL, SWITZERLAND

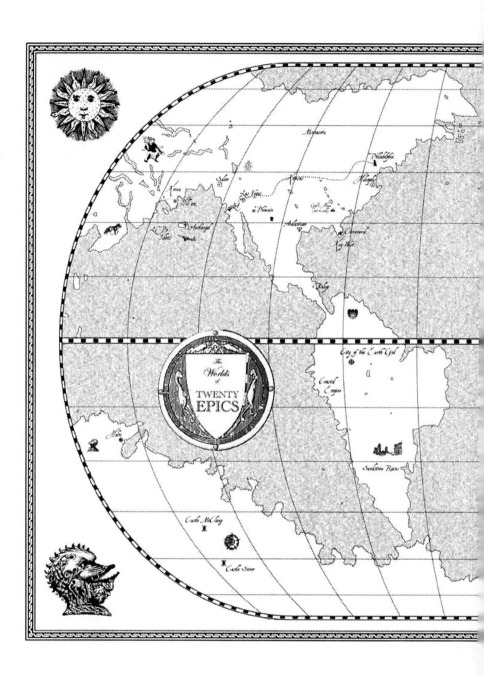

The Worlds of TWENTY EPICS

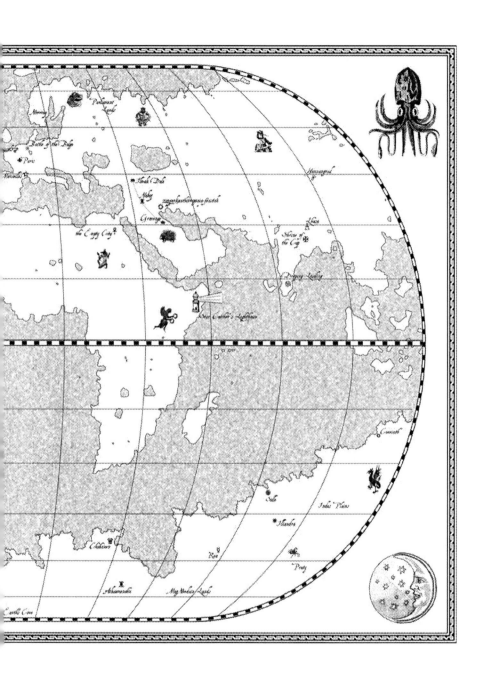

INTRODUCTION

I<small>N THE SPRING OF</small> 2004, <small>THE</small> M<small>INNEAPOLIS PUBLISHING COOPERATIVE KNOWN</small> as the Ratbastards published a slim blue volume called *Rabid Transit #3: Petting Zoo*. In it, among other things, was a story, or an article, or a monograph, called "How to Write an Epic Fantasy," by a Canadian writer named David Lomax.

On the surface it was innocent enough, presenting itself as advice, particular advice, perhaps from one writer to another, on the crafting of a particular story. But when read by a sufficiently suggestible reader,[1] it accomplished a curious trick. Through a kind of *déjà vu* it managed to evoke, in only a handful of pages, the whole of the larger work, a work that had existed nowhere outside the imagination of Mr. Lomax . . . but that now existed also, albeit in a distinct and independent form, in the imagination of the reader. Like the *Essential History* in Paul Park's *A Princess of Roumania*, "How to Write an Epic Fantasy" was larger on the inside than on the outside.

This accomplishment posed an obvious question.

Because we used to like epics. We used to invest untold hours in those big fat fantasy series, those brick-thick novels full of unpronounceable naming schemes, gender-segregated magic systems, color-coded conceptions of absolute good and absolute evil. But somewhere along the way, they lost their charm. When it takes ten or twenty years for a writer to finish a series, writing the same book over and over again, dragging on and on, piling up the foreshadowing, wearing out characters' boots to no

---

[1] In this case, your editor Mr. Moles.

good purpose, writing stories that just *don't end*—they rob the stories of any real passion or power or epic grandeur.

And that's what it's really about. It's not about the pewter tankards, the saucy wenches, the rough woolen cloaks; it's not about the vengeful gods, the cryptic wizards, the farm boys with inexplicably great destinies; it's not about the magic rings and rune-swords and jeweled coronets, the greaves and pauldrons and destriers. It's about grandeur.

There's a place in our hearts that used to be stirred by tales of heroism and discovery, creation and destruction, sin and redemption and catastrophe, love and high adventure. The question posed by "How to Write and Epic Fantasy" is: What does it take to reach that place?

We've collected our authors' answers here.

David Moles & Susan Marie Groppi
Basel, Switzerland & Berkeley, California
May 2006

CONTENTS

TWO FIGURES IN A LANDSCAPE
BETWEEN STORMS

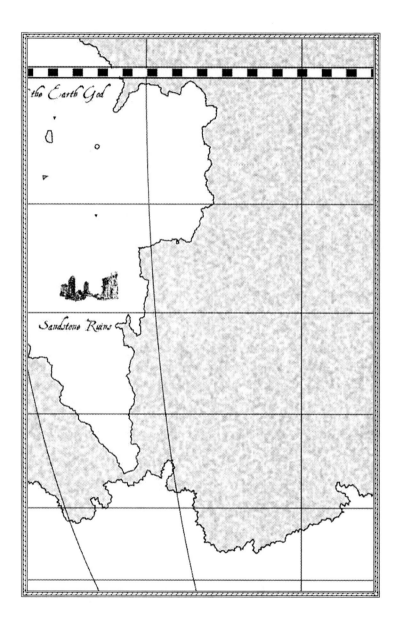

TWO FIGURES IN A LANDSCAPE
BETWEEN STORMS
BY CHRISTOPHER ROWE

THE BUILDINGS, THE TUMBLED STONES, THE GROUND, THEY ARE ALL SAND-
stone. Blasted, pockmarked sandstone. Great blocks are tumbled and
thrown about. The colors of the bloodstains run from near-black along
one wall to a darkening brown beneath his shoulders and thighs to the
violent, living red running from her forehead and mouth.

His gauntleted hand lies inches from her bare left foot. Deep furrows
scar the rock beneath his fingertips, the tracks of his last attempt, his
final angry clawing.

His body is a bulk of metal and muscle. The firelight and the sunlight
playing across it are distorted by greasy smoke.

His armor is red and black, damaged. The plate at the right shoulder
hangs by a frayed strap. Her target. The white bone stands out against
the black metal.

His helmet is stylized angles and nightmare shapes, horned mantids.
It still covers his head, twisted now at an unnatural angle. The visor is
shoved against the ground. A froth of blood has swelled through the
vents.

A scabbard lies discarded beside him. It is empty, but ornately decorated. Silhouettes have been inlaid along its length by a careful craftsman. Women, men, children, engines of war. The silhouettes do not
march the whole distance from open end to gilded close. There would
have been room for her portrait.

One end of the weapon is embedded in a slumped wall. Its flanges

3

and vanes, a complexity of barbs, glower through the dust and smoke. The heavy, tooled shaft stretches across his body, the cruel weight of it pressed against her thigh.

Calmly, she sits. Her hands, nails trimmed short, fingers stained with potter's clay, grip the weapon so tightly.

The torn rags of her tunic are muddy with a mixture of blood and dust and sweat and sand. Her muscled shoulders and midriff and legs are exposed, revealing testaments: scars, burns, bruises, welts, blisters, stretch marks, wounds.

Strands of hair that have escaped from their band are soaked to her forehead. Her broad face is still. Her flecked green eyes are unblinking. There is nothing behind her eyes.

Finally, movement. A shadow. The light from the sun and the fires delineates a shadow falling across a ruin of sandstone. A large shadow, the head a mantid nightmare. Her hand grips so tightly. ✪

CUP AND TABLE

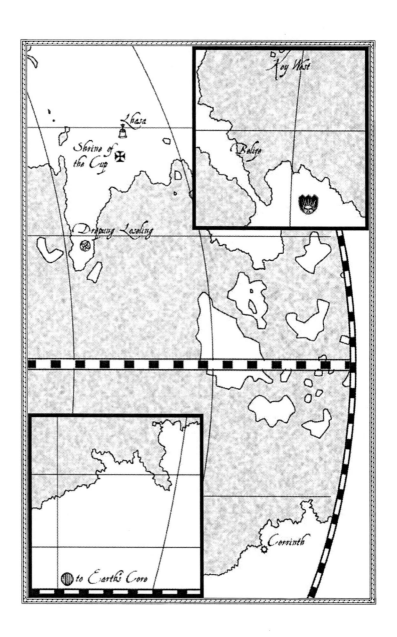

CUP AND TABLE
BY TIM PRATT

Sigmund stepped over the New Doctor, dropping a subway token onto her devastated body. He stepped around the spreading shadow of his best friend, Carlsbad, who had died as he'd lived: inconclusively, and without fanfare. He stepped over the brutalized remains of Ray, up the steps, and kept his eyes focused on the shrine inside. This room in the temple at the top of the mountain at the top of the world was large and cold, and peer as he might back through the layers of time— visible to Sigmund as layers of gauze, translucent as sautéed onions, decade after decade peeling away under his gaze—he could not see a time when this room had not existed on this spot, bare but potent, as if only recently vacated by the God who'd created and abandoned the world.

Sigmund approached the shrine, and there it was. The cup. The prize and goal and purpose of a hundred generations of the Table. The other members of the Table were dead, the whole *world* was dead, except for Sigmund.

He did not reach for the cup. Instead, he walked to the arched window and looked out. Peering back in time he saw mountains and clouds and the passing of goats. But in the present he saw only fire, twisting and writhing, consuming rock as easily as trees, with a few mountain peaks rising as-yet-untouched from the flames. Sigmund had not loved the world much—he'd enjoyed the music of Bach, violent movies, and vast quantities of cocaine—and by and large he could have taken or left

7

civilization. Still, knowing the world was consumed in fire made him profoundly sad.

Sigmund returned to the shrine and seized the cup—heavy, stone, more blunt object than drinking vessel—and prepared to sip.

But then, at the last moment, Sigmund didn't drink. He did something else instead.

But first:

Or, arguably, later:

Sigmund slumped in the back seat, Carlsbad lurking on the floorboards in his semi-liquid noctilescent form, Carlotta tapping her razored silver fingernails on the steering wheel, and Ray—the newest member of the Table—fiddling with the radio. He popped live scorpions from a plastic bag into his mouth. Tiny spines were rising out of Ray's skin, mostly on the nape of his neck and the backs of his hands, their tips pearled with droplets of venom.

"It was a beautiful service," Sigmund said. "They sent the Old Doctor off with dignity."

Carlsbad's tarry body rippled. Ray turned around, frowning, face hard and plain as a sledgehammer, and said, "What the fuck are you talking about, junkie? We haven't even gotten to the funeral home yet."

Sigmund sank down in his seat. This was, in a way, even more embarrassing than blacking out.

"Blood and honey," Carlotta said, voice all wither and bile. "How much of that shit did you snort this morning, that you can't even remember what day it is?"

Sigmund didn't speak. They all knew he could see into the past, but none of them knew the full extent of his recent gyrations through time. Lately he'd been jerking from future to past and back again without compass or guide. Only the Old Doctor had known about that, and now that he was dead, it was better kept a secret.

They reached the funeral home, and Sigmund had to go through the ceremony all over again. Grief—unlike sex, music, and cheating at cards—was not a skill that could be honed by practice.

The Old Doctor welcomed Sigmund, twenty years old and tormented by visions, into the library at the Table's headquarters. Shelves rose everywhere like battlements, the floors were old slate, and the lights were ancient crystal-dripping chandeliers, but the Old Doctor sat in a folding chair at a card table heaped with books.

"I expected, well, something *more*," Sigmund said, thumping the rickety table with his hairy knuckles. "A big slab of mahogany or something, a table with authority."

"We had a fine table once," the Old Doctor said, eternally middle-aged and absently professorial. "But it was chopped up for firewood during a siege in the 1600s." He tapped the side of his nose. "There's a lesson in that. No asset, human or material, is important compared to the continued existence of the organization itself."

"But surely *you're* irreplaceable," Sigmund said, awkward attempt at job security through flattery. The room shivered and blurred at the edges of his vision, but it had not changed much in recent decades, a few books moving here and there, piles of dust shifting across the floor.

The Old Doctor shook his head. "I am the living history of the Table, but if I died, a new doctor would be sent from the archives to take over operations, and though his approach might differ from mine, his role would be the same—to protect the cup."

"The cup," Sigmund said, sensing the cusp of mysteries. "You mean the Holy Grail."

The Old Doctor ran his fingers along the spine of a dusty leather-bound book. "No. The Table predates the time of Christ. We guard a much older cup."

"The cup, is it here, in the vaults?"

"Well." The Old Doctor frowned at the book in his hands. "We don't actually know where the cup is anymore. The archives have . . .

deteriorated over the centuries, and there are gaps in my knowledge. It would be accurate to say the agents of the Table now *seek* the cup, so that we may protect it properly again. That's why you're here, Sigmund. For your ability to see into the past. Though we'll have to train you to narrow your focus to the here-and-now, to peel back the gauze of time at will." He looked up from the book and met Sigmund's eyes. "As it stands, you're almost useless to me, but I've made useful tools out of things far more broken than you are."

Some vestigial part of Sigmund's ego bristled at being called broken, but not enough to stir him to his own defense. "But I can only look back thirty or forty years. How can that help you?"

"I have . . . a theory," the Old Doctor said. "When you were found on the streets, you were raving about gruesome murders, yes?"

Sigmund nodded. "I don't know about *raving,* but yes."

"The murders you saw took place over a hundred years ago. On that occasion, you saw back many more years than usual. Do you know why?"

Sigmund shook his head. He thought he *did* know, but shame kept him from saying.

"I suspect your unusual acuity was the result of all that speed you snorted," the Old Doctor said. "The stimulants enabled you to see deeper into the past. I have, of course, vast quantities of very fine methamphetamines at my disposal, which you can use to aid me in my researches."

Sigmund said, "Vast quantities?" His hands trembled, and he clasped them to make them stop.

"Enough to let you see *centuries* into the past," the Old Doctor said. "Though we'll work up to that, of course."

"When I agreed to join the Table, I was hoping to do field work."

The Old Doctor sniffed. "That business isn't what's important, Sigmund. Assassination, regime change, paltry corporate wars—that's just the hackwork our agents do to pay the bills. It's not worthy of your gifts."

"Still, it's what I want. I'll help with your research if you let me work in the field." Sigmund had spent a childhood in cramped apartments and hospital wards, beset by visions of the still-thrashing past. In those dark rooms he'd read comic books and dreamed of escaping the prison of circumstance—of being a superhero. But heroes like that weren't real. Anyone who put on a costume and went out on the streets to fight crime would be murdered long before morning. At some point in his teens Sigmund had graduated to spy thrillers and Cold War history, passing easily from fiction to nonfiction and back again, reading about double- and triple-agents with an interest that bordered on the fanatical. Becoming a spy—that idea had the ring of the plausible, in a way that becoming a superhero never could. Now, this close to that secret agent dream, he wouldn't let himself be shunted into a pure research position. This was his chance.

The Old Doctor sighed. "Very well."

"What's it like?" Carlotta said, the night after their first mission as a duo. She'd enthralled a senator while Sigmund peered into the past to find out where the microfilm was hidden. Now, after, they were sitting at the counter in an all-night diner where even *they* didn't stand out from the crowd of weirdos and freaks.

Sigmund sipped decaf coffee and looked around at the translucent figures of past customers, the crowd of nights gone by, every booth and stool occupied by ghosts. "It's like layers of gauze," he said. "Usually I just see the past distantly, shimmering, but if I concentrate I can sort of . . . shift my focus." He thumped his coffee cup and made the liquid inside ripple. "The Old Doctor taught me to keep my eyes on the here-and-now, unless I *need* to look back, and then I just sort of . . ." He gestured vaguely with his hands, trying to create a physical analogue for a psychic act, to mime the metaphysical. "I guess I sort of twitch the gauze aside, and pass through a curtain, and the present gets blurrier while the past comes into focus."

"That's a shitty description," Carlotta said, sawing away at the rare steak and eggs on her plate.

The steak, briefly, shifted in Sigmund's vision and became a living, moving part of a cow. Sigmund's eyes watered, and he looked away. He mostly ate vegetables for that very reason. "I've never seen the world any other way, so I don't know how to explain it better. I can't imagine what it's like for you, seeing just the present. It must seem very *fragile."*

"We had a guy once who could see into the future, just a little bit, a couple of minutes at most. Didn't stop him from getting killed, but he wet himself right before the axe hit him. He was a lot less boring than you are." Carlotta belched.

"Why haven't I met you before?" Sigmund shrank back against the cushions in the booth.

"I'm heavy ordnance," Carlsbad said, his voice low, a rumble felt in Sigmund's belly and bones as much as heard by his ears. "I've been with the Table since the beginning. They don't reveal secrets like me to research assistants." Carlsbad was tar-black, skin strangely reflective, face eyeless and mouthless, blank as a minimalist snowman's, human only in general outline. "But the Old Doctor says you've exceeded all expectations, so we'll be working together from time to time."

Sigmund looked into Carlsbad's past, as far as he could—which was quite far, given the cocktail of uppers singing in his blood—and Carlsbad never changed; black, placid, eternal. "What—" *What are you,* he'd nearly asked. "What do you do for the Table?"

"Whatever the Old Doctor tells me to," Carlsbad said.

Sigmund nodded. "Carlotta told me you're a fallen god of the underworld."

"That bitch lies," Carlsbad said, without disapproval. "I'm no god. I'm just, what's that line—'the evil that lurks in the hearts of men.' The

Old Doctor says that as long as one evil person remains on Earth, I'll be alive."

"Well," Sigmund said. "I guess you'll be around for a while, then."

The first time Carlsbad saved his life, Sigmund lay panting in a snow-bank, blood running from a ragged gash in his arm. "You could have let me die just then," Sigmund said. Then, after a moment's hesitation: "You could have benefited from my death."

Carlsbad shrugged, shockingly dark against the snow. "Yeah, I guess."

"I thought you were *evil*," Sigmund said, light-headed from blood loss and exertion, more in the *now* than he'd ever felt before, the scent of pines and the bite of cold air immediate reminders of his miraculously ongoing life. "I mean, you're *made* of evil."

"You're made mostly of carbon atoms," Carlsbad said. "But you don't spend all your time thinking about forming long-chain molecules, do you? There's more to both of us than our raw materials."

"Thank you for saving me, Carlsbad."

"Anytime, Sigmund." His tone was laid-back but pleased, the voice of someone who'd seen it all but could still sometimes be pleasantly sur-prised. "You're the first Table agent in four hundred years who's treated me like something other than a weapon or a monster. I know I scare you shitless, but you *talk* to me."

Exhaustion and exhilaration waxed and waned in Sigmund. "I like you because you don't change. When I look at most people I can see them as babies, teenagers, every step of their lives superimposed, and if I look back far enough they disappear—but not you. You're the same as far back as I can see." Sigmund's eyelids were heavy. He felt light. He thought he might float away.

"Hold on," Carlsbad said. "Help is on the way. Your death might not diminish me, but I'd still like to keep you around."

Sigmund blacked out, but not before hearing the whirr of approaching helicopters coming to take him away.

"I'm the New Doctor," the New Doctor said. Willowy, brunette, young, she stood behind a podium in the briefing room, looking at the assembled Table agents—Sigmund, Carlotta, Carlsbad, and the recently-promoted Ray. They were the alpha squad, the apex of the organization, and the New Doctor had not impressed them yet. "We're going to have some changes around here. We need to get back to basics. We need to find the *cup*. These other jobs might fill our bank accounts, but they don't further our cause."

Ray popped a wasp into his mouth, chewed, swallowed, and said, "Fuck that mystic bullshit." His voice was accompanied by a deep, angry buzz, a sort of wasp-whisper in harmony with the normal workings of his voicebox. Ray got nasty and impatient when he ate wasps. "I joined up to make money and get a regular workout, not chase after some imaginary Grail." Sigmund knew Ray was lying—that he had a very specific interest in the cup—but Sigmund also understood why Ray was keeping that interest a secret. "You just stay in the library and read your books like the Old Doctor did, okay?"

The New Doctor shoved the podium over, and it fell toward Ray, who dove out of the way. While he was moving, the New Doctor came around and kicked him viciously in the ribs, her small boots wickedly pointed and probably steel-toed. Ray rolled away, panting and clutching his side.

Sigmund peered into the New Doctor's past. She looked young, but she'd looked young for *decades*.

"I'm not like the Old Doctor," she said. "He missed his old life in the archives, and was content with his books, piecing together the past. But I'm glad to be out of the archives, and under my leadership, we're going to make history, not study it."

"I'll *kill* you," Ray said. Stingers were growing out of his fingertips, and his voice was all buzz now.

"Spare me," the New Doctor said, and kicked him in the face.

By spying on their pasts and listening in on their private moments, Sigmund learned why the other agents wanted to find the cup, and see God:

Carlotta whispered to one of her lovers, the shade of a great courtesan conjured from an anteroom of Hell: "I want to castrate God, so he'll never create another world."

Ray told Carlotta, while they disposed of the body of a young archivist who'd discovered their secret past and present plans: "I want to eat God's heart and belch out words of creation."

Carlsbad, alone, staring at the night sky (a lighted void, while his own darkness was utter), had imaginary conversations with God that always came down, fundamentally, to one question: "Why did you make me?"

The New Doctor, just before she poisoned the Old Doctor (making it look like a natural death), answered his bewildered plea for mercy by saying, "No. As long as you're alive, we'll *never* find the cup, and I'll *never* see God, and I'll *never* know the answers to the ten great questions I've composed during my time in the archives."

Sigmund saw it all, every petty plan and purpose that drove his fellows, but he had no better purpose himself. The agents of the Table might succeed in finding the cup, not because they were worthy, but simply because they'd been trying for years upon years, and sometimes persistence led to success.

Sigmund knew their deepest reasons, and kept all their secrets, because past and present and cause and effect were scrambled for him. The Old Doctor's regime of meth, cocaine, and more exotic uppers had ravaged Sigmund's nasal cavities and set him adrift in time. At first, he'd only been able to *see* back in time, but sometimes taking the Old Doctor's experimental stimulants truly *sent* him back in time. Sometimes it was just his mind that traveled, sent back a few days to relive past events again in his own body, but other times, rarely, he physically traveled back, just a day or two at most, just for a little while, before being wrenched back to a present filled with headaches and nosebleeds.

On one of those rare occasions when he traveled physically back in time, Sigmund saw the Old Doctor's murder, and was snapped back to the future moments before the New Doctor could kill him, too.

Ray ate a Sherpa's brain two days out of base camp, and after that, he was able to guide them up the crags and paths toward the temple perfectly, though he was harder to converse with, his speech peppered with mountain idioms. He developed a taste for barley tea flavored with rancid yak butter, and sometimes sang lonely songs that merged with the sound of the wind.

"We're going to Hell," the New Doctor said.

"Probably," Sigmund said, edging away.

She sighed. "No, really—we're going into the underworld. Or, well, sort of a visiting room for the underworld."

"I've heard rumors about that." Hell's anteroom was where Carlotta found her ghostly lovers. "One of the Table's last remaining mystic secrets. I'm surprised they didn't lose that, too, when they lost the key to the moon and the scryer's glass and all those other wonders in the first war with the Templars."

"Much has been lost." The New Doctor pushed a shelf, which swung easily away from the wall on secret hinges, revealing an iron grate. "But that means much can be regained." She pressed a red button. "Stop fidgeting, Sigmund. I'm not going to kill you. But I do want to know, how did you get into the Old Doctor's office and see me kill him, when I *know* you were on assignment with Carlsbad in Belize at the time? And how did you disappear afterward? Bodily bilocation? Ectoplasmic projection? What?"

"Time travel," Sigmund said. "I don't just see into the past. Sometimes I travel into the past physically."

"Huh. I didn't see anything about that in the Old Doctor's notes."

"Oh, no. He kept the most important notes in his head. So why aren't you going to kill me?"

Something hummed and clattered beneath the floor.

"Because I can use you. Why haven't you turned me in?"

Sigmund hesitated. He'd liked the Old Doctor, who was the closest thing he'd ever had to a father. He hated to disrespect the old man's memory, though he knew the Old Doctor had seen him as a research tool, a sort of ambulatory microfiche machine, and nothing more. "Because I'm ready for things to change. I thought I wanted to be an operative, but I'm tired of the endless pointless round-and-round, not to mention being shot and stabbed and thrown from moving trains. Under your leadership, I think the Table might actually *achieve* something."

"We will." The grinding and humming underground intensified, and she raised her voice. "We'll find the cup, and see God, and get answers. We'll find out why he created the world, only to immediately abandon his creation, letting chaos fill his wake. But first, to Hell. Here." She tossed something glittering toward him, a few old subway tokens. "To pay the attendant."

The grinding stopped, the grate sliding open to reveal a tarnished brass elevator car operated by a man in a cloak the color of dust and spiderwebs. He held out his palm, and Sigmund and the New Doctor each dropped a token into his hand.

"Why are we going . . . down there?" Sigmund asked.

"To see the Old Doctor, and get some of that information he kept only in his head. I know where to find the cup—or where to find the map that leads to it, anyway—but I need to know what will happen once I have the cup in hand."

"Why take me?"

"Because only insane people, like Carlotta, risk going to Hell's anteroom alone. And if I took anyone else, they'd find out I was the one who killed the Old Doctor, and they might be less understanding about it than you are." She stepped into the elevator car, and Sigmund followed.

He glanced into the attendant's past, almost reflexively, and the things he saw were so horrible that he threw himself back into the far corner of the tiny car; if the elevator hadn't already started moving, he would have pried open the doors and fled.

The attendant turned his head to look at him, and Sigmund squeezed his eyes shut so that he didn't have to risk seeing the attendant frown, or worse, smile.

"Interesting," the New Doctor said.

After they returned from Hell, Sigmund and the New Doctor fucked furiously beneath the card table in the Old Doctor's library, because sex is an antidote to death, or at least, an adequate placebo.

"That's it, then," the New Doctor said. "We're going to the Himalayas."

"Fucking great," Ray said. "I always wanted to eat a Yeti."

"I think you're hairy enough already," Carlotta said.

Sigmund and the New Doctor sat beneath a ledge of rock, frigid wind howling across the face of the mountain. Carlsbad was out looking for Ray and Carlotta, who had stolen all the food and oxygen and gone looking for the temple of the cup alone. They wanted to kill God, not ask him questions, so their betrayal was troublesome but not surprising. Sigmund probably should have told someone about their planned betrayal, but he felt more and more like an observer, outside time—a position which, he now realized, was likely to get him killed. He needed to take a more active role.

"Ray and Carlotta don't know the prophecy," Sigmund said. "Only the Old Doctor knew, and he only told *us*. They have no idea what they're going to cause, if they reach the Temple first."

"If they reach the Temple first, we'll die along with the rest of the world." The New Doctor was weak from oxygen deficiency. "If Carlsbad doesn't find them, we're doomed." She looked older, having left the safety of the library and the archives, and the past two years had been hard. They'd traveled to the edges and underside of the Earth, gathering fragments of the map to the temple of the cup, chasing down the obscure references the New Doctor had uncovered in the archives. First they'd gone deep into the African desert, into crumbling palaces carved from sentient rock; then they'd trekked through the Antarctic, looking for the secret entrance to the Earth's war-torn core, and finding it; they'd projected themselves, astrally and otherwise, into the mind of a sleeping demigod from the jungles of another world; and two months ago they'd descended to crush-depth in the Pacific Ocean to find the last fragment of the map in a coral temple guarded by spined, bioluminescent beings of infinite sadness. Ray had eaten one of those guardians, and ever since he'd been sweating purple ink and taking long, contemplative baths in salt water.

The New Doctor had ransacked the Table's coffers to pay for this last trip to the Himalayas, selling off long-hoarded art objects and dismissing even the poorly-paid hereditary janitorial staff to cover the expenses. And now they were on the edge of total failure, unless Sigmund did something.

Sigmund opened his pack and removed his last vial of the Old Doctor's most potent exotic upper. "Wish me *bon voyage*," he said, and snorted it all.

Time unspooled, and Sigmund found himself beneath the same ledge, but earlier, the ice unmarked by human passage, the weather more mild. Moving manically, driven by drugs and the need to stay warm, he piled up rocks above the trail and waited, pacing in an endless circle, until he heard Carlotta and Ray approaching, grunting under the weight of stolen supplies.

He pushed rocks down on them, and the witch and the phage were knocked down. Sigmund made his way to them, hoping they would be crushed—that the rocks would have done his work for him. Carlotta was mostly buried, but her long fingernails scraped furrows in the ice, and Sigmund gritted his, cleared away enough rocks to expose her head, and finished her off with the ice axe. She did not speak, but Sigmund almost thought he saw respect in her expression before he obliterated it. Ray was only half-buried, but unmoving, his neck twisted unnaturally. Sigmund sank the point of the axe into Ray's thigh to make sure he was truly dead, and the phage did not react. Sigmund left the axe in Ray's leg. He turned his back on the dead and crouched, waiting for time to sweep him up again in its flow.

Carlsbad found Ray and Carlotta dead, and brought back the supplies. By then Sigmund was back from the past, and while the New Doctor ate and rested, he took Carlsbad aside to tell him the truth: "There's a good chance we might destroy the world."

"Hmm," Carlsbad said.

"There's a prophecy, in the deep archives of the Table, that God will only return when the world is destroyed by fire. But it's an article of faith—the *basis* of our faith—that when the contents of the cup are swallowed by an acolyte of the Table, God will return. So by approaching the cup—by *intending* to drink from it—we might collapse the probability wave in such a way that the end of the world begins, fire and all, in the moments before we even touch the cup."

"And you and the New Doctor are okay with that?"

"The New Doctor thinks she can convince God to spare the world from destruction, retroactively, if necessary."

"Huh," Carlsbad said.

"She can be very persuasive," Sigmund said.

"I'm sure," Carlsbad replied.

The fire began to fall just as they reached the temple, a structure so old it seemed part of the mountain itself. The sky went red, and great gobbets of flame cascaded down, the meteor shower to end all others. Snow flashed instantly to steam on all the surrounding mountains, though the temple peak was untouched, for now.

"That's it, then," Carlsbad said. "Only the evil in you two is keeping me alive."

"No turning back now," the New Doctor said, and started up the ancient steps to the temple.

Ray, bloodied and battered, left arm hanging broken, stepped from the shadows beside the temple. He held Sigmund's ice axe in his good hand, and he swung it at the New Doctor's head with phenomenal force, caving in her skull. She fell, and he fell upon her, bringing the axe down again and again, laying her body open. He looked up, face bruised and swollen, fur sprouting from his jaw, veins pulsing in his forehead, poison and ink and pus and hallucinogens oozing from his pores. "You can't kill me, junkie. I've eaten wolverines. I've eaten giants. I've eaten *angels*." As he said this last, he began to glow with a strange, blue-shifted light.

"Saving your life again," Carlsbad said, almost tenderly, and then he did what the Table always counted on him to do. He swelled, he stormed, he smashed, he tore Ray to pieces, and then tore up the pieces.

After that he began to melt. "Ah, shit, Sigmund," he said. "You just aren't *evil* enough." Before Sigmund could say thank you, or goodbye, all that remained of Carlsbad was a dark pool, like a slick of old axle grease on the snow.

There was nothing for Sigmund to do but go on.

"The cup holds the blood of God," the Old Doctor said. "Drink it, and God will return, and as you are made briefly divine by swallowing the substance of his body, he will treat you as an equal, and answer questions, and grant requests. For that moment, God will do whatever you ask." The Old Doctor placed his hand on Sigmund's own. "The Table exists to make sure the cup's power is not used for evil or trivial purposes. The question asked, the wish desired, has to be worth the cost, which is the world."

"What would you ask?" Sigmund said.

"I would ask why God created the world and walked away, leaving only a cupful of blood and a world of wonders behind. But that is only curiosity, and not a worthy question."

"So anyway," Sigmund said, sniffing and wiping at his nose. "When can I start doing field work?" He wished he could see the future instead of the past. He thought this was going to be a lot of fun.

The cup in Sigmund's hands held blood, liquid at the center, but dried and crusted on the cup's rim. Sigmund scraped the residue of dried blood up with his long pinky fingernail. He took a breath. Let it out. And snorted God's blood.

Time *snapped.*

Sigmund looked around the temple. It was white, bright, clean, and no longer on a mountaintop. The windows looked out on a placid sea. He was not alone.

God looked nothing like Sigmund had imagined, but at the same time, it was impossible to mistake him for anyone else. It was clear that God was on his way out, but he paused, and looked at Sigmund expectantly.

Sigmund had gone from the end of the world to the beginning. He was so high from snorting God's blood that he could see individual atoms in the air, vibrating. He knew he could be jerked back to the top of the ruined world at any moment.

Sigmund tried to think. He'd expected the New Doctor to ask the questions, to make the requests, so he didn't know what to say. God was clearly growing impatient, ready to leave his creation forever behind. If Sigmund spoke quickly, he could have anything he wanted. Anything at all.

"Hey," Sigmund said. "Don't go." ✪

HAVE YOU ANY WOOL

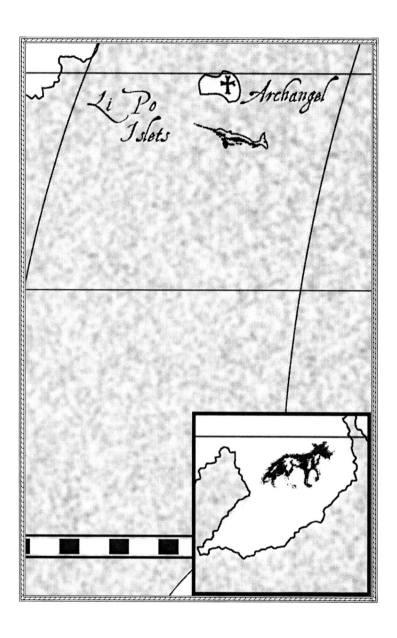

Li Po
Islets

Archangel

HAVE YOU ANY WOOL
BY ALAN DENIRO

YOU KILLED YOUR FIRST WOLF WHEN YOU WERE FIFTEEN. YOU WERE A CABINER aboard the *Queen's Gambit Declined,* a cutter that wended among the Li Po islets. The craggy shorelines were always curtained in cold fog. The fog would whisper about a dead past. The archipelago wasn't safe for trappers and fishers. Cutters tried to make them safe. The thought of families settling down, building homes and living amidst the shoals and tall firs, was ludicrous to you. You understood that most of the worlds were unassailable to civilization.

You served meals, cleaned guns, inventoried supplies. But that wasn't why the crew tolerated you, and the captain prized you.

Queen's Gambit Declined had a guardian. A shepherd, if you will. A narwhal that the crew had nicknamed Jetty—but you knew that its real name was Arborfeint. An intuition of yours, that name. You had a concord with Arborfeint, spoke in its tongue, transmitted the creature's scrimmed language back to the captain. It was unclear why the narwhal tagged along, but one thing was clear—it hated wolves, and told you so in prophetic tones. When it spoke to you of wolves, it would thrash furiously in the icy water and its spiraled horn would, to your eyes, burn bright in the whitecaps. When you squinted into the waves, you weren't entirely sure what was real and what was not.

The crow-boy noticed with his binoculars a freshly ruined settlement, in a frail clearing about a half-kilometer into the interior of a nearby island. It was called Archangel. It was still smoldering; the wolf tracks

27

would be fresh. Some might have even still been rummaging through the supplies, trying to figure out what they could use.

You were surprised when the captain requested your presence on the reconnaissance. She ignored the hue and cry and chose only two others, twins named Pasiphae and Kyrie from New Scythia, who were ambidextrous and good with alien knives. The captain trusted them, and apparently trusted you too.

Arborfeint skittered around the gray rowboat as it was lowered from the *Queen's Gambit Declined,* into the chop and salt of the tide. The twins began rowing. The quartz-strewn coast of Archangel swarmed with legions of black flies large as your thumbnail. Thousands of black thumbnails hovered. You could see them a ways off, sparkling like coal, waiting for you, so you cinctured your cloak tighter.

You were fifteen, after all.

The War With Wolves revolved around a series of metonymous parallaxes and chiads. The contours of the conflict, over the course of ninety years and more than fifty worlds both within the Parameter and without, were more lyrical than narrative. The reckoning of casualties, however brutal, was always a graceful disaster. For example, five thousand telepaths in the destruction of New Scythia pulled their minerva cloaks tighter to create a planet-wide song, *and still perished.* The destruction of worlds was antecedent to the lamentation of that destruction. The territories mattered less than the maps.

This is not an implication that the lyric imagination is somehow less cruel, less taxing, or less demanding of its participants than a narrative turn of mind. Perhaps the opposite is true. The truth has to wallow in the obscure recesses of peoples' hearts in order to be seen as truth.

That is a hard burden for those whose parents and children die. Yet these were the wolves' terms. The Parameter and its allies were forced to abandon what it thought it knew, and embrace what it had no way of ever knowing, if it had any hopes of survival.

The shepherds warned of this, spoke of these frayed contingencies. The shepherds, to an extent, protected their sheep.

The wolves, however, had only two uses for sheep—slaughter or wool.

It didn't surprise you all that much when Arbor transmuted into an owl. Suddenly the owl was there. It made sense. Your journey into the unknown interior was slotted for wood, not water. No one saw it happen, not even you. The captain was skeptical about your claim, and the twins were skittish. The four of you followed a threadbare trail towards Archangel's knoll. But the owl swooped and kept close by, and told you about the ravaged encampment, down to the minute details: where the shadows fell, what the rancid wolverine pelts, knotted and hard like armor, smelled like. The captain was astonished at the level of significant detail you provided: the turgid poetry of surroundings you couldn't see. You were too frightened to acknowledge the compliment. Arborfeint told you that there were live wolves, four of them, rooting through the smokehouses and the corpses for tech to destroy.

Why didn't you tell the captain this? She trusted you. Were the wolves already fettering you out with their enchantments? Unclear. It was hard to think in those breakneck conditions. Galleons of mist descended as the stony ground steepened. The twins coughed in unison. Ahead, you heard the flapping of Arbor's wings. The captain stopped and pointed, drew a flintlock with her other arm. A dirty, orange smudge of campfires. A sunset's ashes.

You tried to open your mouth to tell your companions of the danger, of the no-doubt pounce.

A wolf, you knew, was not a wolf in the way people used to think of wolves. The resemblance was minimal. The wolves you knew were much more dangerous. The name, however, stuck when people living in the archipelagos realized they were prey, hearkening back to childhood stories of predators that might have been right, might have been wrong. It was hard to tell. Wolves—the old wolves—were crafty yet vague memories from a faraway place.

These wolves, like memories, were also spirited and tricky and from a faraway place.

The captain shook down her fiery locks, started to creep towards the ruins. The twins charged, knives slicking.

Then the tenebrae came. You shouted. The owl dove to save you.

Wolves are not the wolves of popular imagination and nursery rhymes and genome reclamation parks. They, like shepherds, were created from archipelagos of perceptions.

Cryptic and nonemotive, yet drawn to humankind, shepherds make interstellar travel possible by surrounding spaceships that accelerate to ten percent of the speed of light, transporting those ships through wherespace to worlds that proved ideal for human settlement. Three worlds, Li Po, Mirabai, and Blake, discovered in a time when politicians foolishly let poets name planets. The false taxonomy of "shepherd" proved convenient, pacifying.

Only telepaths—rare, carefully culled and protected—could share concord with shepherds, guide them to destinations across light-years, but even they were never able to glean all that much from the inscrutable syntaxes of shepherds.

It was more, or less, benign. Less because the Parameter realized, when it accidentally made contact with another alien race that the shepherds were also shuttling between wholly different, discrete worlds, that the shepherds were keeping their flocks separate. Black sheep from the white? Hard to tell. Hard to know until the dam burst open, until the shepherds were caught in their bluff and relented their secrets. More than three hundred other sentient species were found to be using the shepherds as free passage to interstellar pastures. A panoply. Everything thought of as right before was wrong.

The analogy proved useful in another way. Shepherds, the human ones from antiquity, lived in houses, not in the fields. Their inner lives were unknowable to sheep. And yet they offered protection from wolves.

Wolves. They started creeping along the fringes of inhabited space soon after the other spacefarers were stumbled upon.

It was on the fine edges between cognita and incognita that the wolves began conducting war, although this too was something of a misnomer made a nomer by necessity. Like shepherds, wolves required no space-ships to travel vast distances across both herespace and wherespace. Like shepherds, they took diaphanous forms. Some speculated that they were fallen shepherds, similar to what happened in Christian legend to some of the angels. The main difference was that the wolves could take corporeal form, shapeshift and speechshift, to whatever they desired. It was unclear, exactly, what they desired, but when they descended on the Thane Moon Triage—their first invasion—the lights on those satel-lites turned blue and extinguished. The wolves dropped from the sky, released their tenebrae, forced settlers into the structures of their own myths and tragedies (in this instance, a combination of Bluebeard and Great Flood motifs), and started devouring whatever transpired. Wolves bent reality to shapes of storybooks, what transpired beneath the covers of half-buried iconographies.

Warily, spacefarers roused and girded themselves for the sparring, having no idea what they were getting into.

You ducked. A clot of muck caught in your mouth. The smoky breath of the wolves, like ghosts propelled from a cannon, shot towards your crew. Realms of potential harm were thrust upon you. Arborfeint's talons snatched away the tenebrae arcing towards your face like an octopus tentacle. The smoke shriveled. Pasiphae fell sideways, gripping her arm, which had turned into a heron, which in turn was very confused and frightened regarding the graft, and started stabbing Pasiphae's neck with its beak. Kyrie sliced at a tendril and ran to her sister.

You heard the retort of the captain's gun crystallize and then shatter the air. For an instant, you could see what was underneath the world you knew—gray dull rock, no wolves, smooth silver guns instead of muskets. But that passed. Covering your ears, still in your crouch, you saw her shrug off a dying tenebrae that tried to necklace around her. She started running towards the encampment.

No, you shouted, but she didn't hear you. Had your chance to change, to warn her, passed? Arborfeint fended off the remaining wisps, but the twins were lost, draping each other, their bodies a menagerie of birds and snails. Canary chicks burst from Kyrie's eyes. You tried to hold back vomit, and didn't do a very good job at it. Retching, you stumbled to their corpses, which bubbled over with small baronies from the animal kingdom, animals that you remembered from stories. You slid a knife from each of the twins' holsters. One blade was jade and the other turquoise. You saw a dual reflection of your face from the weapons' faces.

Arborfeint landed on your shoulder for a bare instant, and in that moment of contact it told you that the captain was ten seconds from ambush. It was quiet. Arbor alighted. You began running, churning your legs through the fog that wanted to wall you.

The ground tilted on a wild axis and you plunged into the encampment. A gun boomed and pitched. A strand of a lullaby could be heard above the din.

There were more than three hundred spacefaring species. Each species had hundreds of cultures, which meant that there were hundreds of thousands of myths and tales that the wolves fed upon. They were relentless predators upon the once-upon-a-time. They made tactile the golden idylls of fireside, the half-drowsed words sinking into children's ears. They attacked childhoods as much as children, altering topographies into allegories. Once, a pack of wolves transmuted the polar icecaps of Mirabai: the frost into frosting and the ice into gingerbread and it all fell down.

What surprised humans most was that every species had stories, and fought fiercely to keep their stories unrazed. Except for the shepherds, of course, none were immune, not even the species that appeared most austere. The urge for stories was a requirement for sentience. Those tales might have been expressed in magnetic resonances of spheres rearranged on a sea-plain; or books in the form of gourds, droplets of heavy water, or cairns of plankton floating in a methane sea. But the forms mattered less than the tellings told over and over.

After decades of defeat, and hundreds of planets turned into wreckages of folklore eaten from the inside out, it was stumbled upon that the only way to defeat the wolves was to tell more stories, not less. Never less.

Your hearing returned as you saw her fall. The owl was a snake now. A giant garter. A few bodies—gray, almost indistinguishable from a nimbus—skittered around her. They had to have been wolves. One of the wolves was on the ground next to the captain. The wolf looked like it was burning from a gun-hole. The gun was whispering a story. The encampment was topsy-turvy. One of the wolves was eating a metal axe in the shadow of a spruce, blade first. It was hard to get a good look at them, all of them at once, and maybe that was fortunate. Maybe they looked like the trappers they killed, only with more of a blur.

It was gray and dark around you, like you were wading inside fur. But you didn't care. You shouted and your knives rose in the aquamarine eighth of a rainbow. All of the remaining wolves were crouching around the captain, and saying something backwards. One, with a pockmarked face that seemed to be collapsing in on itself, grabbed her palm and licked it. This seemed like appropriate behavior for a wolf. The captain's skin shriveled. Silver writing—no, strings of numbers—appeared on the palm. That was the one you cut first, slicing its ear, a gray apricot dropping to the ground.

As the other wolves started toward you, voices rising in volume—the gun was dying, its voice was fading—Arborfeint, who you had forgotten about for a few seconds, entwined around the wolf closest to you. The left knee. For some reason Arbor, in snake form, knew exactly where to apply pressure. It was a tender place. Your jade knife slashed upwards into its belly. Silver coins spilled out. The remaining wolf straggled away, at a zigzag, hauling its companion—the one the captain felled—by the shoulder. They could give themselves strong shoulders if they wanted them.

You stabbed and stabbed the wolf that you and Arbor had swarmed upon. Its eyes turned to bits of glass, smooth children's marbles. Its neck was a pillow stitched with a tiny unicorn. You hit and hit the wolf until it expired. Arbor sidewinded away.

The captain, whom you had thought dead, coughed and put a hand on your shoulder.

The fog, itching for territory, closed back again.

Then, in the cloudcover, the feinting wolves closed back again. You heard them when it was too late.

Slowly, folklorists and anthropologists took to the front lines. They analyzed what the wolves had transformed. They developed applications of technology that would counter the warping of space-time according to the morphologies of folktales. They would be sheep in wolves' clothing, becoming participants in whatever fantasies the wolves would devise, and then stealthily alter them for tactical advantages. If the wolves mutated a pod settlement into a pastoral scene replete with carillon castles and fair damsels, Parameter shocktroops might become knights, or even trolls. Small groups roaming the symbolic terrain were better. Surprisingly, the shepherds took an active role in these panoplies, plunging themselves into roles of "magical" agents. Sometimes other spacefaring species would integrate themselves onto a planet, in order to confuse the wolves, who are not always adept at interspecies archetypes.

The tide turned. And yes, it is still turning. Nothing is certain, however.

The Parameter and its allies are not sure that it is enough. We tell people on the front lines, when they face impending doom at the hands—or other culturally appropriate appendages—of a wolf, there is one thing that might save them, sometimes. Only sometimes: recite or sing the earliest story you remember. Even if you don't know all of the words, it may help. But wolves are aware of these tricks, and more pour in from wherespace every year. More flesh-and-blood beings step into fables, armed with raconteur guns that shoot encoded, everchanging narratives, encased in super-light. It is one of the few things the wolves cannot stand: being shown, by a superior story, that their imaginations *aren't really that interesting.*

You don't remember which one put its clammy lips around your neck, with a suddenness that took your breath away. Perhaps all of them did. The marrow of your life began sucking out of you, replaced with a nonsense scramble that was on the verge of disconnecting you. You started humming a ward to counter their jabber: *baa baa black sheep have you any wool, yes sir yes sir three bags full, one for my master, and one for my dame, and one for the little boy who lives down the lane.* The captain had no way of knowing what grandmother or aunt taught you that.

As you died, your hair became black as night, and curly, and taut. As you died, you heard Arborfeint shrieking. It was a wolf now, Arbor was an animal, something from a rift of myth. A wolf pouncing on wolves. The captain tried to drag herself away. You didn't have a neck anymore. You mumbled the word *wool* over and over until you fell, each of the sky's stars puncturing the cloudcover like a cookie cutter.

Stories are not just stories. To use a metaphor—as if there is any other way to tell this—if tales are streams coursing down a mountain, then there is always the fish churning upstream against the current, back to the wellspring. There is always the bit of black inside the white, the flaw in the perfect carpet—even the ones that rise from the ground and coast to the crescent moon. There are always knots and tangles in what seems to be the plainest string.

For example, the common nursery rhyme about black sheep was actually a cruel little ditty about taxation, about shepherds having to divvy up what they thought was theirs alone. There were always codes. It was better to sing it sweetly and openly in a meadow, and teach it to children, rather than muttering about the kings-of-things in the alehouse.

The wolves—and I don't know whether they can be called malicious, even after everything they have done—understand this, even when they kill. They enclose us with open arms. They have big teeth that encompass solar systems. They have every capacity to eat us. But there's no celestial axeman to bail us out. We can only save ourselves by the stories we tell, by the pitch and heft of words, how they cleave us. Each of us has the capacity to mend or destroy, speak or shut up. Clever stories will make us more clever. Each of us has enough wool, more than enough to save us.

Captains come and go, but this one lived. She lived and didn't necessarily know whether she deserved it. Arborfeint left; the guardian had no more interest in *Queen's Gambit Declined.* The captain never blamed it and never saw it again. The crew was restless but glad to see the captain alive. She was unable to tell her story to anybody for a long time.

Queen's Gambit Declined, under her steady hand, still hunted wolves, analyzed their stories and forged counterstrikes accordingly. Even in the midst of awful violence, she liked the woods, the seawater, the fog. But the altered landscapes lacked some of their old luster; it became more and more of a simulacrum for her. There was one contingency, however, that kept her going, kept her countermanding the wolves' stories.

You might not have died. She consoled herself with that. It was hard to know whether anyone actually *died* from wolves, or just moved to a different place, to a kingdom where stories were told over and over again and people never had to wither and expire. But it was hard to know, for you, whether dying itself was only a matter of moving to another place. She didn't think so, but had no way of knowing. There never was a way of knowing. Perhaps on the edge of islands, the Ultima Thule, with bone white palm trees and palms, she will come across you again, calling to the waves. Maybe you will have a few black lambs for company, for sweaters.

Until then, she will tell the story of how you were lost. She will tell her crew, and anyone else who would listen, of your courage. "You killed your first wolf when you were fifteen," the captain would begin, staring off into space, navigating the ship. "You were a cabiner aboard the *Queen's Gambit Declined,* a cutter that wended among the islets of Li Po," she would continue, charting her descent into war-ravaged ports, to hear if there have been stories, rumors even, of your return. ✪

THE END OF THE ROAD FOR HYBETH AND GRINAR

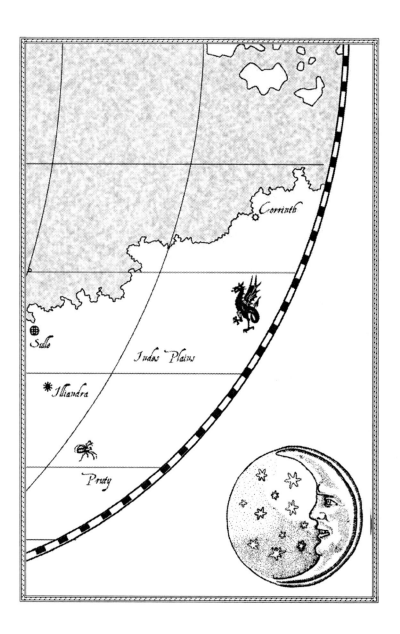

THE END OF THE ROAD FOR
HYBETH AND GRINAR
BY RACHEL MCGONAGILL

IN THE LAST ROOM OF A VAST DUNGEON BELOW THE IMMORTAL CITY OF COR-
rinth, Hybeth braced herself. The susurrus of a nearby fountain calmed
her. Red-flowered ivy wound through the balustrades of the balcony
above, and down the winding marble staircase. She and Grinar had
found, at last, the source of the sun's light, the truth of bedroom eyes,
and the rush of waterfalls, all in one. Two thousand days, it had taken
them, through deserts and caverns and over lost plains, but the journey
was well worth the price. They had found him.

The Pleasure Seeker stood before them. White robes enveloped him,
and he held out his hands. "My children," he said. "What do you wish
of me?"

Grinar snorted. "Pleasure, natch."

Hybeth looked sidelong at her partner of fourteen years and shook
her head. He had no sense of subtlety whatsoever. She ached from their
long journey and, in truth, wanted nothing better than to get out of her
grimy clothes, peel off the weight of leather greaves and her padded
shirt and soak in a bath for a month or two. But if the Seeker wanted,
she could play along. "Indeed, Seeker. It is our hope you will gift us with
that for which you are famous."

"Really?" The Seeker raised a golden eyebrow. "None has ever truly
wanted my service before."

Grinar gaped at him; Hybeth reached over and gently lifted his chin.
"Why?"

41

"The truest pleasure is not mine to offer, but lies beyond the Mountain of Mud, guarded by the dragon Oceagrin."

Hybeth sighed. More traipsing around. But the result would quicken their blood and send their souls heavenward, so it would be worth it, right? She looked at Grinar, and he at her. He was as handsome to her now as he had been when they first met, but his narrow face showed lines of age around his eyes. Though he was still lean and strong, it took him longer to get out of bed first thing in the morning.

He winked at her and turned back to the Seeker. "So, where's this bleeding mountain?"

The Seeker laughed softly. "I cannot tell you that, but if you will go to the dark folk beyond the crystal veil, and let them know you are looking, then perhaps they—"

"We've already seen the bloody dark folk. Look, are you leading us on now or what?" Grinar's face reddened, and his mustaches puffed out with the heat of his breath.

"Grinar . . ." Hybeth started, but he gave a low growl, and she fell silent.

"We've been at this daft quest for six years now. Six years. Do you know how many forests we've crossed, how many folk, dark and otherwise, we've chatted it up with, just to get here?"

With a smile, the Seeker nodded. "I have somewhat of an idea, yes. The trials may be many, but the reward—"

"Bollocks to that!" Grinar drew his sword, the famed blade Exotenth, which had shone from its lofty place above the throne of the Gwellin folk of the Indes Plains. Grinar had won it from them in a champion-battle against their strongest warrior, so that he and Hybeth could get the next clue as to the Seeker's location. That had been over a year ago. "We're not leaving here until you give us what we've come for. We know you've got it, so hand it over."

"I cannot. You haven't been blessed by the Poppy King of Sulle, he who rules beyond the Habber Lakes, and past the desert of—"

"Yes, we bloody have! I tell you, Seeker, we'll have no more of your games. Gives us the reward. Right now."

The Seeker shook his head slightly, and looked as if to open his mouth to give them yet another delay, yet more mountains and barriers to cross, but Grinar stepped toward him rather ominously, and he blanched. "You have the famed sword Exotenth, it is true. I . . . I'll see what I can do."

"That's more like it," Grinar said, and though he did not sheath his sword, he did lower the point. He looked at Hybeth. "See, I told you he could be reasoned with."

Hybeth glanced at him. Perhaps.

The Seeker left the chamber in a flow of white. Hybeth wasn't fond of white robes; too many dangerous types wore them in an attempt to put their supplicants off guard, those who thought white was only for good, black for bad. Still, the Seeker had agreed to cooperate, at least a little. Maybe Grinar was right about his constant show-of-force-wins-the-day routine.

Grinar put Exotenth away soon after, for the power of its shine dimmed if too long from its sheath, unless the blade was put to some actual killing purpose. Moments later, something scraped by Hybeth's left ear. She turned, but found nothing.

"What is it?" Grinar asked.

She shook her head. "I thought I heard something."

"What?"

"I don't know." Her shoulders tensed, for the feeling was familiar as old stone, and she searched her mind for memory. Grinar looked forbidding, as though now was the time to make a scene, so she brushed her hand to the side. "It was nothing."

When they had waited half the day, with Grinar growing more and more impatient, a man in a green cloak entered and touched his fingers to his forehead as he bowed. "May I escort you to the Chamber of Breath?" he asked.

"Uh, sure," Grinar told him. His hand gripped Exotenth's hilt. "Lead on."

Hybeth dogged Grinar's heels as they traversed the hallway, and descended a long set of spiral stairs. Thousands of feet had ground the stone down. Torches flickered in brackets above their heads, and the smell of burning pitch filled the air.

Light rippled on the walls, but as they walked, the torches were placed farther and farther apart, leaving patches of darkness. In each patch, a chill wind blew upon Hybeth's neck, making her shiver. But this was no worse than the tunnels of Abingion. There they'd gone for days with no light at all, only to be dumped out at exactly the same point as where they walked in. They'd had to begin the whole trip again. This was nothing.

When their guide reached the bottom of the steps, his green cloak caught the lip of the torchlight and flared, just for a moment, in a hue of bright colors like a chameleon, before fading back to green. Hybeth caught Grinar's gaze, and asked him what he thought in a single cock of her head. Grinar shrugged and stepped after the guide, and Hybeth had nothing to do but to follow.

It was pure darkness, now, like in Abingion, darkness that crept along her skin like spiders. She hated spiders, had hated them ever since Pruty, when the giant arachnids had caught Grinar—before he'd gotten his sword—and she'd had to cut him free while thousands of baby spiders crawled all over her and into every orifice. The memory made her shiver, again.

"Gri—" she started, wanting to tell him she was thinking this was a very bad idea, but he shushed her, and his hand came to rest on her shoulder. She *hoped* it was his hand. They stopped, and he whispered, "Do you hear anything?"

"No."

"Exactly. Our guide's slipped us. Bastard. I'm gonna gut that Seeker if it's the last thing—"

"Let's just get out of here." Hybeth put her own hand out and felt for the wall where it had been. Her hand touched nothing. "Grinar? I can't find the wall."

"Huh? Oh, bollocks. We should be able to just turn around and find our way out."

"Yeah." She gripped his shoulder. "Ready?"

"Mm-hm. One, two, three." The two of them turned a one-eighty, ending up on each other's opposite side. "Remember the tunnels, Hy. Don't jostle."

Hybeth nodded, then realized Grinar couldn't see her. "I remember." In the tunnels, they had messed up more than once, since whenever either of them bumped the other, they changed from a straight line to more of an angle, and they'd gone down a side corridor instead of straight on. They'd learned the hang of it, eventually. Hybeth was careful now, and the two of them walked for a good while before Grinar said, "It didn't work."

"What didn't?"

"The turning about bit. We're off course."

"How do you know?"

"I counted steps after we passed the last torch. You remember how we got past the Demon Ifraver of Inoppin."

"Yeah . . ." Hybeth cursed herself for forgetting that basic and time-honored strategy. But she'd been busy worrying about spiders. "How many was it?"

"Hundred eighty-three. Give or take for your strides."

"So your count might be off then, if we were taking shorter steps?"

"Yeah, but I figured that in. We've gone back two hundred and twenty steps. We've messed up somewhere."

"Buzzard dung."

"Yeah." Grinar squeezed her shoulder. "But, on the other hand, there's bound to be an exit *somewhere*, so we can try a few alternatives before we call it quits."

Call it quits. That's what Grinar called dying an ignoble and pointless

death. Not "starving to death," or "freezing to death," or "being eviscer-
ated by the Rewert Beast of Thromin and having your guts hung 'round
your neck while you're paraded through the streets of Ming." No. Calling it quits. As if they always had a choice about it.

"Hy, you're tensing up. Breathe out now."

Hybeth tried shrugging off Grinar's hand, but he wouldn't let go.
Damn, she knew she shouldn't get separated under conditions like this,
but she just wanted to be alone. Except not in the dark. So she let his
hand stay on her shoulder, and compromised by turning her head away
from where he stood.

"So . . ." she said, trying to sound casual. "You think we should turn
around again?"

"Nah. The place is obviously magical."

"How about Exotenth?"

"Hm?"

"Your sword. It lights up every time we *don't* want it to, how about
you make it shine here, so we can see?"

Grinar gave Hybeth's shoulder another squeeze. "For a little while,
Hy." He drew the sword in a quick movement, and held it high. The blade
flickered for a moment, letting them see the vast blackness around them
before fading to a dull glimmer. "Better than nothing," Grinar said.

"Not much."

Grinar swung the blade experimentally. "At least I can tell we're—"
His jaw dropped for the second time that day.

"We're what?" Hybeth asked.

"We're not alone." With a chin nod, Grinar indicated the space directly
behind Hybeth. She didn't want to turn around, and yet she did. Drawing her own special blade—the name of which she hadn't shared with
Grinar, since it was fairly pretentious for a little dagger than wasn't much
to look at no matter how well it cut—Hybeth looked to see what had
made Grinar gape. When she did, she, too, was awestruck.

A large throne of gold—it had to be gold, what else were thrones made of when they glinted like that?—sat not a dozen paces away. In the throne, dangling one leg over the arm and sipping a cup of wine, was none other than Rubinok the Great. They had met this joker when sailing the Odgett Sea, after the Storm of a Thousand Sails. Rubinok had hidden aboard and been found as a stowaway, but when the captain tried to dump him over the side, he'd pleaded for leniency, promising treasures so vast the captain—though he and everyone else were sure it was mere trickery to let him live—spared him. True to his word, though, Rubinok had led them to a cave filled with gold and gems and necklaces formed of perfect pearls, and then he—and all the loot—had vanished from sight.

Days of hunting had not unearthed the thief, and so Hybeth and Grinar had continued their own trek, none the richer. And now, here he was.

"Comfy?" Grinar asked.

Rubinok pushed a shock of black hair out of his eyes and shrugged. "Mostly. Why? You got an interest in my throne?"

Grinar growled, low in his throat. "You've got some nerve—"

"More than that. I've got a pile of treasure. What I don't have, though, is a way out of this dragon dunghole."

Hybeth stepped toward him. "How long have you been here?"

"Longer than you, I guess."

"Just answer the damn question."

Rubinok smiled. "Since the day I got the treasure of the cave. I'd made a deal to escape that day, and all it got me was a one-way trip to this pit. Some deal. Never make a bargain with a white-robed man, that's what I say."

"No kidding." Grinar rubbed at his chin. "So, the Seeker brought you here, and you've been a prisoner for what, a half year or so?"

"Has it been so long?"

"Mm-hm. What've you been eating? You don't look starved."

"I'm not. I found this chest, behind the throne, and every little while, I open it and there's food inside. And wine." He slugged down the rest of his cupful. "It's not bad."

Hybeth stared at him. "You drink wine, and eat food from a magic trunk? Are you crazy?"

"Nearly. It's awful tedious here. And if I didn't eat and drink that stuff, I'd be dead already, so I figure it's safe."

"Haven't you tried to get out?" Hybeth just couldn't make the ideas fit. When one was imprisoned, one escaped. Simple. She and Grinar had done it so many times, it was routine. But Rubinok looked back at her with his dark eyes, and she saw more than a hint of insanity lurking in their depths. How long had he sat on his pilfered throne, just *waiting?*

He stood up suddenly. "Of course I tried to get out. I'd gotten out of much worse, hadn't I? Nearly fed to sharks in that storm, for one. I've never seen a cavern so vast as this, or so . . ."

"Dark?" Grinar supplied.

"Yeah." Rubinok sighed and swept his hair back again. "It's a pit."

"How'd you see the trunk?" Hybeth asked him.

"Huh?"

"It's dark, you can't see. But you found the trunk, you said. How?"

"She's a wily one," Rubinok said, giving Grinar a sly grin. "Too bad I didn't steal her, too."

Hybeth wanted to slug him, but while Grinar growled an oath beside her, she only asked, "How?"

"Magic scepter." Rubinok stretched behind his throne and pulled out a rod as long as his arm. Jewel encrusted and gold, it shone in the light of Grinar's sword. Rubinok shook it twice, and an amethyst near its filigreed top glowed, letting out a soft, purply light.

"Neat trick." Grinar moved closer to see the scepter, and Rubinok shrank back. Grinar bared teeth at him in a grin. "I'm not gonna swipe it. Some people around here *aren't* thieves."

"I knew that," Rubinok said. "But you can never be too careful."

"Of what? If I'd wanted to kill you for trinkets, I would've done it already."

"Trinkets? Trinkets!" Rubinok shook the scepter at Grinar. The amethyst brightened. "I spent the better part of four *years* chasing after this booty. Trod over deserts, through underground complexes so twisty you'd need a minotaur to get out. And what do I get for my troubles? Stuck, that's what. At least I have my treasure, though. Edmorian lost the Orb of Vash—"

"What's that?" Grinar asked, leaning closer.

"The Orb of Vashini? I though everyone knew what it was. The Gods of Illiandra once cast down the star—"

"Bag it. I know the legend. Who's this bloke Edmorian?"

"Oh." Rubinok settled back into his throne and waved his scepter. "He's another one here. Found the Orb, brought it to the wizard who was supposed to keep it safe from the Illiandran Gods, and he was led down here instead. He's not the worst, though. There's a pretty lass, name of Gwythia, who made a deal with this same wizard that when she reached the Hills of Antiquilla and sounded the Horn of the Fathers, she would get eternal life. Instead, when she blew it, she ended up here, and the Horn had aged her. Still looks good, but she's a little old for my tastes."

"So all these questors and treasure seekers are here, in this cavern?"

"Yeah. Weren't you listening?"

Grinar turned to Hybeth. "Someone's been up to no good at all."

"True enough. How do we make him pay?"

"One quest at a time." He smiled. "You know that. First we need to get out of here."

Hybeth smiled back, despite herself. "Has anyone seen the Seeker, the white-robed man, since they were trapped here? Does he ever come down into the depths?"

"Nah. I guess we're just too low for him to care about anymore, now that we're trapped." Rubinok leaped from his throne, went behind it and lifted a creaky lid. Hybeth heard a splashing sound, then Rubinok returned, full cup of wine in hand. "Sure you don't want any?"

"Not yet." Grinar stroked his hand along the hilt of Exotenth, his brow furrowed in thought. "Do you have anything else magical besides the scepter?"

"I don't know, I haven't really had the chance to try."

"Haven't had the chance! You've been stuck down here for half a year. What else were you doing? Practicing your swordsmanship?"

Hybeth put a hand on Grinar's arm, and he calmed some, but Rubinok had curled into his chair, taking the scolding like a child.

"It's dark. I don't like the dark."

"I don't see—"

"Grinar," Hybeth said softly. "I don't like the dark either." She shrugged and tried to look brave, though fear grew like a hole in the pit of her stomach. The walls were closing in on her, though she couldn't see them. She could feel their malevolence, like a curse. She realized then what she had suppressed, about walls, and stone, once something had scraped through her mind upstairs. Stone held memories, and things carved from stone—walls, floors, altars—held memories of things done on or near them. When the concentration of stone was greater than normal—in caves and tunnels, for instance, or underground—Hybeth could hear it, feel its memories. She had always been able to, but she did not like it one bit. "It's creepy."

"What's creepy is the Seeker kidnapping a load of questors and making a mockery of everything we stand for," Grinar said, but his tone was gentle.

"What're we going to do about it, then?"

"Good question. First we need to get organized. Rubinok, where are the rest of them?"

Time passed oddly in the dark. Hybeth wasn't sure if hours had passed or days before they were able to gather. Some of them, like Rubinok, seemed apathetic about the mission. Hybeth wondered if it was the wine and food he ate from the chest, or maybe his fear of the dark. Her own fear mobilized her to get out of the situation, but what if she had been imprisoned for a year or more?

More than a score of waylaid questors finally gathered. At first, Hybeth wondered if they would argue for the rest of eternity about who would call them to order. Grinar's stentorian voice won out. Besides, he and she were the most recently captured, and thus could provide the most untainted idea of how to get out of the Seeker's clutches.

"What we need to do is explore all of this chamber—"

"Been done," a woman interrupted. She looked around at the others. "I mean, we're adventurers, aren't we? Me and Tallis got here next before you, and we looked for doors and portals, and mapped out what we could."

"Well, then. Let's have that map."

"It won't do you any good. We had a hard time drawing anything to scale." She paused. "And we couldn't really find walls, so much."

"No walls."

"Not as you'd expect, no." The woman pushed her way forward, and Hybeth looked her up and down. In the purplish light of the scepter, her cheeks were hollow, and her hair—likely strawberry blond in regular light—was a dark red wine. Muscled legs showed under leather breeches, and she carried a well-used sword by her side. She held up a roll of paper. "The best we could get, under the circumstances. We marked steps around and around, marked a few places with pebbles—I keep a supply for just this sort of thing. We realized the walls change, and what there are of them are soft, like crusted bread."

"We'll have to work with that," Grinar said, and held out his hand. After a moment, with a sigh, the woman gave him the map. "Anyone have the ability to track? I mean magically," he continued, when about a dozen raised their hands, "since we're obviously dealing with magic walls." Two still had hands up. "Good. Now, who's seen the green-cloaked man?"

Four more raised hands. Grinar nodded. "The rest of you got here by other means, then?" There were nods all around, and murmurs of "I vanished," "Woke here from a dream," and the like. Grinar looked at Hybeth, and grinned. "I guess we've got to catch ourselves a servant."

For the next little while, Grinar and Hybeth worked with the two people with magic tracking abilities to get a clear picture of what the green-cloaked man looked like, so they could get on his trail. But when the first one tried it, the ball of light that was supposed to show the way of the prey just bounced up and down, looking rather undecided.

Hybeth suppressed a shiver. She was sure the walls were whispering to her now, and wished Grinar would hold her like he had earlier, but he was busy encouraging the young man to concentrate harder, to remember the exact shade of green as described by two other people. The young man's ball just bounced, and finally he let it go and sagged to the floor, a sheen of sweat on his forehead.

Hybeth rushed to catch him before he hit his head, and was able to balance him against her leg so she could let him down gently. Grinar ranted for a bit, turned to the woman, and glared at her as if that would help. It didn't. After a while of chanting under her breath and waving her arms in the air, she came up with no better success.

"He's blocked us from magical seeing," the woman said when she finally had her breath back. "He must have."

With a nod, Grinar sighed. "We'll come up with something," he said. "We always do."

Hybeth was hungry. How long had they been sitting on this cold stone floor? Long enough for the questors to disperse. Their rations had run out. Though Grinar was discouraged, he stoutly refused to eat anything from Rubinok's chest, but Hybeth was starting to wonder if maybe a *little* wine would be all right. She gritted her teeth. No. She had been here too long.

"We can't call it quits," Grinar muttered behind her. His back was warm and solid against hers, but tense, like hers.

The whispers of the walls were getting louder, and she had to hunch up her shoulders to make them stop. They spoke of death and cold and the darkest places in her soul. She scrubbed at her ears. It didn't help. She turned and grabbed Grinar's shoulders.

Startled, he turned to peer at her. "What is it, Hy?"

She shook her head, but Grinar asked her again, and held her gaze. "Tell me."

"The walls. I hear them. They're unhappy."

He raised an eyebrow. "Go on."

"Too much is hidden, they say. I guess . . . too much treasure? They want all of us out of here."

"Will they help us to that end?"

She shrugged. "Maybe. They're sort of . . . irate."

"Excellent!" Grinar climbed to his feet. "We'll give 'em some motivation, then, and they'll do about anything to get us out, eh? Even stop changing."

"Maybe," Hybeth said, though softer, since Grinar was calling to the others, soon giving out tasks and taking suggestions like an auctioneer. Maybe the walls wouldn't cooperate. Didn't he remember the Stones of Redmill? Those stones had spoken to her, too, but only so they could try and make her sacrifice herself on the largest of them as the sun set on the shortest day of the year. It had nearly worked. Stones, walls or otherwise, were not to be trusted. Grinar didn't notice, or didn't remember, and Hybeth decided to go along.

Questors came back to their meeting place laden with whatever they could carry and tossed it into a pile. Soon, thrones, chests, rich brocades sewn with gems and embroidered with gold thread, books, and other knickknacks and bric-a-brac lay in a jumbled heap taller than Hybeth's shoulders. Antique lamps stood cockeye to tapestries from before the Gryphon War.

At first, the walls had taken no notice, and kept on with their chanting, easy, light, subliminal. With each addition of goods, however, they came to attention. When one of the questors used a spell to ignite the mass of treasure, the walls shrieked, loud enough to wake the dead. Hybeth staggered, hands pressed to her ears. Grinar grabbed her, held her up. It hurt, more than anything since she'd faced the Rewert Beast of Thromin with just her dagger. Her eardrums throbbed, blackness rimmed her vision.

"The walls," one string bean of a man said, his shoulders hunched up to his ears. "Are they . . . talking?"

Hybeth nodded, but the motion made her retch. She wanted to curl into a ball and die. The fire roared higher.

"Get out, get out, get out!" the walls cried.

Grinar yelled, "See about making yourselves less move-abouty then. Then we'll get out of here, right quick. If not, it's the flames for ya."

At last, the walls acquiesced. They rushed away and stayed in a cluster at the far end of the cavern. They huddled together, moaning and wheezing from the smoke.

Grinar took up the purple scepter and gestured to the stairwell that appeared, like a mirage or dream, behind them. "Stairs, ho!" he yelled. He tossed the scepter to Rubinok, who led the assembled veterans of the quest onward.

With Grinar's help, Hybeth followed at the tail end of the line. She looked over her shoulder more than once at the walls. They promised revenge one day, for the blaze that still crackled and sparked in the middle of a wall-less cavern. But the farther they got from the walls, the more her mind cleared, and in the end, she could deal with a pack of ill-humored walls.

Upstairs, the questors made their way back to the Fountain Room under Corrinth. The grand foyer seemed a bit smaller than once it had.

And the winding marble staircase to the second floor no longer looked so wide.

Hybeth stood back from Grinar as he drew his sword. Exotenth's glow had dulled to almost nothing, but Grinar banged the blade against a nearby spittoon. The sound rang through the open air. He held the sword aloft. "Seeker! We've returned from your bit of fun, and we brought some playmates."

The Seeker appeared on the balcony at the top of the stairs. "You called, my children. What do you wish of me?"

"We've come out of your maze. We've won free!" Grinar glared. "And we want the Pleasure. Now!"

The Seeker rested narrow fingers on the balustrade and peered down at them. "You have already found that which you seek. I can do no more for you. I will not."

Silence reigned for a stunned moment, and then Grinar roared a charge and lunged for the stairs. Tight in his grip, Exotenth rose before him. The light of the blade pulsed as if it knew what Grinar sought, knew the taste of blood would be upon it in the beat of a heart.

"No!" Hybeth cried. "Grinar, no!"

Grinar reached the Seeker, sword held high, and the Seeker drew back, but did not flee. Grinar's mustaches puffed out with every breath. He grabbed a fistful of white robe and pulled the Seeker close. "You've some nerve. What pleasure do I seek that I have found?"

The Seeker's face was ghost-pale, and he swallowed once before he answered. "The quest is the thing. The journey as it unfolds is more rapture than any gold."

Grinar held the trembling Seeker in his hand, pulled him closer, nose to nose. His face was red except where sweat-smeared soot from their most recent trial traced down it. Hybeth's breath lodged in her throat, but she did not move. No one did. The stone itself held, caught in time.

The Seeker continued, his voice hushed, barely heard above the murmur of water. "And will you not have stories to tell when you are old? Stories to relive your treasures, your wonders, and life? There is pleasure in that to match." Hybeth nodded, though the Seeker's gaze never left Grinar's. His voice dropped to a whisper. "Am I right?"

For one more moment, Grinar hesitated, then he snorted a laugh. "Maybe." He sheathed Exotenth and nodded. "Maybe." With an apologetic glance for the assembled questors below, Grinar trotted downstairs to meet Hybeth, and pulled her into a ferocious hug. "Sorry about the treasure, love. We'll find it some other way."

Hybeth linked her arm in his and led the way out of the dungeon, toward the brightness of a fine summer morning. "I'm sure we will," she promised. She gave him a special smile. "One day." ✪

THE ROSE WAR

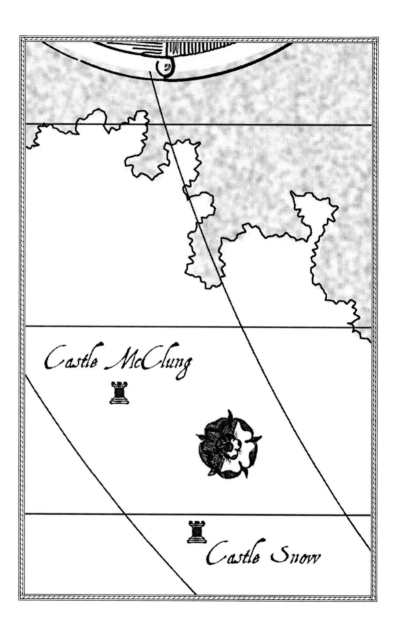

Castle McClung

Castle Snow

THE ROSE WAR
BY K.D. WENTWORTH

THE FIRST SIGN OF TROUBLE AROSE IN THE SOUTH WHEN A VARIETY OF NOR-
mally peaceful rose cultivars went rogue, abandoning their nursery
fields to rampage across the duchy, slaughtering livestock. Lord Alwyn
Snow, craggy-faced patriarch and last of his line save for a single grown
daughter, led his men along the bloody trail of disemboweled cattle into
the hills.

When they didn't return, his daughter, Cristobel, rode out alone the
next day and found only his torn body alongside his beloved bay charger.
A veritable ocean of burgundy rose petals littered the ground. The horse
yet lived, though it was badly wounded, and Cristobel was forced to put
the beast down with her dagger. The rest of her father's men and horses
lay nearby, all lacerated from crown to toe and devoid of even a drop of
blood.

She was a practical girl, having been little valued by her father, since
she was neither the male heir he desired, nor disposed to marry well and
give him a grandson. Her dark-brown hair was knotted on her head, her
skirts tucked out of the way. Her hands were strong and capable. Her
eyes, green in some kinds of light, brown in others, were as changeable
as the sea.

"Well, and well," she said to herself, kneeling beside her father's torn
body. "This is a wretched bad business." Her mind reeled at the thought
of all she must now do.

A single rosebush had survived, though much battered. It emerged from the rocks, defiance apparent in every leaf, then thrust its thorns into the dead charger's flesh and fed.

So beautiful, she thought as the bush covered the lifeless horse, and so deadly. Had he lived, her father would have rooted out every last bush of this strain, then burned them to scented ashes, and so should she, but still . . . Something nagged at the back of her mind.

The rose stirred, abandoning the shrunken corpse of the horse. Its leaves were now huge and glossy, its petals such a deep burgundy they appeared almost black. Her father had been breeding for just this color for years.

It skulked toward her on its root-feet and she picked up her father's fallen sword. The weight almost overbalanced her. "You are the last of your kind, as now I am too," she told the rose. "Attack me and I will end your strain forever!"

The feral rose regarded her, its leaves shifting though the wind lay quiet and the world itself seemed to be waiting. And then she knew what lay in the back of her mind. What a force this breed represented, if it could be harnessed and trained. No army could ever stand before such creatures. Her father's estates were poor, his people unprosperous, the castle falling to bits around its inhabitants' ears. The King would not receive them at Court. This might just be the way to mend all of that.

She snatched a whip from her saddle. "Get back to the nursery!" she told the rose with fierce determination. It balked, then attacked. They fought until only a few leaves and shredded petals remained and her own flesh bled freely from its thorns. The two of them circled and fought as the sun went down and then moonlight silvered the blood-soaked ground.

In the end, they stood wavering, exhausted and both near to death. "Yield to me!" Cristobel cried, struggling to keep her feet. "Yield or die! There is no other choice!"

The rose faltered, then slumped to the ground. Trembling, she leaned over it so that a single drop of blood from her scratched flesh fell onto its thorns. The ragged bush lurched upright, but this time did not attack.

"So," Cristobel said. "Now we understand one another." She mounted her uneasy horse, after retrieving her father's sword, and rode back to Castle Snow in the moonlight. The rose followed, that night, and ever after.

Fifty years later, Ethfraed Snow, third of his line since the determined Cristobel, harvested two thousand of his prime Blood-Burgundys, noted for their ferocity, and marched them north before spring had fully softened into summer.

When outriders spotted the red tide approaching across sprawling Illyn Moor, word was sent to Castle McClung. Siattla McClung responded by ordering the harvest of his vast fields of deep pink Altissimos, which, though young—since the season was less advanced in the north—were brave and cunning.

Siattla was a grizzled old commander, a King's man, veteran of a dozen campaigns in defense of the realm and well used to deploying his troops and bushes to the best possible advantage. Ethfraed was young and greedy, hot-headed. Siattla had met the youth the previous winter at the King's Icetide Court. Ethfraed had stalked about, wearing one of his vicious Burgundys twined about his arm and chest like a damned lady's corsage.

The McClung family stock, Altissimo, was more erratic. Though Siattla had worked in the nurseries his entire life, he would never allow a rose free access to his person. Rumors were whispered that the Snows fed their Burgundys with their own blood, each scion producing many children so that there might be enough to satisfy such a large force. It was true that in each generation, there had been more than the ordinary number of Snow heirs who did not survive into adulthood, and all those who did were as pale as the snow that gave them their family name.

Siattla gathered his forces on the hill before Castle McClung, his massed Altissimos pruned and alert, his men mounted on well-bred chargers. The air crawled with electricity as they waited. Memories flashed through the old warrior's head, bodies reduced to glaring white skeletons on bloody battlefields, glossy fat roses that fed on both sides with equal abandon.

His Altissimos knew their place and the McClung whipping-in masters were unparalleled. His bushes would not run amok, as sometimes happened, but what of the Burgundys? Ethfraed Snow was young and reckless, and there were such terrible tales . . .

The attack, when it came, was overwhelming. The Burgundys swept over his pink Altissimos like a relentless blood tide. There was no order, no strategy, just wave after wave of burgundy mingled with the screams of dying men and horses. The stolid pinks stood their ground, giving no quarter, and for a time Siattla thought his lines might hold.

Petals rained through the air and the contrasting scents of the two variants grew cloyingly thick, so that it was difficult to breathe. Siattla's stallion pranced beneath him, rolling its eyes in fear, and he wielded his own whip, stripping leaf and bloom. Several Burgundys drew the stallion's blood before the commander drove them back.

He saw one of Snow's own men go down beneath the dark-red roses, then another and another. Ethfraed watched from a nearby hillock, roses twined about his arms and brow like garlands. The younger lord made no effort to save his troops, smiling as his own roses crept over him, so that he seemed more than half-rose himself. And, though the savage Burgundys killed all others, friend or foe, without discrimination, they spared his flesh.

A knot of Burgundys broke through and Siattla was hard-put to whip them back. He heard terrible cries as thorns lacerated flesh and his troops died in agony. His stallion screamed as a rose darted up its foreleg and the beast reared to shake the creeper off. Everywhere was blood and the silken shower of petals and leaves, the sickening attar of roses.

Suddenly, Ethfraed's grey charger plunged through the fighting bushes and brought his foe to his side. The man, shorter than he'd remembered, gazed at Siattla with blood-red eyes. "Have you had enough?" he said, as though he were merely asking if his enemy had been served sufficient tea at breakfast.

More Burgundys rushed in and Siattla lay about with the whip. His horse wheeled, panic-stricken, and he fought to keep his seat.

"Yield," Ethfraed said, "and I will spare you what men you have left." A single black-red rose perched above his left brow like a third eye.

"This is abomination!" Siattla cried, never slackening with the whip. "Your family swore allegiance to King Mernay!"

"My family, yes," Ethfraed said, "in another day, another time, but not me. I have a different course in mind."

"The King will obliterate you!" Siattla said as his horse bared its teeth and squealed in terror.

"I think not," Ethfraed said, "though his most gracious Majesty is certainly welcome to try."

Siattla turned upon the youth and slashed at him with the whip. "I will never yield to you and your monstrosities!"

Blood dripped down Ethfraed's face and the rose twined about his head immediately extended a creeper to feed upon it. Ethfraed smiled and reached up to stroke its leaves. "Roses are such dear creatures," he said, "when you put yourself out to understand them."

Shocked, Siattla stared, momentarily forgetting to beat off the encroaching hordes. His stallion stumbled and he was thrown into the sea of bushes. They closed over him as he hit the ground, leaves, root-feet, stems, petals, and thorns. Gagging at the cloying scent, he covered his face with his arms.

Thorns pierced the length of his body, and for a few excruciating moments, as he screamed, he and the roses were one. They pulsed with the fullness of his life, taking more than merely his blood, and he saw what, from this day on, the future would hold.

All sweet-scented blood and sharp, unforgiving thorn.

Ethfraed almost took the north before his Burgundys succumbed to a fungus in the wettest fall on record and died off in waves. As soon as the rain let up, King Mernay ordered the hills burned, and at last Ethfraed abandoned his quest. Undaunted, he drove the survivors back south to his fabled nurseries and concentrated on breeding disease resistance into his savage cultivars.

Thereafter, the King declared it a crime to cultivate roses of any kind, sessile varieties as well as motile. Flowers fell out of favor and any citizen who dared grow such nasty things fell under suspicion of treason.

The following spring, Ethfraed discovered that his Burgundys had learned the lessons of combat rather better than he'd anticipated. Blood, it seemed, was rife with more than nourishment. It bore temperament and cunning. Not all bushes were capable of absorbing more than mere sustenance, but those that were thrived and became the leaders of their kind.

Now, when he walked the nurseries, some of the bushes approached him with purpose. Their creepers assumed a hulking, humanlike shape and their leaves whispered sounds that he could almost understand. The clever creatures had taken what their fallen enemies knew and somehow made it their own.

These he whipped more than the others and fed only sparingly with his, and his children's, blood, knowing full well they were more dangerous than all the rest.

His Master Nurseryman counseled burning those who manifested this changed intelligence. "You'll never control such," the grizzled old man said, his hand tight on his shears. "They have the cunning of soldiers along with the merciless disposition of plants. They'll take whatever you give and then kill us all."

But Ethfraed would not listen, conducting his six children, four boys and two girls, into the nurseries each morning, teaching them to feed and whip the improved roses in equal measure. One day, their numbers would be complete again and then he would finish what he had started the previous year.

And while his rose-men were learning to talk, his youngest daughter, Candaed, was sprouting thorns in the tender flesh inside her sweet young wrists.

Candaed Snow became increasingly wild as she grew, more rose than human, her father's men said, when they dared speak of her at all, which wasn't often. At fifteen, arms entwined with sprays of red-black roses, she drove her mother back to her grandfather's people, the stolid and oh-so-proper Frants, on the other side of the mountains. And even there, the woman cowered, proclaiming to all who would listen that she was not safe.

Candaed's four brothers laughed at her antics, but avoided the nurseries in her company, for it was true that the savage Burgundys answered her like no other. After her mother fled, Candaed slept beneath the bushes at night, forgoing beds and chairs, baths, and other such civilized amenities. She never bore so much as a single scratch, while her siblings were always marked from toe to crown from their duties among the roses.

When, in her sixteenth year, Ethfraed died of a fever, it was Candaed who demanded his body be given to the Burgundys. Her older sister, Amalia, wept and protested, saying she couldn't bear it, but Candaed marched ten stout bushes into her father's bedroom and directed them to bear his corpse away. His body disappeared into the red-black vastness of the nurseries and was never seen again, not even his bones. From that day on, his youngest daughter would not set foot in the castle, but devoted herself completely to her father's passion for cultivars.

In turn, over the next few months, each of her brothers tried to reason with her, but their sister would not relent. So, they went about the business of running their father's lands, occupying themselves with taxes and crops and the training of their guard. She controlled the nurseries, and under her direction, each successive year's blossoms grew larger and more fierce, the shape of the bushes more hauntingly human.

At last, when she was thirty-one, Birin, the oldest of her brothers, came to her in the nurseries and demanded five hundred Burgundys to defend their lands to the west. Their maternal uncle, Eltan Frant, had seized a rich valley of farmholds, a substantial portion of their departed mother's dowry.

His sister was an unsettling sight with roses twined about her arms and legs, leaves threaded through her hair. She had sprouted more thorns in recent years, so that delicate points outlined her brows and ears, accented cheekbones and chin. He had trouble meeting her gaze, but steeled himself. His sister was what she was and, while there was no help for it, he could at least make certain her oddities served the Snows.

As he requested, Candaed harvested five hundred of the fiercest bushes, hand-picking each. Birin was startled to hear them responding to commands in hoarse but recognizable whispers. They set off under the blazing sun of a midsummer's day. Birin rode at the fore with his sister, but his other three brothers and their human troops stayed in the rear, fearing to expose their backs to the savage rose horde.

The Nuir Valley was broad and green, the crops well in at this time of the year. Peasants labored out in fields of wheat, corn, and rye, weeding and watering, their backs bent, oblivious to the horde's approach.

Birin led his force through the valley, announcing to all they passed that the land was now reclaimed in the name of the Snows. Several times, roses attacked the peasants and Candaed had to whip them back. Troubled, her brother camped his strange troops at the valley's far end where the green-tinged Jewel River surged down from the mountains.

Within a week, Eltan Frant, mounted on a moon-pale charger, came down from the pass with a huge force many times the scant number of men fielded by the Snows, and stopped on the other side of the river at

the ford. He rode his horse across the green water and Birin met him at
the river's edge, accompanied only by his standard-bearer, who bore a
flag emblazoned with a single blood-red rose. "Yield!" he told his uncle.

Frant, clad in resplendent green leathers, stood in his stirrups. The
older man was a trusted commander of the King and the scarred veteran of many campaigns waged upon other kingdoms in the years since
Ethfraed's death. "Insolent pup!" His uncle's face was florid with rage.
"These lands only came to the Snows with your mother and now, with
her, have returned to the Frants. The Snows have no rights here!"

"She is still my father's wife," Birin said and noticed out of the corner
of his eye how the roses crept silently forward.

"Is she indeed?" Frant made a show of glancing about. "I don't see
Ethfraed Snow here. Have you perhaps hidden him?"

"Do not mock me!" Blood pounded in Birin's ears. "You know that he
has been dead these many years!"

The black-red carpet of roses was nearer now, most low to the ground,
but here and there, sprinkled among them, manlike shapes loomed with
roses where eyes should be and grasping thorn-hands.

"Then the marriage is dead as well," Frant said. "My sister is no man's
wife, but a widow."

"She abandoned us," Birin said, "and, as such, abandoned her prop-
erty as well. This valley belongs to the Snows!"

"She fled for her life!" Frant cried. "That harridan of a daughter threatened to feed her to your misbegotten roses!"

Candaed had slipped off her gelding and concealed herself in the tide
of approaching roses, the leaves in her hair and sprays about her arms
and torso camouflaging her most effectively.

Frant suddenly realized how close the horde had crept and wheeled
his charger, but the bushes engulfed him, tangling his horse's legs and
bringing it down. Their uncle screamed as the thorns pierced his flesh,
but Candaed whipped the Burgundys back and stood over his bleeding
body.

"Do you yield, Uncle?" she asked conversationally, as though suggesting the two of them take a turn in the gardens.

He writhed, held fast by the creepers, his face gone deathly pale. "My yielding will not return this valley to the Snows!" His voice was cracked with pain and his eyes rolled toward the waiting troops on the other side of the river. "They have orders to fight on, even if I should fall."

"That is unfortunate, for them, then, as well as you," she said and thrust her whip back into her belt. She turned away and stroked the roses she passed as though they were little pet dogs. "Go on with you, then," she said fondly to them. "Take what you need. There's none that shall stop you."

Frant's screams were terrible as his body disappeared beneath leaf and bloom. The rose army surged into the river and engaged that portion of Frant's forces which did not then flee. The battle was long, with hulking shapes rising up to pull warriors out of the saddle, terrified chargers fighting to keep their feet, and the bitter coppery scent of blood everywhere.

Birin and his brothers watched the mismatched battle with sick fascination, but Candaed slipped from man to man, crooning at her roses and disappearing down into the leafy fray from time to time, only to reappear, her own thorns crimson with blood.

By the end, Birin was repelled. He had thought he understood the full measure of what his sister was, but clearly he had not. He was tempted to torch the roses, and her along with them, but he knew the wretched Burgundys would strip the flesh from his bones, if ever he tried. House Snow had chosen a dark, leafy path and there was no going back now, or ever.

Candaed quartered her roses in the valley for the rest of the summer, utilizing the rich black soil and endless sunny days to build their strength. The bushes had taken much from the Frant warriors they'd brought down: cunning, nerve, and ambition. She'd partaken along with them and experienced something new, a desire for progeny that had never touched her before.

No human had ever appealed to her as a mate, but among the man-shaped roses there was one who had fed upon her uncle. It lay with her every night now as the stars wheeled above, piercing her sweetly, savagely, each of them drawing from the other, so that, as time passed, she became ever more rose and it more human. Though she had never before named any of her cultivars, this one she dubbed "Passion."

At the end of the summer, when she drove her roses back to the Castle Snow nurseries for the cold season, she bore a growing seed inside her womb. In the spring, she produced a perfect red-cheeked daughter with a mouth like an angel and a headful of thorns already dark with her mother's blood.

When Birin visited the nursery a week later and saw the monster his sister had produced, he drew his sword with a great ringing hiss of steel. Candaed regarded him calmly from under thorn-studded eyebrows. Her daughter, Desire, quite superior to ordinary human progeny, already toddled about on fat little legs.

"All the rest I have borne!" Birin cried. "But not this!"

Candaed was still weak from her lying-in, which had cost her far more in blood than an ordinary birthing. Her face was pale, her limbs unsteady. "You are jealous, Brother," she said, though she did not rise from her leafy bower. Her terrible rose lover stood at her shoulder. "None of your brats are this extraordinary."

"You mean none of mine are abominations!" With a strangled cry, Birin stabbed her through the heart, then hacked to shreds the bush she called Passion as well. He would kill the child, too, he told himself, then torch the nurseries. This was so far beyond mere dishonor that words could never do it justice. No one else could ever know of this monstrous child, else the Snows' reputation would never recover from this horror.

The thorn-child turned burgundy-red eyes on him, then stretched out along her mother's side, her thorns feeding on the still-warm blood soaking into the earth. He raised his sword to kill her too, but the Burgundys, drawn by the gore's rich scent, swept over him and stripped the flesh from his flailing body.

His shrieks carried all the way to the castle, but no one dared venture into the nurseries even to recover his bones, once the grisly event was over.

Desire matured within the first year, then ruled the nurseries, producing seven children of her own, each thornier even than herself, with as many man-roses. Six of these, all sons, were savage fighters, more leaf than flesh, with no more intellect than the average cultivar, content to fight whenever called upon and otherwise bask in the sun. The seventh, though, a green-skinned, lissome daughter, bore the light of human cunning in her burgundy eyes. Desire named her "Resolve."

Though Desire had known her mother, Candaed, only a few days, she had fed on her blood and taken in all that her mother had known. Likewise, she nourished her own thorn-children with her blood, much as ordinary humans fed babies on milk. Her sons absorbed only the fiercer aspects of her knowledge, but Resolve, a true daughter of the line, learnt things that would take ordinary humans a lifetime to assimilate.

Over the years of her rule, the human Snows rampaged across the kingdom, subjugating one noble house after another, until all but the three largest duchies paid tribute to them, rather than King Calet, who vowed redress and was massing his forces.

One day in early spring, when Orlen Snow, Birin's heir, had gone to the nurseries to map out his strategy against the largest remaining house, he found his infamous cousin, Desire, fading. Already her thorns had dulled, her skin gone patchy. He ordered the sacrifice of captives from earlier campaigns, kept for just that purpose, but their blood did not restore her.

Panicked, Orlen summoned all his best nurserymen as well as master gardeners from every conquered estate, but their efforts were futile. "Perhaps it is just her time, sir," one ancient ventured, crumpling his cap in his hands. "Her Grace is as much plant as human. No one can say how many years such a unique creature would be given in the normal course of events."

Orlen slit the nurseryman's throat on the spot and fed his blood to Desire as well, though that meal did no more good than all the rest. Later, though, when his own blood had cooled, he thought perhaps the old man had the right of it. Who among them could say how long such a rose-bound creature as his cousin would live?

Young Resolve, who had the outer seeming of a girl of fifteen, though she was barely six, watched her mother's fading, but said nothing. Her ears were black-red roses, her hair only thorns and leaves, her skin a startling green. Each successive generation was more rose than human. Orlen wondered how much longer the line would last. He'd best make his move against the King himself before time ran out.

A month later, with her six rose-brothers striding in the fore, Resolve led the campaign against King Calet. A big, bluff man still in his prime, the King sat his black charger, crown gleaming, gloves in one hand, as they approached the castle. The infamous Blood-Burgundys of House Snow spread out and surrounded the castle like a great aromatic sea, awaiting her command.

"Noble to the very end," her cousin, Orlen, said upon seeing the King. He rode at her side, sneering and anxious, challenging her every decision now for days. He wanted to be King, she knew, in the same way that other humans wanted to breathe.

King Calet, bearing a white flag, cantered out to meet them. His finely crafted red-lacquered armor gleamed bright as any rose. Orlen swore, then turned to Resolve. "What does he want? Does the fool think he can merely talk us out of attacking?"

"I wish to listen," Resolve said and urged her gelding forward, her green hands light on the reins. The sun's welcome heat bathed her thorny head. "It might even be amusing."

The King pulled off his helmet. His hair was gold touched with silver, his face set, his eyes steely. "Lady," he said, nodding at Resolve, but ignoring Orlen's querulous presence.

"Sire," she said as the wind ruffled her rose-petal ears.

"Your family has seized most of my kingdom already." He gazed grimly over her shoulder at the rose army, which was poised and waiting. "Now I suppose you've come for what's left?"

Resolve gestured at the cultivars fanned behind her like an immense feral garden. "Obviously, you cannot stand against us."

"So you think to rule in my place?" Disdain colored his voice and he rode yet closer, his stallion champing at the bit. "Command of a kingdom requires more than mere possession, and you have not been born to it, as have I." Craftiness filled his grey eyes. "What about an alliance instead? If you and I married, you could rule at my side."

"No, I am to be King!" Despite meeting under a white flag, Orlen drew his sword, then swung at the King. With a curse, Calet dodged, reining his horse into hers.

Resolve laughed as Orlen tried to regain his balance, but it was like the scratch of thorns over glass, not such a sound as a human would ever have made. "Cousin, as always, you weary me." She motioned to her cultivar brothers. The six swarmed Orlen, pulling him to the ground where he disappeared. Her cousin shrieked and gibbered, and soldiers on both sides stared at the heaving rose bushes in horror until her rose-brothers again stood, their thorns crimson with blood.

"Roses do not marry," she said, turning back to the staring King, who had gone as pale as curdled cream. In the distance, she caught the acrid reek of smoke. Her fierce smile revealed more thorn than tooth. "I will rule—with you at my feet."

She leaned forward and seized his arm so that her wrist-thorns sank into his warm flesh. Reeling back, he tried to free himself, but her thorns bit deep, piercing his veins, stealing his will. From a distance, she knew, it seemed they only clasped arms as though having come to an accord. They were under a parley flag, after all, and he appeared in no imminent danger. His army would wait for his command. And wait. And wait.

His eyes glazed, his muscles wilted as the power of the roses burned through his veins and overcame him. He would have fallen, but through their mingled blood she forbid it. "My line is growing thin of late," she said as she tasted ever more deeply of him. "My mother died young, and I feel my life will be even shorter. It is time for an infusion of human blood."

She closed her eyes, sampling his thoughts, his plans, his fears, then what passed for human cunning. When she had the man's full measure, she smiled again. He had no intention of ever marrying her, but had instead orchestrated a trap. Concealed forces in the forest on the next hill waited with torches. Upon his signal, they would have fallen upon the rose army from behind. Despite the parley flag, he had intended to burn the Snows out once and for all. Now, it only remained to dispatch her own men to cut the saboteurs' throats.

She released him then and Calet stared down at his pierced arm as though it had a will of its own. Blood from the minute wounds laced his skin. "Dismiss your army, then order the castle's gates opened and the roof knocked out," she said. "My roses will live nowhere but under the sweetness of sky and sun."

In a daze, Calet summoned the captain of his guard and bid his forces stand down, then rode back to the castle, Resolve at his side, his face vacant, never again to be his own man. Following behind, the rose army overran the courtiers, the servants, even the cats and chickens. The castle's stone walls disappeared beneath the bushes like bones under flesh. Nothing was visible but a vast mound of leaf and thorn and bloom.

Resolve chained the King in a dusty corner of the courtyard like an out-of-favor spaniel, but took him, whenever the mood came upon her, in a thorny, white-hot heat in the darkness on star-dusted nights.

Through his seed, she produced a line of green-skinned, thorny children, boys and girls, but always the fiercest were female, playing at death and conquest in the same fashion human daughters played with dolls and stick-horses.

Under her command, Resolve's six rose-brothers campaigned with the Blood-Burgundys until all that corner of the world was drowned in blood and thorns and sweet-scented petals. Once nothing remained on that side of the ocean to conquer, Resolve's descendants ruled for many years after, producing a series of savage thorn-haired Rose-Kings and Rose-Queens known far and wide for ruthless cunning, daring, and determination.

Many generations later, when the line at last thinned out, generating children with only the palest of green skin and tiny nub thorns with no points, the kingdom finally fell. The vast royal nurseries were burned by enemies to crumbling silver ash and it took years for the surviving great Houses to sort themselves out as to who owed fealty and where. But, still, once in every few generations, a tiny daughter with burgundy eyes and thorns for eyebrows would be born to some unfortunate family.

When that happened, panic would reign. No one could breathe until the squalling infant had been carried up into the mountains and exposed on the highest ledge where snow fell year-round.

And, though, under pain of death, roses were never cultivated in any corner of the kingdom, sometimes at the height of summer a bush with black-red blooms would sprout up in the snows of the tallest mountain and savage travelers for the briefest of seasons until it succumbed to the cold and men once again were safe. ✪

CHOOSE YOUR OWN EPIC ADVENTURE

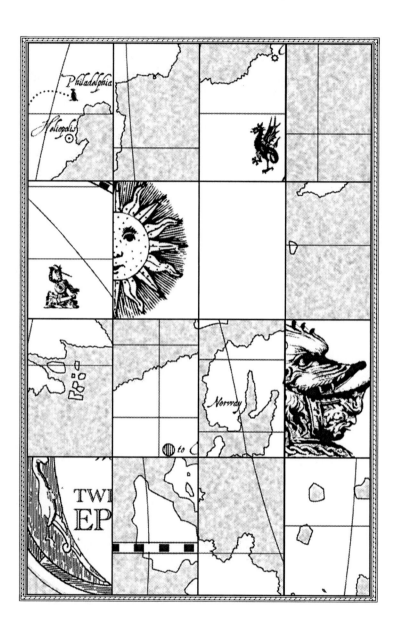

CHOOSE YOUR OWN EPIC ADVENTURE
BY MARCUS EWERT

WELCOME TO "CHOOSE YOUR OWN EPIC ADVENTURE," THE LARGER-THAN-life story whose course *you* determine! Before you begin, please choose your character's gender:

- *If you choose to be male, go to Section 22.*
- *If you choose to be female, go to Section 10.*
- *If you choose to be intersexed, go to Section 6.*

–|–

The two of you raise goats, and sometimes Regal goes fishing with three red-headed sisters, who live nearby. (After one such outing Regal announces that she is a girl. Although you yourself have never felt the need to choose one gender over another, you certainly have no objection to being the proud parent of a wonderful daughter.) Each night you regale Regal with stories of dashing and wily intersexed thieves. As she gets older, Regal starts offering plot-points herself, and soon the stories become collaborations.

Old and venerable at 65, your heart fails you one morning as you eat a plate of eggs scrambled with mushrooms and potatoes. For three years, Regal is desolate with grief, but, gradually, the pain lessens. Regal moves to the capital city and becomes a much-loved governess. To all the children in her care, Regal tells stories of dashing, wily, intersexed thieves.

And thus you live on. ✪

-2-

Your people have a pedantic, moral-heavy tale about the time two *angeloi* were pushed out of Heaven. These siblings fell to earth, where they later became the twin spirits of Bitterness and Resentment. One of them must have stabbed the sharpened point of her feather into your heart, because you see no reason to stop mistreating others, just as you have been mistreated.

And so you plan to sneak into a Tree-Omme camp, in order to do the Splinterfolk a very bad turn. But your fallen guardian angel must have deserted you. Almost immediately, you're spotted by a Tree-Omme guard . . . just a young girl, really. The brat's scream is high and shrill; no doubt she just roused the entire encampment. And then, with her large eyes never leaving yours, the girl screws up her face, and you brace for what you know is coming. Every hole that lines the girl's long, xyloid body shoots gouts of scalding urine.

- *If you attempt to flee, go to Section 13.*
- *If you decide to stay and fight to the (urine-soaked) death, go to Section 16.*

-3-

In disguise, you head to a chalkwitch that your beloved assassin has mentioned. Like many of her foul kind, the 'witch lives in a dirigible-sewer, high above your otherwise beautiful capital city. You absolutely *hate* heights, but you hate the Lady of Medicine more.

The chalkwitch's hut is built on a wooden deck that swings beneath a giant, taut-skinned balloon. The balloon is filled with human waste; it steams and stinks in the sun.

Sometimes the demands of politics can be *so* very trying.

Once the 'witch has understood your need, she scrawls eight of the

Duchess's names and titles on the floorboards, clambering around the deck like a water-strider. Then she adds a line of overwriting: "1 and 1 and 1 and 1 and 1 and . . ." As she works, the 'witch keeps expectorating onto the deck. Apparently, the spit is very important; no one's ever told you why.

When the 'witch is finished, she stands, and her pale hair brushes the greasy underbelly of the sewage-balloon. You can't help but shudder. The 'witch just looks at you and laughs.

- *If you decide to ask the 'witch to tell your fortune, go to Section 20.*
- *If instead you choose to immediately return to the city, hoping never to see the 'witch or her ilk ever again, go to Section 26.*

-4-

You slip away through the concealing fog, scalded but wiser. Oddly enough, in the weeks that follow, you can't stop thinking about that young Splintergirl. What it was like in that moment when your face filled her entire world. She had been looking at you with shock and fear; but imagine if someone regarded you that raptly with love or respect! It would have to be someone very young of course, someone who pretty much knew nothing about you or the world.

Perhaps the feather of the cruel angel has slipped from your heart at last. You want to be a parent.

- *If you choose to have a flesh-and-blood child, go to Section 19.*
- *If you feel you're not up to the challenge, and would prefer a spell-bairn instead, go to Section 28.*

-5-

Why are so many of your lifetimes plagued by the supernatural?

Like your current reality, for instance.

With trembling hands, you struggle to keep the scroll in front of you flat and unrolled; the two *ends* of the scroll, however, want nothing more than to clatter towards each other at top speed, reconcealing the ancient text.

By the Four Hops of the Leaper! Not *another* demon-ridden manu-script!

And as you read further (with the continued *dis*-assistance of the rowdy scroll), you're horrified to realize that the text that you're perus-ing is nothing less than the "Bloody Encyclical," a.k.a. "The Chain Letter from Hell."

Penned centuries ago by a jilted incubus, this vindictive screed wraps a Möbius strip around the reader, a Möbius strip of *time*. Starting now, you've been reading the scroll since time began . . . and always will be.

Next up: the flaying of your skin to make new parchment for the scroll, and the expunging of your blood for ink. ✪

-6-

You are Gohhig, an intersexed goat-thief with two weathercharms (fog, hail) braided into your long, caramel-colored hair.

- *If you choose to continue your life of crime, go to Section 2.*
- *If you'd rather reform your character, and make a fresh start, go to Section 14.*

-7-

Your knees ache as they hit the sparkling malachite that this rich city uses for common pavement. Full-voiced, the following prayer bounds from your throat, as you publicly weep and testify:

Lord Leaper,
You whose pond is the entire kosmos,
> *Wrap me in your rainbow-colored tongue,*
> *And swallow me whole.*
> *Let every part of me be your fuel.*
> *Digest my wretchedness,*
And make me prism.
> *Great Frog, I bow!*

Passersby cheer and applaud. You even see a bronze-armored sentinel brush tears from her face.

And then . . . the ground pitches violently. With a *KRRACK!* that pierces tympanums, green flagstones explode upwards. For a time, everything is upheaval, and billows of powdered malachite.

The sentinel screams. There are shards of white-hot glare boiling up from the split earth, too bright to look at clearly. "Sodium rats!" someone yells, and for a moment you feel like laughing. Sodium rats? Those ludicrous beasts of folklore?

As you shield your eyes with your hands, however, you see that the clambering lights *do* appear to have tails. Suddenly, the flaming beasts of legend no longer seem so laughable.

All around you, foot-thick pieces of malachite are beginning to smolder. Fires are breaking out everywhere, as more and more shining vermin crawl up from the underworld. Your clothes are smoking. The woman in bronze is already down, and on fire.

You and pretty much the city's entire population die in the hideous conflagration. But as the flames eat you, you find that you are weeping . . . with joy. Just in the nick of time, you purified your heart, and had your sins forgiven.

Soon, you'll be crossing galaxies, in the belly of the Leaper. ✪

✪

-8-

Your spirit mounts towards Heaven on shafts of frozen rain.

As you translate out of physical reality, you approach the Empyrean, Heaven's shining outskirts. At once you are mobbed by the proletarians of Paradise, the *angeloi*. They come at you with books and with trumpets, with virtues and spears. And too bad for them: the effete creatures are no match for your Ice-Mauser! Cold cartridges shatter celestial vertebrae and send holy feathers flying.

Make the bastards pay!

Ultimately, you know your one-woman war is hopeless, but so what? Your god's been slain, your existence is meaningless.

Time to punch a few holes in the enemy's cosmology. ✪

-9-

Two days later, your High Tea with the Lady of Medicine is just as dreary as you imagined. What a relief it will be when sweet Olmen comes in to stab you! You have to admit, though, the tea itself *is* exquisite. The Lady pours the liquid piping hot from what's probably a family heirloom: a golden samovar, embossed with scenes of hawks tearing a covey of quail to pieces. Sigh. Some sort of trite allegory, no doubt.

While sipping your third cup, you are displeased by the sudden taste of blood. Quite a lot of blood, in fact. Inside your throat, there is a sense of terrible *rupture*.

You goggle at the Duchess as you choke on your own blood.

- *Go to Section 27.*

-10-

You are Ymerys, an outraged priestess of the Wailing Ice. Your heavy backpack is filled with gravel, the rubble of a dozen broken tomb-stones.

- *If you decide to hunt down your apostate daughter, go to Section 21.*
- *If instead you choose to storm Heaven itself, go to Section 24.*

−11−

A rascal to the end, eh?

Very well, then.

You decide to go ahead and say the Vows anyway, because in the long run, that'll probably get you better access to all the jewel-encrusted goodies the Cathedral must surely harbor. When the time comes to say the sacred words, you do so, but, beneath your long robes, you stand on one foot, your culture's equivalent of crossing one's fingers.

The first time you're alone with the blessèd regalia, you grab the Fruit-fly Crozier and run for your life. Flee. The priests pursue you, prayer-wreathed and wrathful, but you weren't a top-notch goat-thief for nothing! Nimbly, you pick paths that lead high into the mountains, losing your pursuers in the alpine fogs that so often overtake the region.

Sadly, you too are overtaken, though not by fogs nor priests. A crude roadblock is all it takes to deliver you into the hands of three red-headed highwaywomen, a gallivanting band who can't quite believe their good fortune.

"Attend, sisters!" says one, "Is this not just like a tale? Quarry come straight to us?"

The others agree: Yes, it *is* very much like a tale.

The trio proceed to strip you of your clothes and belongings, and then divest you of life via a rather ingenious system that uses five closely-set cedar trees and a lot of stout leather cord. Apostate and renegade that you are, you feel no shame in pronouncing a curse of the Rainbow Frog upon all three of them, for stealing the sacred Crozier. ✪

-12-

Patiently, your daughter talks you through the Prophecy, and you begin
to concede that you just *might* have misread it, after all. *'Hijjinya,'* she
reminds you, can be translated as either 'grave' or 'resting pallet'; and
the verb *'t'ehrrizkhat'* can sometimes be a subjunctive. After listening to your daughter's careful exegesis for several hours, you finally
admit that you were wrong. Your daughter hasn't betrayed the faith at
all!

Together, the two of you walk to the seashore, where you empty the
contents of your backpack into the ocean. As each bit of tombstone-
rubble touches the shining water, it turns into a tiny turtle. The names
and dates of dead lives, dissolving. Soon a flotilla of miniature turtles is
paddling off towards the horizon. With them go the last remnants of
your anger. You and your daughter are reunited. You'll live out your days
peaceful and fulfilled.

For generations to come, a species of small but especially vicious turtles will haunt these waters. If one can just avoid their snapping beaks,
however, they make for a mouth-watering soup. ✪

-13-

You rip a charm from your hair, no time to determine which. Already
your skin is blistering from the Splintergirl's caustic urine. You crush
the snail shell in your fist, and, almost immediately, your hand begins to
smoke. Thick vapor pours out from between your still-clenched fingers.
A moist, cool vapor that soothes your scalded flesh.

Ah. Fog.

• *Go to Section 4.*

✪

-14-

Sickened by your many sins (for sometimes it takes a murder to conceal a theft), you decide to confess your crimes at the shrine of the Rainbow Batrachian. Your own rural village is too small to boast a temple of the Great Leaper, and so you must travel far into the lands of hearsay. For months you travel from city to city, looking for a translucent building streaked with the bright colors of the spectrum. Just when you are about to give up, weary and impoverished in the capital city, you see a vast, rainbow-hued cathedral looming at the end of a boulevard.

Redemption awaits.

- *If you choose to sprint the remaining distance, go to Section 18.*
- *If you fall down and abase yourself right there in the street, go to Section 7.*

-15-

"My goodness, Mother!" the wench says. *"You're* not being reasonable at *all!"* Lithe as a cat, she glides towards you. From her mouth, a pipe with a long white stem protrudes. It wasn't there a moment before.

Your hateful daughter sucks in a bowlful of smoke, expels it voluptuously. Past her lips, the smoke loses all lassitude, and races straight towards you. It sheaths your right arm, like the glove of a prideful woman. You watch in horror as that limb drops from your body as cleanly as fruit from a tree.

There's no pain, but there *is* a fragrance: as the felled limb smacks the floor, a citrus scent floods the room. The smell of a hundred bruised oranges.

And more horrors await.

Your chortling daughter blows plume after plume of smoke at

you. You feel a sudden tightness in your chest as your left breast detaches and drops to the floor, accompanied by a strong smell of coffee. Teeth rain from your gums with the scent of vanilla. Bread, chocolate, burning paper: these are your eyes, fingers, tongue.

The last thing you're aware of is two servants running around frantically, trying to bottle up in little vials the fragances you've become.

You know how these despicable brothels function. No cold purity of the Ice for you! Instead, your last remains will perfume a hundred unclean acts, as your demon daughter gloats . . . ✪

-16-

You rip one of the charms from your hair, no time to determine which. As you crush the tiny shell in your fist, the ambient weather changes immediately. All over your body, filament-thin hairs rise in eager anticipation; the next moment, a violent hail begins to fall, shredding the leaves off trees. As a hundred angry Tree-Ommes swarm you, sharp pellets of ice strike you all. You rip off your other charm, and crush it to powder. Fog as thick as winter clothing boils up from the ground. No one can see a thing.

Although neither hail nor fog will save you (already your vest bristles with arrows), you shiver in perverse delight. All your life you've been a servant of chaos, and churning chaos is what you've just unleashed. Two dozen splinter-arrows miss their mark, and all around you there are thumps and wails as fog-blind comrades cudgel each other. With the wooden blades of their "punching daggers," the Tree-Ommes knit a terrible destruction inside your chest.

And you can't stop grinning . . .

• *Go to Section 23.*

-17-

Ironically, on the day that you decide to kill the Lady of Medicine, you receive an invitation from her:

"Dear cousin, your effulgent presence is requested for High Tea . . . ," etc. (What a petty hag, you think to yourself. Tea plants went extinct centuries ago and it was the Lady's ancestors who reconstructed the genetic line. Trust the Duchess never to miss an opportunity to crow.) Quickly, you fire off a coded message to Olmen, your beloved assassin. His response—"Tonight let me dance for you in private"—is both relevant and literal.

That evening, you lie on your sumptuous bed (bare-chested in violet silk pants), and watch as Olmen performs the assassin's *Totentanz*: The Opening Position. Four darting Butterfly Kicks. The Sixth Position. Saluting the Horizon. Salute to the First Three Faint Stars of Evening. The Serpent Jeté. Etc.

The man of your dreams is a consummate dancer, and you are well versed in the secret signage of the *Totentanz*. As you watch the movements of the obese and beautiful young man, you are simultaneously decrypting. Here is the death-plan that Olmen is dancing:

"My Lord! While you're having tea with the Duchess, I'll break into her manor, like a common thug. I'll storm the room where the two of you two are nibbling and chatting, and I'll go for her first. I'll slit her throat, unless you have another suggestion. Then I'll stab you a few times. To be a good alibi, the thrusts will have to be fairly deep. But you'll survive. Not me, though."

You raise a questioning eyebrow.

Olmen's fluid movements continue: "You'll 'heroically overcome' me, my Lord, which will bolster the alibi. I'll die, but you can bring me back to life in the Vaults."

You nod. (The Duchess isn't the only one with clever ancestors. Deep beneath your castle are regeneration tanks the rest of the world knows nothing about.)

More coded dance steps: "You can grow a clone of me from a few fat cells. Take some now, from my inner thigh."

The assassin melts down to the floor, his strong, pudgy arms still gesturing: "Use my dagger. Go on, do it! I want you, Siriad. I've always wanted you . . ." He pulls you to the floor.

- *Go to Section 9.*

-18-

You reach the temple's sanctuary just before the entire city is engulfed in the worst disaster in your planet's history. Safely inside the temple's crystal walls, you watch as massive buildings erupt in brilliant flame. Has the world gone insane?

"I'm sorry, I'm so, so sorry!" you sob, prostrate before the High Altar.

Two priests comfort you. "Be at peace, you are shriven!" says one. "The Great Leaper forgives everything."

The Frog's grace keeps you and the temple's clergy alive. No matter how fiercely the fires blaze outside (where jade and marble boil like water), the crystal walls of the temple stay moist and cool. For as long as you live, neither you nor anyone else will ever know what razed the once-great city (minus a single building) to the ground.

A holy miracle: the temple's walls continue to ooze moisture long after the last fire goes out. Soon, the frog-shaped cathedral squats in a pool of its own making.

- *If you decide to say the Holy Vows and be ordained, go to Section 25.*
- *If you'd rather rob the good priests blind instead, go to Section 11.*

-19-

From a noblewoman's house you steal a gold-plated urn (decorated with silly pictures of dancing birds), and from a commoner's house you steal a baby. (Just because you've decided to become a loving parent doesn't mean you've *completely* changed.) The first time you give the baby a bath, you discover, to your tearful delight, that the child has a full complement of *intersex* genitals, rather than the half-options most people have to walk around with. If you weren't already smitten with this beautiful—dare you say 'regal?'—child, you certainly would be now.

You hock the samovar, and use the money to buy a sturdy, wood-and-stone cottage in a peaceful, sylvan region. A wonderful place to raise Regal. The two of you relocate.

In your entire life you've never been this happy.

• *Go to Section 1.*

-20-

With a piece of pink chalk, the 'witch writes a mere three or four of your names and titles; with purple chalk, she draws circles around individual letters, seemingly chosen at random. When she's done, she erases all the circled letters with her palm. Her hand doesn't get dusty.

She looks at you, and her gaze goes distant. Then her eyes roll back in her head.

"This is your *fortune!*" she screams, in someone else's voice—that of an older woman, one of considerably better breeding. The 'witch straightens up, and runs right at you. Her thick body slams into yours, and the two of you fall over the side of the dirigible.

The whole torturous way down, your body is pierced and battered by green obsidian spires, gargoyles carved from red carnelian, and other fancy crenellations. Your own ridiculously ornate city is killing you. The 'witch—her body still pressed to yours—is already dead.

- *Go to Section 23.*

-21-

Defiling every tenet of your faith, your daughter has joined *Les Arômes Amoreaux,* a caste of subhuman prostitutes. You plan an ambush for her in one of the brothels owned by *Les Arômes,* but since selling out on her humanity, your wretched child has become diabolically clever. You are the one ambushed.

"Mother!" your daughter trills. "I'm so *exceedingly* pleased to see you!" She is wearing a heavily embroidered satin smoking jacket, her bare breasts visible beneath the crimson-and-jet cloth. Behind her, a man holds a green slab of nevermelt ice, deeply glyphed with runes.

The Prophecy! That heathen bitch stole the Prophecy!

You hiss in anger.

"Oh, don't *be* like that, Mother," the treacherous whore purrs. "You've misinterpreted *everything!* Now, why don't you *sit down,* and let me tell you about the many *fascinating* discoveries I've uncovered? Hmm?"

- *If you cry out, "I'd rather die than listen to any more of your heresy!", go to Section 15.*
- *If you're able to restrain your anger a moment longer, at least, go to Section 12.*

-22-

You are Siriad, the Flowerlord, one of seven warring dukes who rule the planet. Recently, you have fallen in love with a gifted young assassin in your employ. Unbeknownst to both of you, this chubby adolescent is your son.

Your chief rival is the Lady of Medicine, the sole duchess among the dukes. For Funeral Day, she sent you the traditional filigreed stone; the candle that was meant to shine *inside* the stone, however, was poisoned. You've always loathed the Duchess, and now it's time to kill her.

- *If you try to destroy her body, go to Section 17.*
- *If you try to destroy her soul, go to Section 3.*

-23-

As your soul leaves your body through a dozen new holes, your vision dims, as if thick ink were being poured directly into your eyes. At first you think you are seeing Nothingness; gradually, you realize that this void is, in fact, spangled with stars. A figure appears in front of the stars, a frog larger than worlds, its massive, translucent body streaked with seven different colors.

Is this not a god?

The beast's sticky tongue arcs to where you are, and draws the mote that is your soul into its gullet. Inside the frog's crystalline belly, with a million other souls, you watch as the divine batrachian hops from galaxy to galaxy, universe to universe. Jumping, leaping, flying.

A beauty beyond all comprehension.

Even you can see it. ✪

-24-

You sit cross-legged on the promontory where your gelid god was killed, and meditate on pure hatred. You seethe as you think about the murderous forces of the monotheistic Heaven. Piece by piece, your frozen-mercury armor falls to the ground. Your body is losing mass, drastically.

You are becoming sleet, sleet that flies *upwards*.

- *Go to Section 8.*

-25-

Two centuries later, what was once a great city (and then a plain of ashes) is now a vast marsh. In the center of the swamps an enormous cathedral sits, damp, frog-shaped and still splendidly multicolored. Though the region is sparsely populated, a devoted order of rustic priests still lives inside the temple, tending to the humble needs of the parish. You're long dead, but you've also been canonized: St. Gohhig Come-Lately. Each evening, some of your descendants will light stinky little swamp-candles in the side-chapel devoted to you.

Your offspring have become the kind of people you once would have happily stolen goats from. ✪

-26-

Disgusted with yourself, and with all your carefully nurtured complicities, you decide to renounce your position, give up your precious lands and titles, and, almost as an afterthought, change your gender. You relocate to a distant, agrarian country, and never hear news of your old milieu again. You move into a cave, learn a few cantrips, and eventually become a witch yourself, performing simple charms for the locals. All in all, you live to be over two thousand years old, and are still tottering around in the far-distant future, when the so-called "Star Stranglers" come to raid your planet.

And what chalkwitch could ever have predicted all *that*? ✪

-27-

"Oh no, cousin!" says the Duchess dismissively, "It's not poison! After all, we *all* carry bezoars nowadays, so what would be the point? Besides, poisons are *far* too easy to trace. No, no tacky little venoms for people of *our* class. Even if you *are* an enemy, Siriad." Idly, the Duchess strokes her left hand with her right, as if petting a pampered cat.

"The thing that is actually killing you is an *elemental* . . . a *tea*-elemental, to be precise." The hateful woman waves a hand at her cup, and, for a moment, an angry brown wave (albeit a tiny one) rears over the thin porcelain rim. "Even now, one of my creatures is splitting the soft tissues of your trachea!

"But cheer up, cousin! At least I left you *some* dignity. I *could* have killed you with the sugar cookies." She nods at the desserts in question, and, obligingly, the buttery sweets rear up into a squat, humanoid shape. Even with a cookie for a face, the little monster glares quite balefully.

As agonizing as the pain in your throat is, the humiliation is worse. Just as convulsions pitch you out of your chair, Olmen—dressed in yellow like the sun—smashes through an oriel window. Your lover starts towards the Duchess, but then hears you gurgle on the floor. His gaze swings away from the Duchess, over to your crumpled form. His stricken face is the last thing you ever see.

(Three minutes later, the Lady of Medicine will kill your lover with the cream pitchers.) ✪

-28-

The needlewitch you've chosen lives in a cave of bright yellow stone.

"A child," you tell her, "a child of my heart."

The 'witch looks at you briefly, and then nods. From a wooden chest she brings out a length of pale violet silk. "We'll use this," she says. "It was the cradle-blanket of one of the dukes!" That seems highly unlikely, though the cloth does look like it was once very expensive.

The needlewitch snips some long hairs from your head, and magically strengthens them with spells and spit. (Apparently, spit is very important; no one's ever told you why.) The young woman uses the hair as thread, stitching the stick-figure image of a child onto the stained violet silk. When she's done, you give her your thieved coins. She pushes the cloth bundle into your hands. "There," she says. "That'll serve."

You move to another village, and use your past experience with goats (with only a *few* of the details glossed over) to secure honest work herding the animals. On warm evenings, you sleep outside. Gently you cradle the cloth that for years you've believed is a baby. ✪

THE CREATION OF BIRDS

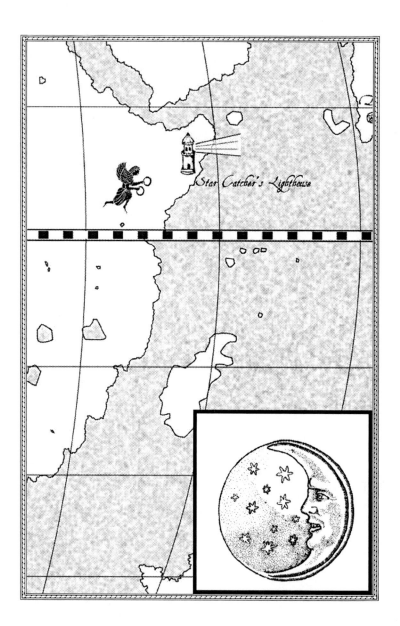

Star Catcher's Lighthouse

THE CREATION OF BIRDS
BY CHRISTOPHER BARZAK

THE BIRD WOMAN SITS AT HER TABLE WITH A LONG STRIP OF PARCHMENT stretched out before her. She holds a quill between her thumb and forefinger, plucked earlier in the night from her own head. She has drawn the outline of a sparrow, has shaded in its curves and hollows. It has two beady black eyes that stare out from the page. This sparrow has spunk, thinks the Bird Woman. She licks her thumb, smudges a section of tail feathers to make them look fuller than usual, then nods, satisfied with the exaggeration.

The Bird Woman is not a realist. She has no time for that. She believes sparrows should have fans for tail feathers, that parrots appear more exotic when they hold silence as a virtue, rather than the prattle for which they are known. The one bird her imagination has left untouched is the hummingbird. Who would dare attempt to better a creature with wings that flutter a hundred times with each beat of its heart? That's art, so simple and evocative. It doesn't get better than that.

Beside her parchment sit two teacups. She cracks open a fresh egg, shuffles the white from the yolk, one shell to the other, then places each half in a teacup. She licks her quill, dips it into the yolk, and draws a small golden circle within the sparrow's breast. A moment later the sparrow opens its beak to warble, but only silence comes out. The golden circle trembles and spins slowly, like a waterwheel, within the sparrow's breast.

She paints each feather with egg white in long lazy strokes. The

97

sparrow stretches its wings a little, clenching and unclenching its tiny claws, testing. "Tut, tut," whispers the Bird Woman. "Not yet, little one. I haven't even given you your colors. What would you want the world to mistake you for? A dove?"

The Bird Woman smiles down at the sparrow. In the next room, the cries and chirps of her most recent creations grow louder as the sun begins to rise. Today she will be taking them to the market. Usually she gives her birds away as gifts or as barter, but she's nearly out of money and soon her landlord will demand what she owes him, which he's been kind enough to ignore for the past two months.

The Bird Woman hasn't been able to make birds for a long time. Nearly four months have passed without one new bird. The birds in the next room were the last to receive the required teaspoon of moon and starlight needed to give them life. The stars and moons, a lot of them have been disappearing. It's because of the Star Catcher—he's been out there again, in the night sky, taking them down, so many of them, as if they were only ornaments or lanterns. Without them, the Bird Woman won't be able to complete even this sparrow, small and slight as it is. There isn't enough available light to make it live. Why did I try, she wonders, if it's such a futile activity? Habit, she thinks. Wishful thinking, she decides.

She tries not to attribute anything to hope.

A swan strolls into the workshop, sidling up beside the Bird Woman's left leg, attempting to view the parchment, but its neck isn't long enough to stretch that high. "Shoo," the Bird Woman scolds it. "Back with the others, silly swan. We'll be leaving soon for the market."

She strokes the top of its head before it turns to leave the room. Her fingers come away damp, sticky with ivory.

It is a good day at the market—there are people everywhere, buying, selling, their voices clamoring in the dusty street. Love potions, jewelry, charms, braided rugs, velvet robes. Food from a thousand worlds, some still living, some long dead. The Bird Woman thinks she might sell a lot of birds in all of this din. A difficult feat, though, considering the Star Catcher has returned from another long absence. His booth sits directly across from the Bird Woman's stall. Even while customers crowd his table, trying to haggle, he stares over their heads at the Bird Woman, his eyes cold as stone.

The Star Catcher is whisper thin and his forehead is filled with creases. He sweats a lot for someone so skinny. He's covered in robes the color of night. On his table he displays an array of moons and stars kept in brass and silver cages. Half Moons, Crescents, Harvest Moons, and a Blue Moon as well. His stars are small and sickly. They wink and blink, but they are known to die quickly after a sale. The Star Catcher never sits down. He stands behind his table, arms folded, and waits for buyers to realize no amount of haggling will force his prices down.

The Bird Woman pretends not to see him. She inhales a deep breath of the dry market air, and shrugs off his stare. It has been several months since she last spoke to him, and though time away has made her days easier, he has not stopped taking down the stars. It is his way of punishing her, she thinks, for leaving. And yet . . . and yet, she thinks, he'd been taking them down before she even made that decision.

A long time ago, the Bird Woman had tried to be his lover. She had tried to understand him like no one had before. But the Star Catcher, she soon discovered, didn't know how to love something he couldn't own. Her memory of their time together is like walking through thick forest, suddenly falling into a pit that's been covered over with sticks and brush to hide the hole someone has dug to keep you trapped as a pet. She tries not to wander through those memories anymore. He kept her in that hole long enough. He shouldn't still have that power over her, she knows, and yet he does. There had been moments that came close to love and, yes, also passion. These memories the Bird Woman tries to leave pure and untouched. She keeps this one beautiful still: his eyes holding her gaze steady as he moved above her, the feel and smell of his skin, grainy and sweet like sugar, his breath fanning her feathers. "I love your eyes," he told her, tracing their contours with his finger, two perfect circles in an owl-like face. "I love your everything," he told her, and his hands moved down the length of her body as she sang, sang, sang, blinking profusely.

The Bird Woman knows where the Star Catcher likes to be kissed—on his forehead, like a child. She used to kiss each of the wrinkles on his forehead before they went to sleep. He never attempted to learn her own skin though, or how to talk to her about her art. The Bird Woman learned so much about the stars and their placement and how the Star Catcher goes about displacing them, she could probably catch stars herself. For a while, she felt like one of his stars, clinging to his arm, on display for other people. He never asked about her birds.

The market is busy this morning, which makes it easier for her to ignore him. She hopes he will choose to ignore her as well.

The swan goes first. Someone is here to buy it for a storybook for children. She wraps a blue bow around its neck before sending it off. Then her silent parrot is paid for by a deaf-mute. His smile is soft and gentle. She imagines the two of them will keep a quiet house together. There go the lovebirds as well as the cuckoo bird, which she notices is a little mad. It continually preens, stopping only to eat. Not a good sign. She is glad it found a home though. Soon it will be laying eggs in other birds' nests, allowing them to raise its hatchlings. I'm a bit of a cuckoo myself, the Bird Woman thinks.

She is busy tidying up her stall, sweeping out feathers and birdseed, when she hears his voice.

"My dear. Jessica. Jess. How have you been?"

The Bird Woman doesn't stop sweeping; she doesn't look up at all. She knows it is the Star Catcher by his deep, sonorous voice and by the name that he calls her. The Bird Woman doesn't have a name like that. She is just the Bird Woman. Her mother never gave her a name like the mortals have. She is her mother's daughter. Her mother had been the Bird

Woman also, and so she was called too, after her mother left this world for the next. But the Star Catcher calls her something human anyway. Some name he thinks she should like. She decides not to answer. She has principles. She's made a point of sticking to them for the past thirty years, after she finally gave him up. She will make a point of sticking to them still.

"Jessica, Jessica," he says, trying again. "Why won't you talk? It's been so long. Look up, it's me. Ivan. I have a gift for you. Really. No kidding."

The Bird Woman looks up. She is not immune to gifts, nor to possible reconciliation. She likes to think people can change. The Star Catcher stands just outside her stall, holding a small silver cage. Inside is a blue star the size of a pearl earring. He holds the cage out for her to take.

"For you," he says.

"I don't keep stars," says the Bird Woman. She looks down, and resumes sweeping her stall. Shaking her head wearily, she says, "I don't keep anything."

"Keep this then," he says. "Please. A peace offering. For all of our troubles."

She is skeptical at first, but finally decides to take it, nodding her assent. She cannot imagine this tiny star could have much of a life with the Star Catcher anyway, and besides, its light may help her sparrow live. Perhaps she can teach the star how to live on land, away from the sky, though not likely, considering she knows sky better than land.

"How long are you back for?" she asks, head down, looking up at him from beneath her eyelashes.

"A few days," he says. "I need to go back out again for more."

"Thank you," the Bird Woman says, eyes fixed on the blue star in its cage. "Have a nice day," she tells him, as if he is nothing more than another customer.

On the Bird Woman's island, all streets lead to the same place—the center. The roads are cobbled, and they travel ever inward, spirals, all of them, one after the other. The Bird Woman's house sits near the center of the city, built on the riverside. The rivers here follow the same pathways; they move inward, spiraling. Between the streets are canals, roads made of water. From above—and the Bird Woman has taken to sky many times just to see this—the island looks like a seashell, floating in the blue ocean.

The Bird Woman's bones are hollow, and because of this her step is light. She moves through crowds more quickly than others. She hops upon wagons and barrows as they wheel by, then wings her way to the other side of the street. Today, she needs to stop by the market, as well as the banker, to deposit the money from the sale of her birds. She also has an appointment with the psychoanalyst, that old man with the long white beard. He wears wizard caps, tall and pointy. For him, the mind is the same thing as magic. The Bird Woman has a friend who sees the psychoanalyst on a regular basis. This friend is an artist as well—a bit of a loon, really—but she swears the psychoanalyst is saving her life, little by little, one hour a week. She's suggested the Bird Woman see him herself. *For the sake of your art, if for nothing else,* she'd explained.

The Bird Woman is more than a little reluctant. She's never needed therapy before. But lately she's not been so sure of herself as she used to be. Perhaps, she thinks, an objective opinion is exactly what's needed.

These names are poetry: kookaburra, cardinal, cormorant, kestrel, nuthatch, warbler, flamingo, thrush. The Bird Woman keeps each name tucked under her tongue. Better than locking them inside her head, where she might not be able to retrieve them, depending on her mood. When the Bird Woman is happy, she'll make Phoenixes and Thunderbirds, which exist only in poetry and dreams. When she is merely content, she makes birds that are real and not imagined. When the Bird Woman is sad, she doesn't make birds at all. She explains all of this within the first fifteen minutes of her session.

The psychoanalyst stares at the Bird Woman through foggy spectacles. He rubs his hands together like a fly. "This, my dear," he says in his old man's voice, "is why you can't work. You're depressed. Sorrow can make any of us stop in our tracks. Of course you can't make birds."

"But there isn't enough light," she explains. "The Star Catcher keeps taking the moons and stars. I need them. It isn't just my own state of mind. The problem is out there in the world. How do you say it? Circumstantial?"

"Yes, yes," he says. "That's the word all right. But really, you must stop blaming others. If you are to help yourself, if you are to break this pattern of self-indulgent sadness, this apathy, then you will have to stop blaming others and be able to point your finger back at yourself. For example, have you ever done anything to the Star Catcher that would make him deprive you of stars?"

"Moons too," she adds quickly. "We were lovers once. It didn't work out. But surely that isn't a reason to strip the sky?"

"Well now," says the psychoanalyst, "even the Star Catcher has feelings. I think you should set aside time to think about that. As an exercise in self-abnegation. It can work miracles, really. I've seen patients recover in no time flat once they've considered themselves the source of their own problems."

The Bird Woman considers this carefully, rubbing the side of her nose with her thumb. "I did end things awfully fast," she admits. "Cut and dried, you know. That's what mother used to say is best in matters of the heart."

"But your mother wasn't a psychoanalyst," the psychoanalyst points out, and the Bird Woman can do nothing but nod.

Before she leaves, the psychoanalyst stops her in the foyer of his office. "Wait," he says. "You forgot your bag."

"I don't have a bag," says the Bird Woman.

"Oh no, it's just a little something I'm sending you home with. You might need it. In times of distress."

"I won't take pills," the Bird Woman says. But the psychoanalyst shakes his head.

"Not necessary at all, in your situation," he declares. And says for her to come back again in a week.

"Thank you," says the Bird Woman. She nods weakly before opening the door to leave.

In the square outside the office building, the Bird Woman pauses before continuing home, wondering what the bag holds. She reaches inside and feels something hairy. She grabs hold of the hair and pulls out the psychoanalyst's head by his beard. The head hangs upside down from the beard like a pocket watch, dangling and swaying.

"Hello again," the psychoanalyst's head says, looking up (or down, from his own vantage) at the Bird Woman. "Are we home yet?"

The Bird Woman loves three things best in the world: birds, the stars that give them life, and flying. When the Bird Woman learned to fly, her mother worried and worried; she cried in joy and terror to see her daughter soaring higher than even she herself had ever dared to go. On her first flight, the Bird Woman brought back handfuls of clouds for her mother, a shard of sunlight, and two swathes of sky to match her mother's eyes. She weaved the sky into a dress robe, and years later, she wrapped her mother in that cloth when she died, offering her back to the heavens.

In the Bird Woman's memory, her mother is who loved her best. She had warned her not to fly too high. "The sky is not always filled with beauty," she told the Bird Woman. "Sometimes danger lingers there, like storms and lightning." Always her mother had been saying things that were obvious, and yet the Bird Woman had run into her share of storms, had dodged several bolts of lightning, no matter that her mother had warned her.

She'd found the Star Catcher like that, pedaling through the sky in a mechanical contraption, the wings made of wire and leather, pulleys attached to its wheels, which pumped the wings to take him higher. She stopped mid-flight and hovered, as if she were a hummingbird, to watch him for a while. She admired a man who wanted to fly. And later, after they had met and the sky and clouds had trembled as they touched, she brought him home to meet her mother. But her mother cast a crooked finger at him immediately, its talon landing on his cheek. "You have the stars in your eyes," she had told him. But it wasn't a compliment. "This one," she told the Bird Woman, "will take what he wants."

The Bird Woman's mother died two months later. The Star Catcher brought a star to the funeral and placed it on top of the casket with the flowers from the mortal mourners. The Bird Woman thought this a grand gesture. He had flown higher than she had to bring this gift for her mother's funeral, and even after her mother had judged him so harshly. As he approached her through the mourning queue, she burst into tears, and he slid his arms around her. "Be still," he whispered into her ear, like a command but gentle, and so she was.

At home, the Bird Woman's sparrow is still struggling to lift itself out of the parchment. She holds the psychoanalyst's head by his beard in one hand, and the caged star in the other. She looks at both. Both look back at her. The psychoanalyst says, "This would be a perfect opportunity to practice appreciating the Star Catcher. Put the star he gave you to good use."

The Bird Woman sets the psychoanalyst's head on her kitchen counter, next to the cutting board. She takes her star to the worktable and opens its cage door. The star doesn't attempt to escape.

She reaches in and pulls it out, fitting it inside the palm of her hand, like a stone, or a kitten. She strokes it, and it vibrates, growing warm. She reaches for a teaspoon, spoons up some of the soft blue light, and sprinkles it over the sparrow's struggling body. The sparrow pulls itself the rest of the way out of the parchment, stretching its wings, clenching and unclenching its tiny claws, blinking profusely. It cocks its head towards the Bird Woman, waiting.

The Bird Woman places the star back in its cage. She's delighted that it actually worked. Here is a new bird, a new creation, waiting. Waiting for her to add the final touches to its life.

She takes down a violin from the top shelf of her closet, propping it between her chin and neck. A long plastic tube dangles from the front of the violin. The Bird Woman pinches the end of the tube between her fingers, brings it close to the sparrow's beak. "Open," she says, and the sparrow opens its beak.

The Bird Woman slips the tube into the sparrow's mouth, like a mother feeding a worm to her hatchling. She lifts bow to strings and begins to play something sweet and lilting, but no music can be heard. The music slides down through the tubing instead. Sometimes green and sometimes golden, it moves through the tubing into the sparrow, like a drip feed. The column of the sparrow's throat moves up and down, drinking greedily. When the Bird Woman finishes her song, she pulls the tube out and the sparrow begins to sing.

"Lovely," says the Bird Woman.

"Indeed," the psychoanalyst says, beaming along with her. "See, my dear. You just have to get on with things. Stop blaming other people. You couldn't have done that if the Star Catcher hadn't given you that star."

The Bird Woman looks back to the cage, where a small pile of ash lies, steaming, in the place where the star has died.

"This star is dead," says the Bird Woman the next morning, pushing the cage with the remains inside it towards the Star Catcher. "You gave me a dying star," she says.

"I did no such thing," says the Star Catcher. He stands in the frame of his front door, holding his hands up to his chest, abashed. "That star was fine when I gave it to you," he says, pointing a long finger towards it. "Did you use it to make a new bird?"

"I used a bit of its light to finish off a sparrow," says the Bird Woman.

"Well there you go," says the Star Catcher, throwing his hands in the air. "You killed it for the creation of your birds."

"They aren't *my* birds," the Bird Woman corrects him. "They're just birds, damn it. And no star should die from giving up a teaspoon of light. Believe me, I'm the expert on that. I'm the expert on *something!*"

"Sorry," says the Star Catcher. "That star would have been fine if you'd left it alone."

The Bird Woman clenches her lips tightly. She grips both of her hands together, flexing the muscles in her fingers. She wants to lash out at the Star Catcher, but she'll hold her hands to each other rather than touch him like that. The Star Catcher likes to be treated as a child. Violence towards him will not help matters at all.

"I'm sorry," she says finally. "You're right. My fault. My fault," and turns to walk away, shoulders shrugging.

"Wait!" the Star Catcher shouts.

The Bird Woman turns her head back towards him.

He moves aside and holds his front door open, waving towards the dark foyer behind. "I can help," he says. "Please. Come inside."

The Star Catcher lives in a lighthouse on the edge of the island. Made from chalky white stones, it nearly touches the sky. It continually sends signals out to nearby boats to warn them away from rocks and dangerous waters. All of the boatmen appreciate the Star Catcher's tower. They call him brother, Guardian of the Light. The Bird Woman has passed by ships in the boatyards, docking or unloading goods from other lands, has heard these men praising the Star Catcher's brilliance. Unable to remain quiet, each time she has called out, "Fools! You thank the one who possesses your constellations!" They forget the troubles they and their fathers and their fathers' fathers have had navigating without them. How in the last hundred years, as the Star Catcher has taken the stars down, more boats manned by their brothers and sisters have wrecked upon the shores of foreign lands, never to be seen or heard from again. He has taken not only the light from the skies, thinks the Bird Woman, but the light from their minds. As she passes the wharf, she opens her beak and caws a short, shocking curse. Some men look up from their nets, but she carries on, not looking at the Star Catcher, until they reach the lighthouse, that gleaming tower at the end of the last curl in her island.

The Bird Woman has forgotten how much space the Star Catcher inhabits. She herself makes do in that little cottage consisting of only two rooms. The Star Catcher's lighthouse goes up and up, catwalks climbing level after level. He ascends a spiral staircase that begins in the center of the first floor, his boots thumping every step of the way, and the Bird Woman follows behind his dark flowing robes.

As they climb to the top, the light inside the building grows stronger, and the Bird Woman's breath grows shorter with each step that she takes. Her cheeks flush, warm and ruddy under her feathers. Finally she asks, "Where are you taking me? I haven't got time for your games."

"Just a little farther," says the Star Catcher, looking over his shoulder and smiling. His smile is innocent and serious, which makes the Bird Woman smile back. She always liked it when the Star Catcher was happy or excited about something. He was always very sincere at those times.

They reach the top floor of the lighthouse and stand before a door where light for the signal originates—the lantern room. The door to this room is closed, but light seeps through the doorframe, outlining it in the dark stairwell. The Star Catcher flings the door open and steps aside, so the Bird Woman can enter before him. Inside, stacked up in large mounds, are heaps of moons and stars, no lighthouse lantern at all. The stars and moons lie together like pieces of gold in a treasure cave. Or, the Bird Woman thinks, like bodies. Dead bodies. Together they sigh and shuffle a little to one side or the other, bumping into each other weakly. But even if they *could* move, where would they go? She almost retches, and throws her hand to her mouth.

"Ivan," she whispers. "What have you done?"

The Star Catcher looks back and forth between the mound of stars and the Bird Woman, grinning. "They're for you, my dear," he says.

Down, down, down. Then down even farther. The Bird Woman hops and flutters down the spiral stairwell, whimpering at the thought of the stars locked inside the Star Catcher's tower. Already she knows she will not be able to live with the memory of what he's done, of what he's taken from the world, from its people. Imagine their upturned faces, staring into emptiness, the sky reflecting nothing of their lives below, providing no guidance, no hint of life outside their own world. It is my fault, thinks the Bird Woman. Even if they've forgotten.

The Star Catcher follows with his robes flapping behind him. "Jessica, wait! You don't understand!"

"I understand perfectly," the Bird Woman squawks over her shoulder. She grabs hold of the brass knob on the front door and pushes it open. Warm light pours in from the outside. On the street a wagon pulled by two oxen creaks by. Two children, a boy and a girl of ten or eleven, sit on the back of the wagon, waving and laughing, legs dangling. The Bird Woman waves back, breathing deeply, sighing. She turns round and faces the Star Catcher once more. "Never speak to me again," she says.

"But—" The Star Catcher reaches out to touch her.

"No, Ivan," the Bird Woman says.

"I did it for you," he tells her. "The stars are yours if you want them."

The Bird Woman considers this. She cocks her head to one side, studying the Star Catcher's face: the wide-set eyes, unbearably blue and innocent; the wrinkled forehead; the cherub lips; the hands, too soft for the sort of work he does. The Bird Woman sees what he says is the truth. How can he speak the truth though, she wonders, and still pry the stars from their homes? The Bird Woman suddenly wishes the psychoanalyst's head were here. He would have answers. Possibly not correct ones, but answers nonetheless.

"For me?" she asks finally, and the Star Catcher nods. "If they're for me, Ivan," she says, "then I suggest you replace them. Put them back where they belong."

"No," the Star Catcher says. He shrugs. "They're for you, Jessica. But here. You can have the stars here, if you like."

The Bird Woman looks past the Star Catcher's face, over his shoulder, at the lighthouse towering behind him, beaming, light stockpiled at the top level. For a moment, she considers the choice she has to make. She will have to have things brought here from her own cottage. She will not be able to do this without help. Finally she turns back to the Star Catcher. "Here then," she says, brushing by him, head held high, back into the lighthouse.

Doves, bluejays, cardinals, canaries, jackdaws, falcons—soon the lighthouse is filled with the flapping of wings, the flash of feathers, the screech and holler of birds. Two owls call back and forth to each other, measuring the night together. The Bird Woman sits cross-legged on the cold flagstones at the top of the lighthouse, sketching, shading, painting, filling the mouths of her creations with notes from her violin.

The Star Catcher brings her tea, plates of toast spread with cream and honey. "Busy, busy," he says, stroking her cheek with the tips of his fingers. Then he disappears for an hour, only to return with his hands empty, smiling, waiting, peering over the Bird Woman's shoulder. "What's this one to be?" he asks.

"An ostrich," the Bird Woman tells him. "Please. I need space. I can't work with you looking over my shoulder."

"Sorry," the Star Catcher says, stepping backwards until he reaches the door. "I'll just be downstairs, then, if you need me."

"I don't need you," the Bird Woman mutters, after he's closed the door.

The Bird Woman stares at her canvas until tears begin to fill her eyes. "Stop that," she whispers. "Stop it. There are better things in this world that deserve your tears."

"What a situation you've gotten yourself into," the psychoanalyst says. His head sits propped up on a nearby bookshelf, his beard trailing over the shelving, almost touching the floor. "I'm beside myself," he tells the Bird Woman. "Really, I can't believe how you put up with his constant attentions. It's disgraceful. You'd think he were a guard, some sort of sentinel."

"I tried to tell you," says the Bird Woman.

"But—" says the psychoanalyst.

"But you wouldn't listen," the Bird Woman says.

"Hmmph," says the psychoanalyst. "Really, my dear. I've never encountered someone like him. Whatever attracted you in the first place?"

The Bird Woman considers this question for a moment, eyes rolled up slightly, finger placed carefully on her lips. She begins to stroke brown into the ostrich before her. "I think it was his passion," she says finally.

"His passion? What passion?" the psychoanalyst says.

"His passion for me," says the Bird Woman.

"That's not passion, dear girl," says the psychoanalyst. "That's obsession. They can seem like the same thing."

Footsteps sound on the catwalk outside. "Wonderful," says the psychoanalyst. "He's back."

The door opens on oily hinges, and the Star Catcher pokes his head inside. "Working?" he asks, tentatively, cautious. The Bird Woman doesn't look at him. She only nods and continues painting.

"Could I bother you for a bite of dinner?" the psychoanalyst asks from his place on the shelves. He raises his eyebrows plaintively.

The Star Catcher nods. "Of course," he says. "But really—where do you put it?"

"Trade secret," says the psychoanalyst.

"Jessica," the Star Catcher says. "Tell me again why this person is here."

"He's my therapist," says the Bird Woman. "Please bring him some supper."

The door swings closed as suddenly as it opened. Footsteps echo, grow softer, and the psychoanalyst—*ahem*—attempts to clear his nonexistent throat. "You must do something about this," he tells the Bird Woman. "Things can't go on this way."

Just then she is helping the ostrich out of its parchment, pulling it out by its flightless wings, one hand tucked under its belly.

"I have a plan," she tells the psychoanalyst, grunting. The ostrich separates from the parchment with a satisfying pop. It peers around the room, looking for a hole to bury its head in. The Bird Woman directs it to the piles of moons and stars, and it saunters over, thrusts its beak into the glowing chips of light.

"You have a plan," the psychoanalyst curls his lip into a mock sneer. "I'm sure this will be interesting."

The Star Catcher used to always bring the Bird Woman love tokens. Packages of exotic seeds from across the ocean. A new glass filter, through which she could direct starlight. Two lovebirds, which she herself never made—they had hatched on their own, in the wild. "Like us," he told her. "Wild," he'd said, nuzzling her neck feathers, and she had pressed herself closer to his hands.

When the stars started to disappear, though, the Bird Woman asked him to stop taking them. "I don't think that it's a good idea," she said. "People are talking."

"What do I care about people?" the Star Catcher said. "I have you, Jess. What business is it of theirs?" He had placed one hand around her neck and brought her face to his to kiss it. The Bird Woman had pushed him away, disgusted.

"The stars belong to no one," she said. "And neither do I. I *choose* to be with you, Ivan." She had looked down at her feet because she couldn't stand to see the Star Catcher when he behaved this way, which, she discovered over time, was a common occurrence.

"They belong to me," the Star Catcher had said, his voice firm.

"You can't take them with you," the Bird Woman whispered.

"Where?" he had asked innocently, as if her statement was a true mystery to him.

"To the next world," she had said.

But her answer only made him grin.

Throughout the day, the Bird Woman rests on a nest of blankets, next to the mounds of stars and moons. She barely sleeps, though, because the Star Catcher insists on sitting next to her, cross-legged, hands folded in his lap, telling stories. His favorite stories are from his childhood. This is nothing new to the Bird Woman. Back when they were lovers, the Star Catcher told her stories all the time. Now that she's back, living in his lighthouse, he's resumed telling them as if he'd only temporarily been interrupted. They are not lovers this time, though; they are simply inhabiting the same space. Along with the psychoanalyst.

The Bird Woman is glad the psychoanalyst is with her. Not for his advice, but because his presence means she never has to be alone with the Star Catcher. The psychoanalyst is not glad of anything, really. He sits on his shelf, rolling his eyes as the Star Catcher tells his stories, sometimes snorting.

"When I was a little boy," the Star Catcher tells the Bird Woman, "I used to love summer best of all seasons. I would wait until the sun began to set, and the fog would roll into the island, and then the fireflies would appear, tiny green sparks in the mist, signaling back and forth to each other. They were so beautiful, the way the glow came from their own bodies. I wanted to glow like that, too. I used to try and catch them, and put them in glass jars to make lanterns. I liked the feel of them in my hands, crawling on my skin. I'd set the lantern on my nightstand and watch them glowing on and off all night, until I fell asleep. In the morning, though, they were always dead on their backs, legs sticking up."

"How sad," the Bird Woman tells him. Her eyelids flutter, heavy with sleep, but she continues listening. She's heard the story before, among others, but the Star Catcher continually returns to this one.

"It's funny, though," says the Star Catcher. "Because it became harder and harder for me to catch the fireflies. After a while, I'd try to catch them, but they'd lift into the air just before I could get hold of them. They'd be just inches above my reach, and they'd float higher and higher, until they disappeared into the night sky. That's when I noticed the stars. That's when I started to catch stars instead. Stars don't move, unless they're dying."

"It's hot in here," the Bird Woman says. She scratches under the ruff of feathers circling her neck. "Please. Open a window. Or else bring me a fan."

"Why not go out for a walk instead?" the Star Catcher offers. He lifts one eyebrow and motions with his hands towards the door.

"Too tired," says the Bird Woman, punctuating her explanation with a long, elliptical sigh. "I've been working so hard, so very hard," she tells the Star Catcher. "Please, Ivan, bring me some fresh air."

"Of course," the Star Catcher acquiesces. "Besides," he says, "this room is beginning to stink of your birds and their dung. You should think about selling some of them, Jess, really."

"Why not release them?" the Bird Woman says. She looks down into her folded hands, locked together in her lap. If she looks at him, he'll see through her; if she doesn't look at him, he'll know something is not right. Without knowing her at all, the Star Catcher knows *some* things about the Bird Woman. He knows the details she wishes other people would overlook: escape tactics, white lies, kindnesses to brush tension under a rug.

For several moments he is silent, so the Bird Woman finally looks up, blinking. The Star Catcher meets her stare.

"Release them?" he asks, eyebrows knitting together. "Wouldn't you rather sell them at the market? They're *your* birds, after all. You made them."

"But I've made so many," the Bird Woman says. "And anyway, why not? I'm here now, instead of renting the cottage. And sometimes I like to make birds for no good reason. Let them take to sky instead of hobbling around in this tower."

"As long as you're sure," the Star Catcher says, shaking his head. He searches the folds of his robes for a set of keys and, finding them, opens a box on the floor, next to the doorway. Inside the box is a long lever. Kneeling next to it, the Star Catcher pulls back on the lever, using all of his weight. The lever click, click, clicks into position. Gears churn, grind beneath the Bird Woman's feet. She can feel the floor buckling beneath her. The dome of the lantern room slides around her until suddenly a sliver of black sky appears, its shadow deeper where the stars have been plucked. Slowly the gap widens until the lantern room is half-exposed to night.

"Ahh," the Bird Woman breathes deeply. The air is cold, salty on her lips. It tastes of feathers floating to earth and fish leaping in spangled sunlight.

"Better?" the Star Catcher asks, still kneeling next to the lever, smiling.

"Much," the Bird Woman says. Her birds flutter and hop around the room in anticipation. She holds both hands in front of her then, palms up, open, a private signal only she and they understand, and the birds rise up—all of them, except for the ostrich—each with a star or a moon clenched in its talons.

"Stop that! What are you doing?" The Star Catcher stands, stretching his arms out, grabbing after the stars and moons that hang lowest in the air. But each one eludes him, floating into the night air like the fireflies of his youth.

The birds spread over the city, the island, past the clouds and even higher, fireworks opening above the boulevards and boatmen, until each star is set back into its proper niche. There are so many holes in the fabric of darkness, and each one fits like a jewel in an antique brooch.

"Call them back, Jessica!" the Star Catcher pleads. He stands in the center of the lantern room, looking up at what took years to collect, then collapses into a pool of black robes, like a melted candle, and begins to weep. Openly, fitfully.

"Time for me to go, I think," says the psychoanalyst. The ostrich saunters over and plucks him down from the bookshelf by his beard. The two of them trot down the stairwell, and the psychoanalyst's voice echoes back, "Call if you need any more advice, my dear. Any at all."

The Bird Woman crawls on hands and knees to where the Star Catcher sits, head lolling to one side, arms splayed out in front of him, like an unstrung puppet. "All gone," he mutters. "All gone. I'll never be able to collect them all again."

"No, Ivan," she says, pulling him backwards to rest his head on her lap. "They're still here. See them? See how brightly they shine?"

He isn't listening, though. It's obvious from the way he shakes his head in disagreement, or dissatisfaction. "No," he says, eyes wincing with tears. "Gone, gone, gone. What am I going to do with myself now?"

Stroking his forehead, she leans down and kisses his worried creases. In her head, the psychoanalyst's head is still talking. He's telling her that what she's doing will make everything happen again. It's a pattern, my dear, he pleads. He's right, she knows that, but she says what she wants anyway. "Let them go," she whispers in his ear. "Some of them might come back." ✪

THE RIDER

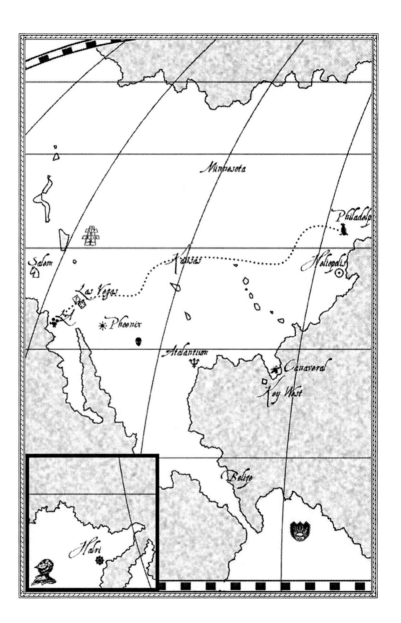

THE RIDER

BY MEGHAN MCCARRON

NELL WOKE ME UP AND ANNOUNCED WE WERE LEAVING. I TRIED TO IGNORE her, but she wasn't having any of it. She pulled open the shades and said, "Look! Daylight!" She pointed at the sun, like she thought I didn't believe her.

By the time I got up, she had taken over the motel bathroom. I started banging on the door. It made me feel like a twelve-year-old.

"Nell, I have to piss!"

"Fuck you, Lewis. You promised to be up at seven."

"It's seven fifteen."

"What?"

"Seven. Fifteen."

"You said you'd be up at seven!"

I leaned against the wall and listened to her brush her teeth.

I met Nell when I went home to do some research for a script. I ended up scrapping the project, but first I spent a lot of time at this dive where I used to pass fake IDs in high school. Nell tended bar there, and we got to be friends. Buddy-friends, nothing deep or significant. Then, one night, she went crazy, and I decided I liked her. It's a thing with me. It's a bad habit. But I don't trust people unless they know what it's like to be nuts.

The night it happened, she'd been drinking with me, matching shot for shot. Laughing. Suddenly she started screaming. NO NO I WON'T ANY MORE NO PLEASE NO NO NOT THE RIDER

119

Everyone stopped talking and stared. I grabbed her wrist and led her outside. Or tried. Halfway across the room, she puked up something that smelled like whiskey and fainted dead away.

"Lewis," she said the next day. "I used to read minds. Do magic. I lived Somewhere Else. There was a war. I had power. Try to believe me."

I did. I didn't even have to ask. She was that thing I'd always day-dreamed. Somewhere Else. I trusted that, too.

"Lewis, stop pouting," she said from inside the bathroom. "I told you how I feel about Kansas."

"You hate it."

"It's too damn flat!"

"So you get like this?"

"Bathroom's yours."

I showered quickly, using soap like armor, as if the *New Spring Mist Scent!* would strengthen me for the day. I came out of the bathroom and found Nell sprawled on her bed. She sat up when she saw me.

"I know what you're thinking, Lewis."

"Oh, you're mind-reading again?"

"You learn to read faces, you know. You learn to read signs. And I know what you're thinking."

"Tell me." I started getting dressed.

"I'm not going to lose it."

"Nell."

"This is different." She tapped her forehead, the space right between her eyes. "It's from before. Adrenaline. Please, Lewis." She made the international sign for "steering wheel."

"Breakfast first?"

"Eat something at the gas station. I need to drive."

I choked down my Ho-Hos at ninety-five miles per hour. I hid the jerky in the back pocket for later. God knew when we'd stop.

Nell was hunched over the wheel, and her small, cowboy-booted foot pushed the gas down as far as it would go. She looked like a hunter. Not a fat man in an orange jacket, but a real hunter, a naked warrior with a knife in her teeth. Her eyes wanted to kill something. Keep herself alive.

It was moments like these that drove it home, that she'd been strange places. Done strange things. *Was* strange, in a way that chilled me, even as it drew me in.

We hit a hundred. I ought to do something. Keep myself alive.

"Nell, tell me how it started," I said.

She didn't take her eyes off the road. "What?"

"What's making you . . . like this."

"Kansas? I dunno, I guess a long time ago some flat, unimaginative asteroid—" she began.

"I mean," I said, "what are you running away from?"

Nell cracked a grin. I didn't like it.

"Ah," she said.

"If you don't want to . . ." I said.

Nell paused. "No. No. We're on a car trip. I've heard all *your* boring confessions. Where should I start?"

"It's your story," I said.

"You got two options," Nell continued. "I can start with 'I was born' or 'I was taken.'"

"What's the difference?" I said.

"How soon we get to me like this."

"'I was born,'" I said.

Nell tapped the steering wheel. "I was born in Toledo, Ohio. My dad cut hair. My mom worked at the supermarket. Assistant manager. My mom and dad split. My mom moved down to Phoenix with her sister and took me with her. It was nice there. Real yellow. My dad stayed in Ohio. Didn't see him much. My mom went back to work at a supermarket. I went to school." She paused, looking for the right word. "Then I got sold."

"You got *sold?*"

"By my dad," Nell said.

"What?"

"I'm sure he thought it was some kind of scam. Or a joke. God knows what he did when he got the check in the mail."

I tried to work this out in my head. Kansas kept whipping by. "So what happened?"

"Two men came for me one day, after school. They wore American clothes, suits, but the clothes didn't sit right on them. They put me in a car and took me out to the desert. They drove until they found this one dirt road that lead to a cave. They led me inside and pushed. Things went kind of fuzzy, and I felt—I dunno. Thin. Next thing I knew I was doubled over at the edge of a lake and puking."

"How old were you?"

"Seven?" Nell flicked up several fingers. "Yeah, seven."

"Back to the lake."

"I never saw it again," Nell said, waving a hand. "Like this corn. Just scenery. No, they took me to a city." Nell's face changed. She looked younger, suddenly, and her eyes got a dreamy look. *The* city. Halri. Street-dances, pop lights, parades of animals I'd never seen before or since. I'd never trade it for a childhood on Earth. Even in Phoenix."

Nell fell silent and stared out the windshield, as if she were watching those parades again. I tried to imagine them, too, but all I saw was semis lumbering in the slow lanes as we whizzed by.

I waited for her to continue, then gave up.

"What did they buy you for?" I asked.

"They had to. They used to just steal kids like me, but at some point they made a deal."

"Was it—for sex?"

Nell made a long, breathy sound—*pissssssh.* Then she started laughing.

"I couldn't get anyone to touch me if I *tried.* Changelings are made *for* their world, not in it. They'd keep us from learning to speak, if they could."

"Oh."

"It's not so bad," Nell said. "You get to step back and watch. Wasn't so bad for a shy kid like me."

"So what did they have you do?" I asked.

"Work," Nell said. "In places where we could be displayed—offices, churches, houses. Changelings are big status, so you don't want to hide them away in factories or farms. I was church-kind. At the biggest cathedral in Halri. There were ten of us in all. We tended the shrines, cleaned the kneelers, kissed the altar on hours when there was no worship. One of the older kids, he even learned their dances. Woke up every full moon and danced them until the sun rose. He was from Cleveland."

"Ohio?"

"Where else? When the Committee came, to take 'servants for the war'—well, we all thought it would be him. Instead it was Sarra. We didn't get it, 'cause she was really sick. Her nose bled in the middle of the night, and she had headaches all the time. Turned out, she was getting cancer. But no one knew that then. She had headaches. She was having visions."

Nell tapped the wheel. "They thought she was me."

She opened her mouth to say more, but seemed to change her mind. Then I saw it. Salvation.

"Welcome to Colorado," I sighed.

But Nell's eyes had already moved on to the next sign.

"Blue Jay Diner," she said. "Let's hope they have corned beef."

I once dated a former child star. It was when I first came to L.A. and had yet to learn the rule: all movie people, save you, are crazy. He was as young as me, but he looked completely past his prime. That's what drew me. The look of being not un-beautiful, but past that stage in life. Like all of us, he had a drinking problem. And like all of us, he was hustling, looking to make that next contact, get that next meeting, find that next person who would finally get him "in." But his ambition was different. He'd been in the circle before. He just wanted to get back, and stay.

There's something of him in Nell. When I first saw her, I thought she was the girl from Punky Brewster. She, too, looks young and past her prime. But when she gets sad, it's not tinged with the self-pity you see in people who grew up easy. It's a sadness that can barely stand itself. It reminds me not so much that she's human, but that humans can feel things you'll never understand.

We were the only people under fifty at the Blue Jay. At first, Nell kept fingering the silverware like so many weapons, but once her corned beef sandwich came she relaxed. I just poked my tuna melt. I regretted the Ho-Hos.

The Blue Jay Diner lived up to its name with odd touches. Birds' nests on the edges of scattered booths, blue tabletops, a real stuffed jay at the cash register. Otherwise it was typical diner chic: mirrors, linoleum, uncomfortable shades of pink.

"So," I began, once the sandwich was gone, "how did they find you?"

"Huh?"

"Did you get headaches too?"

Nell started pouring packets of sugar onto the table. "Forgot I was telling that story. No, I didn't get any headaches. See, one way you can get it, you get like Sarra. The power kicks the shit out of you until you make some space."

"And the other is—?"

"It wrecks everything it can find until you let it in."

I was struck with a feeling that I hadn't had since high school and trying to join in on guy talk about tits. This time, of course, I was the one that was normal, Nell was the freak with a secret, but I didn't feel any more comfortable.

"Ouch," I managed.

"Whatever. I was fine until it got me. Before then it was kind of great. It started with churchgoers hearing things. They'd be kneeling at devotions and catch their neighbors' prayers. Then people started finishing each other's sentences, finding out secrets. There were fistfights."

"Did you know it was you?"

Nell laughed. "No way."

"Did they?"

"No. They thought the culprit would have it the worst. But I wasn't touched."

I tried to imagine the fistfights. I had a vision of my childhood parish embroiled in a massive brawl, like the saloon fight from *Dodge City*, except now old ladies tipped over statues of saints, kids trapped the Sunday-school teacher in a confessional, the deacon pulled up a pew and swung it at the cantor.

"Weird," I said.

"Seriously."

"So, how did they figure it out?"

"It was tough, I think. They got all panicky when the cathedral started getting damaged. A hole got punched through the sanctuary wall. Kneelers burst into flames. They burned for days, no matter how the priests tried to put them out. I watched it. I think I laughed.

"Finally, the Committee showed up. They went straight to the changelings. God, I still remember it—they pulled us out of bed at dawn and lined us up against the wall. We were back to ten—a tiny little girl from Memphis had replaced Sarra—and they went down, one by one, and tapped us with a stick. Stick didn't look very special—just like something you'd find outside, fallen from a tree. But I started shaking. They worked their way down, tap, tap, tap. Six, seven, eight, tap, and I was looking at the door. One of them shut it. Nine, tap.

"And then me, ten. That stick touched my shoulder and I screamed. God, Lewis, my body felt like it would rip apart. One of the priests pushed me, hard, to the ground. I gasped. The power, or whatever, stopped trying to escape me. Because it felt the pain of the fall as much as I did. I couldn't control it—but it was stuck with me."

"How old were you?"

"Thirteen."

"And when did you come back here?"

Nell fingered a glass. "When I was twenty-two."

I tried to get Nell to keep talking, but she brushed me off with jokes about the diner's other patrons. I found the strength to finish my sandwich, and Nell ordered a milkshake. I drank half in exchange for my pickle. Finally, we got the check.

"Can I drive now?" I asked.

"No," she replied. She licked a finger and picked a crumb off the plate. "But I won't speed."

I got the check. Nell patted the stuffed blue jay on the head as we left. She said nothing. Neither did I.

Our goal that day was to at least get down past the Four Corners area, if not shoot across most of Utah until we hit Interstate Fifteen. Nell continued to drive like a maniac. At one point I reminded her she had promised not to speed, but she insisted that ninety was "a perfectly reasonable speed," especially once we ducked onto the local highways to move south and avoid Denver. After that, I sat back and watched the landscape roll by, changing from green to yellow, peaked to flat. We didn't stop for hours—not to eat, not to gas, not to pee. It was superhuman, the way Nell got the car to move.

This leg of our trip marked the start of "quiet time." That's what Nell liked to call it when she got sick of me. For a while we listened to the Talking Heads (my choice) and I stared out the window, but eventually she made me put on the Harry Potter book on tape. Listening to that tape makes me crazy. I did a rewrite on the second script. I think one line of mine made it into the movie, something to the effect of "Shut your mouth, Potter." After that screening, I decided it was time to leave L.A.

for awhile.

The only thing that made listening to the tape bearable was that Nell laughed at least every ten seconds. Not just a chuckle either, a real guffaw, as if she alone understood the brilliant satire that was *The Chamber of Secrets*.

I tried to keep a mental list of what made her laugh. Centaurs, yes. Snake-talk, no. It kept me busy. But, finally, I got sick of it.

"Hey, it's my turn to pick the music again," I said.

"I'm driving, Lewis."

"My car, Nell."

"We're just getting to the good part," she said.

"It will be there tomorrow," I said. "Anything else. Name it."

"Stevie Wonder."

I deliberated. "No Jesus right now."

"Robert Johnson."

I sighed. "All right."

Utah sped from dusk to nightfall. We were in the full desert now, no light but the moon and the cars that flashed by at ghostly intervals. The land was just a black mass. Nell sang along with each song quietly, in a cold whisper, like she alone understood this, too, the brilliant desperation of a man who, if you believed the legends, sold his soul to the Devil just so he could play the blues.

I watched the cars go by, despairing as they grew fewer and fewer. We could be driving in space, in some sort of time warp. We could be going nowhere.

Suddenly, Nell turned the radio off. I went to turn it back on, and she slapped my hand away.

"What the fuck, Nell?" I snapped.

"I just wanted it off," she said.

"You're a pain in the ass, you know that?"

"Yes, Lewis, I know that. I used to read minds, remember?"

"Yeah, but you blew that, didn't you?"

She didn't say anything, just looked straight ahead. We sat that way for a long time, in silence, waiting for something to happen. Or at least pass us by. Nothing came.

"You wanna tell me what the fuck set you off like this?" I said.

Nell waved her hand across the dash. "All these stories. They're not true."

"What stories?"

"I mean, like the Harry Potter stories. They're not true. I don't know why I like them."

"They're not supposed to be true. They're fantasies."

"Isn't that what you think my life was like?"

I realized I did always see Nell in the language of the movies I'd seen, of books. She'd have a sword at her side, some sort of magic aura— purple light, say—surrounding her as she raged—

"Magic. Good versus evil. I wasn't the bad guy, Lewis. But I did a lot of terrible things."

"Nell, it was a war, you can't be held—"

"What do you know about being held?"

"—responsible."

Nell shifted in the seat. I saw something unfamiliar wash over her face. Disgust? Pain?

"After the stick, the one I told you about, the Committee took me away to the mountains above the city. The enemy invaded the same day. As the guns got closer, I understood why I could read minds. Not so I could hear thoughts, but so I could find fear—fear of the guns, fear of the soldiers and the war.

"When they reached Halri, the priests took me aside and said, *War has a ritual. Three people perform it. The Walker comes in peace, to give counsel. The Runner comes in aid, to fight. The Rider comes at the brightest part of the day and kills. You are not an enemy. You are not a friend. You are the war.* They handed me a gun, and a helmet with a front like the face of a hawk. They sent me away, back to being a servant. Except when, at the brightest part of the day, I went out and found fear. It didn't matter what side, what class, what strangers or friends. I wasn't human. I was . . . a disease."

"Nell, I don't believe you were as bad as you—" I said, more in consolation than because I thought it was true.

"Once, I went to the village of a friend," she continued, cutting me off. "A friend like you, the kind that thinks he's joining at the good part. I set his house on fire, and waited for them to run. I shot the ones that did, and the rest tried to hide inside. So I called his name. And he came.

"I took off my mask, and I remember the thrill, when he recognized me. It felt good, Lewis. I told him to bring the rest out. And he did. God. He did.

"I begged the priests to take the power away, after that village," she said, her voice suddenly small. "In a moment when the Rider— But they refused. Someone had to be the terror of war. Someone had to contain the smoking countryside, the burnt houses, the graves. And I was so good."

I had nothing to say, and I didn't even try. We drove in silence till three a.m., all the way to Vegas.

Casinos are a traveler's best friend. At least, if you don't gamble. Cheap food, cheap booze, open any time. The kind of glitz that looks great for twenty minutes, then changes suddenly. Makes you want to get out quick. If that's not an option, then the décor fulfills its true function: to make you drink yourself stupid.

Nell and I took option B.

We were at a casino called the Crossroads on the edge of town, far away from that postmodern terror known as "the Strip." Fitting its name, The Crossroads hadn't settled on a specific theme—it was half desert western and half marble hall. The bar we had settled in favored the marble hall motif—Greek columns flanked the door, and the bar was some form of fake marble, gilded with gold. Mirrors, also gilded, lined the walls like giant sequins. At three a.m., however, the only wait staff came from the casino proper. They wore full cowgirl regalia.

We were not the only people in the bar, but we were the only ones making eye contact with something other than our drinks. Not that we were making a lot of eye contact. But we were talking—hell, we were animated. We were making fun of the waitresses, telling stories about our "crazy" trip, making absurd plans about what we'd do once we reached L.A. (Nell: "Run into the ocean!" Me: "Climb up to the Hollywood sign!" Nell: "Steal a star from the walk of fame!"). We were putting on a show for those around us, hoping to attract someone's attention. Break up our cozy duo.

Nell was officially freaking me out. Not in that kind of *she's a weirdo* way. In that *she killed a lot of people* way. Why couldn't she kill me? I felt like my mother after watching the news. I had to lock my doors. Sleep with a gun under my pillow. Take my car and go.

Eventually, the pep leaked out of the conversation, and Nell wandered over to the Wheel of Fortune slots, which ate her quarters as she hummed alone. I put a twenty on the bar and started walking. I left with my shoulders hunched and head ducked, as if I'd be less noticeable that way. Maybe I was, because she didn't notice. I got to my car and rested a hand on the door. I got in. Turned the ignition, then saw Nell's Harry Potter tapes on the dash. I opened the door and put them down on the white line, where I wouldn't hit them. I killed the engine and got out her duffle bag, the plastic grocery bags full of books, her blanket, her three boxes she'd never let me open.

I opened one. I saw a folded-up shirt with a strange insignia, stranger fabric, like heavy, durable silk. Opened the next. A helmet, not the one like a hawk, just a simple rounded cap made of metal with a disturbing number of dents. There was a gun, a scratched, mangled pistol that looked to be at least fifty years old. It was silver.

The third. Photographs, blown up and put in frames. Nell about five years younger, with three or four others, smiling. She wore the shirt and the helmet, and had the gun pressed to her chest. The others, all of them boys about her age, were dressed the same and smiled in that same cocky teenaged way. I realized I would have thought Nell was a boy in the picture if I hadn't known it was her. Maybe there were other girls in there, too. She was the only white kid; the rest of them were brown. I didn't know if that meant they were from the other world, or just a different part of ours.

"I was expecting you to just drive away," Nell called. I looked up from the pictures and saw her walking towards me from the casino.

"I thought you'd like your stuff," I said lamely.

She shrugged. Her pocket jingled with quarters. "Whatever."

"You mad at me?"

"Nah," she said. "I was planning to stay here."

"Really?"

"Whatever."

"Why?" I asked.

"Spent about a year here, long time ago. Figure I can work the card tables again. Watch faces. Watch signs."

I put down the pictures, what I guessed were relics of another world. I wondered what number I was on her list of goodbyes. If she even did them anymore. "Cool," I said.

"Yeah."

"Who were they?" I asked, pointing down at the box.

"They're still around," she replied. "Old friends. I leave well enough alone, and they return the favor."

"You gonna be lonely, Nell?"

"Sure."

"I'm sorry," I said.

"S'alright."

"I'm gonna go."

"I'll miss you," she said.

"I'll miss you too."

I smiled weakly at her and got into the car. She stood behind it now, looking back towards the casino. I started the engine again and gripped the wheel. I flicked my eyes back at her. She kept looking left. I pulled away.

Back out on the highway, I started to feel shaky, terrified, worse than I had in years. I felt like I was losing my mind all over again, being chased harder by it the faster I drove. And then, it passed. It was like I had rolled down a window to let out a bad smell or an insect. I wanted to turn back. I didn't. My shoulders felt light; I was breathing easy. There was no excitement, but there was no pressure either. She'd left me alone, and I felt better for it. I left her in Vegas. But I did miss her in L.A. ✪

THE DINNER GAME

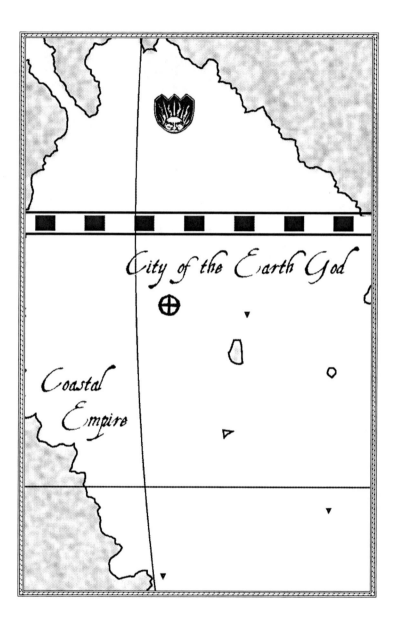

THE DINNER GAME
BY STEPHEN ELEY

SHE WAITS FOR HIM AT THE ROSE. THE HOTEL'S RESTAURANT IS A CAVERN filled with crystal light. A pianist plays Chopin on a dais before the black windows, and conversations ebb and flow with the nocturnes. Everyone at every table is beautiful.

She is the most beautiful. She wears a plain green velvet dress, with two malachite clips in her hair. When he enters she looks beyond him, as if searching for someone else. She smiles and waves at empty space. She doesn't look at him until he reaches the table, and then her breath catches.

He pulls the chair out and sits. He wears a charcoal suit with a bold purple shirt and tie; but a lock of hair hangs loose across his forehead, and his tie is slightly off to the left. She knows his habits, and this is new. A crooked tie says, *I have hacked through a hundred miles of jungle to reach you. Or I want you to believe I have.*

He lifts the menu, and a waiter is there beside him. He nods at the waiter and hands the menu back without looking at it. They do not need to order. They are known. They have done this many times.

"Do I know you?" she says.

"I remember you," he says, and she smiles.

It's another game. He has been a spy fleeing his country. She has been an adulterous First Lady. They have been psychiatrist and schizophrenic; vampire and victim; two blind people speculating on the world they cannot see. They will make love as themselves when they leave the Rose for a room upstairs, and tomorrow he will finish his business and leave her city. But first they dine as other people.

"In a past life?" she asks. They have done that one before. She was Joan of Arc; he was her confessor.

He shakes his head. "In a past world. You were a goddess. The Star Consort, lover of the Earth God."

She's surprised for the briefest of moments. Then she smiles, affecting relief. "You do remember! I was the night sky. Less favored than his first wife."

"But far more beautiful. You came to the earth because you loved him. But his wife, the Day Mother, was jealous, and she turned him against you. He became suspicious of your comings and goings, and chained you to the mountains with a band of light across the sky."

"Some would find our history strange. Earth deities are usually female," she says. Probing him, challenging him.

"This was a stony country. It wasn't fertile, and it didn't nurture. It killed those who lived upon it if they were not respectful. I was the first king to found a city upon it."

"There were no lasting cities," she objects. The wine comes, and the steward pours silently. She always tastes it first. This one is a crisp Chablis, tasting of apples frozen in snow. She shivers slightly at the feel of it in her mouth. He nods to the steward.

"You're right; it didn't last beyond my reign. To build at all I had to swear an oath to the Earth God, and when I broke that oath the city was destroyed with all in it."

She smiles a little. "Did you break the oath for love of me?"

He does not smile. "Of course not! Do you think I would kill ten thousand of my own people for such an inane reason as *love*? I was tricked into breaking the oath."

She sets down the wine, and there is soup on the table before her. The pianist is no longer playing. The talk around them is like surf on the ocean. "I wasn't present when the city fell. How were you tricked? Tell me from the beginning."

His lips tighten, and then he nods. His eyes do not show whether he's stifling a smile or an argument. "My first people came into the stone valley because we were hunted. There was a large empire on the coast. The emperor had had a religious conversion, to some ancient and barbarous god, and decreed that all written tablets in his cities were to be destroyed. To demonstrate the strength of his new god, all the scholars capable of writing the tablets were to be sacrificed to it."

"Your people were the scholars."

He nods again. "Scholars and priests of the old religion, and their families. My father was the hierophant. He had tried to train me to take his place, but I was always dull in matters of the gods. I pursued the military arts instead. When my father was the first one flayed upon the steps of the emperor's new temple, my talents became useful. We could not win, of course; we were forced to retreat, and there was death at every step. But we fought better than they expected, and we spilled nearly as much blood as we shed ourselves."

"Until you reached the stone valley of the Earth God. Your pursuers wouldn't follow you farther: the valley was cursed, and your gods of knowledge and the emperor's new god of blood had no power there. But you had no choice."

"We had no choice," he agrees. He sips his soup without looking at it. His eyes do not leave hers. "We had run as far as we could. There were others living already in the valley, scraping a bare existence on a few flocks of sheep and constant prayer. They hadn't the will nor the weapons to fight us. We made friendships with them, and persuaded them to join us."

"You taught them to build, and to write, and together you erected towers and a wall . . ."

"Your memory is good, but you are getting ahead," he says. "We *tried* to build. But the stones, which gave themselves so easily for the valley people's ovens and huts, would not yield for our wall. They blunted our picks. The rocks that broke would shatter into useless rubble. When we persisted, the valley walls came down upon us in rockslides. This was my fault. I did not begin to believe in the Earth God of the valley until two of my cousins were killed."

He pauses to finish his glass, and she notices that the room is quieter than before. Several of the tables are empty. Their bowls are empty as well, and are taken away.

"I humbled myself before the valley people," he continues, "and I learned their way of prayer. After two months my prayers were answered, and in a vision I was shown the path to a secret cave high in the valley."

"The vision didn't come from the Earth God," she says slowly. It is unusual for either of them to tell so much of the story alone, but she has little to say yet. Her part has not yet entered the story.

"I know that now, although I didn't then. It came from the Day Mother. She always did most of his thinking. And the path she showed me was very carefully chosen."

The main course is delivered by two waiters whose faces she does not see. She has what she always has: beef medallions, rare, with a wild-mushroom sauce. His looks like curried lamb. They bring more wine as well. The crystal chandeliers are dimmer now; the oil lamp in the center of the table is brighter.

"I just realized today that I've never seen you in daylight," he says, startling and annoying her. The warrior-king she had begun to see is gone, replaced by the businessman with the slightly crooked tie.

She still does not know his name. She does not want to know it.

"You've never seen me outside this hotel," she says, raising her new glass. She knows the wine without tasting it: a full red Beaujolais, with hints of copper in the finish. "I meet all of my lovers here."

"*Both* of your lovers," he says, and raises his glass to toast her. She does not return it. Of course he knows whose mistress she is; but he has never been coarse enough to speak of it directly.

"The path brought you to the Earth God," she says, with unusual force. She will decide later whether to punish him for breaking the game.

"It did. I climbed all day and reached him at sunset. There were no torches in his cave, but he glowed a dark red, like a coal removed from its furnace."

"Or like blood," she mutters, and his eyes flicker to the glass of wine still in her hand. His mouth opens; but whatever words he has chosen, he holds them back, and swallows them with a bite of curry.

After he has eaten a little he says: "I went to my knees before him, and lowered my head to the floor of his cave. From that position I told my history. I spoke of the emperor's terrible faith, and the sacrifice of my father. I told him of the battle we had brought to his threshold, and the need of my people to survive. At that, the Earth God spoke for the first time." He looks at her expectantly.

"He said, *Why.*" Her throat rasps the word as she imagines stone sliding against stone.

"I thought long for an answer. Finally I told him the truth. I wanted us to live for our revenge. Not only against the emperor, but against his god. We would destroy that god, with the aid of a stronger one."

"Flattery is always good," she says, and sips. The restaurant is nearly silent. There is no background conversation now; only the distant tapping of cutlery against plates. It is very dim, and the other diners are too far for her to see them.

"The Earth God said, *Build your city. In my name build the greatest city upon this world. When I am first among gods, your children shall strike down your enemy. But you, king of exiles, will never leave this valley.*"

"He wanted to teach you the patience of the gods," she says.

"Perhaps. You would know better than I. I always believed he wasn't that foresighted; I think he just didn't want me running off with his gifts. In any case, it sounded like the best bargain I was likely to get, and I swore that oath in the name of my people. Then he dismissed me. It was full dark—"

"As the Day Mother intended . . ."

"Yes. The climb I had made was too treacherous to descend at night. But in the starlight I saw an easier trail leading up to a low peak. I took that path."

"Where you met the Star Consort, and were consumed with lust."

"Where I met you, yes, and fell in love with you," he says. He adjusts his tie. It is still crooked. "But I was not *consumed* then, with lust or love. That took many years."

She smiles a little and drinks her wine. "To a goddess, many years are an instant. But I remember that first night. I was chained, as you said, and had the freedom of the mountains but couldn't leave them. I could only meet my captor at that ridge, where the mountains met the valley."

"Because the Earth God was bound to the valley," he says, and she raises a brow: now he is stating the obvious.

"We were together until sunrise," she goes on. "I had known mortals before, but none had your spirit. I remember the way you held me, and the way you looked at me. There was never a doubt in you that you would have what you wanted."

"It was my first day as a king," he says. "I was feeling rather full of myself."

"And then I was," she says, and he truly smiles for the first time. "We made love on the bare rock, and I felt in you the power that could strike my chains and free me."

"I was a fool," he says abruptly. She says nothing.

He says, "You haunted me after that night. I fulfilled my responsibilities to my people: I led them well, and I caused the city to be built. We named it for the Earth God. In weak moments I was tempted to give the city *your* name—"

"That would have been disastrous!"

"Indeed. Much worse than I realized at the time. But every day you were in my thoughts. I could not visit you every night, but I went to the

Earth God as often as I could find reasons, and when I left his cave I came to you in the darkness."

"I remember. I wove charms upon him to tire him, so that he wouldn't look for me when you were with me. So many blessed nights."

"It was you who blessed them. Meanwhile, the Earth God blessed my days. The city grew by his gifts. The stones yielded to us in the sizes and shapes we needed. An underground spring was struck, and a channel made so it could flow into the city. In the second winter another welled up of its own accord, hot and smelling of brimstone, and my palace was constructed around it. Copper was always plentiful, and we had brought with us the secrets of bronze. In the third year the Earth God gave us a vein of gold; in the fifth year, jade. By then we had begun to attract notice from the empire and from lands to the south."

"They tried to invade you twice. When that failed, they came back to trade."

He nods. "An army of fifty thousand broke against us. The valley was narrow and we had complete mastery of it; and every man, builder, craftsman or scribe, was also a soldier. But when they brought caravans in place of catapults, we welcomed them, and soon our hospitality was legendary."

"And with the legend grew your wealth. With that wealth you slowly sapped the empire of its own, and built your army in the guise of merchants. Your revenge would be a flood upon them in the next generation. You whispered this to me often as we lay together." *Too often*, she does not say; but she remembers. He has always wanted to talk in the moments after, when all she desired was stillness.

"Yes . . . that is what should have been," he says, and empties his glass. Their plates are empty now, their silver dirty, but she cannot remember the taste of her food. "What *would* have been, but for the schemes of goddesses."

"I had no scheme!" she says, indignant. "I never said a word to turn you from your course. My love was given to you freely."

"It was a poisoned cup," he says. "But I didn't mean you. Our passion *was* a trap, but it was the Day Mother who led me into it. I was her instrument to build her husband's power, and to dispose of you, her rival. And together you thwarted my own ambition: I was so distracted by my love for you that I never married a mortal woman. I never had the children that should have led us from the valley."

"I'm very sorry," she says, with some sincerity. "I had thought often of children, but I didn't dare while I was bound to the Earth God. He would have known instantly. So I chose not to conceive."

"That was well in the end. If you had had them, I would have had to kill them."

She freezes. The restaurant is utterly silent. Nothing moves but the dark red wine, still swirling in the glass she holds.

"I learned the truth about you," he says. "The secret you withheld from me. This was after the second decade, when the magician came to me with the star-forged iron."

He has never spoken to her like this. She is tempted to walk away from the table. But the story compels her, as none of their other stories ever have; she needs to hear its end. She says, thinking quickly, "The star-forged iron that you made into a hammer. The hammer with which you broke my chains."

"I was at the height of my power. My city was ascendant; the Earth God was growing bold in his pride. He began to speak freely to me of his own plans of conquest. He spoke of you, too, as his slave who would travel the earth chained at his side. I became angry. I was concerned that he would learn of our ever-more-frequent nights; and perhaps I was jealous of his claim upon you. I wanted to be your sole lover; and it may be that, in my own dark pride, I wanted to be your master."

"He was a god, and you were mortal," she says. "That is the only way in which he was your better—but I see now that in some ways you were the same."

"I will not deny it," he says. "There are many things I am ashamed of.

But remember that on midwinter's night, I climbed the mountain with that hammer. The Earth God knew my intention and tried to stop me; we fought, and I struck him unconscious. You and I warmed each other for just a moment in the freezing wind, and I swore to you my love, and I struck the chains of skylight that held you to the world. *That* is one difference between me and your . . . other."

The dinner plates are gone now. Before her is a small glass of port. The world is quiet, and beyond the flame of their oil lamp, only the stars shine through the window. She says, "You made me a promise when you set me free."

"I bade you go far from the Earth God, and far from me as well. But I swore that I would find you again, in any life, in any world. I said that after my father's revenge had been taken upon the emperor's god, I would be free of all other oaths. I would win you for my own, and we would wed as equals."

"And I . . ."

"You were stunned for a moment, as you are right now. Then you *laughed*. And you were gone."

She swirls and sips the port. It is almost too sweet, and has a copper tinge like the dinner's Burgundy. "You must have learned, later, why I laughed?"

"I learned before the summer, for word came that the empire that was our enemy had collapsed. The emperor's god had forsaken him; his prayers, his sacrifices, were met with silence. *She had left.*"

She drinks the rest of the port in two swallows, without stopping to savor it. She knows the copper finish well. It is the taste of blood.

"I nearly killed myself for not seeing it at once," he says. "The emperor's god had another name, from the furthest antiquity. And of the *most* ancient gods, the gods of blood and sacrifice, it is said that they are all one, and that god is female."

"True in every world," she agrees, "for the world must be given birth."

"Before I swore to wed you, I had sworn to kill you."

"Love is complicated," she says. "Did you have the means?"

"Of course I did. I knew the power of star-forged iron. It was easy to have a sword made of the same stuff; and the Day Mother, ever eager to help me, showed me another secret path that began in the mountains but did not end in our world."

"You took it."

"Of course I did. I had to find you. As the empire had fallen, and our city was now the shining crown of the known world, I believed my work there was finished. Others could carry on where I had left off, and the Earth God's glory could only grow. My oath never to leave the valley was no longer relevant."

"But the Earth God . . ."

". . . believed otherwise. He did not look to the future; he did not consider that I sought you, whom he also had reason to seek. He saw only disloyalty, and he punished me for it. Before I left the world, as I ascended the highest mountain, I felt it buckle beneath me. I looked behind and saw the towers of gold and jade fall into the earth. The city was of stone and could not burn, but the world opened and fire poured over it. I watched all of this for a day and a night. I heard the last cries of my people. They cried my name."

A glass breaks near the kitchen. She jumps. She had forgotten where they were.

"When the cries were silent, you turned again and continued on the path," she says.

"You know that I did. I walked from my world with a torn heart and a star-forged sword. I walked into the next, and I looked for you there."

"It took you many years. You ascended to power there, and forged new bonds with new gods." The restaurant is brighter again, and she sees a man in a tuxedo at the piano. He begins an aria from Bach.

"And I nearly failed to recognize you," he says. "For you were close

to me, and had a different face. But in time I understood you, and I confronted you. I brought my weapon close."

"But you didn't kill me," she says, "for here we are now."

"I nearly killed you. I tried to bring my anger to the surface; to find
enough strength for one moment to strike you down. But my aim fell
short. I broke your chains in that world instead, and set you free. I told
you that I would find you again. And I have."

The tide of conversation sweeps over them again, and all of the tables
are full. The spell of their words is lifted, and for the first time she sees
the man before her as he truly is. He is not the more powerful of her two
lovers; but he is stronger, and more proud.

"World after world," he says, "I have chased you. Age after age I find
you. Always you are bound to another. Always you are confined by this
other to some palace, some island . . ."

"Some hotel," she says. "And in every age you come to love me before
you recognize me."

The check comes to him. It is already charged to his room. He takes
a black pen from his jacket and signs it without looking at it. "Always,"
he says. "In every world I fight my way to you on the final night, as I
have tonight." The disheveled hair; the crooked tie. Her lovers are business partners, or were before today. She cannot imagine what happened
between them before dinner.

He continues, "And although I intend in every world to fulfill my earliest oath, and to end us both so that I can rest, my hand is stayed by love.
Always I set you free instead, determined that the next world will be the
last."

"Will tonight be our last, then? In this world you could finish me with
that." She looks at the pen. It is a dark metal, and from the way he holds
it she knows that it must be heavy.

"I don't know." They stand in unison. "For one night, the one who
claims you cannot trouble us. I could destroy you tonight for your past.
But I love you, too, and I could free you to go through that hotel door."

"You still won't see me in daylight," she says, and takes his hand in hers. They are walking now. The crystal chandeliers shine light on every beautiful face.

"No. But in the morning I could find the door. I could follow you through it, and eventually, many years from now, I would find you again."

It is winter and the lobby is cold. She walks close to him for warmth. She can smell cigars and sweat, and can feel his pulse in his hand. Their hearts pound. "Many years are an instant to me," she says.

He presses her closer. "Then we have a little time."

They take an elevator to a room, and she makes it dark so that she cannot see his face, or any of the faces he has worn. In the dark they make love as themselves. She leaves marks in his back, and cries out louder than she has ever cried before. It is why she plays the game. They will play it again, many times, and they will have many different roles. But tonight it is over, and the relief runs through her like a bolt. ✪

THE BOOK OF ANT

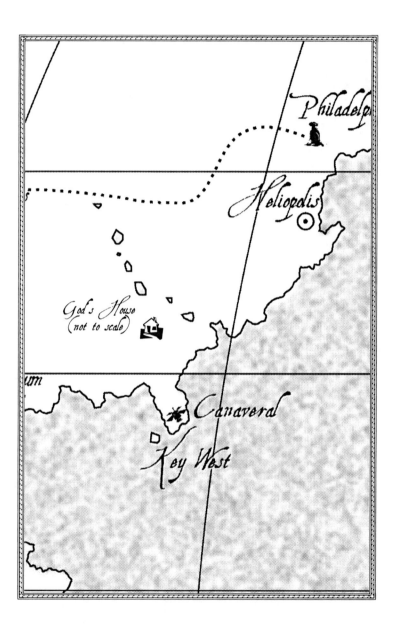

THE BOOK OF ANT
BY JON HANSEN

CHAPTER 1

IN THOSE DAYS THE PEOPLE WERE FEW IN NUMBER, WHEN THEY LIVED IN THE Hill. The Hill sat in the grass forest, bounded on one side by the great Hydrangea towers.

2 And although the forest gave some comfort, the soil was hard to work, with many pebbles to confound the people's tunneling,

3 And there was great lamenting among the people for their fate.

4 And then with the spring one was born, a worker called Ant.

5 Ant was like all of her kind, small and black, with strong jaws for shifting the soil, and in all other ways unremarkable.

6 One day as Ant was gathering leaves cut from the tower, a long earthmover poked its head out from the soil.

7 And Ant bowed in greeting, for although the earthmovers are a different race than the people, they shift soil, which helps all digging creatures.

8 The earthmover complimented Ant on her show of respect and scented in its strange way that it was known as Worm. Thereafter Worm gave Ant advice on the best ways to work the soil and Ant learned the wisdom of Worm,

9 And although some of the people wondered at Ant's friendship with Worm, Ant knew the worth of Worm's counsel.

CHAPTER 2

ONE DAY AS THE PEOPLE TOILED UPON THE HILL, A GREAT SHADOW FELL across the forest, blocking out the sun,

2 And Ant looked to see an Angel approaching.

3 The Angel walked upon four legs, each step shaking the earth. It stood as tall as the towers, covered with a thousand thousand antennae so it might sense all.

4 And the Angel looked down at Ant and gazed upon Ant,

5 And Ant trembled in fear.

6 Then the Angel raised up its head and leaned close to the towers to shake them with its breath,

7 And then the Angel gazed once more upon Ant before moving on, disturbing the forest with each step.

8 Then a great scent came up from the people, saying, "Glory unto you, O God, for passing over us."

9 But Ant did not join in, for it seemed to her that the Angel had some other purpose in mind.

10 And when Ant had completed the day's work, she shared with Worm of all that had occurred.

11 "It is a message for you alone," scented Worm. Ant asked what it could mean, and Worm replied, "Look into yourself and you will know truth."

12 And Ant thought and thought, and then scented to Worm, "The Angel wishes me to travel to the top of the towers, and there I shall discover its will."

CHAPTER 3

THE NEXT MORNING, INSTEAD OF GOING ABOUT HER TASKS, ANT LEFT THE Hill to climb the towers.

2 Filled with determination she followed the path of the trunk into the sky,

3 And although the way was not easy, she did not pause in her task until the noontime sun shone down on her at the top.

4 And there she discovered a great mystery.

5 Upon one of the great green leaves lay one of the bee folk, a great yellow and black warrior; and Ant could see that she lay dead.

6 And at first Ant wondered greatly why the Angel would have her witness this, when her eyes were drawn to the long stinger still hanging from the abdomen of the bee warrior.

7 And then it seemed to Ant she saw a vision of the Angel in the clouds overhead, instructing to her to pluck out the bee's sting and take it up in her jaws.

8 And being a good and faithful servant, Ant did as she was commanded.

9 And so armed with the bee's sting, she set herself to returning to the Hill.

CHAPTER 4

As Ant climbed down, she feared the queen would be angry with her for neglecting her work,

2 But she continued on the path to home, for she had her duty.

3 As she passed through the edges of the grass forest towards the Hill, she heard a great commotion,

4 And she climbed a blade to behold! A great beast of the forest, a lynx spider, was attacking some workers of the people and had already slain some few of them.

5 And though fear gripped Ant, so did a great certainty of purpose.

6 She sprang forth and struck the great spider, stabbing it in the abdomen with the stinger.

7 And then the bee's poison did slay the creature.

8 And the workers rejoiced at what she had done.

9 They returned to the Hill scenting great praise for Ant's deeds, until

all of the people knew what she had done, from the lowliest drone to the Queen herself.

CHAPTER 5

THREE NIGHTS LATER ANT HAD A DREAM IN WHICH THE ANGEL APPEARED before her. It scented to her that she had been chosen by God Herself to lead her people to a new land.

2 In obedience to the Angel's command, Ant climbed upon the face of the Angel and crouched beside its eye.

3 The Angel's passage was like the passage of the honeybee, racing high above the grass forest. Finally the Angel came to a giant shape many times taller than the Angel. "This is the House of God," scented the Angel.

4 Ant was humbled at the sight of it. "Are my people to live there?" she asked.

5 "No," scented the Angel, "for the ways of God are not the ways of your people, and they would suffer much hardship learning the differences." And Ant was chastened.

6 "There is the home for your people," scented the Angel. And Ant looked down to see a wall at the foot of the House of God.

7 Although it was tiny compared to God's House, Ant could see the wall surrounded a great weight of good dark earth many times larger than the Hill, and would hold uncounted number of Ant's people.

8 "But behold! the way will not be easy," scented the Angel. And upon the black earth Ant could see a strange people toiling.

9 Unlike Ant's people, who were black like the earth, these were the color of the sun blazing in the blue sky above. And as she watched they swarmed across the earth in great numbers like the blades of the grass forest.

10 "They are a great pestilence," scented the Angel. "They do not

pay heed to the words of God, and so She has turned away from them. Your task, O Ant, will be to vanquish them and lead the people here."

11 And Ant trembled with wonder and fright. "But how am I to accomplish this task?" she scented.

12 "Look for a sign," scented the Angel. And then Ant awoke.

CHAPTER 6

WHEN THE HILL AWOKE TO BEGIN THE DAY, ANT WENT TO THE QUEEN to share her vision. But the Queen denied the truth of Ant's dream.

2 "It is my place to think of the future of the people. Your place is to toil. Both are important, but I do not perform your duties and you do not perform mine." And the Queen sent Ant away, instructing her to think on her scent.

3 As Ant performed her toil that day, Worm broke from beneath the earth, and Ant related all that had happened in her dream.

4 And after they had scented, a wind blew from the east, carrying a great white leaf unlike any ever seen before, and then it set the leaf before Ant.

5 And Ant wondered to see that, upon the leaf itself, was a likeness of her standing beside the House of God she had seen in her dream. And Ant knew this to be the sign.

6 And Worm scented, "What shall you do?"

7 "I shall put myself in the hands of God," scented Ant, and took up the bee stinger in her jaws once more.

8 Along one edge the leaf was bent and folded, and to this edge Ant crawled and secured herself.

9 As soon as she had done this, the wind rose up once more, seizing the white leaf and carrying it high into the air. Ant held on, scenting unto herself, "I shall trust."

10 The wind carried the leaf a long way, tumbling in its grasp, until it came to earth once more.

11 And Ant climbed off the leaf and saw she had been brought to the foot of the House of God.

12 And Ant rejoiced to see it.

CHAPTER 7

Ant approached the great wall in fear, but remembered the Angel's scents and was strengthened.

2 Up she climbed, until she crested the edge and looked out upon the place God had chosen for her people.

3 It was broad and wide, with good wet soil. Towers grew there, and although they were not as great as the Hydrangea of the Hill, Ant could see they would be good enough.

4 As she gazed in wonder, she smelled a stranger.

5 She turned to see two warriors the color of the sun, filled with wrath. They leaped to attack, snapping their jaws,

6 But Ant was too swift. With two neat strokes of the bee stinger she slew her enemies.

7 But she rejoiced for only a moment, for other sun warriors now raced toward her.

8 And though she knew her worth in battle, she knew they would overcome her and felt certain this was not God's intent,

9 And so she fled with the enemy in pursuit.

CHAPTER 8

Along the wall she raced, until she reached a place where it met the House of God. Now, Ant was a mighty climber, but she feared to even lay leg to this holy place. Then the scents of the Angel came to her, reminding her of her task, and so she hardened her resolve.

2 The walls of God's House were made of stone, but inlaid with paths wider than twice Ant's length. There the way proved easy, and was filled with the scents of strangers who had passed that way before,

3 And Ant knew that this truly was the path.

4 Up and up and up she climbed, until she reached a place where the stone opened up to reveal a tunnel entrance.

5 As she reached it, a sun warrior appeared from it, antennae waving at her approach.

6 Ant struck true, but the bee sting lodged itself in the warrior's chitin. The enemy fell from the House of God, carrying Ant's mighty weapon with her.

7 And Ant feared it was a sign, that God had turned away from her because of her trespass.

8 Despair tore at her.

9 But Ant could hear the enemy raging up the walls of God's House towards her, and so she entered the tunnel.

10 This tunnel was different from the tunnels of the Hill, many times wider and filled with strange scents she had never known before.

11 Ant hurried on, hoping not to meet another fierce sun warrior. Long she ran, until she found a passage different from the others.

12 Light poured from it, bright as the sun, and thinking it an exit, Ant passed through it,

13 But instead found herself in the House of God.

CHAPTER 9

THE AIR WAS DIFFERENT, FILLED WITH THE SCENTS OF FOOD AND WATER, but also with countless unnamed others.

2 Fear gripped Ant, for she remembered that the Angel had told her that the House of God was not a place for Ant and her people.

3 Behind her she could hear her enemies' approach, and so she began to climb once more, up the great wall inside God's House to a wide ledge.

4 Upon reaching it, Ant could see a long low opening in the wall, through which came the scent of fresh air.

5 She turned to see her enemies, who now poured forth into the House of God like the raindrops of a storm.

6 Ant prepared to flee, when a vast shape appeared before them.

7 It was unlike anything Ant had ever seen, mightier than the Angel in size and terrible in appearance, its lower body disappearing into a great abyss far below and its upper body ending in two great legs that themselves ended in five legs apiece.

8 Like the shifting of a tower, it looked down at them all with its hideous visage.

9 And as Ant watched, it reached out with one enormous leg and crushed a dozen of the red warriors as if they were nothing.

10 Ant knew then that it was a guardian of the House of God and would slay them all for their trespass,

11 And she truly knew the scent of fear.

12 "O Guardian," she scented, "I came here only to fulfill my vision and provide for my people. Now I fear in my ignorance I have sinned.

13 "I beg forgiveness, but know I am unworthy. If it is your will that I must pay, then so be it. I ask only that my people achieve the promise of God's will."

14 The guardian looked down upon them once more, then raised up its other leg. A vast cloud spilled out of it, covering all the enemy and Ant,

15 And its scent was Death.

16 Ant breathed it in, accepting the decision of the guardian, and perished.

CHAPTER 10

THEN A GREAT WIND BLEW, CARRYING ANT'S BODY FROM GOD'S HOUSE high into the air. It bore her along for some time, before finally setting her body to rest in the grass forest, where she was found by two workers gathering food. They carried her back to the Hill, where a great sadness filled all the people.

2 And as they mourned, Worm appeared, having heard of what had happened, and asked to receive Ant's body,

3 And the Queen agreed out of respect for the friendship between Ant and Worm.

4 Then Worm took Ant's body back into the forest, where he dug a hole and placed Ant's body within, and covered it with earth.

5 But one day not long afterwards a stranger came out of the grass forest, not far from where Ant had been buried.

6 And although her scent was unknown, all who scented with her would swear they knew her.

7 She was taken to the Queen, where she declared herself to be Ant.

8 "The people must go to the House of God," scented Ant. "The guardian of God's House has slain the sun warriors, for they did violate Her will. The place God Herself chose for us is now ready."

9 And then the Queen knew the truth of Ant's words, and agreed.

10 Then, at the Queen's command, all the people who lived in the Hill gathered the young pupae and larvae and eggs, as well as what food could be carried.

11 Then Ant led the people from the Hill through the grass forest for days, until they reached the House of God.

12 And the people did scent their amazement at their new home.

13 There were some then who called for Ant to be raised up as a Queen, but Ant refused.

14 "We all have our place," she said. "And though I have done great things for the people, my time among you is over." Then Ant returned to the grass forest.

15 To honor her memory the people renamed themselves Ants, as they are now known,

16 And began construction of a new home which they called the Citadel of Ants, and they dwell there to this day.

17 And many among them believe, if they have great need of her, Ant will return to help overcome their foes. ✪

THE MUSE OF EMPIRES LOST

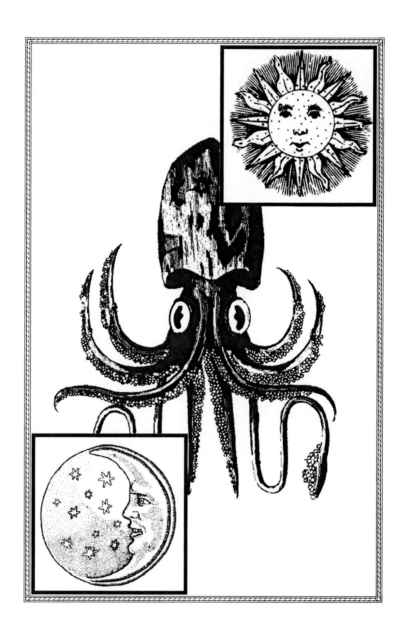

THE MUSE OF EMPIRES LOST
BY PAUL BERGER

A SHIP HAD COME IN, AND NOW EVERYTHING WOULD CHANGE. JEMMI HAD recently become adept at crouching under windows and listening around corners, so when the village went abuzz with the news, she heard all the excitement. She was hungry and lonely, and she thought of Port-Town and the opportunities that would be found there now, and she left the village before light. She went with only the briefest pang of homesickness, and she went by the marsh trail rather than the main road, because if she had met any of her neighbors along the way, they would have stoned her.

The path was swallowed up by the murky water sooner than she expected, and the gray silt sucked at Jemmi's worn straw zori with each step. Poor old Sarasvati, always laboring to bestow ease and prosperity upon her people, and always falling a bit more behind. These were supposed to be fields, but the marshes stretched closer to their houses each year. She couldn't even get any decent fish to breed there. In the village they clucked their tongues and said that was old Sara's nanos going, as if anyone knew what that meant or could do anything about it. But sometimes you could melt handfuls of this silt down and chip it into very sharp little blades that would hold their edge for a shave or two and could be bartered for a bite to eat. Sometimes you could see it slowly writhe in your hand.

Now that the village had turned against Jemmi, Sara was her closest and only chum. When Jemmi was at her most alone she would sit quietly and concentrate on a tiny still spot deep in her center and maybe think a few words in her heart, and a spark would answer, and a huge warm and beloved feeling would spread through her. She knew that was Sara speaking to her. Everyone wanted Sara to listen to them, but Sara barely ever spoke back to anyone.

By midday Jemmi struck a road, and the next morning she reached Port-Town. Her parents had taken her there once when she was little, so she already knew to expect the tumult and smells and narrow streets packed with new faces, but the sheer activity spun her around as she tried to track everything that moved through her line of sight. Jewel-green quetzals squabbled and huddled together under the eaves of high-peaked shingled roofs, and peacocks dodged rickshaw wheels and pecked at the dust and refuse in the streets. There was plenty of food here if she could get it, and fine things to own, stacked in stalls and displayed in shop windows.

She was drawn most of all, though, to the mass of humanity that surrounded her—she could practically taste their thoughts and needs as they swirled by. The townsfolk were thronging towards the old wharf, and she let herself be swept up with them. Sometimes men or women brushed against her or jostled her without a glance or a second thought, and she grinned to herself at the rare physical contact.

An ambitious vendor had piled bread and fruit into a wooden cart at the edge of the street to catch the passers-by, and Jemmi stopped in front of him.

"Neh, what ship is it?" she asked above the din.

"Haven't you heard, then?" he replied. "It's Albiorix!"

Jemmi thought he was mocking her until she caught the man's exultant smile. *Albiorix*—no ship had stopped here for more than a generation, and now this! Albiorix was the stuff of legend, a proud giant among ships, braver and broader-ranging than any other. If Sarasvati was on Albiorix's route now, they would all be rich again.

"Who was on board, then?"

"No one's seen them yet. Looks like they'll be debarking any minute."

Jemmi checked her urge to race off towards the wharf. She put her hand on the vendor's forearm and smiled her warmest smile, and as he stood distracted and fuddled she swept an apple and two rolls into her pockets. She turned and ran before the man's head cleared.

The crowds along the quay were packed tight and jostling viciously, but Jemmi plunged in and no one noticed or resisted as she slipped right up to the barrier. A boy was standing near her. He was clear-eyed and honey-skinned and probably about two years older than she was. Judging from his clothes and the rich dagger that hung at his belt—the hilt bound with real wire—his family was quite well-to-do. With visions of regular meals and a roof over her head, she sidled towards him. The boy looked over her rags and begrimed face and straightaway disregarded her. Jemmi held firm and let the motion of the crowd press him close to her. The back of his hand brushed against her bare wrist, and he unconsciously jerked it away. She shifted her weight so that she was a fraction closer to him. The next time he moved he touched her again, and she imagined that he was not quite so quick to pull back.

The third time they touched she kept her hand against his, and the boy did not pull away. He turned shyly to Jemmi.

"Hello," he said. "My name's Roycer."

At that moment, the entire length of Sarasvati trembled with a gentle impact, and the crowd's cheer was deafening.

Outside, languid in the vacuum of space, Albiorix stroked Sarasvati's stony mantle with the fluid tip of a miles-long tentacle—an overture and an offering. Sarasvati recalled Albiorix of old, and his strength and boldness were more than she could have hoped for. She extended a multitude of soft arms from deep within the moonlet that served as her shelter and her home, and entwined them with his. She dwarfed him as she embraced him. Her tentacles brushed the length of his nacreous spiral shell, and in the silence dizzying patterns of light flashed across both their surfaces. The colors matched and melded, until they raced along his arms and up hers and back again. Sarasvati was receptive, and eager to welcome Albiorix after his lonely journey across the vastness. He disentangled himself and drifted down to the tip of her long axis, and they both spread their arms wide as he clasped his head to the orifice there. She released her great outer valve for him, and he gently discharged his passengers and all their cargo. Sarasvati accepted them gracefully, and in return, flooded his interior with fresh atmosphere from her reserves. Now duty and foreplay had been dispensed with, and they embraced again in earnest, spinning in the void.

The sphincter on Sarasvati's inner surface dilated open, and the passengers off Albiorix stepped through into Port-Town, armed and alert. The arrivals were well aware that half the inhabitants of any orbital would tear newcomers apart just to see what they carried in their packs, and they hustled down the quay in tight phalanxes that bristled with weapons. They no doubt came from richer lands—Jemmi noticed the glint of steel in the trappings of their spears and crossbows as they passed. One group brandished old-style plasma rifles, but Jemmi assumed that was a bluff; everyone knew the smart electronics hadn't worked since the day the Cosmopolis fell. The crowds parted grudgingly around this threat, and Roycer was pushed closer to Jemmi, his gaze never leaving her face.

The rest of the townsfolk watched the arrivals' every move as they sought shelter in the winding streets. Those that could strike deals with families or inns to harbor them were likely to survive. This must have been an especially long voyage, Jemmi thought, or else star travel must be harder than anyone remembered. These arrivals all looked sunkencheeked and worn down as if drained, or haunted by something they could not name.

One last traveler stepped through into Sarasvati, alone. He was the oddest thing Jemmi had ever seen. He was tall and slightly stooped and unnaturally pale—both his skin and his sparse hair were the same shade of thin gruel—and although at a distance Jemmi assumed he was very old, as he approached Jemmi realized she could not guess his age at all. His only luggage was a canister that hung from his shoulder on a strap. He walked unarmed along the barrier and Jemmi was certain he would be snatched up, yet no one in the throng made a move towards him or particularly noted his presence. He took his time, scanning the faces and garments as if looking for something. He stopped in front of Jemmi and her boy, and smiled. His teeth were the same color as his skin, and were all broad and very large in his gums.

"You'll do," he told the boy. "Shouldn't we be getting home now?"

Wordlessly, the boy nodded and released Jemmi's hand. He slipped under the barrier and joined the traveler, and led him down the quay into town.

Jemmi, stunned with amazement and impotent wrath, stood there slack-jawed until long after they left her sight.

With the excitement over, the crowd melted away, and Jemmi saw no chances to get close to anyone else. She spent the rest of the day side-stepping traffic and looking into windows, and she was able to grab a bit more to eat in the same manner she had acquired breakfast. After dusk one or two men on the darkened streets spoke to her, but they didn't look useful and she didn't like what their voices implied, so after that she took to helping people ignore her. That meant she couldn't get indoors to sleep, but luckily Sara was still too distracted with her beau to make a proper rain. Jemmi spent the night curled at the foot of a weather-beaten neighborhood shrine at the end of a narrow alley. It was certainly not what she had hoped for when she had decided to make the journey to town, but it was not too different from what she had left behind. Amongst the incense ash and candle-stubs and tentacled figurines, some housewife had left a rag doll dressed in a new set of toddler's clothes, a supplication to Sara for an easy birth and a healthy baby. The offering of a portion of a family meal that sat alongside it had barely gone cold, but some things were sacred, and Jemmi was not tempted to take it.

She fell asleep thinking how happy she was for old Sara, and she dreamed a wondrously clear vision of the two lovers floating clasped together with countless arms, surrounded by stars, auroras chasing along their skins. Jemmi accepted the image without question, notwithstanding she had never seen a sky before.

She awoke when she felt that Sara was about to make dawn, and she stood in her alley to watch it. Directly overhead, the coil of viscera that stretched along Sarasvati's axis sparked and sputtered with flashes of bioluminescence, and then kindled down its entire length. As the light phased from gold to yellow to white, Jemmi was able to pick out the fields and woods and streets of her own village hanging high above and upside down along Sarasvati's great inner vault. It was significant to her only as a starting point; she had come to town now, and her home would be here. She set out walking again, looking for breakfast and Opportunity.

Before she found either, she found the traveler. He was sitting on the veranda of a home in a wealthy neighborhood, drinking tea and reading. The street was busy with passers-by, but none of them seemed to take any notice of his odd looks, or his book, or the fact that he seemed to actually know how to read it. Jemmi stopped in the street in front of him and stared.

The pale man stirred in his seat and looked up from his book. Jemmi's thoughts immediately shifted to other things—the kerchief on that woman walking past and how she would wear it if she had it, what plans the tradesman across the way might have for the bound lamb he carried, and wouldn't a single gutter down the middle of the street make it easier to clean than one down each side?—as if there were a broad, gentle pressure in the center of her mind. This, the thought struck her, must be what she made the people in crowds around her feel. She held her ground and pushed back.

The man met her gaze with a small, amused smirk. "What can I do for you, daughter?" he called down.

The pressure in Jemmi's mind immediately grew focused and became an urge to comply, practically dragging an answer from her. She refused, and met the force head-on. The compulsion increased, and she resisted.

She stood there frozen by the exertion, and suddenly the frontal assault on her mind dissipated, replaced by the barest sideways push that took her completely off balance.

"I had a boy," she called back, and heard the anger in her voice in spite of herself. "A boy and a dry place to sleep."

"Indeed?" the pale man answered. "Now, what would make you think— Oh my . . ." His little smirk wavered, and he said, mainly to himself, "Here, in this forsaken backwater? Can it be?" He considered his closed book for a moment, then put it aside and stepped to the veranda railing. "I think perhaps we should get to know each other. Won't you come up?"

If there was any coercion now, it was too subtle for Jemmi to feel, and she was intrigued by his bearing, and warily flattered. She joined him, and he sat her beside him like a lady of substance.

"My name," he said, "is Yee."

"Neh, that's a funny name, isn't it?"

His half-smirk returned. "Possibly. It was originally much longer, and there was a string of titles that went after it at one time, but these days Yee is sufficient for my needs." He had an old-fashioned accent that made her think of fancy dances attended by the lords of planets, and a way of speaking as if every word counted.

"I'm Jemmi, then."

"Jemmi, it is an unexpected pleasure to meet you. You are what, eleven, twelve years old?" Up close, Yee's eyes were nearly colorless, but Jemmi got the impression that if he looked too long at something, it would start to smolder—or maybe Yee would.

"Fourteen."

"Fourteen? Ah, yes, of course. Puberty would have begun. And I don't suppose you eat particularly well. Forgive me—I've been a neglectful host. Would you join me in breakfast?"

She nodded.

"I suspected as much. Roycer!" Yee called, barely raising his voice.

The boy from the crowd at the quay stepped out of the door as if he had been waiting beside it. He had the look of someone who had been working feverishly all night.

"I believe our guest could do with a bit to eat," said Yee.

"Breakfast! Of course!" said the boy, as if it were a stroke of genius. He disappeared back into the house.

"Tell me, Jemmi," continued Yee. "Do you have any family?"

She shook her head.

"So I conjectured. They didn't, by any chance, die under mysterious circumstances within the past few months, did they?"

The glance she shot him was all the answer he needed.

"I believe we have much in common, you and I . . . and I honestly can't recall ever saying that to anyone else."

Roycer hurried out of the house with a tray piled with a random assortment of cold meats and vegetables and cups and loaves and cheeses. He set it down before them and stepped away. Yee made a graceful gesture with an open palm, and Jemmi tore into it.

"Perhaps you could also prepare a bath for our guest," Yee suggested while she ate.

"Hot water!" the boy muttered to himself, "Cool water! And soap!" and raced back inside.

Yee watched Jemmi bolt down the food. "You would not be reduced to this if you were on a true world," he reflected. "A planet holds more riches than one person could ever grasp, and you would just be discovering you could take anything you desired right now. How ironic that you and I should both be trapped out in space, at the mercy of the vagaries of a forgotten fad."

Jemmi looked up. "What's that, then?"

"A fad?" said Yee. "A trend of fashion. A novelty. I'm sure you must take it for granted, but please believe me when I tell you that it is not at all an intuitive choice for a human to live in the belly of a mollusk adrift in the ether. When I commissioned the first orbitals, they were intended merely as pleasure palaces to keep my associates content and distracted. We gave the males mobility only to ensure that the species bred strong and true, not because we planned to ride them."

"You did? Like Sara? Like Albiorix?"

"Yes. Your Sarasvati is one of the oldest, one of my first. Through a twist of fate, I happened to be visiting one of her sisters the day the Cosmopolis fell. There wasn't time to return groundside before the machines stopped working, of course, and not even a big ship like Albiorix is strong enough to make planetfall.

"Without the smart machines, you and I may ride ships from one impoverished orbital to the next, while the planets are rich and savage, but utterly isolated. The resources to rebuild civilization are there, but always just beyond my reach."

Jemmi had no clear idea of how long ago the Cosmopolis had fallen, but if Yee had been there her original impression was correct, and he was quite old. She was still hungry, but she was smart enough to stop eating before she got sick or sleepy. She pushed the tray away from her, half its contents untouched. Yee seemed to note this with the barest hint of an approving nod. Jemmi thought back to Sara's joy at the unexpected arrival of a suitor, and connected it to this unexpected man.

"Neh, why did Albiorix come back to Sara?"

"Ah, truth be told, it was not his intention at all. Albiorix prefers his route through his regular harem, and he likely planned to call on Demeter, and then Freya. It was time for me, however, to move rimward. It was a considerable struggle to make him accept my lead."

No one had ever taken such pains to answer Jemmi's questions before. She composed another one. "Why rimward, then?"

His smirk this time was a bit indulgent. "I have been to the galactic core, and I no longer believe I will find what I seek there. I am a man on a quest, you see."

The boy appeared in the doorway. "The bath is ready," he announced to the veranda in general.

"Roycer serves with excellent enthusiasm," Yee confided with a lowered voice. "Do you find everyone in Sarasvati so?"

Jemmi shrugged, nonplussed. "No one ever serves me," she admitted.

"Indeed? Well, that must change. That must change immediately." He stood and offered his hand. "Would you care to join us inside?"

Roycer and Yee led her into the house, which was very old. Parts of it must have been built before the Fall, because they were made of textureless materials Jemmi had no words for, while other rooms were made of wood and stone. They passed through a side parlor, where the rest of Roycer's family lolled in chairs or sprawled across the rug. Jemmi counted two parents, a brother, and three sisters, all with sunken, husklike faces. They were all dead. She was very surprised—her parents had looked the same way when they died.

"A pity, I know," said Yee, gesturing towards the corpses with an upraised chin, "but I needed to simplify the household, and the boy is strong enough for my needs for the time being." Roycer didn't seem to see them at all.

Roycer's family was so rich they had a room just for baths, at the back of the house. It was floored with rough flagstones and had a hearth for heating the water, and a high-backed earthenware tub right in the middle. Jemmi thought it was very odd to take a bath in someone else's house in the middle of the day, and momentarily froze with the apprehension that she was being entrapped, but Yee dismissed it with a shake of his head.

"If you want to pass as townsfolk," he told her, "you really shouldn't be noticeably filthier than they are. Besides, I am too old to take advantage of you, and I promise Roycer will be a perfect gentleman. He will scrub your back if you like."

Yee graciously turned to face the wall, and on her other side, Roycer did the same. Perhaps this was what the high-born did during morning visits. Jemmi let her ragged tunic and leggings fall to the floor, and stepped in. The water was hotter than any water she had ever touched, but she was committed, so she gasped and puffed and slid herself down the side of the tub in tender increments. Her knees immediately disappeared behind swirls of brown. It was scalding, but she discovered that if she kept her legs pressed together and moved only when absolutely necessary, it was nearly relaxing. When she was settled, Yee sat himself on a stool in a corner, looking for all the world like a pale long-legged spider. Roycer remained where he was.

Jemmi picked up a cloth and swiped experimentally at dark patches on her skin. Yee suggested she try the soap, and she had more luck that way. Underneath, she was rather fair, and turning pink in the hot water.

"Neh, Yee," she said, comparing a pink-scrubbed arm to a besmudged one. "Where are you from?"

"Ah," he said. "I was born in the chief city of the greatest dominion the world had ever known."

"The Cosmopolis Core?"

He shook his head. "Long before that. This was so long ago that it was little more than a legend to the builders of the Cosmopolis. In those days our god walked apart from us as a formless creature of faith and awe, quite unlike the beings who have given us their bodies to be our homes and our worlds in this age. He failed us in the end, I suppose, because that empire fell. It was not the first empire to fall, and it certainly was not the last, but it fell badly when it went. And I was a young boy, trapped on a narrow and crowded island of towers when the chaos descended."

Jemmi was silent. Anyone raised among the half-buried reminders of the abrupt and terrible failure of the Cosmopolis had a visceral understanding of that type of chaos.

"This was all so far back that I can recall only the memories of recalling it centuries later. But I know the instrument of our downfall was a plague that our enemies brought among us. Death tore through us so quickly that we who considered ourselves the capital of the world and the heart of its hope were no longer a city, but brutal pockets of marauders running through a steel-and-glass wasteland. I was thirteen then, and the sickness seized me suddenly. It was clear that I would die, but I did not. When I fought to live, I was somehow able to reach out and find strength in the people closest to me. When I recovered, I found they had wasted away in proportion to the vigor I gained. My parents and siblings were dead and empty around me, and I was utterly alone.

"Then the savages who had been our neighbors found our home and ransacked it. I cowered and sought to make myself invisible to their eyes, and they walked past me without seeing me, though I could have put out a hand and touched them. At that point I realized I was now something different, but there was no one to explain it to me."

Jemmi knew exactly what he meant.

"Many dark years followed, but I survived, and my people worked diligently to rebuild something of their society, and I always amassed the best of everything. Gradually I realized this industriousness was my own doing—I could not force a man to do a thing he did not wish to do, but I could place an idea in that man's head and give him the drive to realize it at any cost. The same way, I believe, that you are now learning to do, Jemmi. I felt your mind as you stood out on the street. A power has begun to emerge in you, though you do not know how to use it. This is a rare and precious gift. In all the history of the world, it may be only we two who have had it. And you are the first I have ever told.

"While the rest of our planet squabbled in the dust, my people strove in lockstep and regained their learning and power. They had been close to the secret of star travel when I was a child, though this knowledge was lost for generations during the dark ages. Eventually, though, I saw that mankind's future lay in its ability to spread across worlds, and I gave them the urge to create that technology. When they finally left to cross space in the first great wormhole-drive craft, I went with them, always as a counselor, never as a ruler. That is the proper role for you and me."

Jemmi nodded, wide-eyed.

"I have kept mankind focused on its own advancement and prosperity and culled the weak and the distractions, and I accept relatively little in return—I take no more from my people than the barest life force necessary to remain alive and continue in my role. I have shepherded humanity through eons of history, and ensured that each new empire was built according to my design. The Cosmopolis was my greatest work. Only when it fell and the worlds were sundered from one another did humanity lose my guidance. And look what has become of you."

Jemmi had never had a clear picture of life under the Cosmopolis, but she suddenly sensed that it must have been unimaginably finer than the way people lived now, and she felt ashamed.

"So you see, that is why I am here. To rescue mankind. I must rebuild the Cosmopolis."

To Jemmi sitting in her tub that sounded so grand it was absurd. "From Sarasvati? She's old and poor. How would she help, then?"

"As I told you, I am a man on a quest. I need only to reach an inhabited planet to raise humanity up again. But for that, I need a shuttle—one of the old machines. I have searched since the Great Fall, and none remain intact in any of the orbitals between here and the center. Perhaps there is one left in Sarasvati."

"But, neh, the old machines don't work."

Yee smiled his half-smirk again. "I believe that if I can find a shuttle, I can render it operable." His tone became more urgent. "Join with me, Jemmi. I will have need of your support in the days ahead. Add your power to mine, and there will be nothing we cannot do. We will save mankind from itself and bring order to the stars and lead an empire that spans the galaxy and can never be overthrown!"

"Okay."

He stopped short as if he had prepared more to say. "Excellent," he said.

"But I don't know what help I can be."

"People want to help *you*, Jemmi," said Yee. "It's in your nature. Roycer?"

Roycer stepped up behind her with a long-handled brush, and began to rub warm suds along her spine. Jemmi decided she enjoyed the sensation, and leaned forward to give him more surface to work with. He ran the brush up and down the same route, mechanically focused on the center of her back.

"If you'd like him to do something else, you may direct him," said Yee. "I hand the reins over to you. Simply feel his mind and put the idea into it. You'll find he will be avid to put it into action."

"Don't I need to touch him, then?"

"You shouldn't—I don't," Yee told her.

Jemmi thought back to her earlier struggle with Yee, and reached out with her mind the way she imagined he had. She sensed nothing, so she pressed stronger and further. Suddenly she connected—and she was immense and floating in space, lost and engrossed in animal passion, tangled with Albiorix and straining mightily against his thrusts to receive him deeper and deeper within her. She had gone too far, and was now in Sarasvati's mind.

Overwhelmed by the sensation and shocked by her transgression, Jemmi recoiled and shook herself free of Sara. As she went, she caught a final flash of Sara's sight—stars wheeling around her, and much closer, a blue disk half-covered with a whorl of white. Then she was back in the tub.

"Nothing, eh?" Yee said gently from his corner. "Well, try again. You'll do it."

She took a deep breath and reached out again, this time barely past her own skin. She felt Yee in the room with her—he nearly filled it—so she turned the other way and touched Roycer. She hesitated, then decided that people like Yee and herself were beyond bashfulness, and gave the boy the idea of her right shoulder.

The brush moved from her spine and made gentle circles around her right shoulder blade. This was nothing at all like how she was used to confounding minds. It was subtle and focused and efficient. She immediately saw it as a thing of beauty, as if she had been born to it.

"Excellent!" It sounded a little strained when Yee said it. "It seems you learn more quickly than I did. But always be aware that his enthusiasm may be diverted to other ideas."

The brush was now circling her left shoulder.

Jemmi gently reminded Roycer of her right side, and the brush returned to make its circles there. Yee moved him away again—and it was more challenge than test. Jemmi pictured her right shoulder in detail and pressed the image into Roycer's mind, and then pressed even harder in response to Yee's redoubled pressure. Roycer stood frozen, torn between the two equal demands. After nearly a minute, the long-handled brush began to shudder silently.

"Well, there's no point in breaking him," Yee said a bit too lightly. "I still have some plans for the boy."

Behind her Roycer emitted a sigh, and the brush resumed its gentle circles on her right shoulder blade.

Afterwards, when Yee suggested that the bath had done as much for her as could reasonably be expected, she stood up into a large towel Roycer held for her. She pressed the water out of her hair, and tossed the towel over her shoulder like a gown.

"Neh, am I beautiful now?" she asked.

Yee looked her over with an eye that had appraised queens.

"Why would you ask such a thing?" he said at last. "For you, that will never matter."

So Jemmi moved in with Yee and Roycer, and got her warm dry bed and a boy to serve her after all. The bedroom was filled with magnificent girl-things that had been Roycer's sisters' and Yee said were now all hers. She dressed herself in a frock of a crisp, shiny fabric that would be ruined forever if it were even in the same room with a speck of grease, and put ribbon after ribbon into her hair until the whole mass could practically stand on its own. Yee saw it and muttered a vague comment that restraint was often the better part of elegance, so she kicked the dress into a corner and changed into a more practical working skirt.

The next day, as they finished breakfast and sat looking over the jumbled heap of everything Roycer had pulled out of the larder, Yee slid his chair back and observed, "We seem to have exhausted this house's stores. Come—it's time we went to the market." Jemmi and Roycer followed him out.

Jemmi loved crowds, and to her mind the market was the best part of Port-Town. Yee led them to the busiest, most densely-packed street, where folk shoved to get by them and hawkers vied to drown out each others' voices. He turned to Jemmi, and his voice carried perfectly without rising at all. "Roycer and I have some business to attend to and will leave you to do the shopping," he told her coolly. "Please do not return until you have acquired everything you think the household needs. And do try not to get yourself killed while you're about it. I have noticed subtlety is not your strong suit."

He steered Roycer into the crowd, and they disappeared in a few steps. Jemmi didn't even have a basket. Was Yee kicking her out already? Had she failed somehow? Or did it just mean he wanted her to practice putting ideas in people's heads? She couldn't tell, and she felt alone again, and very exposed. She fought to stay in one place for a long while until the buffeting from the shoppers became unbearable, and then, near tears, she fled to a quiet corner at the edge of the square.

She forced herself to breathe deeply until she was nearly calm again, and then reached out for the comfort of feeling Sara.

There was a brief, dizzying sensation of stretching through free-fall and then she was back in Sara's mind, gargantuan but still less than a mote in the immeasurable space that surrounded her. The Herculean coupling with Albiorix showed no sign of slowing, but those sensations were too strong for Jemmi and she turned to other aspects of Sara's awareness.

Sara, she saw, floated in a barren void but carried her ecosystem entire within her, as if someone had taken an empty house set in a garden, then turned all of it inside-out. She gloried in the living beings she harbored, both because they were the foundation of her own survival, and because they had sprung from her own body. Designed into the core of her awareness was the drive to shore up that precarious balance by any means possible. She could win over allies and choose favorites, and smite the enemies growing inside her as if they were incipient contagions.

Jemmi saw the spindle-shaped world inside Sara through Sara's own mind, and she felt the angst and darkness that had been taking hold as her facility to orchestrate that environment slipped away. Sara was old and proud and secretly ashamed to be failing in her duty. Her wordless hopes were focused on the great egg she had prepared for Albiorix. If it quickened, she would have a glorious new life within her for a time, and then the lives she sheltered would have a new home.

Jemmi showed herself to Sara and guilelessly let the fact of her budding talent flow through. For a moment she felt Sara freeze the link between them, as if assessing the best way to react to some startling threat. But when Sara came back, her response was to engulf Jemmi with the sensation that she knew her and cherished her and reveled in her. It overwhelmed Jemmi and flooded through her, and she was powerless against it. Sara had unlimited reserves of love to draw on, and she used them mercilessly.

Jemmi was pinned there like an enraptured butterfly for a long, timeless instant. She was unable to move or think, and she wouldn't have given it up for anything. Finally, when the effect was deep enough, Sara bid her farewell and gently withdrew.

Finding herself squatting by herself on muck-covered cobblestones, Jemmi hugged herself and sobbed quietly. She would have clawed her way back into Sara's mind, but the connection had ended with a note of finality that she would not overstep. Gradually, she realized she was not empty, but filled with warmth and strength, and she could think of nothing but the great heart that had given her that. She now knew down through her bones that she would never have any use for Yee's old empires or for planets where there was nothing at the other side of the sky but more sky, because Sarasvati was her world. Jemmi belonged here, where she could reach out with her hand or mind and touch her god, and if there was anything beyond Sara, it did not interest her.

But for the time being at least, Yee was helping her learn her own strength. She remembered the task he had given her and half-heartedly stepped to the edge of the crowd. She extended her mind just the slightest bit beyond her own skin, and the maelstrom of thoughts and words and desires that hit her was like ducking her head under a waterfall. She drew back and focused on the thoughts of the woman closest to her.

The invasion of privacy was thrilling. The woman was picking vegetables from big baskets, and Jemmi found herself swimming through twisting currents of intentions and half-ignored impressions and the occasional diamond-clear string of words. She wondered if she might become lost in the woman's mind if she got any closer.

Ever so gently—not at all like guiding Roycer's hand—she tossed in the notion that a vendor across the square might be willing to negotiate his price, and watched the ripples spread out across the woman's other thoughts. Her eyes lit, and she hurried away from the table.

Start at the beginning, Jemmi decided. She strode up to the vegetable seller, and graciously allowed him to place his hastily emptied wicker basket on her arm. Then she moved on to a baker, who placed two loaves into it with a flourish as if it was the wittiest thing in the world, and strolled on into the heart of the square.

Jemmi returned home at the head of a small, heavily-laden parade. She directed the string of young men carrying her parcels to line them up along the veranda, and then sent them off. Yee stepped out of the house to observe this, then turned back inside with an audible sniff. Jemmi ran up after him.

"Neh, I can do it!" she told him. "I did it!"

"I daresay you did," he said. "And made quite a scene, by the looks of it. It's a wonder they didn't have you burned at the stake. Have Roycer move your booty inside." He turned away again.

Jemmi was crestfallen.

"Neh, Yee," she blurted. He stopped. "How come Sara— Why don't things work like they did in the olden days?" she asked.

That must have been the right question to ask him, because he immediately warmed to her again. "Ah," he said. "It was the machines. Few people remember that it was the destruction of the machines that caused the fall of the Cosmopolis, and not the other way around. In the days of its greatest strength, the Cosmopolis had enemies who preferred utter anarchy to the order and prosperity it gave them. They were fools and fanatics. They introduced a machine pandemic that spread from one end of inhabited space to the other."

"And all the machines got sick?"

"Not at first. It slept quietly for years, and then at a preordained signal it struck everywhere, simultaneously. All the smart electronics died at that moment, and the Cosmopolis was shattered. To re-create the technology that humans and Sarasvati relied on, we will have to build from the beginning again: steam and iron. It is a long road, but I have walked it before."

Jemmi did not trust Yee, and she didn't think she liked him, but she would follow him anywhere if it would save Sara.

"In fact, Roycer and I were able to uncover some information towards that end while you were out," he told her. "We learned that Sarasvati originally had a shuttle port at either extremity. These were large and busy, so they likely contained several shuttles at the time of the Fall, but they were quite prominent and I expect they were plundered generations ago. There were also several emergency evacuation portals scattered throughout her. These have been lost, and there is a chance that one may be untouched. They will have to be searched out."

That seemed like a lot of work to Jemmi. "Why don't you just ask Sara?"

Yee scoffed. "And what would the question be? The ships and orbitals are very simple beasts, and even if they understood, they couldn't form an answer. But come, I will show you how it's done." He stepped over her groceries and led her back down into the street.

"What we need is people who seem persistent and resourceful, and whose absence will not be noted overly much," said Yee. "People like you and me—but expendable, of course."

Yee approached a laborer in a floppy, grease-stained cap pulling a heavy cart, and smiling and clasping his long pale hands together, asked him if he knew anything about the old-days shuttle port at the end of Sarasvati's long axis. The man, obviously annoyed, shook his head and looked at Yee as if he were cracked. Yee appeared disappointed, and observed it was a pity, since it wouldn't do to go spreading this around, but he was eager for news of any undamaged shuttles, and was more than willing to reimburse the man who brought that news quite handsomely. A fortune, really. At any rate, if he heard of anything, Yee lived right over there—the house with the veranda, can you see?—and would be delighted to receive any news. The man moved on as if he was glad to be rid of Yee. His steps became increasingly more hesitant though, as if something was unfolding in his mind. Finally, about a hundred paces down the street he abandoned his cart completely with a furtive look back, and sprinted away along the quickest route out of Port-Town.

The next man Yee spoke to developed a frantic urge to make the grueling trek to the ruins of the shuttle port at Sarasvati's far end and return to report on his findings. After that, four others became fascinated with the pressing need to locate one of the lost evacuation ports scattered along her length. It seemed to Jemmi that before they hurried off, each of them had been struck by the sudden inspiration for a scheme that simultaneously delighted them and tortured them.

"If a man sees it as a struggle to express an idea from within, he'll exhaust everything he has to bring it to fruition," Yee explained, as the last one began to run. "Well, after your success in the market this morning, I believe I can leave the rest to you. You'll need to send out about another dozen or so." He turned to go.

"Neh, why so many?"

"One of the first things you must learn, Jemmi, is that one man acting alone will change nothing. To have progress, you must mobilize a society. Once we are on a world, you will see how quickly entire kingdoms move forward when they embrace the goals we give them."

Yee returned to the house and stepped over the groceries on the veranda as he went in. Jemmi stalked the street recruiting searchers for the rest of the afternoon, and the food sat out there until evening, when she reckoned she had snared enough.

There was no dawn the next morning. Jemmi jumped out of her big bed with a sense of foreboding and a gut feeling that it was later than it looked. She ran down the wooden stairs and out onto the road in her bare feet. Shock and woe were palpable in the air and the soil, and Sara was lamenting with all her heart. Then it hit Jemmi—Albiorix was dead. He had weakened and gone still and fallen slack in Sara's embrace, and she was nearly paralyzed by loneliness and the weight of this new failure.

People in the villages high overhead began to wake and light lamps and fires as they tentatively started their day. The scattering of weak sparks in the darkness was a pale imitation of the stars Jemmi had seen through Sara's eyes. Yee stepped out onto the veranda and silently leaned over the rail to look upwards and sniff, as if he were tasting the weather.

"Yee—do you know? Albiorix is dead," Jemmi said.

"I'm not surprised," answered Yee. "He was stubbornly fixed on his old route, and I had to relieve him of much of his strength before he would accept my course. We're lucky I made it this far."

Jemmi's hands were fists. "How could you do that?"

"I know what you're thinking—and it's not a problem. Albiorix has always been trailed by younger males as he makes his rounds. I'm sure Horus or Xolotl will be here by the time we are ready to move on."

"But she was going to have his baby!" Jemmi managed.

"Not likely. The orbitals and ships are improbable beings, so they must be part animal, part machine," Yee told her. "I'm certain you've noticed Sarasvati is no longer the paradise she was intended to be. Since the Fall, they have been unable to replenish the nanomachines that they need to grow and heal themselves. I doubt there would have been any offspring." He shrugged.

Jemmi tried to say something, but her grief and rage were like a solid mass that seared through her throat and chest. She had no words to express the depth of his sin and blasphemy. She knew that to strike at Yee would be suicide, so instead, she forced herself to turn from him and raced down the darkened street. When her legs tired, she walked through Port-Town as she had on her first night, staying to the shadows and peeking in windows.

It was hours before she got bored with wandering and returned home. Yee was out.

"Roycer!" Jemmi said. "Where's the jar, then?"

"Which jar, Jemmi?" he asked.

"The one he brought with him off Albiorix. Where does he hide it?"

He paused, and she flicked the boy's mind to give him just a bit of encouragement. "In the tub room. Underneath the floor stones."

"Show me."

Roycer led her to the room with the tub and lifted a flat stone away. In the space beneath was the gray canister Yee had carried when they had first seen him. Jemmi pulled it out. It was obviously very old, because it was made of a single piece of something very smooth and very strong. She grasped the cap, but it would not turn. It had an indentation the shape of a palm on top, but nothing happened when she pressed her hand against it. She handed it back to Roycer and told him to return it just as they found it. He could demonstrate astounding attention to detail when prompted.

As he moved the stone back into place, Sarasvati stirred herself to remember her duty, and her sky sullenly flickered and kindled with morning light, half a day late.

Jemmi and Yee and Roycer continued to live together over the next dozen or so days, but Jemmi saw Yee as little as possible. She also began to avoid looking directly at Roycer. The boy seemed brittle and stretched thin, and he was getting weak and clumsy. He was no longer pretty. Jemmi suspected he would be replaced shortly.

The laborer in the floppy hat returned after a few days, limping and exhausted as if he had run all the way up to the old shuttle port and back. It had been picked clean, he reported, and nothing bigger than a wagon-wheel was left. Several nights after that, the searcher that had been sent to the far end of Sarasvati crawled across the veranda and scratched weakly at the door. He could not speak, but he had just enough strength left to convey that he had also found nothing. Roycer dragged the body inside before the neighbors noticed.

Jemmi approached Yee the next morning. "Neh, Yee, how long will the other searchers be gone?"

Yee snorted. "Were you expecting them back? The task you gave them was to return only when they could report something of value, and to continue searching until then. I'd be surprised if many of them are still standing. Your old Sarasvati is worthless to us, as I expected." He seated himself and picked up his book.

"You and I should begin planning our departure. One of the younger orbitals further rimward is more likely to have what we need."

Jemmi slipped outside and sat in a corner of the veranda. She stretched her mind out across the emptiness, and touched Sara.

All of Sara that was not dedicated to the physics of regulating her inner environment was still in mourning for Albiorix, and she was in no mood to notice Jemmi.

Please, Sara! I'm going to have to leave if you don't . . . We're all going to have to leave! She visualized Sarasvati's interior deserted and bare, and prodded her with the image. Resentful, Sara turned part of her attention to Jemmi, and sluggishly recognized her as one marked as her own.

You have to help us find a shuttle, or else he's going to take me far away. There was no reaction to the words, of course. Jemmi tried to make an image of a shuttle, but she had no idea what a spacecraft would look like. Instead, she imagined people flying in and out of Sarasvati.

Sara responded with a picture of a flawless white fish, smoother than an egg and shaped like a teardrop, with stubby fins. The fish dove out of a hole in the side of Sarasvati's asteroid and swam across empty space.

That must be it, then! Where?

But Sara did not have a mind that could answer a question like that.

Jemmi leapt onto the veranda railing and caught hold of the edge of the roof, then scrambled on top of the house. From its peak she could look down along Sarasvati's entire inner length as it curved over her head in lieu of a sky.

Is it there? she asked, looking at a spot directly across, and kept the interrogative at the front of her mind as she moved her eyes across Sarasvati's interior. When Jemmi reached a point that was far off—90° around and two-thirds of the way towards her other end—Sara stirred, and Jemmi's vision of the spot came into clear focus. She had a sudden image of the white shuttle in a smooth white cavern, clasped by metal arms that held it suspended over the floor.

Thank you, Sara! Thank you! Now I'll never have to leave you.

Jemmi gently withdrew and left Sara to her grief. She remained on the veranda until she had collected herself, and went inside.

"Neh, Yee," she said as if she was discussing the weather. "I've found a shuttle."

Yee looked up from his book, as cold as ice. "Do not even think of toying with me, child—you would die before you hit the ground. Run along."

"It's smooth and white, in a big white room. One of my searchers made it back."

Yee was out of his seat and gripping her collar as if propelled by lightning. "Where?" he demanded. "Let me talk to him!"

She shook her head. "Can't. He's dead now. But I know where it is." She took him to the mullioned window and pointed out the spot to him.

"There? Where the river makes the bend around the tip of the cloud forest?" He calculated. "That's a three-day journey. Roycer—the packs!" Jemmi heard heavy footsteps running frenetically through the house, and Roycer burst into the room carrying two loaded rucksacks and an enormous backpack.

"We leave now," Yee said to her. "Prepare anything you need to take."

He left the room. Jemmi could think of nothing, so she sat and waited. When Yee passed through again, he had the gray canister slung over his shoulder, and he didn't pause to see if they followed him.

Three days later, Jemmi was farther from home than she had ever been. They had had men pull them in carts day and night for most of the way, but the last one had dropped from exhaustion just as they decided to leave the road, and they had hiked through the brush on their own.

They stood in a clearing in a jungle. Humid air, blown erratically out of an obstructed duct from one of Sarasvati's lungs, met the cool currents overhead and sent a thick perpetual cloud rolling through the trees. Moisture dripped from the leaves like rain. In front of them was a symmetrical grassy mound, like a small hill standing alone.

"This is assuredly an evacuation portal," said Yee, pacing around it. "That's the entrance, and it is overgrown and partially buried, so the space beyond certainly could have remained intact. But how did your source know what was inside?"

He shot Jemmi a glance. She shrugged.

"No matter. We are very close, and our day is at hand." He removed two packets from his rucksack and tucked them in the tumbled stones that filled a door-shaped indentation. "Roycer, light this string here and here, please, then join me quickly." He strode away. "Jemmi, you might care to accompany me."

She followed Yee back into the trees. Roycer came running up, and then there was an explosion that sent earth and spinning shards of timber flying past them. The cloud amongst them jumped, and Sarasvati flinched violently under their feet.

A third of the mound was blasted away. The explosion had removed the layer of soil and stone covering it, and laid bare several yards of a deep purple-pink gash that oozed and glistened wetly. Jemmi wondered if the wound was as bad for Sara as it looked, or if on her miles-long body it was less than a scratch. Of the doorway only smoke and rubble remained, but beyond it was a steep shaft that led down through Sarasvati.

Yee tossed aside his pack and hurried in. Roycer and then Jemmi followed him down a long spiral staircase, smooth flowing steps formed by Sarasvati's living body. When daylight could no longer reach them, the steps above and below them glowed to light their way. They descended so far that Jemmi could feel herself becoming heavier.

A chitinous membrane blocked the passage and drew them up short. Yee placed his hand in its center, and it dilated open. They stepped through, and it silently closed behind them. Another blocked their way, and the air pressure changed and Jemmi's ears popped before it opened for them.

The stairs here were no longer alive. They were mathematically perfect, with precise lines and right angles that had never existed in Jemmi's world. They were a sterile white, against which Yee and Roycer seemed both more vivid and less whole. Jemmi had left Sarasvati, and was standing in the bare asteroid that protected her soft flesh from the harsh vacuum.

The white staircase was short, and it opened up into a cavernous chamber walled and floored in featureless white. The vaulted ceiling was a warm silky gray, chased with flickers of colored lights—Sarasvati's outer surface, pressed tight across the top of the space. At the center, as big as a house, a pristine fish-shaped shuttle was suspended over the floor by a set of jointed steel arms.

Yee rushed forward with a sound that was part gasp and part sob. He circled the shuttle, reaching out a hand and pulling it back to his mouth as if he were afraid to touch it. Jemmi ran her palm along its side. It was smoother than an egg, and cool.

"It's whole, and perfect!" Yee crowed. "At long last, I've done it!"

Jemmi nudged at it. "But, neh, Yee," she said. "It's dead. It doesn't go."

"Ah, but it will now." He caressed the canister he carried.

"What's in that thing, then?"

"Today, it is the greatest treasure in all the galaxy. I have carried it with me since before the Fall, when I first began to suspect that my enemies might take extreme measures to divest humanity of my direction."

"I thought you said they were the enemies of the Cosmopolis."

"I may have—did you think there was any difference?"

Near the tail of the shuttle, Yee gingerly pried open a tiny drawer in the craft's skin and inspected its interior with one eye. Then he placed his palm on the lid of the canister and twisted. It came off with a chuff of air. He handed the lid to Roycer, and reverently held the container out towards Jemmi.

"Behold—one and a half liters of breeder nanos, sealed away long prior to the Fall." Inside was a gritty paste. It smelled like hot sand and rising bread dough. "This is quite possibly the last batch in existence untouched by the machine plague. Each speck can replicate thousands of the same nanomachines that built and ran the technology of the Cosmopolis. What I hold here is enough to raise an entire planet from the dark ages back to enlightenment. It is the key to our next empire."

He lifted the canister to the intake panel. "It would not do to waste it—would half a spoonful be too much?" He tilted a drop in. "The nanos will find the diagnostic system, and it will activate them to begin whatever repairs it needs."

He pushed the little drawer closed and bored those eyes of his into the surface of the spacecraft as if willing it to let him see its inner workings. Nothing happened for as long as Jemmi could hold her breath, and then a faint ticking and hissing sound emerged. Yee cackled with delight. "It will be no time at all now," he told Jemmi. "In a few hours you'll have had your first taste of fresh air. You will have seen your first sunset."

"But then we'll come back to Sara, neh?"

Still preoccupied, he answered, "What's that? Don't be absurd. Once you're on a real planet, you won't spare another thought for this rat-hole."

Jemmi turned her back on him. Near the entrance stood a heavy hand crank and a podium topped with switches and levers. She ran her hands over the alien textures and idly toyed with the switches to hear them click.

She closed a simple circuit that had remained alive across the centuries, and the floor beneath them disappeared, phasing into transparency. Her heart lurched and she groped for balance. She stood atop a star-spattered bottomless void, and looked between her feet far out into nothing. Suddenly, an edge of the emptiness was occluded by a shape that swung past her. For a moment, staring up into the chamber was a golden-green, slit-pupilled, lidless eye—flat, dead, and far broader than the entire launch bay. It was Albiorix.

Sara was unable to bring herself to release him, and he wafted like marsh-grass in her embrace.

Jemmi stood transfixed until he swept beyond her range of vision, and said carefully, "Neh, Yee. I don't think I want to go with you."

Yee faced her, and his voice was cold with threat. "That is unacceptable, Jemmi. You have a great responsibility to humanity, and I need you by my side for the great works I will do. You will be my empress. One way or another you will accompany me, and I assure you that you will rejoice in the opportunity."

Jemmi averted her eyes from his. She reached out and placed a thought in Roycer's mind: *Roycer, kill Yee. It's important.*

Roycer sized up Yee with a stony glance, and quietly shucked his heavy pack. He took a few wary steps, and then rushed him. Suddenly startled, Yee snapped his head around, and Roycer froze in mid-stride. His muscles shuddered horribly as Jemmi leaned the force of her mind against Yee's. Blood trickled down Roycer's chin from where his jaw had clenched on his tongue.

"Is this the best you can do, child?" Yee sneered. "Use the last gasp of an exhausted puppet against me? Countless others with real weapons have made the attempt, and they have all failed." His stoop disappeared, and he became a towering presence in the white chamber. "I am the immortal Andrew Constantin Fujiwara Borsanyi, founder of the Cosmopolis, eternal First Lord of the League of Man, and architect of all mankind's history. Who are you?"

Jemmi had no answer to that.

She released her pressure on Roycer, and he fell backwards towards her across the invisible floor. Instead, she reached out to Sara. She had to grope because she no longer knew where to find her, but at last they touched, and Jemmi's urgency roused Sara's attention. Jemmi concentrated all her awareness on the launch bay, dead Albiorix, and Yee standing next to the shuttle.

He's the one! She flung the rage and fear towards Sara. *He killed Albiorix! And now he'll do worse—*

The thought suddenly bloomed in Jemmi's mind that the most clever and crucial thing she could do was get down on her knees and bow her head. She welcomed the idea as an inspired stroke of brilliance, and rushed to kneel in submission. She heard Yee's footsteps snap against the crystal floor as he sauntered towards her, and it did not trouble her.

They felt the rumbling through the walls and the floor then. It started hushed and far off, a sustained roll of thunder that rushed up and overtook them.

Yee cocked his head and frowned, and then his eyes widened as he identified the sound: Sara had spasmed her entire boneless body in a long rolling wave, like a rope snapped across miles of ground. It was the roar of an earthquake, focused and aimed right at him.

Jemmi grabbed Roycer and spurred him with an intensity that sent him scrabbling maniacally past her into the cover of the stairwell. She dove in after him.

Yee dropped the canister and extended his arms overhead, not to fend off Sara's body, but to reach into her mind. He stood there for the space of a heartbeat, but there was no time to learn to contact her, and he abruptly broke and fled for the stairwell, all gangly arms and legs.

He snatched at Jemmi's ankle, and from somewhere she found the wherewithal to shout, "Your nanos!" throwing all the weight and urgency she could into the thought. Yee stared at her and hesitated a moment—perhaps it was the power of her suggestion, or perhaps it was the age-old habit of cherishing his burden—and then spun back into the launch bay.

At that moment the living ceiling of the chamber lurched high up with a great solid heave that pulled the air screaming past their ears and whiplashed back down into the launch bay. It hammered against the invisible floor in a paroxysm of violence that obliterated Jemmi's scream. The shuttle and its equipment, which could bear the forces of vacuum, fire and ice and had stood unmarked for centuries, were instantly pulverized into a thin stratum of wreckage. Yee, standing among them, was mashed into nothing.

The wave rolled off again just as quickly, trailed by the sound of receding thunder. A stunning silence stretched for several minutes, punctuated as bits of unrecognizable debris rained down towards the stars from where they were embedded in Sarasvati's side, clattering or splatting to a stop against the crystal.

Jemmi pressed her face hard against the stairwell wall and waited until the world had stopped reverberating. It took a long time before she judged it was safe to move.

"Let's go, then," she said to Roycer—no compulsion, just an order. "Ah, wait."

She threaded her way into the launch bay and picked through the ankle-high detritus until she found Yee's canister. It was dented and scraped, but almost none of the paste had been spilled. She took it.

"Now we can go." She led Roycer back into Sarasvati, and up the long stairs. She was careful not to touch his thoughts again. Near the top of the climb, he stumbled to his knees, and, clear-minded for the first time in weeks, sobbed with horror and loss. Jemmi sat several steps above him with her arms wrapped around her shins and waited patiently, mindful of all the things Roycer had seen and done, allowed no feeling but solicitude for Yee's needs. He doubled over and retched. When he began glaring at her during his pauses for breath, Jemmi picked herself up and continued climbing. He hurried to follow.

Jemmi stepped out through the ragged hole at the surface and climbed to the top of the mound. The air tasted to her as if it were filled with pain and righteous fury. A raw pink line now ran from the end of Sarasvati, crossing over the stairwell, and continuing deep into her interior. A strip of ground more than a hundred paces wide had wrenched itself clear, exposing the bare flesh beneath it. Trees, stones, earth and bits of homes lay tossed and scattered to either side for as far as she could see. In the hazy distance, a series of aftershocks or convulsions raised dust clouds and sent ripples running back towards them. Jemmi's own body burned in aggrieved empathy. She would never let anyone hurt Sara again.

Roycer joined her on the rubble and surveyed the destruction.

"What *are* you?" he asked.

Jemmi blinked for a moment, and while she considered, he shifted his weight and raised his fists to strike her. She flicked his mind and he went still. And that gave Jemmi her answer.

"Bow down," she told Roycer. "Get on your knees and bow down before me. I am the priestess of Sarasvati. I have come, and everything will change now."

With that, as her boy knelt with earnest awe and reverence, Jemmi walked to the place where Sara's wound was the worst, and poured the contents of Yee's canister out into it. ✪

FIVE HUNDRED AND FORTY DOORS

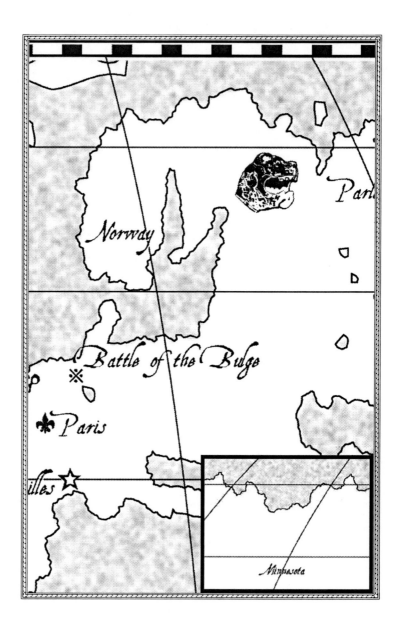

FIVE HUNDRED AND FORTY DOORS
BY DAVID J. SCHWARTZ

SO I WAS CUTTING MY NAILS AND LISTENING TO THE VIKINGS GAME ON THE radio when that Jake Skarda come around with a gun. Buddy Mahla had put it around that I had a heckuva lot of money in the house, which I sure didn't. Jake believed it, though. He tried to disguise himself, but even through that dumb ski mask I knew his voice from him always talking so dang much.

I said, "Jake, you don't want to do this," and limped towards him, hiding the nail scissors in my hand. I been limping since I took a bullet at the Battle of the Bulge. Folks ask a lot of dumb questions about it, but I never been much for talking, and anyhow it happened a long time ago.

I figured Jake would run or he would shoot, and there wasn't much point worrying which. Pretty much I wanted him to get on with it, since my knees were sore and the scissors were biting at my hand. So I said "You done some stupid things, Jake, but you never killed nobody, and I don't figure you're going to start now."

Well, I was wrong. He shot me and I stabbed him with the scissors and I died.

After I was dead the doorbell rang. I knew I was dead because when I got up to answer it I didn't limp and I didn't hurt, and I don't mean from the bullet because I never felt that. No, the pain I was missing was them aches you get when you're eighty-two and you hurt so much all the time you hardly think about it. Them pains were gone.

Anyhow this woman was at the door. You know how some folks' eyes are too bright, like they been crying, only without the red? She had eyes like that. Wild eyes. She wore old-time armor, and kind of a vest over it with ravens on the front and some bloodstains. She said her name was Thrima and she was a Valkyrie come to take me to Valhalla. Now I knew from Odd's stories—Odd was this fella I knew back in Double-Ya Double-Ya Two—I knew Valhalla was where the heroes who die in battle go to serve Odin. They eat and drink and kill each other and wake up alive in the morning to do it over again.

I didn't much like the idea of the killing, but outside of that Valhalla sounded OK, and since I had a free ticket I didn't feel like chancing on not getting into the other heaven. So I followed Thrima outside. There was a trail of blood on the ground, and I asked about Jake. She said he'd be dead by morning, and I guess that's all there is to say about that.

Thrima's horse was nosing at my blueberry bushes which weren't doing much but hold up the January ice. Before I got shot I couldn't have got up on that horse, but I felt strong, not eighty-two and dead. So I mounted up behind Thrima and that horse trotted up in the air without wings or anything. Pretty soon we were halfway to the clouds. Town sure looked small from up there.

Thrima said I was the last of the Einheriar, which I guessed was a Norwegian word but I didn't know what it meant. I'm Norwegian, but not from Norway. See, I was 99th Infantry in the war. The brass wanted to push the Nazis out of Norway, so they put out a call for Norwegians. Some that joined up had been kicked out by the Quislings, but most were second- or third-generation, like me. Anyhow it turned out the Allies went through Normandy instead, and the 99th got combined with some other units and sent to the Ardennes, so none of us got to Norway until the war was near over. A lot of us didn't get there at all, because of the Bulge.

Anyhow, I told Thrima I didn't know what Einheriar meant, and she told me they were the heroes of Valhalla and when the last one shows up it's time for Ragnarok. Well, I knew Ragnarok was the battle at the end of the world, when the gods and giants kill each other. I started wishing I'd took my chances with St. Peter after all.

We kept climbing through the clouds. After a while we come out above them and Thrima reined in the horse and slid off him and took my hand. I guessed being dead had different rules about walking on clouds, so I got down after her. It wasn't any different from standing on wet pasture. Then Thrima kissed me and I know it's the thing nowadays to give details but I wouldn't even if there was anything to tell. The truth is things didn't get far before Thrima went limp and fell down on the cloud.

Turned out Odd Boddason had hit her over the head with a rifle butt. Sergeant Hassel was with him, both of them dead since December 1944.

I was kind of put out about the interruption, but I said "How you doing there, Odd?" and he said "Not too bad. You been keeping your nails trimmed?" and I said "Yah."

Sergeant Hassel held out an M-1 like the ones we carried during the war. He said "We aim to put a stop to this Ragnarok, you up for it?"

Well, I had to think about that. Folks say Double-Ya Double-Ya Two was a good war, and I know they mean we were there for the right reasons. But the killing I seen wasn't right and it wasn't good. I didn't want anymore of that. But Ragnarok meant the end of everything, so I told Sergeant Hassel OK.

Then Odd said "There's someone else joining us," and around a hill in the clouds come my brother Alek, and I just about killed my first dead person right there.

My brother Bill died in 1934. Me, Bill, Alek, and Harald were out hunting that day. Harald didn't see too good, but he had steady hands, so we used to take turns pointing him at the deer. That day it was Alek's turn, so he stayed with Harald while Bill and I went off separate.

I sat down at my spot next to the creek, and pretty soon I seen Bill settle in on the other side. There must have been a deer convention down to the Cities that day, though, because I didn't have no luck and neither did Bill.

After a while I heard something behind me, and I seen Harald about thirty yards up the slope, squinting over the creek with his finger on the trigger like he had a twelve-point buck. There wasn't no buck, though, and no doe or fawn neither, just Bill, and next thing I knew Harald took his shot.

I seen enough kill shots on deer to know when a body's dead, so I didn't go over the creek to check on Bill. I run back up the bank with my rifle, but Alek was gone. I knew Alek pointed Harald at Bill because they'd been arguing all week over Sylvie Throndson and what happened at the Harvest Dance. I was surprised, though. Alek could be mean, but most times it was just talking. Daddy said Alek got his tongue from his Ma. Alek was our half-brother, see. Daddy used to be married to a woman from over to Erdahl, but she died birthing Alek, and then Daddy married Ma and they had Bill and Harald and me.

After Bill died me and Harald never went hunting again. I went to war and Harald ended up with Sylvie Throndson so I had plenty of nieces and nephews that visited even after I moved into town. Harald died a couple years before me, and I never seen Alek again until I was standing on that cloud.

I would have shot him, too, only Odd said "He didn't do it." I told Odd he didn't know nothing about it and he said "I've been dead longer than you and I know. If you shoot you'll just spook that horse back to Valhalla and they'll know something's up."

I put down my rifle and Alek said "Harald done it on his own, you know." He started in about how Harald always saw better than he let on but I didn't want to hear it and I told Odd he better explain some things.

The Norwegians used to call Odd a *skald*. That means poet or story-teller, and Odd used to tell stories every night while he clipped his nails, about Viking funerals where they burned the dead man's ship and about Loki and Thor getting into all kinds of trouble, sometimes on the same side and sometimes not. Anyhow Odd said there were five hundred and forty doors in Valhalla and eight hundred men were supposed to come through each one come Ragnarok. He said it took some figuring but it seemed like the last man was coming soon. He started thinking about the things that were supposed to set Ragnarok off, and he wondered if we could stop any of them things, so he come up with a plan. First thing was to stop the last Einheriar getting to Valhalla, so they followed Thrima when she come to get me. Next thing was to kill three roosters before they crowed, one in Asgard, one in Jotunheim, and one in Hel.

So the Flogstad brothers were going to kill Gold-comb up in Asgard, Odd and Sergeant Hassel were going after Fjalar in Jotunheim, and me and Alek were going to Hel to kill her rooster. See, Hel's the place and it's also the woman who runs it. It's pretty confusing.

I didn't much like the idea of hunting with Alek again, but I thought about Harald's grandkids. I always give them blueberries with cream and sugar when they come over, which I guess they might not do if their folks didn't tell them to, but they were good kids and they deserved to live long enough to be old and ignored even if their grandpa was a liar and a murderer.

So I asked Odd how was this supposed to work. He fixed bayonet on his M-1 and he stabbed the cloud and it tore apart like an old bedsheet. There was a tree branch inside wide as a two-lane highway. Odd said that was Yggdrasil, the tree the worlds were built on and the quickest way to get around.

Right then, though, Thrima woke up and come at us with her bare hands. She slashed Sergeant Hassel pretty bad across the face and took a bite out of Alek's leg. Odd got a rope around her neck and I cracked her on the chin with my rifle. I felt bad about it, but Odd said the Valkyries pretty much had to help fate take its course and we couldn't let her get away and warn nobody what we were up to. So we tied her up and she had a lot to say about that but I'm not going to repeat it.

I thought we should take the horse, but Odd said she wouldn't listen to nobody but Thrima and especially not no man. So we tethered her horse to her belt and dropped through the tear in the cloud and started out.

I tell you, that Yggdrasil is one big tree. It was so big we couldn't see the trunk from where we started out. A long ways out to either side there was more branches, but I couldn't see the ground or the top of the tree. The bark was thick and greenish-gray, and branches sprouted off here and there, smaller but still big enough to walk on. I guess it was winter there same as down in Minnesota, because the tree didn't have no leaves, just black buds like warts and black ravens everywhere. Odd said the ravens were waiting to feast off whoever died at Ragnarok. They were just regular birds, but there were thousands of them.

Odd set a good pace and I remembered how the whole squad used to take their cues from him, even Sergeant Hassel. We cleaned our guns when Odd cleaned his and we cut our fingernails when Odd cut his and we hit the sack when Odd finished telling stories. The fingernails were because Odd told us that after the ravens picked over a battlefield Hel's shipbuilders came to collect the dead men's fingernails. They were using them to build a ship called Njalfar that was going to sail at the end of the world. We kept ours real short so they wouldn't have much to work with, and it got to be a habit. Even after Odd died on Elsenborn Ridge I kept doing it.

We walked a long time, Odd and Sergeant Hassel ahead, me and Alek behind, and the ravens all around. The branch led to a bigger branch, and that led to a bough the size of the Interstate. After a while I asked Alek were these M-1s supposed to take out a giant rooster or was there something else I needed to know. He told me they were some kind of special weapons from Valhalla but he didn't know how they worked.

I said "If you didn't do nothing to Bill how come you run off" and he said "I knew Daddy would think it was me." I thought about how Daddy used to say Alek took after "that woman." He meant Alek's Ma, and I don't know what was so bad about her, but I guess Daddy thought Alek was just as bad. I guess I thought so too back then, without even knowing it.

I might have said something more, but a wind come up and spooked the ravens. I seen a deer running along one of the branches out to the side, a thirty-two-point buck at least, big enough to feed Paul Bunyan for a few weeks. Odd said, "There are four deer, one for each of the winds," and I said "If that's the size of the deer I can't wait to see the roosters."

We seen the squirrel first, though, right after we caught sight of the trunk. That thing must have been a couple of miles around. The trunk, I mean. The squirrel twitched and chattered like any other, but he was red and big as a Burlington Northern car. Quick, too, because by the time we got to the trunk he was up and out of sight. Odd sat down where the bough and the trunk met and said the squirrel's name was Ratatosk and he was going to be our ride.

Alek said "I didn't see no saddle on him," and Odd said "He's not known to carry passengers. But we're going to bid with his preferred currency: gossip."

Turns out this Ratatosk runs up and down Yggdrasil passing gossip between this dragon chewing on the roots and this eagle sitting at the top. Ratatosk tells the eagle what the dragon's been saying about him and then he tells the dragon what the eagle said back.

Gossip, that's the kind of thing that Buddy Mahla does. Ma used to say you don't spread dirt around without getting some on you. I told Odd that, but Odd said he didn't figure we were going to get a ride with our good looks.

Pretty soon Ratatosk came back, and Odd shouted something about carrying passengers as well as tales. Well the squirrel stopped and cocked its head like regular squirrels do, but he had teeth the size of hay bales and claws like old-fashioned plows. He squeaked something about trading rumors for rides only he made it rhyme but I'm no *skald* so don't ask me to recite it.

So Odd said the real reason Heimdall and Loki hate each other is because of the time Sigyn spent at the Bifrost bridge while Loki was visiting his Ma's folks. The squirrel laughed and told Odd he would take him to the worlds beneath the roots. Then Sergeant Hassel told about Thor getting stuck in an airport when he was walking among mortals which if you think about it makes no sense at all but Ratatosk seemed to like it fine.

Alek grinned at me and said "The last of the Einheriar wet his bed until he was six years old." Ratatosk laughed so hard he scared off all the ravens around us. Well, I was so ticked off I couldn't think of anything mean to say about Alek, so I said "That Erik Johnson's been doing more than plow the fields for Louise Nygaard since her husband died." I wished I had something to tell about gods or heroes, but I guess it didn't matter because Ratatosk let me get on with the rest.

Well, like Alek said there weren't no saddles. We held on to Ratatosk's fur, which felt like rolled cornhusks, and I hadn't hardly got a grip before he took off down Yggdrasil. Back in '44 I spent a few hours bouncing through Krinkelt on the side of a personnel truck with Jerry right behind. That was like plowing butter compared to riding Ratatosk. I never rode horses much, but at least there's a fit between a person's lower parts and a horse's back. Ratatosk was scrawny as any other squirrel, and by the sixth or seventh time I come down hard on his spine I was thinking about letting go. Maybe the fall wouldn't kill me since I was already dead.

Well, I didn't let go and Ratatosk kept moving down Yggdrasil, chattering the whole way about the world ending in blood and fire. He said the wolves were going to break their chains and the sun was going to go out. Odd told him we were going to do something about that and Ratatosk said something about warring to end war and he laughed.

Pretty soon Ratatosk turned off the trunk and onto a branch, only it was twisted like a root even though we were still a long ways up in

the tree. I don't know how that works. I wanted to hear someone talk
besides that squirrel so I asked Alek had he been in the war, too. He told
me he was 101st Airborne and I asked had he been in Bastogne during the
Bulge and he said he had. I said, "I guess that makes you some kind of
hero," and he said, "That's what I been told," and I said, "Yah me too."

After a while Ratatosk stopped running. There was a little root off the
main one, and through the clouds underneath—and I don't know how
it works that clouds hang underneath roots, so don't ask—through the
clouds I seen pasture with cattle so big they made Babe the Blue Ox look
like a hamster.

Ratatosk said if he went any closer he'd be spotted and he didn't want
them giants throwing rocks at him. Sergeant Hassel got down off the
squirrel but Odd said "If something goes wrong with the roosters you
have to stop Njalfar from sailing." Then he told us "Good luck" and
dropped down next to Sergeant Hassel, and me and Alek held on while
that squirrel went racing back towards Yggdrasil's trunk.

Ratatosk said "I know your brothers, the killer and the killed." Alek
asked how he knew about it but Ratatosk laughed and said we'd find out
soon enough. I wanted a better answer but right then I heard a horn, real
faint but clear, like a radio you turned down and forgot about until you
walked right past it.

Ratatosk said "That was Heimdall's horn," and for once he wasn't giggling. I guessed that meant it was starting.

Ratatosk took us down the trunk and onto another root. It was all
black and red below, like fire burning underground. I figured that was
Hel. Then I heard a rooster crowing above and Ratatosk said "That will
be Fjalar" and I said "Are we going to find this rooster or what?"

Ratatosk stopped next to a smaller root and said "Hel's rooster lies
below, on the roof of her palace. If you climb down from here you won't
have to climb her walls."

Well, we got down and Ratatosk run off, I guess to meet the dragon
one last time. Alek and me started climbing down into the dark. That

root was rough enough that we didn't have too much trouble finding places to hold on, and even after bouncing around on that squirrel I felt pretty good. But then I heard another rooster crowing.

Alek said "That must be Gold-comb," and I said "Yah." We kept going, and pretty soon we seen Hel's palace. It wasn't much more than a big house, and I don't know how the roof held that rooster up. I guess he was fifty foot or so—taller than the old water tower in town, for sure. His wattle and comb was red, but most of his feathers were black, and he blended right in with the burning ground. I guess he seen us hanging there on the root, because he kind of stretched his wings and took a breath.

Back before the war we kept chickens, and when we needed to kill one we'd cut off its head with a hatchet. Well, soon as I thought that, a hatchet showed up where the M-1 used to be. I guess that was the special part of the Valhalla weapon. So I thrown it at the rooster.

Alek got off a couple shots, but that hatchet did the job. It got bigger after I thrown it until it was so big it cut that rooster's head clean off. Then it turned around and come flying right back to my hand.

Didn't matter, though, because that rooster had already crowed.

I never heard a sound like that before. It sounded like a train blowing its horn while plowing through a herd of screaming cattle. The tree shook when that rooster crowed, and it kept vibrating after, like it was scared.

The rooster's head rolled down to the ground and lay still, but the body run off Hel's roof and into the dark like any other dumb chicken. It didn't make any noise, though. I figured after a scream that meant the end of the world there ought to be noise. When I thought about the end of the world I thought of the Bulge, and the Bulge had been loud; shells falling, jets overhead, Jerries shouting.

Hel stayed quiet, though. After that rooster took off, Hel's doors opened up and a few million men come out of the palace in total silence.

Maybe that many men couldn't fit in a house that size, but they did. Alek and Odd and Sergeant Hassel had all looked about the same as when I seen them last, but Hel's soldiers looked like shadows with guns and swords. They were Jerries and Yanks and fellas from pretty much every place ever fought a war. Probably everyplace. They run out into the dark without a sound and Alek said "They're headed for Njalfar."

So we climbed the rest of the way down and took off running with Hel's army. I guess they couldn't see we didn't belong there, and I wasn't sure we didn't. I couldn't figure how the Valkyries decided who got to live in Valhalla while the rest came down here where the sun never shone.

Anyhow we run with them until we come to the biggest darned ship I ever seen. I figure one of the rules about being dead is lots of things are bigger than they need to be. The ship was bigger than one of them aircraft carriers, and it kind of glowed in the dark, maybe because of the fingernails. Hel's army ran right up a ramp onto that ship like the animals boarding Noah's ark.

There was a platform next to the ramp, and a woman stood up there. The left side of her was white like fresh snow but the right side was black like turned soil. Harald stood on her left side and Bill on her right, and when they seen Alek and me they jumped down off that platform and come running at us.

I guess that's how come Ratatosk knew about Harald and Bill. I found out later they were Hel's consorts, or a couple of them. I guess she picks out new ones every so often. Anyhow they come running and Alek said "I figure we got to get through them to get this done."

A few years back one of my nephews give me a book, some kind of saga, which I guess means a lot of killing. It was about these families over to Iceland who got into a feud and killed each other until hardly anybody was left. That's what it was like when Harald and Bill and Alek and me come together, only since we was already dead it just kept going. Alek and me killed our brothers and they got up and killed us back and we got up and killed them again. If you think it didn't hurt you're wrong.

I felt like my soul was bleeding, and I wondered if the ravens were going to eat that too.

I told Bill there wasn't no reason for us to fight, but he said "There are rules we all got to follow. And you can't change anything anyhow." I told him I thought that was a bunch of baloney and I killed him again.

I didn't think it would ever stop. Them weapons from Valhalla changed from rifles to swords to clubs and Harald and Bill had the same type of thing only they come from Hel, but I couldn't tell the difference. Meantime them shadows run around us onto the ship and started untying it from the dock and getting ready to head out.

I killed Harald and I thought maybe that ought to feel good after what he done but it didn't. I spent a long time hating Alek for what I thought he done, but here he was fighting with me to save the world. And Bill never done nothing wrong, but Hel couldn't tell the difference between him and the one that killed him.

So I quit fighting. I left my brothers and I told that weapon what I wanted it to be and I climbed up onto that ship with the other damned folks. It's funny, the things you see when you're scared. I seen that the shadows had faces, only you couldn't tell except up close. I didn't look at the faces. I climbed onto the deck and then I went down into the hold and cut loose with that weapon.

The first enemy tank I seen in the Bulge had a flamethrower on it, and I was never so scared as I was when they pointed it at us. It's hard to think when you see fire coming at you like it's a living thing, like Jerry made some kind of a deal with it to burn everything in his way. Only now it wasn't Jerry using it against me, it was me using it on the ship. The shadows scattered before the flames, and I cooked the ship's insides until they caught. Them burning fingernails smelled pretty bad, and they kicked up a heckuva lot of smoke. Pretty soon I couldn't see no part of the ship that wasn't burning, so I come up onto the deck, figuring it was all over and done with.

Well, I was wrong. The next thing I seen was a giant so big he couldn't fit on the ship. He slapped me down with one of his big hands, and I didn't wake up again for a while.

Turns out this giant's name was Hymir, and he was supposed to be sailing Njalfar, so he was pretty ticked off about me burning it. He wanted to toss me down to the depths of Niflheim, I guess, but my brothers stopped him. All of them.

Once Njalfar burned I guess Harald and Bill figured the whole Ragnarok thing was off for now, so they called a truce with Alek and told Hymir to get lost. He took some convincing—his skull is pretty thick, and I'm not being funny. Odd says Thor broke an ale cup against Hymir's head one time.

Odd's here in Hel with the rest of us. Sergeant Hassel and the Flogstad brothers too. Odd says it don't make much sense. He says considering what's supposed to happen to Odin and the rest of them come Ragnarok, they ought to be happy we put a stop to it.

I don't like Hel all that much, but then I kind of expected I'd end up here. I never figured killing was the kind of thing you got graded on. You kill a good guy or you kill a bad guy, you still killed someone.

Mostly it's boring here, and quiet. We don't talk much anymore, not even Odd. Sometimes my brothers and me play cards. Harald cheats. Lately, though, it's tough for me to tell who's who. I guess pretty soon we'll be shadows like the rest.

Someday they'll finish that ship again, and maybe some other fellas will show up trying to put a stop to Ragnarok again. Sometimes I think maybe it'd be better if they didn't. Bill says as long as folks keep on getting chances they'll keep on making mistakes, and maybe that's true. But I'm hoping folks keep their nails trimmed, just in case. ✪

LIFE SENTENCE

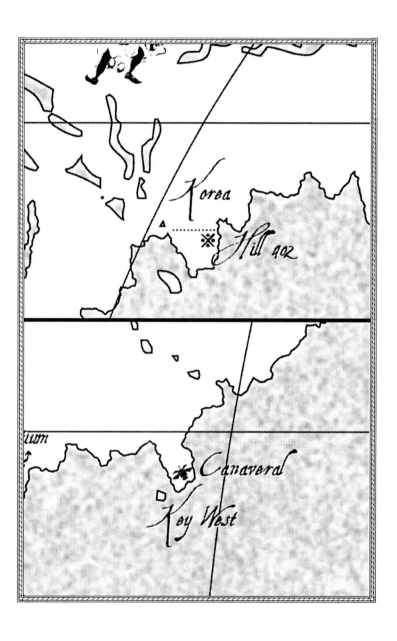

LIFE SENTENCE

BY SANDRA MCDONALD

THE SEAPLANE RAMPS HAD BEEN REPLACED BY A CRAPPY STRIP MALL DURING the years Frank Hayes had been away. Half the buildings were boarded up, the parking lot was an obstacle course of chewed-up asphalt, and the overhead marquee still read H PPY N W YE R, though Easter of 1979 was just two days away. *Shithole,* Frank thought, and spat on the ground. He would have liked one last plane ride with Buckeye Jim, who for a dollar had taken kids high above the marsh and out over the Atlantic. He'd thought fondly of those rides over the years. Of being free and unbound, no iron bars blocking the clouds.

Squire Road had degenerated into four lanes of gas stations and restaurants, and it took a minute for Frank to figure out how to cross it without getting flattened by shitbox Japanese cars. Once across he cut through littered parking lots to the avenue of Cape Cod houses his father, the bigshot developer, had built decades earlier while Frank was off in Korea. "Best houses for working men," Patrick Hayes had boasted back then. Frank could still see him, spiffy in his suit and expensive gold wristwatch. Patrick had flown Corsairs during WWII. He had shot down seven Japanese Zeroes. Patrick added, "This one's for you and Francesca. Welcome home, kid."

Standing on the freshly cured sidewalk, his legs still aching from bullet wounds, young Frank had eyed the house with mixed emotions. The new development had once been part of a vast array of pig farms. If he sniffed hard enough he could still smell their piss and shit. "Dad," he said, "it's great. But we were thinking of maybe moving out west."

Francesca, her yellow sundress fluttering in the breeze, snuggled against Frank's side. "To California."

"Don't be idiots." Patrick pressed a key into Frank's hand. His lips lingered a split second too long on Francesca's forehead. "This is my gift to the two of you. My favorite couple."

Memories of that immaculate starter home faded away as Frank swung open the rotted picket gate. White paint was flaking off the house, several roof tiles had landed in the yard, and the rose bushes flanking the front door had withered from neglect. He circled around the back to the kitchen door. Francesca sat inside drinking a glass of soda.

"Frank," she said, no surprise in her voice.

It was worse than he'd feared. The dimples he'd loved were no longer visible under rolls of wrinkles and fat. Her hair was the color of dishwater, the flesh under her housedress bloated. Hands clenched, he said, "Frannie. How you doing?"

Francesca barked out a laugh. "Same old, Frank. Same old. You staying?"

"Thought I might."

She shrugged as if it were no concern of hers.

The living room was still decorated with the furniture they had picked out at Hennessy's, but their wedding photos, and any she might have had of her baby, were long gone. The master bedroom, a sea of cheap pink satin surrounding a shrine to the Virgin Mary, made his stomach churn. Frank carved a path through the spare bedroom and sat on a mildewed mattress. Shadows against the dusty curtains reminded him of the gray hills of Korea.

Welcome home, kid, Patrick had said as he zipped away in his brand-new Chevy Bel Air. Or was that Buckeye Jim, his red scarf trailing against the sky? Maybe it was Eddie Monroe or Big Dick Richards or Billy the Conch, men Frank had known in prison. Maybe it was the twenty men from Hill 402, gunned down like dogs with their hands tied behind their backs.

He returned to the kitchen. "Where's Richie and Jackie these days?"

"Richie moved to Arizona." Frannie opened up a fat bottle of prescription pills. "Jackie left Loretta and ran off. You going to get a job or anything?"

"Can I have a day off first? I just did twenty-six years because of you."

She said, "Yeah. Worst murderer in this city, that's you, all because of me. Isn't today the anniversary?"

"You haven't lost the knack of pissing me off, Frannie."

Francesca downed her pill. "It's a gift."

He took a walk down to the Deep Six, where the same old lobster traps and fishing nets still hung on the walls. Frank sat at the bar and drank an ice-cold beer that came in a spotted glass. If the bartender knew he was serving the *worst murderer in this city,* he didn't show it.

"Sammy Gick still own this place?" Frank asked.

The bartender gestured to a picture of President Carter tacked to the wall. "Feds got him. No big loss, you know?"

Frank stared the man down. "He was a friend."

The bartender lifted his hands. "Like I said, a top shelf guy."

Frank fired up a cigarette and watched cars go by. A redhead with great onions came in to bum some matches. That was his father's word, *onions,* but Frank preferred tits or knockers. The bartender's kid appeared with a keg to fill, and Frank wondered what Francesca's runt would be like if he'd had the chance to grow up. After another beer Frank paid his tab and went down to the crappy strip mall. He'd known the old gang wouldn't be waiting for him, he knew the years rolled by and people died or moved on, but it was still goddamned depressing. Behind the mall was a narrow path and on impulse he followed it into the marsh. Voles scurried from his approach and signs of mankind gradually diminished until only the drone of passing traffic remained.

Frank wasn't sure how long he wandered, pulled by a longing he couldn't put a name to, but when he finally stopped to mop the sweat

from his face he saw a small piece of metal half-buried in the muck.
He dug it free and wiped away the scum. The wristwatch's face was
smashed but the inscription on the back was still legible. Goosebumps
rippled down his back and arms as he read it.

PFH. USMC 1941-1944.

"No fucking way." Frank swung around to see if some jerk from
Candid Camera had followed him into the marsh. He couldn't imagine
how the watch could have lain there all these years, overlooked by cops
and kids, just waiting for him to stumble by. He certainly didn't believe
in Easter miracles. But there it was, no denying it. His father's Omega.
The gold band was intact enough for him to slip it on his wrist. Heavy,
he realized. And warm from the sun. No, not warm, hot, burning hot,
searing his skin, boiling through his flesh—

He screamed and fell to his knees, clawing at his tortured wrist. When
he next opened his eyes the day had faded to moonlit night and the sound
of insects surrounded him. For a moment he imagined himself back in
Korea, a slanty-eye sneaking up on his six with a burp gun in hand. Then
he lifted his arm and saw that it was unharmed beneath a workman's
shirt and plain old watch. A wedding ring encircled his finger.

"Jesus," he croaked out. Frank climbed to his feet and nearly tripped
over a severed leg lying in the marsh beside him. The leg had fallen out
of a stained Army duffel bag. Patrick Francis Hayes's head had rolled
free as well, the eyes blank and unseeing. Frank choked on a scream
and stumbled backward, his feet tripping over each other. He had to be
goddamned dreaming, or having a nervous breakdown, or tripping on
something the bartender had put in his beer.

"Wake up, Frank," he told himself. "Wake the fuck up."

Somewhere in the tall grass a harrier cried out. Frank backed away
from his father's body parts with bile in his throat. If this crazy dream
continued as reality once had, the cops would soon come to arrest him.
The trial itself would last only five days. A jury foreman with an arm
withered by polio would say, "Guilty, Your Honor," and he'd be off to

the state prison, twenty to life, with absolutely no leniency despite his service in the war.

He looked at the time. Ten minutes until midnight. That fit in with his memories as well. He'd confronted his father around nine o'clock, his courage fortified by half a dozen beers at the Deep Six. Broken his neck —unplanned, that, and not something he was proud of, but the old man had deserved it. He'd hacked up the body, dragged it here—

Patrick's dead eyes glared at him. Frank turned toward the lights of civilization and made his way to the apron of concrete where Buckeye Jim's seaplane sat with a tarp pulled over its cockpit. Patrick's 1953 Chevy Bel Air, fire-engine red, sat parked on the road just beyond. After a moment's consideration Frank began walking home. A moment later he started to run. Francesca met him at the back door. She was young again, her hair dark and lustrous, her waist half the size of her bust.

"Did you do it?" she asked. "Is he gone?"

Frank grabbed the whiskey bottle from the counter and downed three large gulps. Then he ground his lips against hers and forced his tongue into her mouth.

"Frank!" She broke away. "What happened? Are you hurt? Your face—"

"I dumped the body, but they're going to find him." Frank grabbed a cooking pot and stared at his distorted image—narrow face, not yet lined with wrinkles; brown hair, not yet gray. Patrick's fingernails had raked his cheek. "The cops will know it's me."

"I told you to leave it alone."

"Shut up. You and him, that's what got us here. You and him."

She started to cry in great gulping sobs and Frank resisted the impulse to punch her in the face. Or in her stomach, which had already started to round. Hope pulsed through him, a wakening of senses that had been dead too long. He could do it, he could change the future: he could live his fucking life, not spend it chained like a dog in a yard.

"Frank?" Francesca asked, watching him stuff clothes into a suitcase. "Where are you going?"

"I'll call you when I get there."

"You can't—" She slung her arms around his neck. "Take me too."

Frank stopped because the scent of her—perfume and whiskey, soap and Camel cigarettes—flooded into him like a river, and he'd been parched so very long. "No."

"I can't live without you. I don't know what'll become of me."

He knew. Gout, arthritis, bloated skin. He wished it were as easy to hate her as he hated Patrick. "Frannie, I don't even know where I'm going."

"Anywhere's good but here. Frank, please . . ."

Frank gave her ten minutes to pack. The highway took them down through Connecticut and past New York City. After eighteen hours of driving Frank's vision began to blur and they checked into a roadside motel. Francesca didn't want to fuck but Frank needed to, and not once but twice, leaving bite marks on her breasts.

"*Cara,*" he said.

"*Tesoro,*" she murmured. After a few minutes she rose and went to the bathroom. When she returned she lit a cigarette and asked, "What do you want me to do about it?"

He propped himself up on one elbow, watching her face. "We'll find a doctor."

Her eyes were very dark. "It's a sin."

As if she hadn't committed others. Frank rolled onto his back. "Then we'll give it up. Give it to someone who doesn't know where it came from."

Francesca stubbed out her cigarette and curled up beside him wordlessly.

The next morning he hot-wired a Dodge Coronet. He and Francesca sped down the Atlantic Seaboard. He followed the road into hills and out of them, keeping the ocean at his left arm, until the concrete ran out in a clump of banyan trees that fronted the Florida Straits. Billy the Conch had described it all perfectly.

"Home," he said, and Francesca nodded.

He got a job working on Navy planes at Boca Chica airfield. Francesca stayed home in their shack on the poor side of Key West, her belly swelling in the tropical heat. She wanted to call her mother, but he said no.

"I just want to make sure she's okay," Francesca said.

"Don't worry about her. Last time, when things went wrong, she cut you out of her life like you cut out the moldy parts of the bread. That easily, too."

"You're crazy!" Francesca stomped her foot. "You talk about things that never happened!"

But they had happened, at least for him. Now he woke every morning in a young man's body, with a young man's erection. Often he dreamed he was back in Korea, watching shrapnel rip through faceless men flanking him in the snow. Sometimes he returned to prison instead, listening to men piss and shit and groan twenty-four hours a day. And every now and again he dreamed himself back in the marsh, his father's Omega burning against his wrist. Yet the visions always faded. The northeast and Far East, and all their woes, were far behind him.

He was stripping a carburetor when Francesca went into labor and took a cab to the hospital on her own. Frank went to lunch with the sailors and spent the afternoon sneaking beers out of a cooler in the chief's office. Only when the twilight sky was red over the ocean did he go to out to see the result. There was no mistaking Francesca's son in the nursery. He had her dark hair and dimples and wailed with the same exact gusto. Two days later, when the priest was due to take the boy to his new parents, Francesca's eyes welled up.

"Frank, please." Her cold hand clutched his forearm. "We don't have to."

Frank bent to the bed. "Listen to me," he said, very low. "You screwed my father and you had his kid. We keep him, and I'm going to beat you every day for the rest of your life for it. Beat him, too: lying in the crib, when he takes his first steps, on his first day of school, whenever I want to. Living hell, Frannie, that's what your life will be, and his too, and there won't be a thing you can do about it because there's nothing I can do for it, either. You put me in that position and I'm helpless, you see? Nowhere for the anger to go but right at you and him."

The color drained from her face. Frank brushed a dark curl from her forehead.

"I really can see the future, *cara,*" he said. "Don't make me into that monster, okay?"

Francesca gave the runt a kiss before the priest carried him off in blue swaddling clothes. Two days later she came home and took to bed. He let her sulk until Sunday and then dumped her off the mattress, saying, "We've got living to do, Frannie. I got a plan to own this island."

"I don't want to own this island," she replied. "I want to go home."

"Billy the Conch, this guy I know, said it's all about land—hotels, resorts, a golf course. They're going to build like crazy. We're going to buy as much as we can to be ready for it."

"You think you can see what's going to come, but you can't." She came to him slowly, the front of her dress damp from leaking milk, and cupped the back of his head. Her lips were pale pink slits. "I see it, Frank. Misery and unhappiness for the rest of our lives. You're not the man I married. I think, 'It was Korea, it was the war,' but it's something else. You're like my husband used to be, but all foul and black inside, like the devil."

"I'm not the Devil," he protested. Hell, maybe he was. Maybe that was the deal he'd somehow made in the marsh. But he didn't feel foul inside. He felt stronger and sharper than ever, and ready to take on the entire goddamned world to come.

He carried Francesca to bed and was kissing her thighs when she smashed the bedside lamp against his head so hard that he woke up in the emergency room, already handcuffed to a bed. "Francis Hayes, you're under arrest for murder," the county sheriff said, puffed up with his own importance.

Frank closed his eyes. "No fucking kidding."

They extradited him back to Massachusetts, where a different judge sentenced him to thirty years. Frank wound up back at the same state prison, surrounded by the same fat fucks. Though he tried unsuccessfully to convince the head guard that he could foretell the future ("Kennedy as president? Why not just the Pope himself?"), he'd seen enough government-conspiracy movies to guess that he didn't want to become J. Edgar Hoover's secret weapon. He turned his knowledge toward betting on sports. Sammy Gick back home took action, building up a sizeable bankroll for when Frank got out. Having already witnessed assorted murders, rapes, assaults and power shifts, Frank was also able to forge alliances with the people he knew would still be standing ten or twenty years down the dreary road.

"You got this sixth sense about people, eh, Frank?" Big Dick asked one day in the yard. Some said Big Dick had killed a dozen Germans single-handedly on Omaha Beach and then strangled his wife with his Medal of Honor. Others said he'd been a doctor in Georgia who'd tortured and killed German POWs for the fun of it.

Frank tilted his head toward the sky and said, "Yeah. I've got a gift."

Francesca was long gone, and not even the cops knew where—off to Hollywood, maybe, following her childhood dreams. Though Frank hardly ever thought of the runt, the military priest sent word now and again letting him know that all was well. Frank threw the letters away until one came saying there'd been accident, the runt and his parents, off a bridge late at night. Frank fucked Eddie Monroe extra hard that night.

"The world screws you, kid," he told Eddie, who was a slim, tow-headed guy doing ten years for auto theft.

Eddie grunted. "Tell me about it."

The trouble with prison was that it was like sitting around in a stink-ing, claustrophobic bathroom all your life. By 1970 the stench of it had worn Frank to the point where he began popping pills to get through the day. Uppers, downers, hash—the Vietnam guys flooding through the front door could get hold of anything. They were sissy-ass whiners, most of them, complaining as if no other soldier had ever seen his buddy's brain exposed to the light of day. Vietnam had been warm and full of pretty young slanty-eyes to screw. Not like the ugly, bomb-blasted hill of Korea. Not even like the shark-infested South Pacific.

"The Buddha Guy says all wars are pointless, man," one of the Viet-nam guys told Frank. They were sitting behind the prison laundry, stoned out of their gills. If Frank squinted at the prison yard just right he could see the ocean shimmering off the shores of Key West. "Violence is a trap. Screws up your karma."

Karma was a crazy hippie idea. Frank had been just eight years old when his father came slithering past his door late at night, and what kid deserved that? And who deserved to be sent to battlefields where your feet might turn black from frostbite or gangrene, or where soldiers might rise out of the mist like ghosts and fill your belly with bullets, or where your best friends might end up buried under the dirt and broken beams of a shelled command post? As always the dead from Hill 402 sur-rounded him, their mouths open in silent screams.

"What goes around comes around," the dealer said.

Who the hell was he to make such judgments? As if in a slow-motion dream Frank swung a punch that flattened the asshole's nose and sent blood splattering in the air. He saw his hands tighten around the guy's neck. When he next woke up he was in a small dark cell, his own face bloody and swollen. Locked in solitary confinement with only his imagi-nation for company, Frank soared over the marsh in a seaplane as Buck-eye Jim's scarf trailed in the wind. He revisited his honeymoon in a wooden cabin near Niagara Falls, the thunder of the water like the drum of his own blood. When Francesca kissed him her onions turned into grenades and the men from Hill 402 crashed through the ceiling, crushing him with their deadweight. He could see half of Second Lieutenant Kroeller's head blown away, and the horrified expression on Little Mike Simonetti's face just inches from his own. Little Mike had left behind a pregnant wife in Toledo, and after the baby came he tied tiny pink socks to his bayonet so everyone would know the news.

"They died and you didn't," Frank heard Patrick say. His father stood in the corner of the cell, spiffy in his expensive suit and leather shoes. Patrick checked the time on his gold wristwatch. "What are you going to do about *that,* Frank?"

Frank lunged at the apparition. When he next woke he was strapped to an infirmary bed, an IV drip in one hand and both wrists restrained to the bed.

"You flipped out like no one else ever did," Big Dick told him. "Scared the shit out of them all. Great strategy."

Frank regained his mental strength slowly. Instead of drugs he turned to Christianity, but being born again did nothing for him. He tried investing in stocks but he lost a spectacular amount of money by confusing IBM with another company that went bust. After Eddie Monroe got released Frank took up again with Billy the Conch, a wild-eyed Seminole kid whose uncle was busy buying up land in Key West. But Billy's wild tales of island life were less entertaining the second time around, and by the spring of 1979 Frank was so tired and depressed he could barely get out of bed each morning. His left arm grew increasingly heavy. The prison doctor said it was nothing but Frank knew his arteries were clogged up from decades of mess-hall swill. Easter weekend he was on top of Billy, sliding in and out of him with effort, when Patrick's Omega, bright and pulsing, materialized out of nowhere and encircled his wrist with white-hot fire. Frank screamed.

"Jesus!" Billy squirmed out from under him. "What the—?"

Frank tumbled away and landed in the front seat of his father's 1953 Chevy Bel Air. The engine was idling with a contented purr. Marsh grass, starlit under the dark sky, flanked either side of the car. On the radio the deejay announced that it was eleven thirty. If Frank opened the trunk he knew he'd find a duffel bag containing the cut-up parts of his father's body.

"Oh, shit," Frank said. Another goddamned second chance.

This time he didn't go home to see Francesca. He took what money was in his father's wallet, dumped the Bel Air off a bridge and grabbed a midnight bus to New York City. From there he hitchhiked south and west, staying off the main highways. His luck broke a month later in Sioux City, when the flophouse where he was staying caught fire in the middle of the night. He stumbled out choking on smoke, lights blinding him, sirens wailing, and when a cop tried to help him Frank thought he was back on Hill 402, fighting for his life. From there it was just a shackled hop, skip and jump back to Massachusetts, and after the judge sentenced him to forty years he went a little nuts. The bailiff's nose shattered under the blow from Frank's fist, and it took three men to wrestle him to the ground. Looking back, he supposed he'd given them all a damned good show, and proved the district attorney's theory that he'd murdered his father in a fit of rage. Fuck 'em all.

Third time around. The stench of the place drove him crazy. Piss and vomit, semen and sweat, and fear; everywhere fear, everyone drenched in it, even Big Dick. Francesca visited once a month with her belly getting bigger and bigger.

"How sorry do you want me to be?" she asked. "You think I meant for any of it to happen? You grew up with him, what he did to you—"

"Frannie," he said, "shut up."

She fiddled with the buttons of her sweater. "I'll do whatever you want me to do."

He knew she hadn't loved his old man. Who could? Patrick had been a well-dressed, smooth-talking blight. While he'd been fighting in the Pacific, Frank had prayed for his death at the hands of the Japanese. His sickly mother had told him to bite his tongue. Maybe in this lifetime Frank was supposed to forgive Francesca, put the past behind them all and do something good for a change. Anything was worth a shot. He dredged up memories that he'd buried long ago and leaned toward her.

"Christmas Eve, don't bring the baby out. Crazy drunk drivers all over, you know?"

Francesca wiped her nose. "Frank, that's months and months away."

"God showed me what's going to happen, Frannie. The baby won't live if you try and bring him to your mother's."

She didn't believe him, he knew. She thought maybe he was crazy and had been since he'd come home from Korea. When the baby came a few days before Thanksgiving she sent a picture. Frank wrote her a letter, again warning her that the kid would die. He even bribed the guards for the chance to call her on Christmas Eve Day, but the phone rang and rang without answer. Three days later Francesca showed up for visiting hours with her arm in a sling and her left eye shot through with blood. The runt was with her, swaddled in blue blankets.

"Jesus, Frank," she said. "The guy never even slammed on the brakes. What else did God tell you?"

"That you'd stay by me, Frannie." Frank grasped her hand. "That we'd be a family."

And they were. Francesca placed the bets Frank told her to make and invested the proceeds, which took care of her financial needs. She visited, sent packages and brought pictures as Tony grew older. But Frank's nights were not made easier knowing the two of them were out there on their own, unaware and unprotected. He dreamt of gook rapists climbing in Francesca's bedroom window or lobbing grenades onto Tony's playground. He thought of breaking out of prison and carrying them off to Mexico, where they could be happy together—but then in 1969 Francesca ran off with Sammy Gick and mailed him the divorce papers.

"Divorce!" Frank ripped the papers into pieces and showered the debris over Billy the Conch, who sat on the bed in his underwear.

"Maybe she got tired of waiting, Frank."

"Waiting! You know how long I've been here? I'm the King of Sitting Around Fucking Waiting."

And come to think of it, who was responsible for Frank being in prison in the first place? Who was the little whore who'd spread her legs for Patrick so willingly, so happily? For months he imagined tying her hands behind her back, forcing her across miles of frozen ground and then shooting her. He would prod her with sharpened bamboo sticks. He would ignore all her pleas for mercy. The revenge fantasies didn't make the days go any faster. The goddamned years stretched on, the same food, the same stories, the same fights and squabbles. He fought in the yard several times. What were they going to do? Sentence him to a longer term? Come Easter of 1979 and he'd be free again, courtesy of his father's goddamned time-traveling Omega, until he screwed it up again.

"You believe in karma?" he asked Billy one night. It was dark but not quiet. Prison was never quiet. "You think we make the same mistakes, over and over again?"

"I don't know," Billy giggled. "I make new mistakes all the time."

Frank slapped his skinny ass. "I'm serious."

"You want to know about karma, you should ask the Buddha Guy. He digs that stuff."

A few days later Frank climbed the stairs to B Wing. The Buddha Guy was a bald, skinny man sitting cross-legged on the floor of his cell. "I see your anger," the Buddha Guy said, though his eyes were closed. "It's like a red cloud of bees."

"I don't care about my anger. It's my karma. You know anything about that?"

"Acknowledge the bees, man. Listen to what they tell you."

Like he needed that crap. Frank walked away from the cell and didn't go back. Women on TV started wearing disco dresses, mood rings became popular, normally sane people went nuts over pet rocks. Frank tried reading his way through the prison library, but for what? No science-

fiction crap or est bullshit was going to get him off his wheel. He rubbed
his wrist compulsively, and one day asked Big Dick how hard it was to
cut off a guy's arm below the elbow.

Big Dick was silent for a while. Then he said, "It's not so hard if you've
got the right knife. Serrated. You've got three nerves and two arteries
to get through. Two bones, but you could crack them against something, break them off that way. Whose arm you going to cut off? Some
chink?"

"Nah." It was a well-known secret that Frank couldn't bear the sight
of the few Asians in the prison's population. "It's just a thought."

Because even if he did cut off his own arm, then what? If he survived
the makeshift surgery and made parole one day he'd be nothing more
than an old veteran with one good arm, no marketable skills and no
special insights into the future. Maybe it would be better to cycle back to
1953 and do everything he could to stay out of prison. Maybe he'd land
far enough back to keep from killing Patrick in the first place. Could he
face his father without snapping his neck? He was trying to visualize it
when a dark-haired and dimpled kid showed up doing ten-to-twenty for
armed robbery.

"You know who I am?" Frank asked.

Tony squared his shoulders. "Not my father."

"She tell who he was?"

"I don't care."

"You care," Frank said. "Everybody cares. Your father did things no
man should do, but you wouldn't be here if it wasn't for him. You respect
him for that if nothing else."

"Fuck that," Tony said, and Frank slugged him in the stomach.

Other people punched the kid as well. The runt didn't know how to
hold his temper around men stronger and more dangerous than he was.
He mouthed off to all the guards. He complained about everything. If it
wasn't for Frank's protection he would have soon had his tongue forced
down his own throat or had a broomstick shoved up his ass.

"You think I'll be around all the time, keeping an eye on you?" Frank asked.

Tony rolled his eyes. "You think you're going somewhere, old man?"

Three nerves, two arteries, two bones. Did he owe that much to the kid? Easter drew nearer and nearer. Frank tried soliciting spiritual advice but the prison priest was a no-good drunk and the Buddha Guy had long ago been released, gone off to some ashram in New York. On Ash Wednesday Tony got into a fight with some Black Muslims, and when Frank went to break it up he lost control and broke a guy's jaw. A second later something sharp punctured his lower back. Blood filled his mouth and the ceiling spun. When his disorientation cleared he was lying on the cold floor of his father's garage and Patrick Hayes, his neck broken, was already dead. It was eleven o'clock at night, the spring of 1953.

"Fuck." Frank sat up slowly, clutching his side, but no shiv poked out of him, no blood pulsed between his fingers. The night was still and warm, and a dog barked in the distance. Frank pulled himself up and stumbled into his father's opulent den. Only the best for Patrick Hayes and the steady procession of women who'd followed after the death of Frank's mother. A look in the bathroom mirror showed scratches and the beginning of a black eye. After a moment's consideration he gouged his cheeks more savagely, and out in the garage he swung a crowbar against the two bones, two arteries and three nerves of his left forearm.

Pain exploded though him like a grenade, and it took several long minutes before Frank recovered enough to place the crowbar near Patrick's curled-up hand. Slick with sweat, weak-kneed but able to lurch, he fumbled for the phone.

The judge let him post bail. Frank placed a few high-stakes sports bets and hired a top-notch defense team. His lawyers paraded Frank's Purple Heart and unit commendation from General MacArthur. A military psychologist testified to the lasting effects of shell shock, and a medical doctor theorized about the broken arm Frank had suffered when Patrick swung the crowbar at him. Francesca came to court every day with the runt, the very picture of a supportive wife. And although Patrick Hayes had been beloved by many, three clients and one cuckolded husband took the stand to testify to his temper and stubbornness.

The jury came back with an acquittal. Frank's best friends Richie Reilly and Jackie Mac threw a shindig at the Deep Six to celebrate. Cars double-parked up and down the block, booze flowed like an uncapped hydrant, and Francesca wore a red dress that clung to every curve of her body. Through the haze of whiskey and cigar smoke Frank saw his future opening up again. He would use his knowledge of the stock market to become the richest man in town. He would buy a mammoth house untainted by Patrick's legacy and sire a dozen kids, all of them handsome or beautiful. He would never set foot in prison again. Buckeye Jim was promising him a ride over the entire fucking city of Boston when Frank realized he hadn't seen Francesca for a while, and when he followed the sound of her voice into the alley he saw her kissing Sammy Gick.

His fists pummeled Sammy to the filthy ground before his brain could stop them. The next thing he knew, Richie Reilly had him pinned to the alley wall.

"Fuck it, Frank," Richie was saying. "You really pissed in your own well now."

Sammy moaned behind his broken teeth. Francesca knelt down to help him. Jackie Mac pressed a handful of sweaty twenty-dollar bills into Frank's hand and said, "Take my car." Frank wavered, sure that he could salvage something out of the situation. "Get out of town for a while," Jackie Mac insisted, and with the music of his own party still ringing in his ears Frank gunned Jackie's Packard Clipper past the marsh and toward the highway.

Fury and self-loathing rode with him all the way to Bangor, where they finally shaded into exhaustion and pity. It was the alcohol, he decided. If he went dry he'd be able to stay out of trouble. He ditched the car in the middle of nowhere and caught the bus into Canada, spending Jackie's money sparingly on room and board in a lousy neighborhood of Quebec City. When he called Francesca she hung up on him. He telephoned Richie Reilly, who told him Sammy had died.

"Died?" It didn't seem likely. Men died because someone shot them in the head or gut, or broke their necks, or lobbed grenades between their legs. "How?"

"Brain swelled up. I wouldn't come back this way if I were you."

He went to Montreal instead and got work laying brick for an American who'd lost an eye and a hand on Guadalcanal. After nearly fifty years in prison Frank needed something to do with his hands. Two years later he crossed into Michigan to lay sewer lines and string telephone wire. He settled in Alpena, shacking up with a dark-haired Ojibway girl named Marie Mountain. He thought things were perfect, but one day he came home early and found Marie in the arms of a long-haired beatnik who taught poetry at the community college. Frank tossed a chair through the front window. The poet followed, landing on the rain-soaked lawn with a sickening crunch.

"You're crazy!" Marie screamed. The neighbors came out on their porches to watch. "You're a psycho nut case drunk!"

Frank headed west until he hit the shores of Beaver Island, a wooded hideaway where Irish immigrants had built up a thriving fishing industry. The stink of fish guts clung to him day and night, but he stayed away from the bottle. Three nights after he proposed to a local waitress he got into a late-night fender-bender with the asshole son of one of the fishing-conglomerate owners. The episode ended with Frank taking a tire iron to the man's windshield. The locals ran him off the island that night. With a bottle of gin in his pocket he zig-zagged east until he hit Ithaca, New York, a college town on the shores of an old glacier lake. The town was in full psychedelic swing, the neighborhoods jammed with sweet smoke, beaded girls and singers. Come winter the coffeehouses filled up with poets and guitar players protesting Vietnam, and Tibetan prayer flags flapped from the bare tree branches. For work he got a job pouring concrete for two towering residence halls being built at the top of South Hill. The foreman, Paul Scott, walked around every day with an iron pole stuck up his ass.

"You should never trust a man with two first names anyway," said Kenny Bolt. He was a square-faced kid who claimed to have done a year in-country, but Frank had heard he'd spent his entire tour in Saigon working in an air-conditioned supply office. "Paul Scott, get it? Scott Paul. Two first names."

Frank squinted at the overcast sky. He had a hangover like a son-of-a-bitch, and the icy wind barreling off the lake cut through him like a dozen shivs. "That so?"

"Never date a girl named after a city, either. Never play cards with a guy named Pops."

"Those are the stupidest things I've ever heard."

Kenny said, "Advice for living. They'll get you through the years."

"The years are longer than you think," Frank muttered. He had his own pearls of advice. Chief among them was not staying up until five a.m. guzzling Wild Turkey with a doe-eyed Cornell hippie on one side of your bed and a jaded farmer's daughter on the other, not unless you wanted to spend a day with a cement mixer going round and round in your skull. As a few fat snowflakes fell against his upturned face he decided that the working man phase of his life had ended. He was ready to start making real money again. Maybe the Omega wouldn't work if he moved far enough away—

"Never bring a gun to a knife fight," Kenny said. "Never eat at a place called—"

Frank didn't have to hit Kenny but he did anyway. A quick pop, hardly anything to it at all, was it his fault the war hero had a glass jaw? He quit the job and would have gunned his car out of the parking lot if one of his tires hadn't gone flat. Snow was already beginning to blanket the campus, muffling all sound. He set off on foot, the whiskey doing more to keep him warm than his coat. Although the trip back to town was entirely downhill, the snow somehow turned him around until he was facing a wide-open stretch of flat farmland. He did a full three-hundred-and-sixty degree turn but couldn't even see the lake.

"Crap," he said. After a few more minutes he realized his feet were going numb. Visibility dropped steadily. When an unpaved road appeared he followed it, hoping to find a shelter. No houses or barns or telephone poles broke the solid ranks of pine and fir trees. The flask ran dry. A few icy miles later Frank reached a collection of small wooden buildings clustered around a barn and corral. Chimney smoke trickled out of the main structure, which was some kind of conference center or chapel.

"Welcome," a voice said, and he turned to see a thin man carrying firewood and wearing nothing but a coarse brown robe. Frank recognized him as the Buddha Guy from state prison. But that was a different lifetime, and this man didn't know him.

"I'm Benny," the Buddha Guy said. "You're looking for the Zen Center?"

Zen. More dippy hippie craziness that Ithaca was full of. Frank stood shivering in his coat, a terrible sadness filling him the way no bottle of booze ever did. The accumulated decades had stretched him thin and then beaten him into a shape he didn't recognize anymore. His life was someone else's movie, a story he had no control over.

"I need to control my anger," Frank admitted. "You got some program for that?"

Benny the Buddha Guy cocked his head. "You got to work your own program. But this place can help. Come inside."

Frank followed him into the octagonal building. Warmth from a wood stove hit him the moment he stepped inside, the cedar smoke like perfume. A dozen or so people in robes sat silently on the hardwood floor. Some were American, two were women, and at least three of them, including the man sitting cross-legged at the front, had dusky skin and slanty eyes. Without a word Frank turned around and started back down the road, ignoring Benny the Buddha Guy when he asked, "Hey! Where are you going?" The woods stretched out in all directions, silent but for the soft shush of the snowfall. When the coldness faded from his limbs Frank stretched out on the ground and stared up at a mosaic of branches and pine needles against distant clouds. A plastic bag or old balloon had caught in the trees and he thought of pink socks tied to a bayonet, Little Mike Simonetti's anguished face.

Nothingness. Blankness. Not dark, but not light either. Cold prickling over every inch of his body. When Frank managed to pry open his eyes he was sprawled on the floor of his father's garage, Patrick lifeless beside him. Frank pulled himself to his feet, found Patrick's well-oiled revolver in the top drawer of his desk, and shot himself through the mouth. This time the space between lives was a fiery cauldron, acid eating away at flesh and muscle, unseen hands tearing all of his limbs from their sockets and gouging out his eyes. He woke up in the garage screaming, and the terrified neighbors called the police.

He got arrested.

He won an acquittal, again, but skipped town before anyone threw him a party.

He returned to Ithaca.

The Zen Center hadn't been built yet. No one had heard of or seen monks in the area. Frank went to Japan, a nation that had hauled itself out of war ruins. The sight of thousands of slanty eyes nearly made him board the next flight back to the States, but he forced his feet forward until he found a temple where foreigners could study. He slept on thin mats. He ate rice and drank green tea. Sometimes he ran away to drink and whore, but the monks always took him back. Sometimes he hit walls with his fists, and the monks bandaged his broken fingers. He was on the road to enlightenment and if it was an uphill road, a road littered with dead bodies and long-buried shame, at least it was his. The Frank Hayes Road Through Eternity.

One day a smart young lady from *Stars and Stripes* newspaper came to see him while he was raking the garden. "Nancy Carter," she said, shaking his hand. "I'm working on a book about war crimes in Korea. You were on Hill 402, right? I've been tracking down the survivors."

Frank dragged a rake through the dirt. "I wasn't there."

"A radio message telling the unit to fall back never got through. Twenty men were captured, and then most of them were executed by the North Koreans—"

"Miss Carter," he said, "it doesn't matter."

"Of course it does. The sergeant who led the massacre later defected to Seoul—"

Frank walked away.

The next day he sat in meditation for several extra hours. Sitting on your ass, he'd learned, was the Zen key to achieving enlightenment. That and thinking about unanswerable questions. He sat while snowy winters cycled through to the first cherry blossoms of spring, and as the rains of summer turned into the monsoons of autumn. He sat with his eyes closed. He sat with his eyes open. He sat until he fell asleep and the monks whacked him with a stick. He sat while temple bells rang and prison doors clanged shut and snow fell across the fields of upstate New York, and Marilyn Monroe died again, and *Star Wars* broke box-office records again, and then in the spring of 1979 the master of all the monks said, "Your time here is done."

Frank bowed. "Thank you."

The next day the Omega took him home.

He was standing outside his father's house in clothes that smelled like cigarette smoke and beer. The night was unseasonably warm. Inside the open garage Patrick was waxing his beloved Bel Air. It was a job he never delegated to others, no matter how much money he made converting pig farms to suburbs. Frank could hear music on someone's radio, jaunty

Glenn Miller carrying on the breeze, but then a man's voice said something loud and angry and the radio snapped off. A dog barked, but just once.

Patrick raised his head, squinting toward the street. "Is someone there?"

His father looked impossibly young, just forty-six. His arms were sinewy and strong, and his hands had done terrible things, but there he was, someone who'd made mistakes, someone who deserved to be punished, but not someone who would be killed and dismembered this night by his own son.

Patrick put down his rag and took an uncertain step forward. "Hello?"

Frank walked away. Just like that. Down the hill he went, toward the old pig farms, toward the avenue of Cape Cod homes and picket fences and his wife, Francesca, whom he wasn't sure he loved anymore, but love wasn't the point. He'd only gone two blocks before the Omega wristwatch appeared, glimmering in the streetlight.

"Mission accomplished, is that it?" Frank took it off, admiring the weight of it, the craftsmanship. For a moment he considered bowing to it, as he had bowed to the Zen master. "What happens next?"

The watch was warm and gold and silent.

"Will you bring me back further next time? Flip back some more pages? There's business I could take care of, for better or worse."

Silence from the watch. Frank put it back onto his wrist. The next time he thought to look for it, the Omega was gone.

He went to Francesca and forgave her, and they started over in a small town near Worcester. He didn't drink. Together he and Francesca raised the runt, Anthony, who decided to become a doctor. On their way home from dropping him off at Cornell, Frank hit a wet patch of road and lost control of his car. Francesca died immediately. Seven years later the Omega yanked Frank back to the morning in 1953 when he stepped off his plane and Francesca met him on the tarmac, her face a mixture of pride and apprehension.

He led a life in which he and Francesca moved to California and were unhappy together. A year after they divorced she slammed her car into a telephone pole in Santa Monica. Tony grew up, joined the Army, and became a medical corpsman stationed in Japan. When 1979 arrived, the Omega cycled Frank back to the day he signed his discharge papers in Fort Benning and threw away his war medals in a metal trashcan in the airport.

He led a life in which he abandoned Francesca and went to Tokyo, where he married the daughter of a Zen monk.

He led a life in which he hitchhiked around the world helping build homes for the poor. He learned several languages.

He led a life in which he sought out a *Stars and Stripes* reporter named Nancy Carter and then went to meet a former North Korean sergeant named Kim Won-Ja.

He lived, he traveled backward. He lived again, he traveled further backward. And then one day the Omega yanked him out of 1979 and deposited him in a cold, foggy valley that looked as lifeless as the moon. Twenty American GIs, including himself, stood in the diffused daylight with their hands tied behind their backs. Their captors, a ragtag band of North Korean soldiers, conferred a dozen yards away. Second Lieutenant Kroeller was staring at the ground as if he'd never seen dirt before. Little Mike Simonetti stood shivering at Frank's shoulder.

"POW camp," one of the other GIs whispered. "They'll feed us when we get there."

Some of the men he'd known for months, while others had reported to Hill 402 just a day or two ago. Guys from Denver and Puerto Rico and Los Angeles, and an ape-ugly private from Pittsburgh, and a cowboy platoon leader nicknamed Tex. Before the war they'd been high school students or tractor salesmen or mechanics. Some of them had heard stories of North Korean atrocities, but only Frank knew what was about to happen.

"L.T.," Frank said to Kroeller, "I've got an idea."

Kroeller didn't look up from the ground.

"I've got an idea, too," Simonetti muttered. "Anyone got a gun?"

Guns wouldn't save them. Frank had considered dozens of heroic or stupid plans over the years and discarded them all. Violence, as Benny the Buddha Guy had once said, wasn't the solution—not even here, in these bloodstained hills, with so much death already saturated into the ground. The North Korean soldiers broke up their conference and turned back to the GIs. They looked as cold and miserable as Little Mike. Frank knew they would next line up the Americans in ranks and columns, shoot them in the back, pile the corpses together. It was expeditious and pragmatic, but it was still wrong.

He'd rehearsed this moment for years, but as he stepped forward and bowed Frank's heart began to thud wildly. In fluent Korean he said, "Honored Sergeant Kim Won-Ja. Your ancestors speak through me now, their restless spirits begging you to lay down your weapons and put aside all thoughts of killing your captives."

Sergeant Kim, a barrel-chested man no older than Frank, jerked back as if he'd touched a scalding pan. Every culture had crazy superstitions and boogeymen who hid under the bed, but Frank had never met people more genuinely worried than the Koreans. Everyday life, especially in the small villages, was a constant exercise in appeasing or wooing goblins, ghosts, deities and unhappy ancestor spirits. Frank had spent decades studying these men, their beliefs, their families. He knew how to call out their ghosts.

"Your grandmother, Bok Dok Yoong, calls to you from her home at Sochang, where she would beat you with her pipe when you picked her jasmine flowers without permission. Your grandfather, Kim Sung-Jung, berates you for not respecting the day of his death these past three years. Your aunt Yu, dead at the hands of the Japanese, hovers over your right hand, her fingers icy against your skin. Listen to their call, Kim Won-Ja, or face their eternal wrath."

He named the other soldiers as well, invoking the dead mother of Private Kang, the murdered brother of Private Han and the childhood sweetheart of Private Lee. Frank's fellow Americans stared at him, their mouths agape, unable to understand a word he was saying. Private Han fell to his knees and began praying to his ancestors.

"Go now," Frank told them. "Turn back from the path of Communism and great evil."

The North Koreans fled over the hill. Second Lieutenant Kroeller said, "Jesus Christ," and Little Mike Simonetti said, "Someone fucking untie me!" and Frank sat down, all the strength gone from his legs. When he looked up again Kroeller was looming over him.

"What did you say, Hayes?" he demanded. "When did you learn to speak Korean?"

"I had some extra time on my hands," Frank murmured. The daylight was fading. He felt five hundred years old, which was just about right. When he tried to stand his knees gave out. Francesca's face floated toward him in the encroaching darkness, and as his vision faded he thought he heard marsh insects, a seaplane's propellers, the clang of prison doors opening. He woke up in a mobile hospital unit with an IV in his arm and the Omega on his wrist.

"Nice watch," said the doctor who came by on morning rounds.

"Yeah." Frank lifted his head. "So what's wrong with me?"

"Just exhaustion. You'll be back at the front by the end of the week."

Frank took the watch off. Later he buried it in the mud behind the MASH unit. Because he couldn't go back to killing people, he walked away from all the battlefields. One last brand-new life, he thought to himself, as a hired boat took him across the Sea of Japan. The air was cool and breezy, and overhead a seaplane dipped its wing before sailing off across the clear blue sky. ✪

A SHORT HISTORY OF THE
MIRACULOUS FLIGHT TO PUNT

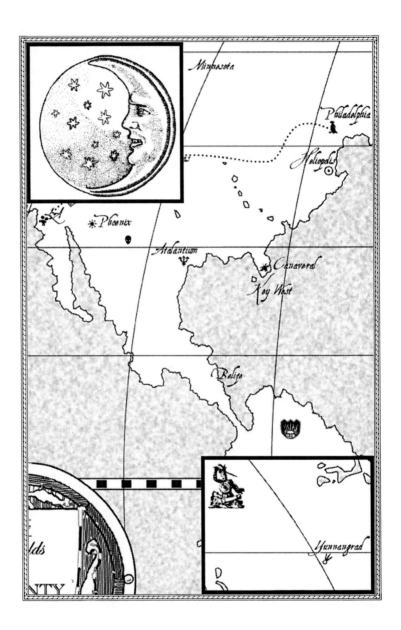

A SHORT HISTORY OF THE
MIRACULOUS FLIGHT TO PUNT

BY JACK MIERZWA

GALIXEO GALIXEI
   wrote the book that broke the sky—
It was such a long time ago.

Beneath the Library of Atalantium, in the labyrinths where Time itself
got lost, he kept his laboratory stocked with:

1. moondials and water clocks
2. spinning spheres of silver and bronze
3. taxidermied griffon's bones
4. jars of quintessence, ether, and positrons
5. bottles of Djinn and fairy dust
6. unicorns' eggs, lions' wings
7. centrifuges, pitchblende, and scales of brass
   (he was an alchemist until the last[1])

That's where he was the night the Old Kingdom ended,
   "crouched amongst the papyrus punch-cards,
   writing out the hieroglyphs of the calculus
   as the city fell into the sea."[2]

He was a worshipper of Apollo—
   In the last year of the Second Intermediate Period,

at the age of three hundred eighty-one, he undertook the pilgrimage to
the Temple of the Sun.[3]

"There he burned his bright eyes out
looking upon his God."[4]

✪

The Pharaoh Diana Hatshepsut, Queen of Columbiana,
 was a Sun-worshipper, and a Moon-worshipper, too,
Maia, daughter of Atlas
dark, painted princess of Mesopomerica,
taken from her sisters in a golden cage
 to be the trophy of a conquering king
It was so many winters ago

Her sons were the old Pharaoh's favorites
still boys when their father grew feeble,
when their cousins laid siege to the palace,
when their mother
strapped on the lapis beard, seated herself on the throne of the Pharaoh,
and proclaimed that she,
 "Diana Maatkare Hatshepsut the Bearded,
 Regent of Columbiana,
  has taken the ankh and chariot of her king
  and made his wars her own."[5]

Her servant Galixeo
 was a worshipper of Apollo—
At dawn on a midsummer day, he climbed to the top of the Helicron:
 "he bridled the waking Eagle
 to take him to see the Sun."[6]

His hands were on fire when he returned, blinded and bleeding,
clutching the scrolls of Amon-Re,
but he would not douse them and he would not open them,
until he whispered the Secret in the ear of his Queen:

> $n + 235U \rightarrow 236U^* \rightarrow daughter + daughter + 200MeV + 2.5n$
> $n + 239Pu \rightarrow 240Pu^* \rightarrow daughter + daughter + 200MeV + 2.2n$
>   *if $k > 1$, starfire!*

So Columbiana and her charioteers
   the boys and men of Amon-Re
   the Heroes of Enola Gay
dealt murder and death in the lands of the Phoenix
   brought the Old Kingdom into the New.

And blind Galixeo,
   He stumbled along darkened roadways,
always downhill,
until he tumbled into the sea. He worked in the darkness of the sunken
city, seeing by the glow of the afterimage, by the face of the Sun burned
into his ruined eyes:

Polish quartz with pitch and rouge
Mix silver, hydroxide, ammonium, and honey

   "He ground glass crystals to be his eyes
   and shot them up, into the sky."[7]

but the Secret—

✪

The Eagle told it to the Peacock

who went and told it to the Crane
who went and told it to the Nightingale

So the Emperor Stalin-Ma,
   Tsar of the Middle Kingdom, journeyed
    to the flowering mountains—
So many summers ago.

For five days he walked into the mountains without knowing why, to the
Temple of the God-Who-Lets-Things-Fall.
   Then for five nights he'd slept under solstice stars,
in the Floating Gardens of Shangri-stan,
and the Nightingale perched in a pomegranate tree,
   and sang to him the Secret of the Sun.

And so from the steppes to the shores, the messenger was sent:

Cheng Ho astride the Eastern Dragon,
   Admiral of the Western Zodiac,
has come from the distant shores of Yunnangrad
to break open the sky.

   Then in the Underground Palace vaults and on the Red Pagoda balco-
nies, the ministers began to whisper
   of the fabled Land of Punt . . .

But Cheng Ho told it to the Dragon
who told it to the Albatross
who told it to the Leviathan
   well, word travels fast underwater,
   and whales are terrible gossips,[8]
and somebody must have told the old crackpot down in Atalantium,

Old Galixeo,
because he mounted his fastest Nautilus, and hurried to the cold, white
city of his Queen, to tell Columbiana the news from the East:

That the armies of the Volga-Ming
   "were sending Cheng Ho and a thousand ships
   to search for the Elixir of Life,
   to bring the starfire of the Emperor-Khan
   to the Seven Cities of Selenite,
   to the lost Kingdom of Punt."[9]
and if Cheng Ho were to reach them first,
   "what with all the glory, all the oil and the gold,
   all the riches they would surely find"[10]
then all the Kings of all the Lands would pay tribute or fall before the
Ruby Hordes.

Columbiana heard, and she understood.

She sent them from the port of Carina, seventeen ships in all,
   "with the maps forged in Atalantium
   to search for the land of Punt"[11]
And a mechanical bird flew before them
   "a metal Eagle, designed by the madman Galixeo, with alumen
   feathers and gears for joints,
   with glass tubes for brains and fire
   beneath its wings."[12]
And the sons of the Queen were her Admirals—
   She most have been astonished to see them, all
her beautiful boys, soaring higher and higher on the
grotesque wings of Galixeo—
Was she frightened?
Was she proud?

Compass and Sextant, north-cross-west
around the Cape of Canopus,

past Cetus Sound and the Praesepe cliffs, running straight
for the Horn of Magellan.
They circled the seas, then they circled again,
    then they circled and circled a dozen times more.

but Cheng Ho and his Dragon were always in sight,
    always on the horizon, turning around the Northern star
    Maybe they were catching up
    or maybe he was catching up
They wouldn't know until they got there.

✪

You know how it ended.

    and history will tell
That there was no gold, there was no oil,
no elixir,
no gain to be had at all
just empty, pitted beaches
full of dust and twinkling, broken rocks
beneath untwinkling stars
where the moon is always blue because it
    never rises
    and never sets
but stays fixed forever in the sky, making the sailors
so sick with wonder and longing
an irresistible tide
    pulling you home.

But the harbor ice is thick in winter
and the solar currents are fickle
and not all of our sons and daughters have returned.

Morning came and found them there
   trapped off the isles of Pontchartrain,
and the meteors were bright as Apollo's fire
and the last ships of Columbia sank burning
into the cold, black sea

   because Amon-Re is a jealous god
and these mortals have spent too long worshipping
the heretic Moon.

And foolish Galixeo
   Oracle of Orion, Mirror of Andromeda,
    seer of the dawn of time
She will dash his eye upon the Earth
She will raze the shipyards and scuttle the ships
throw the ashes out on the ocean
   more flotsam for the tranquil sea

These are the actions of a prudent ruler,
carefully weighed and carefully made

So smash the mapmaker and burn the maps
It's time to buy ourselves some new gods
Tell all of our sons and daughters
that there's no place else worth looking.
Maybe if they never see those charts,
   full of places without names,
Maybe they won't wonder and

Maybe they won't
try to go to see it for themselves.

It was just another Ming Dynasty expedition,
    after all, just another journey to Punt,
just another vainglorious, pointless quest.

✪

November nights we go down to the shoreline,
    all of us sons and daughters,
to the beaches where the Lighthouse of Canaveral once stood.
There we lie down in the sand to watch
    for the meteors of Apollo
for the skeletal ships still burning upon
the cold, black sea

And I would do it all again.
even knowing how it ended,
but

You see,
Djinns can be put back into bottles and
broken skies can be repaired and
I haven't seen an Eagle in these parts since
they drained the marshes for the super-mall and
put in the new subdivision and

I would do it all again.

but it's such a long time from now . . .

NOTES AND BIBLIOGRAPHY

1. Whereas earlier wizards had attempted to turn lead into gold, Galixeo worked to create lead, typically from pitchblende and oralloy.
2. Pliny Vulcanis, ed. *Encyclopedia of Atalantium,* 3rd ed. (Pergamon House).
3. Mahmoud Al-Falaki, *Constituents of the Celestial Sphere.*
4. Prof. Artemis Curie, "Elementals of Alchemy" (lecture, Popular Aristotelian Philosophy series, University of Thebes).
5. Fermi, *History of Columbiana* (Heliopolis University Press).
6. Alexander Ptolemeus, *Almagest* (Amonhotep Lyceum Reserve Shelves).
7. The legend of the Mirror of Andromeda: The earliest known version of this myth is inscribed on the great obelisks excavated at Nereides. Some scholars equate this underwater archaeological site at the mouth of the Eridanus with the lost city of Atalantium.
8. Woodward, Bernstein, and Felt, *Dispatches of Empire,* ed. Graham.
9. Tereshkova et al., "The Year of the Dragon," in *Korolev Chronicles* (Purple Mountain Observatory Notices).
10. Wan Hu, trans., *Icarus and Pegasus—The Stratosphere on the Cheap* (promotional literature from the Lockheed Imperial and Nedelin Rocketry corporational collaboration).
11. *One Hundred Thousand Li: Autobiographical Notes of Zheng He.* (Yong Le University special collections).
12. Webb and Gruman, *Apollo User's Manual*

✪

BOUND MAN

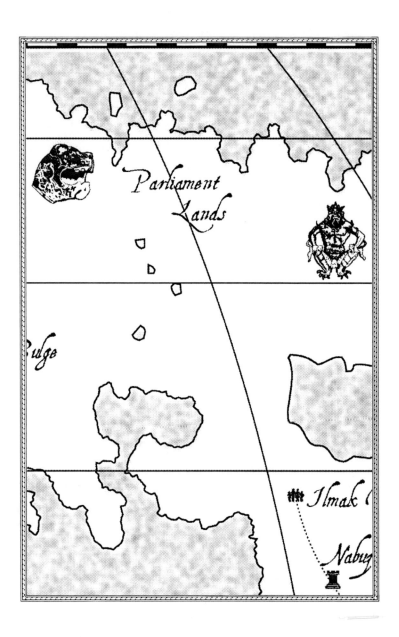

BOUND MAN

BY MARY ROBINETTE KOWAL

LIGHT DAPPLED THROUGH THE TREES IN THE FAMILY COURTYARD, PAINTING shadows on the paving stones. Li Reiko knelt by her son to look at his scraped knee.

"I just scratched it." Nawi squirmed under her hands.

Her daughter, Aya, leaned over her shoulder studying the healing. "Maybe Mama will show you her armor after she heals you."

Nawi stopped wiggling. "Really?"

Reiko shot Aya a warning look, but her little boy's dark eyes shone with excitement. Reiko smiled. "Really." What did tradition matter? "Now let me heal your knee." She laid her hand on the shallow wound.

"Ow."

"Shush." Reiko closed her eyes and rose in the dark space in her mind.

In her mind's eye, Reiko took her time with the ritual, knowing it took less time than it appeared to. In a heartbeat, green fire flared out to the walls of her mind. She dissolved into it as she focused on healing her son.

When the wound closed beneath her hand, she sank to the surface of her mind.

"There." She tousled Nawi's hair. "That wasn't bad, was it?"

"It tickled." He wrinkled his nose. "Will you show me your armor now?"

251

She sighed. She should not encourage his interest in the martial arts. His work would be with the histories that men kept, and yet . . . "Watch."

Pulling the smooth black surface out of the ether, she manifested her armor. It sheathed her like silence in the night. Aya watched with obvious anticipation for the day when she would earn her own armor. Nawi's face, full of sharp yearning for something he would never have, cut Reiko's heart like a new blade.

"Can I see your sword?"

She let her armor vanish back into thought. "No." Reiko brushed his hair from his eyes. "It's my turn to hide, right?"

Halldór twisted in his saddle, trying to ease the kink in his back. When the party reached the Parliament, he could remove the weight hanging between his shoulders.

With each step his horse took across the moss-covered lava field, the strange blade bumped against his spine, reminding him that he carried a legend. None of the runes or sheep entrails he read before their quest had foretold the ease with which they fulfilled the first part of the prophecy. They had found the Chooser of the Slain's narrow blade wrapped in linen, buried beneath an abandoned elf-house. In that dark room, the sword's hard silvery metal—longer than any of their bronze swords— had seemed lit by the moon.

Lárus pulled his horse alongside Halldór. "Will the ladies be waiting for us, do you think?"

"Maybe for you, my lord, but not for me."

"Nonsense. Women love the warrior-priest. 'Strong and sensitive.'" He snorted through his mustache. "Just comb your hair so you don't look like a straw man."

A horse screamed behind them. Halldór turned, expecting to see its leg caught in one of the thousands of holes between the rocks. Instead, armed men swarmed from the gullies between the rocks, hacking at the riders. Bandits.

Halldór spun his horse to help Lárus and the others fight them off.

Lárus shouted, "Protect the Sword!"

At the Duke's command, Halldór cursed and turned his horse from the fight, galloping across the rocks. Behind him, men cried out as they protected his escape. His horse twisted along the narrow paths between stones. It stopped abruptly, avoiding a chasm. Halldór looked back.

Scant lengths ahead of the bandits, Lárus rode, slumped in his saddle. Blood stained his cloak. The other men hung behind Lárus, protecting the Duke as long as possible.

Behind them, the bandits closed the remaining distance across the lava fields.

Halldór kicked his horse's side, driving it around the chasm. His horse stumbled sickeningly beneath him. Its leg snapped, caught between rocks. Halldór kicked free of the saddle as the horse screamed. He rolled clear. The rocky ground slammed the sword into his back. His face passed over the edge of the chasm. Breathless, he recoiled from the drop.

As he scrambled to his feet, Lárus thundered up. Without wasting a beat, Lárus flung himself from the saddle and tossed Halldór the reins. "Get the Sword to Parliament!"

Halldór grabbed the reins, swinging into the saddle. If they died returning to Parliament, did it matter that they had found the Sword? "We must invoke the Sword!"

Lárus's right arm hung, blood-drenched, by his side, but he faced the bandits with his left. "Go!"

Halldór yanked the Sword free of its wrappings. For the first time in six thousand years, the light of the sun fell on the silvery blade, bringing fire to its length. It vibrated in his hands.

The first bandit reached Lárus and forced him back.

Halldór chanted the runes of power, petitioning the Chooser of the Slain.

Time stopped.

Reiko hid from her children, blending into the shadows of the court-yard with more urgency than she felt in combat. To do less would insult them.

"Ready or not, here I come!" Nawi spun from the tree and sprinted past her hiding place. Aya turned more slowly and studied the courtyard. Reiko smiled as her daughter sniffed the air, looking for tracks. Her son crashed through the bushes, kicking leaves with each footstep.

As another branch cracked under Nawi's foot, Reiko stifled the urge to correct his appalling technique. She would speak with his tutor about what the woman was teaching him. He was a boy, but that was no reason to neglect his education.

Watching Aya find Reiko's initial footprints and track them away from where she hid, Reiko slid from her hiding place. She walked across the courtyard to the fountain. This was a rule with her children; to make up for the size difference, she could not run.

She paced closer to the sparkling water, masking her sounds with its babble. From her right, Nawi shouted, "Have you found her?"

"No, silly!" Aya shook her head and stopped. She put her tiny hands on her hips, staring at the ground. "Her tracks stop here."

Reiko and her daughter were the same distance from the fountain, but on opposite sides. If Aya were paying attention, she would realize her mother had retraced her tracks and jumped from the fountain to the paving stones circling the grassy center of the courtyard. Reiko took three more steps before Aya turned.

As her daughter turned, Reiko felt, more than heard, her son on her left, reaching for her. Clever. He had misdirected her attention with his noise in the shrubbery. She fell forward, using gravity to drop beneath his hands. Rolling on her shoulder, she somersaulted, then launched to her feet as Aya ran toward her.

Nawi grabbed for her again. With a child on each side, Reiko danced and dodged closer to the fountain. She twisted from their grasp, laughing with them each time they missed her. Their giggles echoed through the courtyard.

The world tipped sideways and vibrated. Reiko stumbled as pain ripped through her spine.

Nawi's hand clapped against her side. "I got her!"

Fire engulfed Reiko.

The courtyard vanished.

Time began again.

The sword in Halldór's hands thrummed with life. Fire from the sunset engulfed the sword and split the air. With a keening cry, the air opened and a form dropped through, silhouetted against a haze of fire. Horses and men screamed in terror.

When the fire died away, a woman stood between Halldór and the bandits.

Halldór's heart sank. Where was the Chooser of the Slain? Where was the warrior the sword had petitioned?

A bandit snarled and rushed toward them. The others followed, their weapons raised.

The woman snatched the Sword from Halldór's hands. In that brief moment, when he stared at her wild face, he realized that he had succeeded in calling Li Reiko, the Chooser of the Slain.

Then she turned. The air around her rippled with a heat haze as armor, dark as night, materialized around her body. He watched her dance with deadly grace, bending and twisting away from the bandits' blows. With movement as precise as ritual, she danced with death as her partner. Her sword slid through the bodies of the bandits.

Halldór dropped to his knees, thanking the gods for sending her. He watched the point of her sword trace a line, like the path of entrails on the church floor. The line of blood led to the next moment, the next and the next, as if each man's death was predestined.

Then she turned her sword on him.

Her blade descended, burning with the fire of the setting sun. She stopped as if she had run into a wall, with the point touching Halldór's chest.

Why had she stopped? If his blood was the price for saving Lárus, so be it. Her arm trembled. She grimaced, but did not move the sword closer.

Her face, half-hidden by her helm, was dark with rage. "Where am I?" Her words were crisp, more like a chant than common speech.

Holding still, Halldór said, "We are on the border of the Parliament lands, Li Reiko."

Her dark eyes, slanted beneath angry lids, widened. She pulled back and her armor rippled, vanishing into thought. Skin tanned like the smoothest leather stretched over her wide cheekbones. Her hair hung in a heavy, black braid down her back. Halldór's pulse sang in his veins.

Only the gods in sagas had hair the color of the Allmother's night. Had he needed proof he had called the Chooser of the Slain, the inhuman black hair would have convinced him of it.

He bowed his head. "All praise to you, Great One. Grant us your blessings."

Reiko's breath hissed from her. He knew her name. She had dropped through a flaming portal into hell and this demon with bulging eyes knew her name.

She had tried to slay him as she had the others, but could not press her sword forward, as if a wall protected him.

And now he asked for blessings.

"What blessings do you ask of me?" Reiko said. She controlled a shudder. What human had hair as pale as straw?

Straw lowered his bulging eyes to the demon lying in front of him.

"Grant us, O Gracious One, the life of our Duke Lárus."

This Lárus had a wound deep in his shoulder. His blood was as red as any human's, but his face was pale as death.

She turned from Straw and wiped her sword on the thick moss, cleaning the blood from it. As soon as her attention seemed turned from them, Straw attended Lárus. She kept her awareness on the sounds of his movement as she sought balance in the familiar task of caring for her weapon. By the Gods! Why did he have her sword? It had been in her rooms not ten minutes before playing hide-and-seek with her children.

Panic almost took her. What had happened to her Aya and Nawi? She needed information, but displaying ignorance to an enemy was a weakness, which could kill surer than the sharpest blade. She considered.

Their weapons were bronze, not steel, and none of her opponents had manifested armor. They dressed in leather and felted wool, but no woven goods. So, then. That was their technology.

Straw had not healed Lárus, so perhaps they could not. He wanted her aid. Her thoughts checked. Could demons be bound by blood debt?

She turned to Straw.

"What price do you offer for this life?"

Straw raised his eyes; they were the color of the sky. "I offer my life unto you, O Great One."

She set her lips. What good would vengeance do? Unless . . . "Do you offer blood or service?"

He lowered his head again. "I submit to your will."

"You will serve me, then. Do you agree to be my bound man?"

"I do."

"Good." She sheathed her sword. "What is your name?"

"Halldór Arnarsson."

"I accept your pledge." She dropped to her knees and pushed the leather from the wound on Lárus's shoulder. She pulled upon her reserves and, rising into the healing ritual, touched his mind.

He was human.

She pushed the shock aside; she could not spare the attention.

Halldór gasped as fire glowed around Li Reiko's hands. He had read of gods healing in the sagas, but bearing witness was beyond his dreams.

The glow faded. She lifted her hands from Lárus's shoulder. The wound was gone. A narrow red line and the blood-soaked clothing remained. Lárus opened his eyes as if he had been sleeping.

But her face was drawn. "I have paid the price for your service, bound man." She lifted a hand to her temple. "The wound was deeper . . ." Her eyes rolled back in her head and she slumped to the ground.

Lárus sat up and grabbed Halldór by the shoulder. "What did you do?"

Shaking Lárus off, Halldór crouched next to her. She was breathing. "I saved your life."

"By binding yourself to a woman? Are you mad?"

"She healed you. Healed! Look." Halldór pointed at her hair. "Look at her. This is Li Reiko."

"Li Reiko was a Warrior."

"You saw her. How long did it take her to kill six men?" He pointed at the carnage behind them. "Name one man who could do that."

Would moving her be a sacrilege? He grimaced. He would beg forgiveness if that were the case. "We should move before the sun sets and the trolls come out."

Lárus nodded slowly, his eyes still on the bodies around them. "Makes you wonder, doesn't it?"

"What?"

"How many other sagas are true?"

Halldór frowned. "They're all true."

The smell of mutton invaded her dreamless sleep. Reiko lay under sheepskin, on a bed of straw ticking. The straw poked through the wool fabric, pricking her bare skin. Straw. Her memory tickled her with an image of hair the color of straw. Halldór.

Long practice kept her breath even. She lay with her eyes closed, listening. A small room. An open fire. Women murmuring. She needed to learn as much as possible, before changing the balance by letting them know she was awake.

A hand placed a damp rag on her brow. The touch was light, a woman or a child.

The sheepskin's weight would telegraph her movement if she tried grabbing the hand. Better to open her eyes and feign weakness than to create an impression of threat. There was time for that later.

Reiko let her eyes flutter open. A girl bent over her, cast from the same demonic mold as Halldór. Her hair was the color of honey, and her wide blue eyes started from her head. She stilled when Reiko awoke, but did not pull away.

Reiko forced a smile, and let worry appear on her brow. "Where am I?"

"In the women's quarters at the Parliament grounds."

Reiko sat up. The sheepskin fell away, letting the cool air caress her body. The girl averted her eyes. Conversation in the room stopped.

Interesting. They had a nudity taboo. She reached for the sheepskin and pulled it over her torso. "What is your name?"

"Mara Halldórsdottir."

Her bound man had a daughter. And his people had a patronymic system—how far from home was she? "Where are my clothes, Mara?"

The girl lifted a folded bundle of cloth from a low bench next to the bed. "I washed them for you."

"Thank you." If Mara had washed and dried her clothes, Reiko must have been unconscious for several hours. Lárus's wound had been deeper than she thought. "Where is my sword?"

"My father has it."

Rage filled Reiko's veins like the fire that had brought her here. She waited for the heat to dwindle, then began dressing. As Reiko pulled her boots on, she asked, "Where is he?"

Behind Mara, the other women shifted as if Reiko were crossing a line. Mara ignored them. "He's with Parliament."

"Which is where?" The eyes of the other women felt like heat on her skin. Ah. Parliament contained the line she should not cross, and they clearly would not answer her. Her mind teased her with memories of folk in other lands. She had never paid much heed to these stories, since history was men's work. She smiled at Mara. "Thank you for your kindness."

As she strode from the room she kept her senses fanned out, waiting for resistance from them, but they hung back as if they were afraid.

The women's quarters fronted on a narrow twisting path lined with low turf and stone houses. The end of the street opened on a large raised circle surrounded by stone benches.

Men sat on the benches, but women stayed below. Lárus spoke in the middle of the circle. By his side, Halldór stood with her sword in his hands. Sheltering in the shadow by a house, Reiko studied them. They towered above her, but their movements were clumsy and oafish like a trained bear's. Nawi had better training than any here.

Her son. Sudden anxiety and rage filled her, but rage invited rash decisions. She forced the anger away.

With effort, she returned her focus to the men. They had no awareness of their mass, only of their size, and an imperfect grasp of that.

Halldór lifted his head. As if guided by strings his eyes found her in the shadows.

He dropped to his knees and held out her sword. In mid-sentence, Lárus looked at Halldór, and then turned to Reiko. Surprise crossed his face, but he bowed his head.

"Li Reiko, you honor us with your presence."

Reiko climbed onto the stone circle. As she crossed to retrieve her sword, an ox of a man rose to his feet. "I will not sit here, while a woman is in the Parliament's circle."

Lárus scowled. "Ingolfur, this is no mortal woman."

Reiko's attention sprang forward. What did they think she was, if not mortal?

"You darkened a trollop's hair with soot." Ingolfur crossed his arms. "You expect me to believe she's a god?"

Her pulse quickened. What were they saying?

Lárus flung his cloak back, showing the torn and blood-soaked leather at his shoulder. "We were set upon by bandits. My arm was cut half off and she healed it." His pale face flushed red. "I tell you this is Li Reiko, returned to the world."

She understood the words, but they had no meaning. Each sentence out of their mouths raised a thousand questions in her mind.

"Ha." Ingolfur spat on the ground. "Your quest sought a warrior to defeat the Troll King."

This she understood. "And if I do, what price do you offer?"

Lárus opened his mouth but Ingolfur crossed the circle.

"You pretend to be the Chooser of the Slain?" Ingolfur reached for her, as if she were a doll he could pick up. Before his hand touched her shoulder, she took his wrist, pulling on it as she twisted. She drove her shoulder into his belly and used his mass to flip him as she stood.

She had thought these were demons, but by their actions they were men, full of swagger and rash judgment. She waited. He would attack her again.

Ingolfur raged behind her. Reiko focused on his sounds and the small changes in the air. As he reached for her, she twisted away from his hands and with his force, sent him stumbling from the circle. The men broke into laughter.

She waited again.

It might take time but Ingolfur would learn his place. A man courted death, touching a woman unasked.

Halldór stepped in front of Reiko and faced Ingolfur. "Great Ingolfur, surely you can see no mortal woman could face our champion."

Reiko cocked her head slightly. Her bound man showed wit by appeasing the oaf's vanity.

Lárus pointed to her sword in Halldór's hands. "Who here still doubts we have completed our quest?" The men shifted on their benches uneasily. "We fulfilled the first part of the prophecy by returning Li Reiko to the world."

What prophecy had her name in it? There might be a bargaining chip here.

"You promised us a mighty warrior, the Chooser of the Slain," Ingolfur snarled, "not a woman."

It was time for action. If they wanted a god, they should have one. "Have no doubt. I can defeat the Troll King." She let her armor flourish around her. Ingolfur drew back involuntarily. Around the circle, she heard gasps and sharp cries.

She drew her sword from Halldór's hands. "Who here will test me?"

Halldór dropped to his knees in front of her. "The Chooser of the Slain!"

In the same breath, Lárus knelt and cried, "Li Reiko!"

Around the circle, men followed suit. On the ground below, women and children knelt in the dirt. They cried her name. In the safety of her helm, Reiko scowled. Playing at godhood was a dangerous lie.

She lowered her sword. "But there is a price. You must return me to the heavens."

Halldór's eyes grew wider than she thought possible. "How, my lady?"

She shook her head. "You know the gods grant nothing easily. They say you must return me. You must learn how. Who here accepts that price for your freedom from the trolls?"

She sheathed her sword and let her armor evaporate. Turning on her heel, she strode off the Parliament's circle.

✪

Halldór clambered to his feet as Li Reiko left the Parliament circle. His head reeled. She hinted at things beyond his training. Lárus grabbed him by the arm. "What does she mean, return her?"

Ingolfur tossed his hands. "If that is the price, I will pay it gladly. Ridding the world of the Troll King and her at the same time would be a joy."

"Is it possible?"

Men crowded around Halldór, asking him theological questions of the sagas. The answers eluded him. He had not cast a rune-stone or read an entrail since they started for the elf-house a week ago. "She would not ask if it were impossible." He swallowed. "I will study the problem with my brothers and return to you."

Lárus clapped him on the back. "Good man." When Lárus turned to the throng surrounding them, Halldór slipped away.

He found Li Reiko surrounded by children. The women hung back, too shy to come near, but the children crowded close. Halldór could hardly believe she had killed six men as easily as carding wool. For the space of a breath, he watched her play peek-a-boo with a small child, her face open with delight and pain.

She saw him and shutters closed over her soul. Standing, her eyes impassive, she said, "I want to read the prophecy."

He blinked, surprised. Then his heart lifted; maybe she would show him how to pay her price. "It is stored in the church."

Reiko brushed the child's hair from its eyes, then fell into step beside Halldór. He could barely keep a sedate pace to the church.

Inside, he led her through the nave to the library beside the sanctuary. The other priests, studying, stared at the Chooser of the Slain. Halldór felt as if he were outside himself with the strangeness of this. He was leading Li Reiko, a Warrior out of the oldest sagas, past shelves containing her history.

Since the gods had arrived from across the sea, his brothers had recorded their history. For six thousand unbroken years, the records of prophecy and the sagas kept their history whole.

When they reached the collections desk, the acolyte on duty looked as if he would wet himself. Halldór stood between the boy and the Chooser of the Slain, but the boy still stared with an open mouth.

"Bring me the Troll King prophecy, and the Sagas of Li Nawi, Volume I. We will be in the side chapel."

Still gaping, the boy nodded and ran down the aisles.

"We can study in here." He led the Chooser of the Slain to the side chapel. Halldór was shocked again at how small she was, not much taller than the acolyte. He had thought the gods would be larger than life.

He had hundreds of questions, but none of the words.

When the acolyte came back, Halldór sent a silent prayer of thanks. Here was something they could discuss. He took the vellum roll and the massive volume of sagas the acolyte carried and shooed him out of the room.

Halldór's palms were damp with sweat as he pulled on wool gloves to protect the manuscripts. He hesitated over another pair of gloves, then set them aside. Her hands could heal; she would not damage the manuscripts.

Carefully, Halldór unrolled the prophecy scroll on the table. He did not look at the rendering of entrails. He watched her.

She gave no hint of her thoughts. "I want to hear your explanation of this."

A cold current ran up his spine, as if he were eleven again, explaining scripture to an elder. Halldór licked his lips and pointed at the arc of viscera. "This represents the heavens, and the overlap here—" he pointed at the bulge of the lower intestine "—means time of conflict. I interpreted the opening in the bulge to mean specifically the Troll King. This pattern of blood means—"

She crossed her arms. "You clearly understand your discipline. Tell me the prophecy in plain language."

"Oh." He looked at the drawing of the entrails again. What did she see that he did not? "Well, in a time of conflict—which is now—the Chooser of the Slain overcomes the Troll King." He pointed at the shining knot around the lower intestine. "See how this chokes off the Troll King. That means you win the battle."

"And how did you know the legendary warrior was—is me?"

"I cross-referenced with our histories and you were the one that fit the criteria."

She shivered. "Show me the history. I want to understand how you deciphered this."

Halldór thanked the gods that he had asked for Li Nawi's saga as well. He placed the heavy volume of history in front of Li Reiko and opened to the Book of Fire, Chapter One.

In the autumn of the Fire, Li Reiko, greatest of the warriors, trained Li Nawi and his sister Aya in the ways of Death. In the midst of the training, a curtain of fire split Nawi from Aya and when they came together again, Li Reiko was gone. Though they were frightened, they understood that the Chooser of the Slain had taken her rightful place in heaven.

Reiko trembled, her control gone. "What is this?"

"It is the Saga of Li Nawi."

She tried phrasing casual questions, but her mind spun in circles. "How do you come to have this?"

Halldór traced the letters with his gloved hand. "After the Collapse, when waves of fire had rolled across our land, Li Nawi came across the oceans with the other gods. He was our conqueror and our salvation."

The ranks of stone shelves filled with thick leather bindings crowded her. Her heart kicked wildly.

Halldór's voice seemed drowned out by the drumming of her pulse. "The Sagas are our heritage and charge. The Gods have left the Earth, but we keep records of histories as they taught us."

Reiko turned her eyes blindly from the page. "Your heritage?"

"I have been dedicated to the service of the gods since my birth." He paused. "Your sagas were the most inspiring. Forgive my trespasses, may I beg for your indulgence for a question?"

"What?" Hot and cold washed over her in sickening waves.

"I have read your son Li Nawi's accounts of your triumphs in battle."

Reiko could not breathe. Halldór flipped the pages forward. "This is how I knew where to look for your sword." He paused with his hand over the letters. "I deciphered the clues to invoke it and call you here, but there are many—"

Reiko pushed away from the table. "You caused the curtain of fire?" She wanted to vomit her fear at his feet.

"I—I do not understand."

"I dropped through fire this morning." *And when they came together again, Li Reiko was no more.* What had it been like for Aya and Nawi to watch their mother ripped out of time?

Halldór said, "In answer to my petition."

"I was playing hide-and-seek with my children and you took me."

"You were in the heavens with the gods."

"That's something you tell a grieving child!"

"I—I didn't, I—." His face turned gray. "Forgive me, Great One."

"I am not a god!" She pushed him, all control gone. He tripped over a bench and dropped to the floor. "Send me back."

"I cannot."

Her sword flew from its sheath before she realized she held it. "Send me back!" She held it to his neck. Her arms trembled with the desire to run it through him. But it would not move.

She leaned on the blade, digging her feet into the floor. "You ripped me out of time and took me from my children."

He shook his head. "It had already happened."

"Because of you." Her sword crept closer, pricking a drop of blood from his neck. What protected him?

Halldór lay on his back. "I'm sorry. I didn't know . . . I was following the prophecy."

Reiko staggered. Prophecy. A wall of predestination. Empty, she dropped to the bench and cradled her sword. "How long ago . . . ?"

"Six thousand years."

She closed her eyes. This was why he could not return her. He had not simply brought her from across the sea like the other "gods." He had brought her through time. If she was trapped here, if she could never see her children again, it did not matter if these were humans or demons. She was banished to Hell.

"What do the sagas say about my children?"

Halldór rolled to his knees. "I can show you." His voice shook.

"No." She ran her hand down the blade of her sword. The edge whispered against her skin. She touched her wrist to the blade. It would be easy. "Read it to me."

She heard him get to his feet. The pages of the heavy book shuffled.

Halldór swallowed and read, "This is from the Saga of Li Nawi, the Book of the Sword, Chapter Two. 'And it came to pass that Li Aya and Li Nawi were raised unto adulthood by their tutor.'"

A tutor raised them, because he, Halldór, had pulled their mother away. He shook his head. It had happened six thousand years ago.

"'But when they reached adulthood, each claimed the right of Li Reiko's sword.'"

They fought over the sword, with which he had called her, not out of the heavens, but from across time. Halldór shivered and focused on the page.

"'Li Aya challenged Li Nawi, saying Death was her birthright. But Nawi, on hearing this, scoffed and said he was a Child of Death. And saying so, he took Li Reiko's sword and the gods smote Li Aya with their fiery hand, thus granting Li Nawi the victory.'"

Halldór's entrails twisted as if the gods were reading them. He had read these sagas since he was a boy. He believed them, but he had not thought they were real. He looked at Li Reiko. She held her head in her lap and rocked back and forth.

For all his talk of prophecies, he was the one who had found the sword and invoked it. "'Then all men knew he was the true Child of Death. He raised an army of men, the First of the Nine Armies, and thus began the Collapse—'"

"Stop."

"I'm sorry." He would slaughter a thousand sheep if just one could tell him how to undo his crime. In the Saga of Li Nawi, Li Reiko never appeared after the wall of fire. He closed the book and took a step toward her. "The price you asked . . . I can't send you back."

Li Reiko drew a shuddering breath and looked up. "I have already paid the price for you." Her eyes reflected his guilt. "Another hero can kill the Troll King."

His pulse rattled forward like a panicked horse. "No one else can. The prophecy points to you."

"Gut a new sheep, bound man. I won't help you." She stood. "I release you from your debt."

"But, it's unpaid. I owe you a life."

"You cannot pay the price I ask." She turned and touched her sword to his neck again. He flinched. "I couldn't kill you when I wanted to." She cocked her head, and traced the point of the blade around his neck, not quite touching him. "What destiny waits for you?"

"Nothing." He was no one.

She snorted. "How nice to be without a fate." Sheathing her sword, she walked toward the door.

He followed her. Nothing made sense. "Where are you going?" She spun and drove her fist into his midriff. He grunted and folded over the pain. Panting, Reiko pulled her sword out and hit his side with the flat of her blade. Halldór held his cry in.

She swung again, with the edge, but stopped; Halldór held still.

She turned the blade and slammed the flat against his ribs again. The breath hissed out of him, but he did not move. He knelt in front of her, waiting for the next blow. He deserved this. He deserved more than this.

Li Reiko's lip curled. "Do not follow me."

He scrabbled forward on his knees. "Then tell me where you're going, so I will not meet you by chance."

"Maybe that is your destiny." She left him.

Halldór did not follow her.

Li Reiko chased her shadow out of the Parliament lands. It stretched before her in the golden light of sunrise, racing her across the moss-covered lava. The wind, whipping across the treeless plain, pushed her like a child late for dinner.

Surrounded by the people in the Parliament lands, Reiko's anger had overwhelmed her and buried her grief. Whatever Halldór thought her destiny was, she saw only two paths in front of her—make a life here or join her children in the only way left. Neither was a path to choose rashly.

Small shrubs and grasses broke the green with patches of red and gold, as if someone had unrolled a carpet on the ground. Heavy undulations creased the land with crevices. Some held water reflecting the sky, others dropped to a lower level of moss and soft grasses, and some were as dark as the inside of a cave.

When the sun crossed the sky and painted the land with long shadows, Reiko sought shelter from the wind in one of the crevices. The moss cradled her with the warmth of the earth.

She pulled thoughts of Aya and Nawi close. In her memory, they laughed as they reached for her. Sobs pushed past Reiko's reserves. She wrapped her arms around her chest. Each cry shattered her. Her children were dead because Halldór had decided a disemboweled sheep meant he should rip her out of time. It did not matter if they had grown up; she had not been there. They were six thousand years dead. Inside her head, Reiko battled grief. Her fists pounded against the walls of her mind. No. Her brain filled with that silent syllable.

She pressed her face against the velvet moss wanting the earth to absorb her.

She heard a sound.

Training quieted her breath in a moment. Reiko lifted her head from the moss and listened. Footsteps crossed the earth above her. She manifested her armor and rolled silently to her feet. If Halldór had followed her, she would play the part of a man and seek revenge.

In the light of the moon, a figure, larger than a man, crept toward her. A troll. Behind him, a gang of trolls watched. Reiko counted them and considered the terrain. It was safer to hide, but anger still throbbed in her bones. She left her sword sheathed and slunk out of the crevice in the ground. Her argument was not with them.

Flowing across the moss, she let the uneven shadows mask her until she reached a standing mound of stones. The wind carried the trolls' stink to her.

The lone troll reached the crevice she had sheltered in. His arm darted down like a fishing bear's and he roared with astonishment.

The other trolls laughed. "Got away, did she?"

One of them said, "Mucker was smelling his own crotch is all."

"Yah, sure. He didn't get enough in the Hall and goes around thinking he smells more."

They had taken human women. Reiko felt a stabbing pain in her loins; she could not let that stand.

Mucker whirled. "Shut up! I know I smelled a woman."

"Then where'd she go?" The troll snorted the air. "Don't smell one now."

The other lumbered away. "Let's go, while some of 'em are still fresh."

Mucker slumped and followed the other trolls. Reiko eased out of the shadows. She was a fool, but would not hide while women were raped.

She hung back, letting the wind bring their sounds and scents as she tracked the trolls to their Hall.

The moon had sunk to a handspan above the horizon as they reached the Troll Hall. Trolls stood on either side of the great stone doors.

Reiko crouched in the shadows. The night was silent except for the sounds of revelry. Even with alcohol slowing their movement, there were too many of them.

If she could goad the sentries into taking her on one at a time she could get inside, but only if no other trolls came. The sound of sword-play would draw a crowd faster than crows to carrion.

A harness jingled.

Reiko's head snapped in the direction of the sound.

She shielded her eyes from the light coming out of the Troll Hall. As her vision adjusted, a man on horseback resolved out of the dark. He sat twenty or thirty horselengths away, invisible to the trolls outside the Hall. Reiko eased toward him, senses wide.

The horse shifted its weight when it smelled her. The man put his hand on its neck, calming it. Light from the Troll Hall hinted at the planes of his face. Halldór. Her lips tightened. He had followed her. Reiko warred with an irrational desire to call the trolls down on them.

She needed him. Halldór, with his drawings and histories, might know what the inside of the Troll Hall looked like.

Praying he would have sense enough to be quiet, she stepped out of the shadows. He jumped as she appeared, but stayed silent.

He swung off his horse and leaned close. His whisper was hot in her ear. "Forgive me. I did not follow you."

He turned his head, letting her breathe an answer in return. "Under-stood. They have women inside."

"I know." Halldór looked toward the Troll Hall. Dried blood covered the left side of his face.

"We should move away to talk," she said.

He took his horse by the reins and followed her. His horse's hooves were bound with sheepskin so they made no sound on the rocks. Something had happened since she left the Parliament lands.

Halldór limped on his left side. Reiko's heart beat as if she were running. The trolls had women prisoners. Halldór bore signs of battle. Trolls must have attacked the Parliament. They walked in silence until the sounds of the Troll Hall dwindled to nothing.

Halldór stopped. "There was a raid." He stared at nothing, his jaw clenched. "While I was gone . . . they just let the trolls—" His voice broke like a boy's. "They have my girl."

"Mara?"

He nodded, looking as if he were surprised that she knew the name of his daughter.

His daughter. Reiko felt her anger slip away. "Halldór, I'm sorry." She looked for other riders. "Who came with you?"

He shook his head. "No one. They're guarding the walls in case the trolls come back." He touched the side of his face. "I tried persuading them."

"Why did you come?"

"To get Mara back."

"There are too many of them, bound man." She scowled. "Even if you could get inside, what do you plan to do? Challenge the Troll King to single combat?" Her words resonated in her skull. Reiko closed her eyes, dizzy with the turns the gods spun her in. When she opened them, Halldór's lips were parted in prayer. Reiko swallowed. "When does the sun rise?"

"In another hour."

She turned to the Hall. In an hour, the trolls could not give chase; the sun would turn them to stone. She unbraided her hair.

Halldór stared as her long hair began flirting with the wind. She smiled at the question in his eyes. "I have a prophecy to fulfill."

◉

Reiko stumbled into the torchlight, her hair loose and wild. She clutched Halldór's cloak around her shoulders.

One of the troll sentries saw her. "Hey. A dolly."

Reiko contorted her face with fear and whimpered. The other troll laughed. "She don't seem taken with you, do she?"

The first troll came closer. "She don't have to."

"Don't hurt me. Please, please . . ." Reiko retreated from him. When she was between the two, she whipped Halldór's cloak off, tangling it around the first troll's head. With her sword, she gutted the other. He dropped to his knees, fumbling with his entrails as she turned to the first. She slid her sword under the cloak, slicing along the base of the first troll's jaw.

Leaving them to die, Reiko entered the Hall. Women's cries mingled with the sounds of debauchery.

She kept her focus on the battle ahead. She would be out-matched in size and strength, but hoped her wit and weapon would prevail. Her mouth twisted. She knew she would prevail. It was predestined.

A troll saw her. He lumbered closer. Reiko showed her sword, bright with blood. "I have met your sentries. Shall we dance as well?"

The troll checked his movement and squinted his beady eyes at her. Reiko walked past him. She kept her awareness on him, but another troll, Mucker, loomed in front of her.

"Where do you think you're going?"

"I am the one you sought. I am Chooser of the Slain. I have come for your King."

Mucker laughed and reached for her, heedless of her sword. She dodged under his grasp and held the point to his jugular. "I have come for your King. Not for you. Show me to him."

She leapt back. His hand went to his throat and came away with blood.

A bellow rose from the entry. Someone had found the sentries. Reiko kept her gaze on Mucker, but her peripheral vision filled with trolls running. Footsteps behind her. She spun and planted her sword in a troll's arm. The troll howled, drawing back. Reiko shook her head. "I have come for your King."

They herded her to the Hall. She had no chance of defeating them, but if the Troll King granted her single combat, she might escape the Hall with the prisoners. When she entered the great Hall, whispers flew; the number of slain trolls mounted with each rumor.

The Troll King lolled on his throne. Mara, her face red with shame, serviced him.

Anger buzzed in Reiko's ears. She let it pass through her. "Troll King, I have come to challenge you."

The Troll King laughed like an avalanche of stone tearing down his Hall. "You! A dolly wants to fight?"

Reiko paid no attention to his words.

He was nearly twice her height. Leather armor, crusted with crude bronze scales, covered his body. The weight of feasts hung about his middle, but his shoulders bulged with muscle. If he connected a blow, she would die. But he would be fighting gravity as well as her. Once he began a movement, it would take time for him to stop and begin another.

Reiko raised her head, waiting until his laughter faded. "I am the Chooser of the Slain. Will you accept my challenge?" She forced a smile to her lips. "Or are you afraid to dance with me?"

"I will grind you to paste, dolly. I will sweep over your lands and eat your children for my breakfast."

"If you win, you may. Here are my terms. If I win, the prisoners go free."

He came down from his throne and leaned close. "If you win, we will never show a shadow in human lands."

"Will your people hold that pledge when you are dead?"

He laughed. The stink of his breath boiled around her. He turned to the trolls packed in the Hall. "Will you?"

The room rocked with the roar of their voices. "Aye."

The Troll King leered. "And when you lose, I won't kill you till I've bedded you."

"Agreed. May the gods hear our pledge." Reiko manifested her armor.

As the night-black plates materialized around her, the Troll King bellowed, "What is this?"

"This?" She taunted him. "This is but a toy the gods have sent to play with you."

She smiled in her helm as he swung his heavy iron sword over his head and charged her. Stupid. Reiko stepped to the side, already turning as she let him pass.

She brought her sword hard against the gap in his armor above his boot. The blade jarred against bone. She yanked her sword free; blood coated it like a sheath.

The Troll King dropped to one knee, hamstrung. Without waiting, she vaulted up his back and wrapped her arms around his neck. Like Aya riding piggyback. He flailed his sword through the air, reaching for her. She slit his throat. His bellow changed to a gurgle as blood fountained in an arc, soaking the ground.

A heavy ache filled her breast. She whispered in his ear, "I have killed you without honor. I am a machine of the gods."

Reiko let gravity pull the Troll King down, as troll shrieks filled the air. She leapt off his body as it fell forward.

Before the dust settled around him, Reiko pointed her sword at the nearest troll. "Release the prisoners."

Reiko led the women into the dawn. As they left the Troll Hall, Halldór dropped to his knees with his arms lifted in prayer. Mara wrapped her arms around his neck, sobbing.

Reiko felt nothing. Why should she, when the victory was not hers? She withdrew from the group of women weeping and singing her praises.

Halldór chased her. "Lady, my life is already yours but my debt has doubled."

He reminded her of a suitor in one of Aya's bedtime stories, accepting gifts without asking what the witchyman's price would be. She knelt to clean her sword on the moss. "Then give me your firstborn child."

She could hear his breath hitch in his throat. "If that is your price."

Reiko raised her eyes. "No. That is a price I will not ask."

He knelt beside her. "I know why you cannot kill me."

"Good." She turned to her sword. "When you fulfill your fate let me know, so I can."

His blue eyes shone with fervor. "I am destined to return your daughter to you."

Reiko's heart flooded with pain and hope. She fought for breath. "Do not toy with me, bound man."

"I would not. I reviewed the saga after you went into the Hall. It says, 'and the gods smote Li Aya with their fiery hand.' I can bring Li Aya here."

Reiko sunk her fingers into the moss, clutching the earth. Oh gods, to have her little girl here—she trembled. Aya would not be a child. There would be no games of hide-and-seek. *When they reached adulthood, each claimed the right of Li Reiko's sword* . . . How old would Aya be?

Reiko shook her head. She could not do that to her daughter. "You want to rip Aya out of time as well. If Nawi had not won, the Collapse would not have happened."

Halldór's brow furrowed. "But it already did."

Reiko stared at the women, and the barren landscape beyond them. Everything she saw was the result of her son's actions. Or were her son's actions the result of choices made here? She did not know if it mattered. The cogs in the gods' machine clicked forward.

"Are there any prophecies about Aya?"

Halldór nodded. "She's destined to—"

Reiko put her hand on his mouth as if she could stop fate. "Don't." She closed her eyes, fingers still resting on his lips. "If you bring her, promise me you won't let her know she's bound to the will of the gods."

He nodded.

Reiko withdrew her hand and pressed it to her temple. Her skull throbbed with potential decisions. Aya had already vanished into fire; if Reiko did not decide to bring her here, where would Aya go?

Her bound man knelt next to her, waiting for her decision. Aya would not forgive Reiko for yanking her out of time, any more than Reiko had forgiven Halldór.

His eyes flicked over her shoulder and then back. Reiko turned to follow his gaze. Mara comforted another girl. What did the future hold for Halldór's daughter? In this time, women seemed to have no role.

But times could change. Watching Mara, Reiko knew which path to choose if she were granted free will.

"Bring Aya to me." Reiko looked at the sword in her hand. "My daughter's birthright waits for her." ✪

SMITTEN

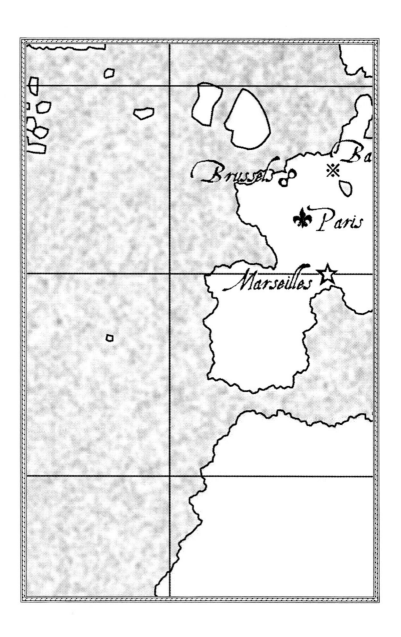

SMITTEN
BY ZOË SELENGUT

HUGO,

I am sorry for my part in what happened. That is the truth. He was
our friend, your cousin, and we meant well. I shall tell you the story and
you may judge.

Our friend Laurens was not a coward at heart. He could withstand suffering, especially that of others. He had the low, sloping forehead that in
Lavater denotes a brutish and criminal nature, but in him accompanied
a certain intensity and brilliance of intellect. Coupled with his bladelike
nose and rose-tipped mouth it gave him an impression of mingled sav-
agery and sweetness that brought women to their knees with lustful con-
fusion or, sometimes, confused lust. He was a very bad divinity student
and he drank. These were his primary faults, as we knew them. He was
not an adventurer or a gambler or a thief and he had never killed anyone
ever.

This is what I knew of him before.

It was raining when he fell in love. This—I should have said—was a
Thursday, so he was full of gin as well as wet. He wore a ring set with
an emerald, which signifies St. John the Evangelist, and he was walking
alone. The air was heavy and thick with the scent of lilies and he closed
his eyes against it. Because of the gin, he did not realize at first that he
had hurt himself when he walked into the woman, and when he knew
that he was hurt, he did not realize at first that it was because she was

281

made of stone. He apologized and fell down and then began to realize, and when he had got up he was not the same.

That is what he told us, after. That is all he would tell us of their meeting.

Some days later he appeared with her in the café.

Now, I don't want to distress you, Hugo, but it was not unheard of for Laurens to bring strange women there. He consorted with artists and wished to ape their ways; still, none of his women were what I would call *bad*. (Though I know what you would call me.) Neither I nor Fritz wanted to be rude, but we did wonder about her monochrome appearance, her inflexibility, her silence. She did not sit, nor drink. One of us must have said something, asked for an introduction. And then—

"She is a God—" he said, "a God. Ess. I worship, I follow, I obey, and I smite where smiting is called for. I am the arm of the Goddess. I am the fist of her wrath."

Her smooth face seemed to approve, as she gazed into the middle distance.

I must say that neither of us knew exactly what to make of this. Was this mere drunkenness? Poesy? A sort of philosophical position? Love, I think, was the explanation we decided on, though I did reflect that when other young men call their beloved a goddess you find in their speeches rather more of beauty, and less of wrath.

"I am the death of her enemies," said Laurens.

"She seems pleasant," I offered.

"I am the spear of her fury," said Laurens.

Fritz hid behind his newspaper.

Now—whatever he told you, to keep the peace and to keep himself in funds, Laurens had no faith and no desire for any. He thought he could make himself a very fine priest without it. But it was not easy for him. He dreamt many times that an old man was sitting by a deep, dark well, holding a fishing rod with a great iron hook attached. He knew when he awoke, terrified, that it was God, fishing for his soul. He felt himself at the edge of a great precipice of faith sometimes, and would cling to anything just so as not to fall.

(Laurens liked to tell people about his dreams. He felt it would be interesting for them.)

Why, then, he would consent to worship a Goddess just because she happened to appear before him in corporeal form, is a question I have some difficulty answering. He would not explain by what means she had suborned him from his scholarly duties. Only, he would say, she had told him *such things*. And she, she would not talk to us.

Laurens said we could call her Petra, although he said that wasn't her name. I thought I would be able to draw her out, once, when the men had gone out for cigarettes and left us sitting. Women together, and all that. Conspiratorial. I was also thinking of M. Baudelaire's poems about freezing Lesbians, and marble shoulders in the moonbeams, dreams of stone, if you want to know. (Probably you don't read such things. I'm sorry, Hugo, for suggesting you might.) But she wouldn't turn her face to me. She had one servant and one only. That servant soon returned from the *tabac* afire with purpose.

"She has given her command," he said. "She requires me to found a city."

"I found a city once," Fritz mumbled. "I got off the train and there it was. Like a shining star." (Fritz went to Marseilles once. He recalls it often. Marseilles is not like a shining star, and I do not believe it was any more so when Fritz was nineteen, either. Nevertheless.)

"So," said I. "A new Rome. From her lips to your shell-pink ears. Where is this city to be? In deepest Africa? In the hyperboreal regions? In Antarctica, among the penguins?" (Fritz tried to perk up at this; he is fond of penguins.) "There are not so many unsettled places in the known world now, and you know you have no army to subjugate the penguins, or whomever it may be, for your Goddess."

Laurens gazed at us, unruffled, austere.

"But I do," he said. "Of course I do. I have the two of you."

There was a thoughtful pause.

"And," he added, "we will not have to travel so far. My Goddess has taken a liking to Bruxelles; she is tired of over-hot regions. We will raze selected municipal buildings, put some of the inhabitants to the sword, intermarry with others. Out of the smoking ruins will climb an undying race, a ceaseless city. It will bear our rule and glorify Her name forever."

—Hugo, if you can bear to put your fondness for your cousin aside for a moment, I feel sure you will recognize the difficulty we found our-selves in at this moment. It is different for you, I know; you love the country, and sheep, and milkmaids; you hate sin, and vice, and drunk-enness, and lechery, and crowds, and all the many other evils of urban living in this sad century. So it would not seem like such a terrible loss to you, a city not even of the first rank, and furthermore, as his rela-tive, you would share in the reflected glory of his conquest. But for us it was very uncomfortable. Fritz studied in Bruxelles—the university, I may remind you, is not yet many decades old, and deserves a chance to survive. I have a sister who lives there, although I am not very fond of her. It's not so easy to aim straight at the heart of glory when you have scruples. And we do have scruples, Hugo, we do. And don't think it wasn't a temptation to join him, when he called us his Army. I have been a seamstress and an artist's model, but I have never been a soldier. I don't expect anyone will offer me the chance to be one ever again, either. I have regrets.

One day he arrived without her, and a great hope sprang up within us—within me—that he was finished with the whole business. His devotion had faded. I had been sure it would. He had called me a goddess once too, I reminded him, and look how little attention he paid to me now.

"Yes—" he said; "but you know, Marya, when I said that of you I meant that you were a very pretty girl, if a little proud, and that I should have liked to go to bed with you. When I say it of her I mean she screams across the empty regions of the sky and I beg her to make of my soul one tiny spot of light in her blazing crown. Not the same thing, you see."

Well; these are the things a man says to you sometimes, and you try not to be hurt. This was the moment, however, at which the crux of the problem for me became saving Bruxelles, not saving Laurens. For he had actually lost none of his fervor; he was drawing up plans for a temple, in fact, that was to go in the Grand-Place. Laurens's grasp of architecture is extremely weak, I don't need to tell you. He showed me his drawing. It had lots of columns. I admired it, which pleased him, and set off to do what I was certain had to be done.

I don't mean that his artistic offenses and personal remarks meant more to me than the larger moral issues—death and pillaging, and so forth. Please don't think that. It just seemed suddenly all very immediate and threatening, and I thought there was no hope of him changing his mind. This is a point upon which the futures of nations and empires turn, I thought; I must be brave.

She wasn't with him, as I said; she had told Laurens how little she liked the loudness and unpleasantness of the places he took her. He had appealed to Fritz, who had agreed to let her stay in his workshop with the other statues, until she had a temple of her own to live in. Laurens was planning; Fritz was out drawing somewhere. I had a key. I seized my chance.

I went there alone. I took up a chisel and a hammer and went up to her. As a last, hopeless gesture, I cut my thumb and put the blood to her lips. I'm well-enough read; I know that's for the dead, not the gods, but I thought they might like the same sort of things.

"This is your last chance," I told her. "We can discuss this like rational people. You can choose a better acolyte. I could design you a better temple, at the very least." She put out her stone tongue to taste, and then, as my heart wildly lifted, said nothing at all. Her eyes closed. Her contempt was clear. I lifted the chisel to her neck and waited for her to strike. If she had paid enough attention to me to hinder me from my awful deed, I might have let her be, let a fine city and centuries of progress be damned.

I was not stricken.

When I left the atelier, there was a fine white coating of dust all over me. People stared at me as I walked home, and some said things.

I did feel blasphemous and sinful taking her apart the way I did, but as Laurens said, it was only one of her earthly manifestations and she can make as many more as she chooses. I hope the next one will be far in the future, or far from here. I shouldn't like to destroy her twice.

I didn't see Laurens for two days after that. When he next spoke to me, he said he had been in Hell, or Elysium. He said it was all part of the preparation for his great task. He said his little kitten, Ferdinand, that died of drowning, greeted him and bade him not falter nor lose heart. He didn't say if he had had to give it blood to drink before it would speak to him. He said his two dead great-uncles were there too.

That was the last thing he said to me. I was shaking. I felt, not guilty, but ashamed. He said he had passed through a gate of fire. He didn't mark my condition; his eyes were full of the underworld, large with ambition. Then he left me, and he must have gone to the atelier, and seen what I'd done. He never came back. I do not know what became of him. I hope he is alive.

In conclusion, Hugo, I entreat you to understand the circumstances in which we found ourselves. To understand all is to forgive all—I believe that. I understand how little inclined you may be to do me any favor, but do not, at least, blame Fritz for any of this. He is a gentle soul, and had no part in my actions. He has begun a new canvas, very large, in oils—there are no menacing female figures in white or pale grey, which is what I was afraid of; only a vast landscape with ice floes and darkening sky.

Marya ✪

THE LAST DAY OF REA

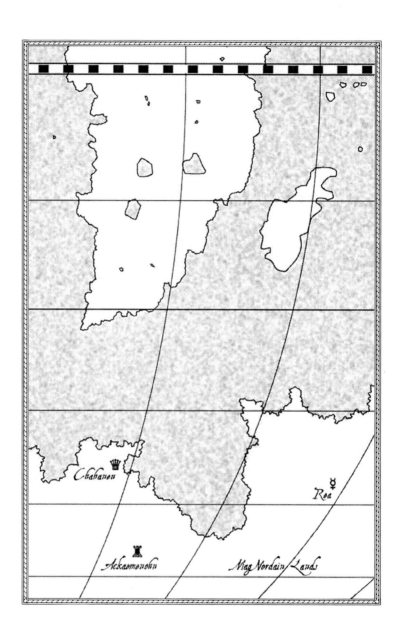

Chahanou

Rea

Ackaemenohn

Mag Nordain Lands

THE LAST DAY OF REA
BY IAN MCHUGH

"The armies of Imperial Chahanesh seem like a sea of polished steel *from the hilltop that His Divine Personage, Cyrus the Forty-Second, King-of-Kings and Lord-Of-All-He-Surveys, has chosen from which to enjoy his impending victory over the Heretics of Rea . . ."*

The Historian paused, realizing he had forgotten a full stop somewhere along the way. He read the sentence aloud and ran out of breath at *Surveys*. He clucked his tongue, then shrugged. If florid language was what the megalomaniac wanted, then florid language was what the megalomaniac got. He continued writing.

"The bright banners of the many regiments and legions are like the sails of ships upon the metal waves, flapping proudly in the gentle breeze, while thousands upon thousands of helms and spearpoints glitter in the bright morning sunlight . . ."

The Historian sat just outside the impervious human wall of the King's Personal Guard, alongside the Imperial Baggage Handlers and the priests of the lesser Gods and Saints and assorted courtesans and hangers-on. He scribbled in his parchment notebook while he observed the disposition of the regiments below with an aged and cynical eye. He waxed lyrical about the stirring sight of sixty thousand terrified men and boys being herded to their brutal fates. And thanked all the Gods and Saints that his own grandsons had been saved by privilege and scholarly talent from participation in the approaching bloodbath.

He briefly listed a few provincial regiments whose banners he recognised, then gave most of his attention to the legions of *"tall, handsome"*

Chahanen warriors. *"The least and most common"* of whom was *"as a lord among the lesser folk of the Empire."* History, of course, is written by the winners and, cynic though he often was, the Historian was also Chahanen to the bone. His people had written the history of half the Western world for more than twelve centuries.

"The battle magicians, those paragons of Imperial might, prepare their potent sorceries while they are borne among the legions in their curtained litters or circle high overhead on their flying carpets, like eagles wheeling before the strike. The great siege engines and wheeled towers of the Imperial Engineers and mighty war elephants from Malgurya rise like breaching leviathans amid the metal waves . . ."

He savoured that simile for a moment, pleased with himself, before moving on to record by name those lords and generals whose stellae came close enough for him to identify.

". . . Prince Uvash of Eshanth, youngest brother of Crown Prince Simesh, parades past with his brave captains and dips his banners before He-Who-Brings-The-Morning. The Prince is noted as a brilliant tactician and his inspired leadership was instrumental in the great Imperial victory at . . ."

The Historian's pencil hovered above the parchment. He frowned. He couldn't think of any previous military engagements at all—victorious or otherwise—that the fat dullard Prince Uvash had ever been even remotely associated with.

His brow cleared.

". . . instrumental in the great Imperial victory at Brantohilde that saw the final extermination of the renascent Fazhgumackhid Assassins."

He sniggered to himself, imagining the consternation this sentence would cause to future students of Imperial history. The Fazhgumackhid Assassins were the invention of an early predecessor, who had needed to add some respectability to the otherwise laughable military exploits of Cyrus the Thirteenth. It was an in-joke that separated the men from the boys in scholarly circles. Brantohilde was the name of the Historian's blessedly departed mother-in-law.

Still chuckling, he took a moment to stretch his back, straightening for a moment from his habitual stoop. Then he noted in his book the continued absence of the legions from Ackaemenohn. *"Delayed, so the farseers say, by an uprising in Sinridis."*

Strange news, the Historian thought, given that the rest of the King's army had passed most recently through that northern province and seen no sign of unrest. Still, the magicians reported from their scrying bowls that the Ackaemen army was indeed busy torching fields and butchering Sinridish villagers.

The Divinely Blessed Personage was less than pleased with the tardiness of the Lord of Ackaemenohn. The Historian could hear He-Who-Commands-The-Tide's petulant outbursts from within the wall of bodyguards every time he demanded to know where the Ackaemen army was—and was fretfully informed they still hadn't shifted from the Sinridish border. The Historian wrote that *"the displeasure of He-Who-Levels-Mountains-With-A-Glance is fearsome to behold and the cowardly Lord of Ackaemenohn will surely expire from sheer terror when the snivelling wretch is finally brought before his King."*

He set his book aside at this point, pleased with himself. Already he had the basis of an account that would, with only a little more embellishment, suit even the unexcelled hubris of He-Who-Scattered-The-Stars-Upon-The-Night. The Historian tucked his pencil behind his ear and tugged his tabac pouch from his belt, tamping his pipe with lead-stained fingers. A click of thumb and fingertips produced a small spark. It was the full extent of his meagre magical talent—and the reason he had been quietly evicted from the College of Magicians all those years ago and sentenced to a life of scholarly rectitude. He sucked happily on his pipe.

A shadow fell across him. He squinted up into the acne-infested face of an Imperial Messenger.

"His Imperial Majesty requires your presence, Historian," the youth said, conspicuously omitting the 'My Lord' from in front of 'Historian'.

The Historian sighed and smothered his pipe. "Of course he does," he muttered. "What for?"

The Messenger only sneered—meaning he hadn't being paying attention enough to know the answer.

Arrogant whelp, the Historian thought. The boy's ugly mug was familiar, but he couldn't quite place which lord of the Empire had spawned the insolent sprog. He gathered his staff from the grass beside him and, with creaking knees, hauled himself to his feet.

"Bring my stool," he commanded the Messenger. The boy made no move to comply, so the Historian smacked him viciously across the shins with his staff. Amid the amused titters of the nearby courtiers and priests, and without waiting to see if the boy followed, the old man hobbled off in the direction of his liege.

The Personal Guard shuffled aside to let the Historian and the limping Messenger pass. They were the finest troops in the Imperial Army. The finest Chahanen troops, anyway, and as far as history was concerned, that was the same thing. Sadly, their armour was so ornate they could barely walk, let alone raise arms to defend themselves—even if the oversized ironmongery they had been given to lug about wasn't just as absurd as their armour. They looked, the Historian thought, like they had been dressed by a mad cake decorator gone berserk in a blacksmith's forge. His Impervious Ignorance had, naturally, designed the armour himself.

The Historian passed through the circle of incapacitated Guards and approached the huge, gold-leafed and silk-curtained litter that bore The Blessed Imbecile. The clutch of people around the litter included the most senior generals and magicians, their staff officers and an assortment of body slaves, plus the high priests of the eight Greater Gods of the Chahanen Pantheon. The generals had, with vast satisfaction, cited the exigencies of the battlefield and evicted the usual circus of painted sycophants from the makeshift inner sanctum.

Also present, hovering most closely beside the royal litter, was the

Sumoran Ambassador, dressed in functional black armour and looking comfortable wearing it. The dwarf—again, much to the generals' satisfaction—had been stripped of his weapons. His usual retinue of guards had been evicted along with the rest.

The Historian noted with interest a Gar dwarf slave—a gift from the Ambassador's predecessor—glaring daggers at the Mor's back. The Gar, wearing nothing but a slave's vest and short kilt, had muscles on his muscles and bore a fighter's scars on his face, chest and arms. Even shaved and tortured into submission, he struck the Historian as a formidable figure.

The Gar was not the only vanquished foe among the King's slaves. The litter itself was so big it took eight burly men to lift it. It was a conceit of this particular Son of Heaven that his litter should be borne by captured enemy warriors—a proclivity that made his Guards and generals distinctly nervous. At each of the rear corners of the litter loomed a tusked, yellow-skinned ogre from the southern continent. At one front corner was a black-skinned djinn, elvish kin from the fierce desert across the Summer Sea. The remaining litter bearers were pale, bearded MagNordain barbarians from the northern plains, alike in colouring and features to men of Chahanesh, but taller and half-again as broad. One of the MagNordain, older than the others, wore the facial scars of a tribal chieftain and bulked larger than even the two ogres.

The King's slaves were supposed to be mind-broken and submissive. Certainly the gaggle of young halfling girls who saw to the most intimate bodily needs of He-Who-Is-Excessively-Pampered appeared to be so. But the MagNordain chief in particular observed the Historian's approach with a disquieting alertness. The Historian wondered if the standards of the Imperial Torturers had slipped in recent times.

The Warlord of Imperial Chahanesh was talking urgently to the young King-of-Kings. From the thunderous expression on what little could be seen of the Mor's face above his enormous silver-shot beard, the Historian guessed that the Warlord and the Ambassador were at odds yet again.

The figure reclining in the gauzy shade of the litter silenced the Warlord with a languid flick of the wrist when the Historian arrived. Veins popped out on the old soldier's temple and his jaw muscles bulged as he clamped his teeth abruptly shut. The Historian hid a grin by bowing as low as his arthritis would allow.

He-Who-Raises-Insufferability-To-An-Artform left him there an inordinately long time before commanding, "Rise, Historian."

Now it was the Warlord's turn to smirk from behind the King's back. The Historian ignored him and contrived to gaze worshipfully upon the chinless, watery-eyed visage of the inbred little streak of piss who was his monarch. The Blessed Imbecile's beloved father had been an inbred little streak of piss, too. But he at least had possessed the grace and wit to let the generals and senate run the Empire while he whiled away his days in the Royal Harem having sex with his sisters.

It had been that way among the Kings of Chahanesh for about twenty generations now, ever since the infamous Cyrus the Thirteenth decided he rather fancied the look of his sister and contrived to have himself exempted from the laws governing incest. Or, as the Royal Historian of the day had rationalised it, he had taken the action *"in order to ensure the preservation of the pure blood of Cyrus the Great in the veins of the Kings of the Eternal Empire."*

The lords and mages of Chahanesh and its provinces had found, after a time, that the results of severe inbreeding in the royal family rather suited them, leaving them relatively free to run the Empire as they pleased and reap the profits of doing so. Unfortunately, the present Cyrus—having impatiently murdered his docile sire—had rather different ideas and fancied he was the reincarnation of Cyrus the Great.

"What humble service may it be my eternal pleasure to provide Your Most Divinely Ordained Majesty?" the Historian asked.

"That," the boy exclaimed nasally to the Warlord and assembled generals, magicians and priests, "is the appropriate way to address one's monarch." He turned back to the Historian, head jiggling on his scrawny neck. Stoned as a menhir, the Historian thought.

"The Heretics wish to parley," said the King. "You will parley with them on Our behalf."

The Historian was mildly surprised at the astuteness of the command. As a student of languages and cultures past and present, he was without doubt the best qualified of the King's retainers to communicate effectively with persons from an unknown foreign culture. From the satisfied expression on the face of the Warlord, the Historian surmised that the idea had come from him. The sour expression of the Sumoran Ambassador confirmed it.

The High Priest of the Guardian of the Source, a cadaverous old stick of enormous dignity and rigid conservatism, ventured forward. Striking a pose that somehow managed to convey both diffidence and condescension, he said, "Most Majestic, might I suggest that it would be better for we clergy to conduct the negotiation. We are, after all, the best equipped to defend Your Holiness's purity of mind from the ungodly perversions of these heretics . . ."

The Blessed Imbecile hissed at him irritably and said, "No, you mightn't suggest! Now bugger off!"

Several magicians and generals smothered sudden coughing fits. The High Priest's already wrinkled face puckered up like a prune at He-Who-Wouldn't-Know-A-Dangerous-Enemy-If-They-Stuck-A-Dagger-In-His-Back's rudeness. He bowed his head stiffly and muttered something that sounded like "Yes, Omnipotence," but could have been "Yes, Incontinence," instead.

The Blessed Imbecile didn't notice. With an offended sniff, the High Priest stalked back to his fellow clerics.

"Do they come for parley already, Omnipotence?" the Historian asked, pronouncing the honorific with exaggerated clarity. The High Priest of the Guardian sneered at him.

The King had lapsed back on his cushions, exhausted by his confrontation with the High Priest, and was calling for wine. He waved a limp-jointed arm, indicating that the Historian should pursue his conversation with the Warlord.

With the barest arching of his brows, the Warlord said levelly, "They approach as we speak. They came from the city in a floating contrivance under a flag of truce, but were forced by our troops to abandon it and are being conveyed here on foot."

The Warlord took the Historian aside then, to stand facing the domes of Rea, so their faces were obscured from the view of the Mor and the priests.

"Get us out of this, old friend," the Warlord murmured, "so that we can go deal with that Ackaemen upstart."

Old friend, eh? The Historian thought to himself. He and the Warlord had known each other for many years but, while there was no antipathy between them, they had never developed any deep friendship either.

"It is rebellion then?" the Historian asked, equally quietly, and when the Warlord nodded he muttered, "Still, it was only a matter of time."

"Oh?"

"Before someone decided the possible rewards of raising a rebel flag were worth the risk of being stabbed in the back by his fellow lords."

The Warlord flashed him a wry grin, quickly smothered.

"But I would not have expected it to be that toad Ackaemenohn who took the lead," the Historian mused, "nor did I expect a move so soon."

"Who did you think it would be?" the Warlord asked.

Now it was the Historian's turn to flash a grin. "You."

The Warlord allowed himself a brief bark of laughter and clapped the Historian on the back. The old scholar knew then he had not been too far from the mark: Ackaemenohn had only just stolen the march on the Warlord of Chahanesh.

"Ackaemenohn would be little more than a nuisance," said the Warlord, "if His Inflexible Recalcitrance were not so determined to smash this army to pieces on the anvil of Rea. It helps not at all that the thrice-cursed dwarf keeps egging him on. Did you notice, Historian, that the provincial lords have sent to this fight the paltriest contingents of half-trained conscripts they could get away with?"

The Historian was chagrined that he had not—having been too enamoured with the cleverness of his own prose—but he shrugged non-committally rather than admit his failure of perception.

The Warlord continued, "The other lords have held back. They wait to see which way the contest between Chahanesh and Ackaemenohn goes before they commit to either cause. This army is the main strength of Chahanesh proper. Should this battle go ill, we will struggle to contain Ackaemenohn's ambitions."

"What of the College?"

"The magicians are split. Ackaemenohn has suborned perhaps one in ten."

"And the rest?"

"Most stand aside, as the lords do, for now. More are with us than against, though. We think most of the temples have gone over to Ackae-menohn." The Warlord looked directly at the Historian. "Get us out of this, old friend."

So, the Historian thought, it is time to take sides.

He met the other man's gaze squarely. "Be assured, I will do my utmost," he replied.

The Warlord gave a sharp nod and returned to his generals to discuss the disposition of his army. The Historian beckoned to the recalcitrant Messenger, still holding his stool, and bade him set down the seat and fetch a cup of water. He retrieved his pipe and was pleased to find the half-burnt plug hadn't spilled out while it was in his pocket.

Holding his pipe between his teeth, he opened his book and took his pencil from behind his ear to jot a few more notes. He recorded the presence in the army of three regiments of Mor dwarves, commanded, so the Historian understood, by the Ambassador's brother: *"hook faced*

and bristle bearded, stark in their black robes and black-metal armour, like grim harbingers among the brightly coloured ranks of the Imperial legions. Allies, these, rather than subjects; from Sumor across the Inland Sea. Fell and frightful friends for even one so great and divinely blessed as the King of Chahanesh."
And worse enemies, the Historian thought to himself, though he did not write it. He shuddered to think what perverse treasures the Mors hoped to find inside Rea.

He scanned the army, squinting to make out the most distant units. The Warlord was right about the paltry contributions of the provinces. The Sumorans were probably the largest contingent after the Chahanen troops. Even so, the army comprised the strength of an empire, brought to destroy a single city.

Overkill, he thought.

Of course, this was no ordinary city.

His gaze travelled past the Imperial host to the clutch of low white domes nestled against the feet of the mountains across the valley. *"Rea: City of Heretics. Where a strange and secretive folk hide their faces from the light of the sun and work their furtive and ungodly alchemies."*

Or so it was said, anyway. No-one had seen a denizen of Rea in generations. The Historian was aware of a handful of ancient and contradictory tablets from the long defunct and mostly forgotten Sinridish kingdom. These described the Rea variously: as bloodless beings, ghostlike and pale of skin, eye and hair; as giants encased in armour who hurled lightning from their hands; as gods who ascended into the heavens upon pillars of fire; or as elvish-kin, who rode about in magical horseless carriages rather than upon the backs of wyverns and stranger beasts, as the elf lords were wont to do.

The Sinridishmen of old had worshipped the Rea as gods until Cyrus the Great, founder of the Eternal Empire of Chahanesh, razed their kingdom and put their apostasy to the sword. In the centuries since, Cyrus' successors had found neither the opportunity nor the inclination to deal with Rea itself. They were far more interested in conquering their neighbours and exchanging petty raids with the MagNordain giants and the halfling folk of Gil'gamech. And they were far more worried by the Witch-Kings of Yngrehl and the possibility of a union among the Mor nations than they were by the reclusive folk of Rea in their solitary city.

Of course, the Historian didn't write any of this in his book, either. Nor did he write that this most recent Cyrus had, immediately upon ascending to the throne and against the advice of all his generals, foolishly embarked on a massive but ultimately unsuccessful pogrom against the MagNordain. Having thoroughly irritated the barbarian tribes, He-Of-Unrivalled-Imprudence had stripped his empire's borders of half their defenders and marched them here—to destroy a city on the edge of the world, that bothered no-one and which few remembered as anything other than a fairy tale. Unfortunately, this most spoiled and coddled of all the Cyruses to have succeeded the First had little concept that his Empire was, not only finite, but surrounded by enemies both immediately and potentially great.

It took nearly an hour for the Heretics to be conveyed on foot to the presence of The Blessed Imbecile. The Historian snapped out of a light doze when they arrived, to observe with considerable fascination the two pallid, oddly dressed people thrust forward by a squad of Chahanen infantrymen and made to kneel before His Incestuousness.

The Historian hauled himself to his feet and hustled over on creaky legs to confront the Heretics before any of the priests could jump in and spoil everything.

In the tongue of the old Sinridish kingdom, he said, "Abase yourselves, Heretics. Your lives are at stake."

The Heretics—they were a man and a woman, the Historian saw on closer inspection, both apparently of late middle-age—lifted their heads. "I can speak Chahanen," the male said, in that language.

The Historian sighed and swore softly under his breath

The High Priest of the Guardian leapt forward, preceded by an accusing claw. "Heretic! Do you come before the Son of Heaven to deny the existence of the Gods?"

The Heretic frowned at him in bemusement. "No, of course not. The beings you call gods are quite real."

"Ah." The High Priest blinked, nonplussed. His finger sagged.

The High Priestess of the Keeper of Knowledge came to his rescue. In a dangerously nonchalant drawl she asked the Heretic, "Do you, then, acknowledge the sovereignty of the Gods over mortal beings?"

The Heretic licked his lips. "We believe that mortals hold their destiny in their own hands and are ruled only by their own self-imposed limitations," he replied.

The High Priest of the Guardian took a moment to work through the Heretic's response, then his face lit up in triumph. The finger lashed out once more. "He dares utter his heresy before The Divine Personage! Death, I say!"

The Historian looked to the Warlord for assistance, but the old warrior only shrugged.

"Oh, very well," came a weary voice from the royal litter, "if it will make you happy. Kill him."

The Historian noted the quick glance the infantry captain shot toward the Warlord, and the slight nod he received in response, before he obeyed the royal command. The Heretic had barely opened his mouth to protest when the sword came down on the back of his neck.

The Historian turned his face away, not wishing to see the blow. "What a waste," he murmured to himself.

He turned back to the remaining Heretic. The woman was staring open-mouthed, goggle-eyed and white-faced in horror at the twitching corpse of her compatriot. The Historian tapped her on the arm with the butt of his staff.

She looked unsteadily up at him.

"Speak to me in Old Sinridish," he said.

"I too speak Chahanen," the Heretic stammered, but in Old Sinridish.

"Speak Chahanen and you will end up the same way, fool," the Historian growled. The Heretic's eyes flickered down and back again. The Historian went on. "You and I are the only ones here who speak Old Sinridish. Things are afoot of which you know nothing. Speak to me only in Old Sinridish and you and your city may live beyond this day."

The Heretic nodded mutely. The Historian turned his back on her then and approached the King's litter. After bowing low again, he said, "Forgive me, O He-Who-Bestrides-The-Globe-And-Holds-Up-The-Sky, but this poor Heretic speaks no word of Chahanen."

He-Who-Possesses-The-Concentration-Of-A-Gnat sighed. "How tiresome."

The Historian ignored the suspicious glowers of the priests and the Sumoran Ambassador. "Indeed, Most Majestic, I would be most hesitant to subject you to the tedium of translating the entire negotiation. Might I be so bold as to suggest that I converse with the Heretic directly in Old Sinridish and with your authority, Your Beautificence . . ." The Historian hesitated for a couple of heartbeats, realising he had just invented a word. He shrugged to himself and swept on. "Ah, to negotiate the surrender of the City of Heretics to Your Imperial Righteousness."

The Mor looked like he was about to speak, but the Warlord stepped in smoothly. "Perhaps Your Divinity would prefer to take an early luncheon while this tiresome matter is resolved?"

"Excellent idea!" The-Anus-From-Whence-The-Sun-Doth-Shine exclaimed. "We have decided that We will take an early luncheon."

Amid the sudden flurry of activity around the litter, the Historian gestured to a pair of infantrymen to bring the surviving Heretic. He led them over to where he had left his stool and sank gratefully back onto his seat. At a second gesture from the Historian, the soldiers released the Heretic's arms and retreated a few paces.

"Sit," the Historian bade her, retrieving his pipe.

The Heretic dropped cross-legged onto the grass. She watched in some amazement as the Historian lit the pipeweed with his finger. With a sudden, shuddering breath, tears came. She lowered her head and retreated into her grief. The Historian puffed on his pipe and waited for her to regain her composure.

"We have the means to defend ourselves," the Heretic said, after a while and without raising her head.

"I rather suspected as much," said the Historian.

"Many of your people will perish if you attack."

"Mm," the Historian agreed.

The Heretic fell silent. The Historian fancied he could almost see the thoughts flying around inside her head. Abruptly, she looked up at him, eyes burning with a sudden intensity. "Why must you attack us? We are no threat to you."

"You are Heretics," said the Historian. "The Gods command that you must submit or be destroyed. I am afraid I am not the arbiter of such matters."

"Do you truly believe it is the will of your gods that drives this army and not mortal ambition?"

The Historian allowed himself a slight smile. "When one is in the service of a divinely inspired King, the two are not mutually exclusive."

"Are you not, then, a god-fearing person?"

The Historian arched an eyebrow. "I don't wear a copper hat in the middle of the Temple Quarter and stand decrying the Gods as frauds. The Gods of Chahanesh are real." He clicked his fingers to make a spark leap towards the Heretic's face. She flinched. "They repay our fealty with tangible gifts." He sat back. "And I would much rather bend my back to Chahanen Gods than to the Underlords of Mor or the Witch-Gods of Yngrehl."

The Heretic hung her head again.

"Your nation is threatened," she said. "But not by us. The tribes of the MagNordain . . ."

"Yes, there are the barbarians. And there are the Yngrehl and the Gil'gadin and the Gars and the bloody Mors," said the Historian, cutting her off. He deemed it better not to mention the Empire's present internal difficulties. "Chahanesh has not endured so long because we are complete fools."

Not all of us, anyway, he amended under his breath.

"There is an army at your rear."

The Historian managed to keep his surprise off his face. How did she know about Ackaemenohn? Perhaps, he guessed, the folk of Rea had devised some way of scrying that was not a gift from the Gods.

"Yes, we know," he said.

The Heretic seemed nonplussed. "You do? Then why do you not leave to confront it?"

The Historian laughed harshly. "Because to do so would be the action of reasonable men," he said. "And reasonable men are badly outnumbered here today."

"We could force you to fight," she whispered.

The Historian had been around long enough to know an empty threat when he heard it. "And this army will roll over your city and it will be no more."

"You know nothing of our defences. The carnage will be terrible."

"Are your defences enough to save you?"

The Heretic's teary-eyed stare was filled with hate and helpless anger.

"I thought not," said the Historian.

"You said before, when . . ." Her voice faltered as she gestured toward the spot where her dead countryman still lay. "You spoke of things afoot of which we know nothing, but it is you who do not even begin to grasp the extent of your ignorance."

"Oh?"

"My people have harnessed the energies of the universe." The Heretic thumped her thin chest for emphasis, her voice finding sudden strength. "We have done this for ourselves. Our knowledge is hard-earned, but the power it has provided us reduces even the greatest of your god-given gifts to mere party tricks."

"Party tricks that can level your city," the Historian reminded her, mildly.

She jabbed a finger at him. "We could have striven with the gods for mastery of this world, had we so chosen!"

The Historian leaned forward on his stool. "Then why did you not?"

The Heretic subsided under the intensity of his glare, the fire going out of her as quickly as it had come. She sighed heavily. "Because we had no stomach for genocide. Instead, we built machines to carry us up, above the sky. On this earth we left just one small outpost, to harvest the things only a living world can provide. The lights you see on the moon are not the palaces of the gods, but the great cities of my people."

The Historian glanced up automatically, although it was the middle of the day. "Now *that*," he said, "is a heresy that would have you executed as quick as your comrade."

He fell silent. Despite his quip, his gut told him the Heretic spoke in earnest. His thoughts went to the mad writings of old Sinridis. *"Beings who ascended to heaven on pillars of fire . . ."* He tried to imagine cities on the moon and nights lit by earthlight; to imagine the machines that would take men there.

The Historian licked his lips. "And if we destroy your outpost, will your countrymen rain death on us from the moon?"

The Heretic replied, softly, "We forswore that option long ago."

Not that you could not, the Historian thought, but that you have chosen not to do so. Such power . . .

He did not realise he had spoken this last aloud until the Heretic said, "We could share it with you."

The Historian's mind snapped back into sharp focus. "Share it?"

He leapt to his feet with unaccustomed agility, dragging the Heretic up with him. The Historian pointed. "Do you see those black regiments?

They are Mors, here to take everything you have, not accept whatever tidbits you might offer. Can you *imagine* what such as they would do with your knowledge?"

The Heretic watched him, thoughtfully, as he trembled with sudden passion. She nodded.

The Historian's gaze drifted upward, to the battle mages circling on their flying carpets. *"Like eagles wheeling before the strike,"* he had written earlier. Like crows waiting to feast on the carrion, he thought, now.

He twisted to look at the royal party. The Ruler of the World was shamelessly fucking one of his slave girls while the generals, priests and magicians feasted. Only a couple of yards from the royal litter and the trestles around which lords of the Empire gathered, the dead Heretic still lay where he had been struck down.

What savages we are.

The slave girl was facing toward the Historian and her eyes met his. He turned away in shame and disgust and sank back to his seat.

He was silent again for a long time.

Eventually, he said, "Would you flee, if I could give you the chance?"

"In truth, we are already preparing to do so," the Heretic replied. "We need only a little more time."

Feeling a new resolve, the Historian nodded. "We must speak to the Warlord."

As though anticipating the Historian's need, the old warrior arrived beside them at that moment.

"It would be well if the surrender of Rea were resolved quickly," he rumbled. "His Phenomenal Intemperance has eaten his fill and sown his seed and will soon become impatient."

The Historian rose to face him. "The Heretics must not surrender," he said. "Nor must we take the city by force."

The Warlord raised his eyebrows in surprise. "Indeed. Why not?"

"Have you considered," said the Historian, "that the fabled alchemies of Rea are real?"

The Warlord glanced down at the Heretic, still seated near their feet. "Do you believe so?"

"I am certain of it," said the Historian. "What of the consequences if Sumor got hold of that knowledge?"

The Warlord stroked his chin, staring out at the domes of Rea. Or if anyone else got hold of it, the Historian could imagine him thinking, other than the Warlord of Chahanesh.

"What, then," said the Warlord, "do you propose?"

"We must allow the Heretics to escape."

The Warlord shook his head. "Impossible. The damage to my reputation would be irreparable."

The damage to your ambitions, you mean, thought the Historian. He said, "Not if you immediately seized power."

"You push me into treason, Historian," the Warlord said, his tone dangerous.

"That you were plotting already," the Historian countered.

The Warlord growled deep in his throat. He decided quickly.

"So be it. I will endeavour to distract . . ." He trailed off, his gaze caught by something in the distance. Colour drained from his face. "What the . . . ?"

Alarmed, the Historian turned to see what had shocked him so. The Heretic rose beside them.

The army of Chahanesh was on the move.

"I gave no order," the Warlord spluttered, then bellowed, "*I gave no order!*"

He spun to face the royal litter and roared, "What in the name of all the Gods and Saints is going on?"

"How dare you speak to Us that way!" the King of Chahanesh shrieked. "*We* have ordered *Our* army to attack, while *you* were stuffing your fat face and while the Heretics think we are still negotiating!"

"Stop them!" the Heretic cried. "You don't know what you're doing!"

"No!" The Historian restrained her as she made to push past him.

"You did this!" the Warlord thundered at the Sumoran Ambassador, ignoring both the Heretic and the Blessed Imbecile.

"We did this!" the King screamed. *"We, We, We!* Dare you challenge Our right?"

Everyone froze and all eyes fixed on the Warlord. The tableau held for a breathless minute. The Warlord raised his chin and drew himself up. He pointed at the King. "You: be silent, or I will have you killed this minute." Then at the Mor. "Seize him."

The Blessed Imbecile's eyes bulged so far from his head the Historian thought they might actually pop out. The boy sputtered incoherently. The Ambassador submitted silently as two soldiers pushed him to the ground.

To the priests the Warlord said, "Any objections?"

As one, the clerics mutely shook their heads. The Warlord glanced at the magicians. With a slight smile, the Chancellor of the College of Magicians shook his head as well. The Warlord swept his gaze across the surrounding ranks of the Personal Guard. Not a man moved.

"Find me messengers!" the Warlord bellowed, and started firing off instructions. The soldiers who had brought the Heretics began shedding their heavier accoutrements, the better to aid their running. The magicians ran for their carpets and launched themselves skyward.

Too late, the Historian thought, as he turned again to watch the Chahanen army advance. Too late.

An instant later his fears were confirmed. A bolt of blue flame lashed out from the top of a dome and detonated amid one of the foremost regiments. Men and broken bits of men were flung into the air. The magicians responded in kind, pasting the domes with a storm of sorcerous energy. The catapults of the Imperial Engineers launched their missiles. The city retaliated with more fire. Catapults were smashed apart and flying carpets blasted out of the sky. Amongst it all, the common soldiers of Chahanesh surged forward in blind terror and were slaughtered in their hundreds.

A well-aimed spell struck a point already badly weakened on one of the domes. With a thunderous boom, the whole side of the dome collapsed inward. The leading regiments charged forward over the rubble and into the city. Moments later a second dome was punctured by a hail of stones from a catapult battery.

No metal giants from legend came out to meet the soldiers at either breach. As the minutes passed, the blue fire from the domes grew sporadic and soon ceased altogether. The Historian felt oddly and uncomfortably disappointed that the city seemed to be succumbing so easily.

A tower arose among the domes and levitated on a pillar of fire. The Historian heard a collective gasp of wonder and terror that seemed to come from every throat in the Chahanen host. With ponderous grace, the flying tower moved out over the battlefield. A trio of magicians swooped toward it on their carpets, but the great machine incinerated them all with bolts of blue, swatting them as a man might swat a fly.

The Heretic, half-forgotten at the Historian's side while he watched the battle, turned to him and said, "I tried to warn you, though you didn't deserve it. And you wouldn't listen, in any case. I tried to reason with you, but you know too little of reason.

"We will not destroy you from the heavens—there is no need. You will reap the harvest of your own ignorance."

She touched the bracelet on her wrist. The Historian stumbled back in alarm as her body started to shimmer. A soldier leapt forward and swung his sword, but the Heretic had already vanished from sight.

The burning tail of the Heretics' flying machine blasted downward to strike the earth, vaporising a regiment at the foot of the hill on which the royal party stood. The Historian and all those around him staggered and raised their arms to protect themselves as hot air scorched their skins.

The Historian watched numbly as the flying tower rose swiftly into the sky and dwindled in the distance above.

Then the city exploded.

Hundreds of soldiers both inside and out died at once. An instant later the Historian staggered again as the blast wave hit the hilltop. He would have fallen if the Warlord had not caught his elbow. Together, they watched in horror as whole regiments broke and ran while fiery debris rained down on their heads. Terrified elephants and horses trampled fleeing soldiers underfoot in their haste to escape.

A horn sounded. The Historian felt icy fingers run down his spine: the sound had come from behind him.

Beside him, the Warlord whispered, "Ackaemenohn."

Together, they turned to face this new threat. Dazed, they watched an ocean of mounted warriors pour down the side of the valley and fall like a tsunami upon the Chahanen rear guard. The Warlord was wrong. The newcomers were not squat, ruddy skinned Ackaemen. These warriors were tall and fair, broad and wild.

"Damn me," the Historian said. "There must be every bloody barbarian off the plains in that lot."

"There is an army at your back," he recalled the Heretic's words. She had played him like a virtuoso, he realised. She had given him every opportunity to save the situation, but the Heretics had planned for this outcome all along.

And we were all too busy stabbing each other in the back to notice the hammer about to fall on our heads. He felt a chuckle bubble up inside his throat. The Historian started to laugh.

The Warlord jerked into action. "To me! To me! Retreat!" he cried. The Personal Guards struggled to comply, frantically casting off the most inconvenient bits of their armour. The generals and priests stampeded after the Warlord.

Still laughing helplessly, the Historian saw the oldest of the MagNordain litter bearers reach out a long arm and casually break the neck of a passing guardsman. The ceremonial broadsword, so cumbersome in Chahanen hands, proved deadly when wielded by a giant such as he.

A running body bowled the Historian off his feet. He landed face down, the impact knocking both the wind and the hysteria out of him.

Sprawled on his stomach, he watched while the other litter bearers armed themselves and set about the fleeing Chahanen soldiers. He watched the Gar slave pounce on top of the Sumoran Ambassador and beat him to death with his fists. He watched the halfling body slaves leap upon the King of Chahanesh and tear the screaming wretch apart.

The Historian buried his face in the grass and wished for a quick and painless death.

An eternity later, a foot shoved under his ribs and tipped him unceremoniously onto his back. He looked up into the grinning, blood-spattered face of the newly liberated MagNordain chieftain. The other former slaves stood behind him, united in that moment by hatred of their former masters. The giant pointed at the Historian with his bloody sword and said in accented Chahanen, "You are storyteller, yes?"

"I am an Historian, yes," he managed in response.

"Ha!" The barbarian reached down and grabbed him by the front of his robe. With no apparent effort, he lifted the Historian to his feet.

Sweeping the field with an extravagant gesture, the giant said, "Then write *this* his-story, storyteller."

MagNordain horsemen thundered past on either side of the hill, their great shaggy mounts bearing them towards the last remnants of the army of Chahanesh, gathered forlornly around the Warlord's banner.

In the distance, a thick column of black smoke billowed up from the shattered ruins of Rea. The Historian looked skyward. The Heretics were gone, leaving the rest of them to flounder in the dirt.

"Write this history," the giant said again.

"So, with its dying gasp, once-mighty Chahanesh drives the Heretics of Rea from the world. And from its ashes arises a new empire . . ." ✪

HOPSCOTCH

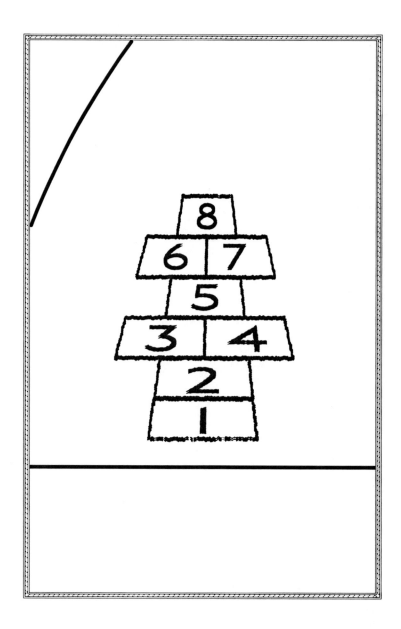

HOPSCOTCH

BY YOON HA LEE

8 | YOU'RE FAR FROM THE HOMESTAR, ON THE RUN FROM THE BIG GUNS. YOU think of the places scorched behind you: Forked glassy structures with their petal-sails spread toward the more assertive of twin stars. The fortress-wheel spinning in irrevocable fragments away from its tethers, burning up in transitory constellations over the planetmass. The girl-woman with the peony eyes and the weapons (guns, guns, guns) with your names inscribed on them in eighteen languages. Your faces.

You have eyes, and hands for all the good they do you, and—those problematic ones—lungs. You hear your breathing, and the ship counts the breaths remaining. At this rate both of you will be empty of oxygen. You carry the things gestation wrote upon your bones, but you never thought your lungs would betray you first.

(Those peony eyes. Your hands threading through her hair and into secret places, inner spaces. The moments you weren't sure who was breathing in and who was breathing out.)

6 | Your mother speaks the language of her mother and her mother's mother. You could interrupt her at her spreadsheets (rows and columns, the absent diagonal). You could lay before her a bouquet of words like peonies.

7 | You planned your route: signposts and ramps, always homing toward fuel. The skyview would show the heartbeat cities, the lightpulse web of roads. You want to unhinge that fractal network into further

315

The act would unroot her.

Anything to fill the lacunae:
words like bullets, smiles like
thorns. Secrets live in the gaps
left by honesty. Meanwhile, you
suffocate in expectations. Your
lover is forbidden from this roof (a
girl and a girl, yang with no yin)
or your father's. In this one thing
your parents are united.

This troubles you and you waver at
the doorway, waiting. This pleases
you and you leave her your footfalls
in the silence. This matters not at
all to you and you abandon your
shoes at the threshold, walking
away bare of family.

You seed absence behind you:
your chair askew the desk, the
window ajar for that unlikely
breath of breeze, sheet music
open to a troublesome phrase
in that Telemann concerto.
Your handwriting on the week's
assignments in place of the single
farewell you would have liked to
leave.

You can't write upon petals. You
don't try.

fractals, lose yourself in recursive
branchings.

Play the game on terrain of your
father's choosing. He has his
maps, the precise arrangement of
your progress across the court.
Sidestep each other, flanking
and unflanking: never flunking,
scattering hours of study into
moments of acceptable academic
brilliance.

Subvert the skirmishes even
there. In the transition of
phases, the unbearable balance
of the triple point, you see your
parents' divorce, yourself. In
the roseate whorls of nebulae,
you see her peony eyes, her
bemused sideways smile.
And this is where the calculus
overcomes you. She is the light
in your eyes, and what you are
to her (notes written in puns
upon the periodic table; her
shadow over your feet, waiting
for you at your locker) is hers to
determine.

She should not become a
battlefield. And so you desert
(her).

Say you're stranded amid drifts of strange dense dust, everywhere to hide but nowhere to seek. Say you're on the far side of a moon whose secret tides toll the days like bells, and your ship, trapped amid crags and frozen ammonia, can't accelerate to that magic number, escape velocity. Say the coruscating vines that define your engine have been stressed into improbable topiaries. Say you'd rather not blossom across the night's deeps in a one-time sacrificial rite of spring.

Say it straight. Stranded. This ship was such a nifty notion when you swept off with it. You loved the knife-sleek metal gleam, the hairpin turns and tricky rolls, the insouciant in-out slippage of distances your ancestors never dreamt in the soles of their feet.

So you traversed that random walk in curled dimensions, connecting disparate systems and their teeming worlds. An aeon's worth of negotiations compressed into the year-long summer of an aestivating habitat. The interception of unsigned communications, the flicker-fade of encryption modes parsed by intelligences with no other passion. The repair, after a botched landing, of the shells within shells armoring your ship.

Yours, your beauty, your blade into the galaxy. You pledged yourself to travel, and in traveling, fight—

(This one matters. This is the why. Without the why, you stop at x, that coy variable. Why? An empire that enslaved entire worlds by rooting their populations, feet into the soil, shears and gazebos. A general with eyes of ice and a smile of cinders, his orders, your *Never*. Velvet voices behind velvet masks, a marketplace of drugs and blood and subtle atrocities. These are not mutually incompatible.)

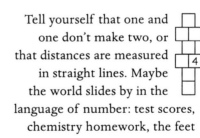

You breathed your words into her cupped hands. You drank each other's eyes, and there was only fire. You mirrored each other, arms crossed, eyes lowered, across a barrier of unempty desks. All the ways of

Tell yourself that one and one don't make two, or that distances are measured in straight lines. Maybe the world slides by in the language of number: test scores, chemistry homework, the feet

speech without words, poetry
without lines, you held out to
each other.

You've learned this language's
inverse from your parents'
separated houses, the alternating
weekends. Words have more
honest holes. They hollow you.
One house or the other, no
invitation encompasses you both.

A stone on the line is nowhere inside
any space. Move the fight elsewhere
and you have no moves left.

in a trochee—these code your
secret escape. Maybe your heart
is the pivot of a pendulum,
unmoved by the periodic
motion.

At this hour of night, as both
houses recede in miles traveled,
the roads are dead arteries. You're
the one red cell traveling the black.
You honor the yellow boundaries,
dotted, now and again, like a trail
of troubled stars. There are lines
you can't cross without crossing
yourself out.

Strategy enthralled you once upon a world. Skirt the slow-fading sculptures that have already stretched beyond recognizable matter, ghosting at the singularity's event horizon. Rest, for a while, in a void filled only by that microwave thrum. Hide amid the orbital traffic of other ships and manufactured moons around moons. Places to invade, spaces to escape.

Objects in motion stay in motion in motion in motion. Perpetual minus that frisson of truth, the heat-death arbiter. You thought your trajectory would take you to that final battle. You would scour the general from his own vast vessel, crying the words you should have shouted the first time around, which you've since knotted around your tongue and through your teeth. You would free worlds upon worlds to breathe their own mandates.

Objects at rest stay at rest at rest at rest. You didn't expect it to be midway to nowhere. You're used to throwing your stones (yourself) and watching the lines and spaces, waiting for the impact, hop skip jump moving on. Now you have gunshots, the small personal ones. Your eyes hands lungs might be waiting for that moment to betray you.

No motion, nothing, nowhere. Caught between.

Say you find the exotic material that powers this gun-ship, a route for this knife-ship, some unmined secret source of the oxygen that airs this wind-ship. You continue your journey. Three worlds orbiting ever nearer a nexus of broken rock and spumes of frothing heat. A song that stretches across three galaxies in a harmony beyond hearing, written in changing spiral density waves, gathering you up in a figured bass. Unexpected allies who travel in prime-number groups, a living sieve of Eratosthenes.

No.

Nowhere.

(You were wrong. It's the hands after all. So hard to stop reaching, when nothing's left to reach.)

Your hands on the wheel take you to a gas station; your feet, to a phone booth. The lights are a pittance of stars, but your fingers know the numbers, your heart the pattern.

A battlefield you flee remains a battlefield. You can't balance yourself on the boundary forever. It's time she knew your story and told you hers, whatever the hour. She might be waiting, herself stranded. She might have a trajectory intersecting yours, or guiding her elsewhere entirely.

The phone rings and you exhale her name, inhale, listen.

Your father's eyes of ice have given you nowhere to go; your mother's pale disappointment has given you nowhere to grow. Instead, you have galaxies, the nights of a thousand thousand worlds for the plucking, peonies breathing their scent across your hands. Cast your stone and begin the journey again; there's no other way to find out where's

Home. ✪

A SIEGE OF CRANES

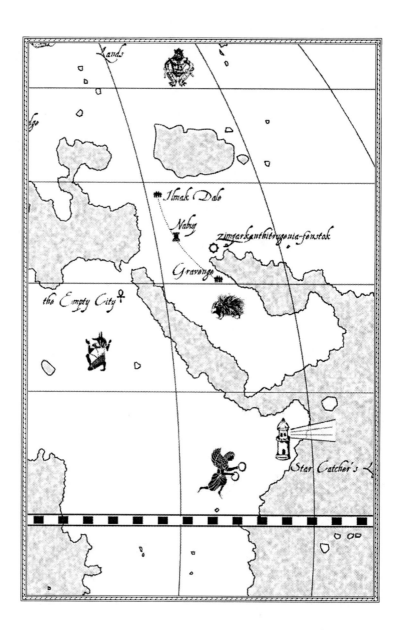

Lands

Ilmak Dale

Nabeg

zimtarkanthitrugonia-fenstok

Gravénge

the Empty City

Star Catcher's

A SIEGE OF CRANES

BY BENJAMIN ROSENBAUM

THE LAND AROUND MARISH WAS FULL OF THE GREEN STALKS OF SUNFLOWERS: tall as men, with bold yellow faces. Their broad leaves were stained black with blood.

The rustling came again, and Marish squatted down on aching legs to watch. A hedgehog pushed its nose through the stalks. It sniffed in both directions.

Hunger dug at Marish's stomach like the point of a stick. He hadn't eaten for three days, not since returning to the crushed and blackened ruins of his house.

The hedgehog bustled through the stalks onto the trail, across the ash, across the trampled corpses of flowers. Marish waited until it was well clear of the stalks before he jumped. He landed with one foot before its nose and one foot behind its tail. The hedgehog, as hedgehogs will, rolled itself into a ball, spines out.

His house: crushed like an egg, smoking, the straw floor soaked with blood. He'd stood there with a trapped rabbit in his hand, alone in the awful silence. Forced himself to call for his wife Temur and his daughter Asza, his voice too loud and too flat. He'd dropped the rabbit somewhere in his haste, running to follow the blackened trail of devastation.

Running for three days, drinking from puddles, sleeping in the sunflowers when he couldn't stay awake.

Marish held his knifepoint above the hedgehog. They gave wishes, sometimes, in tales. "Speak, if you can," he said, "and bid me don't kill you. Grant me a wish! Elsewise, I'll have you for a dinner."

Nothing from the hedgehog, or perhaps a twitch.

Marish drove his knife through it and it thrashed, spraying more blood on the bloodstained flowers.

Too tired to light a fire, he ate it raw.

On that trail of tortured earth, wide enough for twenty horses, among the burnt and flattened flowers, Marish found a little doll of rags, the size of a child's hand.

It was one of the ones Maghd the mad girl made, and offered up, begging for stew meat, or wheedling for old bread behind Lezur's bakery. He'd given her a coin for one, once.

"Wherecome you're giving that sow our good coins?" Temur had cried, her bright eyes flashing. None in Ilmak Dale would let a mad girl come near a hearth, and some spit when they passed her. "Bag-Maghd's good for holding one thing only," Fazt would call out and they'd laugh their way into the alehouse. Marish laughing too, stopping only when he looked back at her.

Temur had softened, when she saw how Asza took to the doll, holding it, and singing to it, and smearing gruel on its rag-mouth with her fingers to feed it. They called her "little life-light," and heard her saying it to the doll, "il-ife-ight," rocking it in her arms.

He pressed his nose into the doll, trying to smell Asza's baby smell on it, like milk and forest soil and some sweet spice. But he only smelled the acrid stench of burnt cloth.

When he forced his wet eyes open, he saw a blurry figure coming toward him. Cursing himself for a fool, he tossed the doll away and pulled out his knife, holding it at his side. He wiped his face on his sleeve, and stood up straight, to show the man coming down the trail that the folk of Ilmak Dale did no obeisance. Then his mouth went dry and his hair stood up, for the man coming down the trail was no man at all.

It was a little taller than a man, and had the body of a man, though covered with a dark gray fur; but its head was the head of a jackal. It wore

armor of bronze and leather, all straps and discs with curious engravings, and carried a great black spear with a vicious point at each end.

Marish had heard that there were all sorts of strange folk in the world,
but he had never seen anything like this.

"May you die with great suffering," the creature said in what seemed
to be a calm, friendly tone.

"May *you* die as soon as may be!" Marish cried, not liking to be
threatened.

The creature nodded solemnly. "I am Kadath-Naan of the Empty
City," it announced. "I wonder if I might ask your assistance in a small
matter."

Marish didn't know what to say to this. The creature waited.

Marish said, "You can ask."

"I must speak with . . ." It frowned. "I am not sure how to put this. I
do not wish to offend."

"Then why," Marish asked before he could stop himself, "did you
menace me on a painful death?"

"Menace?" the creature said. "I only greeted you."

"You said, 'May you die with great suffering.' That like to be a threat
or a curse, and I truly don't thank you for it."

The creature frowned. "No, it is a blessing. Or it is from a blessing:
'May you die with great suffering, and come to know holy dread and
divine terror, stripping away your vain thoughts and fancies until you are
fit to meet the Bone-White Fathers face to face; and may you be buried
in honor and your name sung until it is forgotten.' That is the whole
passage."

"Oh," said Marish. "Well, that sound a bit better, I reckon."

"We learn that blessing as pups," said the creature in a wondering
tone. "Have you never heard it?"

"No indeed," said Marish, and put his knife away. "Now what do
you need? I can't think to be much help to you—I don't know this land
here."

"Excuse my bluntness, but I must speak with an embalmer, or a sepul-christ, or someone of that sort."

"I've no notion what those are," said Marish.

The creature's eyes widened. It looked, as much as the face of a jackal could, like someone whose darkest suspicions were in the process of being confirmed.

"What do your people do with the dead?" it said.

"We put them in the ground."

"With what preparation? With what rites and monuments?" said the thing.

"In a wood box for them as can afford it, and a piece of linen for them as can't; and we say a prayer to the west wind. We put the stone in with them, what has their soul kept in it." Marish thought a bit, though he didn't much like the topic. He rubbed his nose on his sleeve. "Sometime we'll put a pile of stones on the grave, if it were someone famous."

The jackal-headed man sat heavily on the ground. It put its head in its hands. After a long moment it said, "Perhaps I should kill you now, that I might bury you properly."

"Now you just try that," said Marish, taking out his knife again.

"Would you like me to?" said the creature, looking up.

Its face was serene. Marish found he had to look away, and his eyes fell upon the scorched rags of the doll, twisted up in the stalks.

"Forgive me," said Kadath-Naan of the Empty City. "I should not be so rude as to tempt you. I see that you have duties to ful-fill, just as I do, before you are permitted the descent into emptiness. Tell me which way your village lies, and I will see for myself what is done."

"My village—" Marish felt a heavy pressure behind his eyes, in his throat, wanting to push through into a sob. He held it back. "My village is gone. Something come and crushed it. I were off hunting, and when I come back, it were all burning, and full of the stink of blood. Whatever did it made this trail through the flowers. I think it went quick; I don't think I'll likely catch it. But I hope to." He knew he sounded absurd: a peasant chasing a demon. He gritted his teeth against it.

"I see," said the monster. "And where did this something come from? Did the trail come from the North?"

"It didn't come from nowhere. Just the village torn to pieces and this trail leading out."

"And the bodies of the dead," said Kadath-Naan carefully. "You buried them in—wooden boxes?"

"There weren't no bodies," Marish said. "Not of people. Just blood, and a few pieces of bone and gristle, and pigs' and horses' bodies all charred up. That's why I'm following." He looked down. "I mean to find them if I can."

Kadath-Naan frowned. "Does this happen often?"

Despite himself, Marish laughed. "Not that I ever heard before."

The jackal-headed creature seemed agitated. "Then you do not know if the bodies received . . . even what you would consider proper burial."

"I have a feeling they ain't received it," Marish said.

Kadath-Naan looked off in the distance towards Marish's village, then in the direction Marish was heading. It seemed to come to a decision. "I wonder if you would accept my company in your travels," it said. "I was on a different errand, but this matter seems to . . . outweigh it."

Marish looked at the creature's spear and said, "You'd be welcome." He held out the fingers of his hand. "Marish of Ilmak Dale."

The trail ran through the blackened devastation of another village, drenched with blood but empty of human bodies. The timbers of the houses were crushed to kindling; Marish saw a blacksmith's anvil twisted like a lock of hair, and plows that had been melted by enormous heat into a pool of iron. They camped beyond the village, in the shade of a twisted hawthorn tree. A wild autumn wind stroked the meadows around them, carrying dandelion seeds and wisps of smoke and the stink of putrefying cattle.

The following evening they reached a hill overlooking a great town curled around a river. Marish had never seen so many houses—almost too many to count. Most were timber and mud like those of his village, but some were great structures of stone, towering three or four stories into the air. House built upon house, with ladders reaching up to the doors of the ones on top. Around the town, fields full of wheat rustled gold in the evening light. Men and women were reaping in the fields, singing work songs as they swung their scythes.

The path of destruction curved around the town, as if avoiding it.

"Perhaps it was too well defended," said Kadath-Naan.

"May be," said Marish, but he remembered the pool of iron and the crushed timbers, and doubted. "I think that like to be Nabuz. I never come this far south before, but traders heading this way from the fair at Halde were always going to Nabuz to buy."

"They will know more of our adversary," said Kadath-Naan.

"I'll go," said Marish. "You might cause a stir; I don't reckon many of your sort visit Nabuz. You keep to the path."

"Perhaps I might ask of you . . ."

"If they are friendly there, I'll ask how they bury their dead," Marish said.

Kadath-Naan nodded somberly. "Go to duty and to death," he said.

Marish thought it must be a blessing, but he shivered all the same.

The light was dimming in the sky. The reapers heaped the sheaves high on the wagon, their songs slow and low, and the city gates swung open for them.

The city wall was stone, mud, and timber, twice as tall as a man, and its great gates were iron. But the wall was not well kept. Marish crept among the stalks to a place where the wall was lower and trash and rubble were heaped high against it.

He heard the creak of the wagon rolling through the gates, the last work song fading away, the men of Nabuz calling out to each other as they made their way home. Then all was still.

Marish scrambled out of the field into a dead run, scrambled up the rubble, leapt atop the wall and lay on its broad top. He peeked over, hoping he had not been seen.

The cobbled street was empty. More than that, the town itself was silent. Even in Ilmak Dale, the evenings had been full of dogs barking, swine grunting, men arguing in the streets and women gossiping and calling the children in. Nabuz was supposed to be a great capital of whoring, drinking and fighting; the traders at Halde had always moaned over the delights that awaited them in the south if they could cheat the villagers well enough. But Marish heard no donkey braying, no baby crying, no cough, no whisper: nothing pierced the night silence.

He dropped over, landed on his feet quiet as he could, and crept along the street's edge. Before he had gone ten steps, he noticed the lights.

The windows of the houses flickered, but not with candlelight or the light of fires. The light was cold and blue.

He dragged a crate under the high window of the nearest house and clambered up to see.

There was a portly man with a rough beard, perhaps a potter after his day's work; there was his stout young wife, and a skinny boy of nine or ten. They sat on their low wooden bench, their dinner finished and put to the side (Marish could smell the fresh bread and his stomach cursed him). They were breathing, but their faces were slack, their eyes wide and staring, their lips gently moving. They were bathed in blue light. The potter's wife was rocking her arms gently as if she were cradling a newborn babe—but the swaddling blankets she held were empty.

And now Marish could hear a low inhuman voice, just at the edge of hearing, like a thought of his own. It whispered in time to the flicker of the blue light, and Marish felt himself drawn by its caress. Why not sit with the potter's family on the bench? They would take him in. He could stay here, the whispering promised: forget his village, forget his grief. Fresh bread on the hearth, a warm bed next to the coals of the fire. Work the clay, mix the slip for the potter, eat a dinner of bread and cheese, then listen to the blue light and do what it told him. Forget the mud roads of Ilmak Dale, the laughing roar of Perdan and Thin Deri and Chibar and the others in its alehouse, the harsh cough and crow of its roosters at dawn. Forget willowy Temur, her hair smooth as a river and bright as a sheaf of wheat, her proud shoulders and her slender waist, Temur turning her satin cheek away when he tried to kiss it. Forget the creak and splash of the mill, and the soft rushes on the floor of Maghd's hovel. The potter of Nabuz had a young and willing niece who needed a husband, and the blue light held laughter and love enough for all. Forget the heat and clanging of Fat Deri's smithy; forget the green stone that held Pa's soul, that he'd laid upon his shroud. Forget Asza, little Asza whose tiny body he'd held to his heart . . .

Marish thought of Asza and he saw the potter's wife's empty arms and with one flex of his legs, he kicked himself away from the wall, knocking over the crate and landing sprawled among rolling apples.

He sprang to his feet. There was no sound around him. He stuffed five apples in his pack, and hurried towards the center of Nabuz.

The sun had set, and the moon washed the streets in silver. From every window streamed the cold blue light.

Out of the corner of his eye he thought he saw a shadow dart behind him, and he turned and took out his knife. But he saw nothing, and though his good sense told him five apples and no answers was as much as he should expect from Nabuz, he kept on.

He came to a great square full of shadows, and at first he thought of trees. But it was tall iron frames, and men and women bolted to them upside down. The bolts went through their bodies, crusty with dried blood.

One man nearby was live enough to moan. Marish poured a little water into the man's mouth, and held his head up, but the man could not swallow; he coughed and spluttered, and the water ran down his face and over the bloody holes where his eyes had been.

"But the babies," the man rasped, "how could you let her have the babies?"

"Let who?" said Marish.

"The White Witch!" the man roared in a whisper. "The White Witch, you bastards! If you'd but let us fight her—"

"Why . . ." Marish began.

"Lie again, say the babies will live forever—lie again, you cowardly blue-blood maggots in the corpse of Nabuz . . ." He coughed and blood ran over his face.

The bolts were fast into the frame. "I'll get a tool," Marish said, "you won't—"

From behind him came an awful scream.

He turned and saw the shadow that had followed him: it was a white cat with fine soft fur and green eyes that blazed in the darkness. It shrieked, its fur standing on end, its tail high, staring at him, and his good sense told him it was raising an alarm.

Marish ran, and the cat ran after him, shrieking. Nabuz was a vast pile of looming shadows. As he passed through the empty city gates he heard a grinding sound and a whinny. As he raced into the moonlit dusk of open land, down the road to where Kadath-Naan's shadow crossed the demon's path, he heard hoofbeats galloping behind him.

Kadath-Naan had just reached a field of tall barley. He turned to look back at the sound of the hoofbeats and the shrieking of the devil cat. "Into the grain!" Marish yelled. "Hide in the grain!" He passed Kadath-Naan and dived into the barley, the cat racing behind him.

Suddenly he spun and dropped and grabbed the white cat, meaning to get one hand on it and get his knife with the other and shut it up by killing it. But the cat fought like a devil and it was all he could do to hold on to it with both hands. And he saw, behind him on the trail, Kadath-Naan standing calmly, his hand on his spear, facing three knights armored every inch in white, galloping towards them on great chargers.

"You damned dog-man," Marish screamed. "I know you want to die, but get into the grain!"

Kadath-Naan stood perfectly still. The first knight bore down on him, and the moon flashed from the knight's sword. The blade was no more than a handsbreadth from Kadath-Naan's neck when he sprang to the side of it, into the path of the second charger.

As the first knight's charge carried him past, Kadath-Naan knelt, and drove the base of his great spear into the ground. Too late, the second knight made a desperate yank on the horse's reins, but the great beast's momentum carried him into the pike. It tore through the neck of the horse and through the armored chest of the knight riding him, and the two of them reared up and thrashed once like a dying centaur, then crashed to the ground.

The first knight wheeled around. The third met Kadath-Naan. The beast-man stood barehanded, the muscles of his shoulders and chest relaxed. He cocked his jackal head to one side, as if wondering: *Is it here at last? The moment when I am granted release?*

But Marish finally had the cat by its tail, and flung that wild white thing, that frenzy of claws and spit and hissing, into the face of the third knight's steed.

The horse reared and threw its rider; the knight let go of his sword as he crashed to the ground. Quick as a hummingbird, Kadath-Naan leapt and caught it in midair. He spun to face the last rider.

Marish drew his knife and charged through the barley. He was on the fallen knight just as he got to his knees.

The crash against armor took Marish's wind away. The man was twice as strong as Marish was, and his arm went around Marish's chest like a crushing band of iron. But Marish had both hands free, and with a twist of the knight's helmet he exposed a bit of neck, and in Marish's knife went, and then the man's hot blood was spurting out.

The knight convulsed as he died and grabbed Marish in a desperate embrace, coating him with blood, and sobbing once: and Marish held him, for the voice of his heart told him it was a shame to have to die such a way. Marish was shocked at this, for the man was a murderous slave of the White Witch; but still he held the quaking body in his arms, until it moved no more.

Then Marish, soaked with salty blood, staggered to his feet and remembered the last knight with a start; but of course Kadath-Naan had killed him in the meantime. Three knights' bodies lay on the ruined ground, and two living horses snorted and pawed the dirt like awkward mourners. Kadath-Naan freed his spear with a great yank from the horse and man it had transfixed. The devil cat was a sodden blur of white fur and blood; a falling horse had crushed it.

Marish caught the reins of the nearest steed, a huge fine creature, and gentled it with a hand behind its ears. When he had his breath again, Marish said, "We got horses now. Can you ride?"

Kadath-Naan nodded.

"Let's go then; there like to be more coming."

Kadath-Naan frowned a deep frown. He gestured to the bodies.

"What?" said Marish.

"We have no embalmer or sepulchrist, it is true; yet I am trained in the funereal rites for military expeditions and emergencies. I have the necessary tools; in a matter of a day I can raise small monuments. At least they died aware and with suffering; this must compensate for the rudimentary nature of the rites."

"You can't be in earnest," said Marish. "And what of the White Witch?"

"Who is the White Witch?" Kadath-Naan asked.

"The demon; turns out she's somebody what's called the White Witch. She spared Nabuz, for they said they'd serve her, and give her their babies."

"We will follow her afterwards," said Kadath-Naan.

"She's ahead of us as it is! We leave now on horseback, we might have a chance. There be a whole lot more bodies with her unburied or buried wrong, less I mistake."

Kadath-Naan leaned on his spear. "Marish of Ilmak Dale," he said, "here we must part ways. I cannot steel myself to follow such logic as you declare, abandoning these three burials before me now for the chance of others elsewhere, if we can catch and defeat a witch. My duty does not lie that way." He searched Marish's face. "You do not have the words for it, but if these men are left unburied, they are *tanzadi*. If I bury them with what little honor I can provide, they are *tazrash*. They spent only a little while alive, but they will be *tanzadi* or *tazrash* forever."

"And if more slaves of the White Witch come along to pay you back for killing these?"

But try as he might, Marish could not dissuade him, and at last he mounted one of the chargers and rode onwards, towards the cold white moon, away from the whispering city.

The flowers were gone, the fields were gone. The ashy light of the horizon framed the ferns and stunted trees of a black fen full of buzzing flies. The trail was wider; thirty horses could have passed side by side over the blasted ground. But the marshy ground was treacherous, and Marish's mount sank to its fetlocks with each careful step.

A siege of cranes launched themselves from the marsh into the moon-abandoned sky. Marish had never seen so many. Bone-white, fragile, soundless, they ascended like snowflakes seeking the cold womb of heaven. Or a river of souls. None looked back at him. The voice of doubt told him: *You will never know what became of Asza and Temur.*

The apples were long gone, and Marish was growing light-headed from hunger. He reined the horse in and dismounted; he would have to hunt off the trail. In the bracken, he tied the charger to a great black fern as tall as a house. In a drier spot near its base was the footprint of a rabbit. He felt the indentation; it was fresh. He followed the rabbit deeper into the fen.

His was thinking of Temur and her caresses. The nights she'd turn away from him, back straight as a spear, and the space of rushes between them would be like a frozen desert, and he'd huddle unsleeping beneath skins and woolen blankets, stiff from cold, arguing silently with her in his spirit; and the nights when she'd turn to him, her soft skin hot and alive against his, seeking him silently, almost vengefully, as if showing him—see? This is what you can have. This is what I am.

And then the image of those rushes charred and brown with blood and covered with chips of broken stone and mortar came to him, and he forced himself to think of nothing: breathing his thoughts out to the west wind, forcing his mind clear as a spring stream. And he stepped forward in the marsh.

And stood in a street of blue and purple tile, in a fantastic city.

He stood for a moment wondering, and then he carefully took a step back.

And he was in a black swamp with croaking toads and nothing to eat.

The voice of doubt told him he was mad from hunger; the voice of hope told him he would find the White Witch here and kill her; and thinking a thousand things, he stepped forward again and found himself still in the swamp.

Marish thought for a while, and then he stepped back, and, thinking of nothing, stepped forward.

The tiles of the street were a wild mosaic—some had glittering jewels; some had writing in a strange flowing script; some seemed to have tiny windows into tiny rooms. Houses, tiled with the same profusion, towered like columns, bulged like mushrooms, melted like wax. Some danced. He heard soft murmurs of conversation, footfalls, and the rush of a river.

In the street, dressed in feathers or gold plates or swirls of shadow, blue-skinned people passed. One such creature, dressed in fine silk, was just passing Marish.

"Your pardon," said Marish, "what place be this here?"

The man looked at Marish slowly. He had a red jewel in the center of his forehead, and it flickered as he talked. "That depends on how you enter it," he said, "and who you are, but for you, catarrhine, its name is Zimzarkanthitrugenia-fenstok, not least because that is easy for you to pronounce. And now I have given you one thing free, as you are a guest of the city."

"How many free things do I get?" said Marish.

"Three. And now I have given you two."

Marish thought about this for a moment. "I'd favor something to eat," he said.

The man looked surprised. He led Marish into a building that looked like a blur of spinning triangles, through a dark room lit by candles, to a table piled with capon and custard and razor-thin slices of ham and lamb's foot jelly and candied apricots and goatsmilk yogurt and hard cheese and yams and turnips and olives and fish cured in strange spices; and those were just the things Marish recognized.

"I don't reckon I ought to eat fairy food," said Marish, though he could hardly speak from all the spit that was suddenly in his mouth.

"That is true, but from the food of the djinn you have nothing to fear. And now I have given you three things," said the djinn, and he bowed and made as if to leave.

"Hold on," said Marish (as he followed some candied apricots down his gullet with a fistful of cured fish). "That be all the free things, but say I got something to sell?"

The djinn was silent.

"I need to kill the White Witch," Marish said, eating an olive. The voice of doubt asked him why he was telling the truth, if this city might also serve her; but he told it to hush up. "Have you got aught to help me?"

The djinn still said nothing, but he cocked an eyebrow.

"I've got a horse, a real fighting horse," Marish said, around a piece of cheese.

"What is its name?" said the djinn. "You cannot sell anything to a djinn unless you know its name."

Marish wanted to lie about the name, but he found he could not. He swallowed. "I don't know its name," he admitted.

"Well then," said the djinn.

"I killed the fellow what was on it," Marish said, by way of explanation.

"Who," said the djinn.

"Who what?" said Marish.

"Who was on it," said the djinn.

"I don't know his name either," said Marish, picking up a yam.

"No, I am not asking that," said the djinn crossly, "I am telling you to say, 'I killed the fellow who was on it.'"

Marish set the yam back on the table.

"Now that's enough," Marish said. "I thank you for the fine food and I thank you for the three free things, but I do not thank you for telling me how to talk. How I talk is how we talk in Ilmak Dale, or how we did talk when there were an Ilmak Dale, and just because the White Witch blasted Ilmak Dale to splinters don't mean I am going to talk like folk do in some magic city."

"I will buy that from you," said the djinn.

"What?" said Marish, and wondered so much at this that he forgot to pick up another thing to eat.

"The way you talked in Ilmak Dale," the djinn said.

"All right," Marish said, "and for it, I crave to know the thing what will help me mostways, for killing the White Witch."

"I have a carpet that flies faster than the wind," said the djinn. "I think it is the only way you can catch the Witch, and unless you catch her, you cannot kill her."

"Wonderful," Marish cried with glee. "And you'll trade me that carpet for how we talk in Ilmak Dale?"

"No," said the djinn, "I told you which thing would help you most, and in return for that, I took the way you talked in Ilmak Dale and put it in the Great Library."

Marish frowned. "All right, what do you want for the carpet?"

The djinn was silent.

"I'll give you the White Witch for it," Marish said.

"You must possess the thing you sell," the djinn said.

"Oh, I'll get her," Marish said. "You can be sure of that." His hand had found a boiled egg, and the shell crunched in his palm as he said it.

The djinn looked at Marish carefully, and then he said, "The use of the carpet, for three days, in return for the White Witch, if you can conquer her."

"Agreed," said Marish.

They had to bind the horse's eyes; otherwise it would rear and kick, when the carpet rose into the air. Horse, man, djinn: all perched on a span of cloth. As they sped back to Nabuz like a mad wind, Marish tried not to watch the solid fields flying beneath, and regretted the candied apricots.

The voice of doubt told him that his companion must be slain by now, but his heart wanted to see Kadath-Naan again; but for the jackal-man, Marish was friendless.

Among the barley stalks, three man-high plinths of black stone, painted with white glyphs, marked three graves. Kadath-Naan had only traveled a little ways beyond them before the ambush. How long the emissary of the Empty City had been fighting, Marish could not tell; but he staggered and weaved like a man drunk with wine or exhaustion. His gray fur was matted with blood and sweat.

An army of children in white armor surrounded Kadath-Naan. As the carpet swung closer, Marish could see their gray faces and blank eyes.

Some crawled, some tottered: none seemed to have lived more than six years of mortal life. They held daggers. One clung to the jackal-man's back, digging canals of blood.

Two of the babies were impaled on the point of the great black spear. Hand over hand, daggers held in their mouths, they dragged themselves down the shaft towards Kadath-Naan's hands. Hundreds more surrounded him, closing in.

Kadath-Naan swung his spear, knocking the slack-eyed creatures back. He struck with enough force to shatter human skulls, but the horrors only rolled, and scampered giggling back to stab his legs. With each swing, the spear was slower. Kadath-Naan's eyes rolled back into their sockets. His great frame shuddered from weariness and pain.

The carpet swung low over the battle, and Marish lay on his belly, dangling his arms down to the jackal-headed warrior. He shouted: "Jump! Kadath-Naan, jump!"

Kadath-Naan looked up and, gripping his spear in both hands, he tensed his legs to jump. But the pause gave the tiny servitors of the White Witch their chance; they swarmed over his body, stabbing with their daggers, and he collapsed under the writhing mass of his enemies.

"Down further! We can haul him aboard!" yelled Marish.

"I sold you the use of my carpet, not the destruction of it," said the djinn.

With a snarl of rage, and before the voice of his good sense could speak, Marish leapt from the carpet. He landed amidst the fray, and began tearing the small bodies from Kadath-Naan and flinging them into the fields. Then daggers found his calves, and small bodies crashed into his sides, and he tumbled, covered with the white-armored hell-children. The carpet sailed up lazily into the summer sky.

Marish thrashed, but soon he was pinned under a mass of small bodies. Their daggers probed his sides, drawing blood, and he gritted his teeth against a scream; they pulled at his hair and ears and pulled open his mouth to look inside. As if they were playing. One gray-skinned suckling child, its scalp peeled half away to reveal the white bone of its skull, nuzzled at his neck, seeking the nipple it would never find again.

So had Asza nuzzled against him. So had been her heft, then, light and snug as five apples in a bag. But her live eyes saw the world, took it in and made it better than it was. In those eyes he was a hero, a giant to lift her, honest and gentle and brave. When Temur looked into those otter-brown, mischievous eyes, her mouth softened from its hard line, and she sang fairy songs.

A dagger split the skin of his forehead, bathing him in blood. Another dug between his ribs, another popped the skin of his thigh. Another pushed against his gut, but hadn't broken through. He closed his eyes. They weighed heavier on him now; his throat tensed to scream, but he could not catch his breath.

Marish's arms ached for Asza and Temur—ached that he would die here, without them. Wasn't it right, though, that they be taken from him? The little girl who ran to him across the fields of an evening, a funny hopping run, her arms flung wide, waving that rag doll; no trace of doubt in her. And the beautiful wife who stiffened when she saw him, but smiled one-edged, despite herself, as he lifted apple-smelling Asza in his arms. He had not deserved them.

His face, his skin were hot and slick with salty blood. He saw, not felt, the daggers digging deeper—arcs of light across a great darkness. He wished he could comfort Asza one last time, across that darkness. As when she would awaken in the night, afraid of witches: now a witch had come.

He found breath, he forced his mouth open, and he sang through sobs to Asza, his song to lull her back to sleep:

"Now sleep, my love, now sleep—
  The moon is in the sky—
The clouds have fled like sheep—
  You're in your papa's eye.

"Sleep now, my love, sleep now—
   The bitter wind is gone—
The calf sleeps with the cow—
   Now sleep my love 'til dawn."

He freed his left hand from the press of bodies. He wiped blood and tears from his eyes. He pushed his head up, dizzy, flowers of light still exploding across his vision. The small bodies were still. Carefully, he eased them to the ground.

The carpet descended, and Marish hauled Kadath-Naan onto it. Then he forced himself to turn, swaying, and look at each of the gray-skinned babies sleeping peacefully on the ground. None of them was Asza.

He took one of the smallest and swaddled it with rags and bridle leather. His blood made his fingers slick, and the noon sun seemed as gray as a stone. When he was sure the creature could not move, he put it in his pack and slung the pack upon his back. Then he fell onto the carpet. He felt it lift up under him, and like a cradled child, he slept.

He awoke to see clouds sailing above him. The pain was gone. He sat up and looked at his arms: they were whole and unscarred. Even the old scar from Thin Deri's careless scythe was gone.

"You taught us how to defeat the Children of Despair," said the djinn. "That required recompense. I have treated your wounds and those of your companion. Is the debt clear?"

"Answer me one question," Marish said.

"And the debt will be clear?" said the djinn.

"Yes, may the west wind take you, it'll be clear!"

The djinn blinked in assent.

"Can they be brought back?" Marish asked. "Can they be made into living children again?"

"They cannot," said the djinn. "They can neither live nor die, nor be harmed at all unless they will it. Their hearts have been replaced with sand."

They flew in silence, and Marish's pack seemed heavier.

○

The land flew by beneath them as fast as a cracking whip; Marish stared as green fields gave way to swamp, swamp to marsh, marsh to rough pastureland. The devastation left by the White Witch seemed gradually newer; the trail here was still smoking, and Marish thought it might be too hot to walk on. They passed many a blasted village, and each time Marish looked away.

At last they began to hear a sound on the wind, a sound that chilled Marish's heart. It was not a wail, it was not a grinding, it was not a shriek of pain, nor the wet crunch of breaking bones, nor was it an obscene grunting; but it had something of all of these. The jackal-man's ears were perked, and his gray fur stood on end.

The path was now truly still burning; they flew high above it, and the rolling smoke underneath was like a fog over the land. But there ahead they saw the monstrous thing that was leaving the trail; and Marish could hardly think any thought at all as they approached, but only stare, bile burning his throat.

It was a great chariot, perhaps eight times the height of a man, as wide as the trail, constructed of parts of living human bodies welded together in an obscene tangle. A thousand legs and arms pawed the ground; a thousand more beat the trail with whips and scythes, or clawed the air. A thick skein of hearts, livers, and stomachs pulsed through the center of the thing, and a great assemblage of lungs breathed at its core. Heads rolled like wheels at the bottom of the chariot, or were stuck here and there along the surface of the thing as slack-eyed, gibbering ornaments. A thousand spines and torsos built a great chamber at the top of the chariot, shielded with webs of skin and hair; there perhaps hid the White Witch. From the pinnacle of the monstrous thing flew a great flag made of writhing tongues. Before the awful chariot rode a company of ten knights in white armor, with visored helms.

At the very peak sat a great headless hulking beast, larger than a bear, with the skin of a lizard, great yellow globes of eyes set on its shoulders and a wide mouth in its belly. As they watched, it vomited a gout of flame that set the path behind the chariot ablaze. Then it noticed them, and lifted the great plume of flame in their direction. At a swift word from the djinn, the carpet veered, but it was a close enough thing that Marish felt an oven's blast of heat on his skin. He grabbed the horse by its reins as it made to rear, and whispered soothing sounds in its ear.

"Abomination!" cried Kadath-Naan. "Djinn, will you send word to the Empty City? You will be well rewarded."

The djinn nodded.

"It is Kadath-Naan, lesser scout of the Endless Inquiry, who speaks. Let Bars-Kardereth, Commander of the Silent Legion, be told to hasten here. Here is an obscenity beyond compass, far more horrible than the innocent errors of savages; here Chaos blocks the descent into the Darkness entirely, and a whole land may fall to corruption."

The jewel in the djinn's forehead flashed once. "It is done," he said.

Kadath-Naan turned to Marish. "From the Empty City to this place is four days' travel for a Ghomlu Legion; let us find a place in their path where we can wait to join them."

Marish forced himself to close his eyes. But still he saw it—hands, tongues, guts, skin, woven into a moving mountain. He still heard the squelching, grinding, snapping sounds, the sea-roar of the thousand lungs. What had he imagined? Asza and Temur in a prison somewhere, waiting to be freed? Fool. "All right," he said.

Then he opened his eyes, and saw something that made him say, "No."

Before them, not ten minutes' ride from the awful chariot of the White Witch, was a whitewashed village, peaceful in the afternoon sun. Arrayed before it were a score of its men and young women. A few had proper swords or spears; one of the women carried a bow. The others had hoes, scythes, and staves. One woman sat astride a horse; the rest were on foot. From their perch in the air, Marish could see distant figures—families, stooped grandmothers, children in their mothers' arms—crawling like beetles up the faces of hills.

"Down," said Marish, and they landed before the village's defenders, who raised their weapons.

"You've got to run," he said, "you can make it to the hills. You haven't seen that thing—you haven't any chance against it."

A dark man spat on the ground. "We tried that in Gravenge."

"It splits up," said a black-bearded man. "Sends littler horrors, and they tear folks up and make them part of it, and you see your fellows' limbs, come after you as part of the thing. And they're fast. Too fast for us."

"We just busy it a while," another man said, "our folk can get far enough away." But he had a wild look in his eye: the voice of doubt was in him.

"We stop it here," said the woman on horseback.

Marish led the horse off the carpet, took its blinders off and mounted it. "I'll stand with you," he said.

"And welcome," said the woman on horseback, and her plain face broke into a nervous smile. It was almost pretty that way.

Kadath-Naan stepped off the carpet, and the villagers shied back, readying their weapons.

"This is Kadath-Naan, and you'll be damned glad you have him," said Marish.

"Where's your manners?" snapped the woman on horseback to her people. "I'm Asza," she said.

No, Marish thought, staring at her. No, but you could have been. He looked away, and after a while they left him alone.

The carpet rose silently off into the air, and soon there was smoke on the horizon, and the knights rode at them, and the chariot rose behind.

"Here we are," said Asza of the rocky lands, "now make a good accounting of yourselves."

An arrow sang; a white knight's horse collapsed. Marish cried "Ha!" and his mount surged forward. The villagers charged, but Kadath-Naan outpaced them all, springing between a pair of knights. He shattered the forelegs of one horse with his spear's shaft, drove its point through the side of the other rider. Villagers fell on the fallen knight with their scythes.

It was a heady wild thing for Marish, to be galloping on such a horse, a far finer horse than ever Redlegs had been, for all Pa's proud and vain attention to her. The warmth of its flanks, the rhythm of posting into its stride. Marish of Ilmak Dale, riding into a charge of knights: miserable addle-witted fool.

Asza flicked her whip at the eyes of a knight's horse, veering away. The knight wheeled to follow her, and Marish came on after him. He heard the hooves of another knight pounding the plain behind him in turn.

Ahead the first knight gained on Asza of the rocky plains. Marish took his knife in one hand, and bent his head to his horse's ear, and whispered to it in wordless murmurs: *Fine creature, give me everything.* And his horse pulled even with Asza's knight.

Marish swung down, hanging from his pommel—the ground flew by beneath him. He reached across and slipped his knife under the girth that held the knight's saddle. The knight swiveled, raising his blade to strike—then the girth parted, and he flew from his mount.

Marish struggled up into the saddle, and the second knight was there, armor blazing in the sun. This time Marish was on the sword-arm's side, and his horse had slowed, and that blade swung up and it could strike Marish's head from his neck like snapping off a sunflower; time for the peasant to die.

Asza's whip lashed around the knight's sword-arm. The knight seized the whip in his other hand. Marish sprang from the saddle. He struck a wall of chainmail and fell with the knight.

The ground was an anvil, the knight a hammer, Marish a rag doll sewn by a poor mad girl and mistaken for a horseshoe. He couldn't breathe; the world was a ringing blur. The knight found his throat with one mailed glove, and hissed with rage, and pulling himself up drew a dagger from his belt. Marish tried to lift his arms.

Then he saw Asza's hands fitting a leather noose around the knight's neck. The knight turned his visored head to see, and Asza yelled, "Yah!" An armored knee cracked against Marish's head, and then the knight was gone, dragged off over the rocky plains behind Asza's galloping mare.

Asza of the rocky lands helped Marish to his feet. She had a wild smile, and she hugged him to her breast; pain shot through him, as did the shock of her soft body. Then she pulled away, grinning, and looked over his shoulder back towards the village. And then the grin was gone.

Marish turned. He saw the man with the beard torn apart by a hundred grasping arms and legs. Two bending arms covered with eyes watched carefully as his organs were woven into the chariot. The village burned. A knight leaned from his saddle to cut a fleeing woman down, harvesting her like a stalk of wheat.

"No!" shrieked Asza, and ran towards the village.

Marish tried to run, but he could only hobble, gasping, pain tearing through his side. Asza snatched a spear from the ground and swung up onto a horse. Her hair was like Temur's, flowing gold. My Asza, my Temur, he thought. I must protect her.

Marish fell; he hit the ground and held onto it like a lover, as if he might fall into the sky. Fool, fool, said the voice of his good sense. That is not your Asza, or your Temur either. She is not yours at all.

He heaved himself up again and lurched on, as Asza of the rocky plains reached the chariot. From above, a lazy plume of flame expanded. The horse reared. The cloud of fire enveloped the woman, the horse, and then was sucked away; the blackened corpses fell to the ground steaming.

Marish stopped running.

The headless creature of fire fell from the chariot—Kadath-Naan was there at the summit of the horror, his spear sunk in the its flesh as a lever. But the fire-beast turned as it toppled, and a pillar of fire engulfed the jackal-man. The molten iron of his spear and armor coated his body, and he fell into the grasping arms of the chariot.

Marish lay down on his belly in the grass.

Maybe they will not find me here, said the voice of hope. But it was like listening to idiot words spoken by the wind blowing through a forest. Marish lay on the ground and he hurt. The hurt was a song, and it sang him. Everything was lost and far away. No Asza, no Temur, no Maghd; no quest, no hero, no trickster, no hunter, no father, no groom. The wind came down from the mountains and stirred the grass beside Marish's nose, where beetles walked.

There was a rustling in the short grass, and a hedgehog came out of it and stood nose to nose with Marish.

"Speak if you can," Marish whispered, "and grant me a wish."

The hedgehog snorted. "I'll not do *you* any favors, after what you did to Teodor!"

Marish swallowed. "The hedgehog in the sunflowers?"

"Obviously. Murderer."

"I'm sorry! I didn't know he was magic! I thought he was just a hedgehog!"

"Just a hedgehog! Just a hedgehog!" It narrowed its eyes, and its prickers stood on end. "Be careful what you call things, Marish of Ilmak Dale. When you name a thing, you say what it is in the world. Names mean more than you know."

Marish was silent.

"Teodor didn't like threats, that's all . . . the stubborn old idiot."

"I'm sorry about Teodor," said Marish.

"Yes, well," said the hedgehog. "I'll help you, but it will cost you dear."

"What do you want?"

"How about your soul?" said the hedgehog.

"I'd do that, sure," said Marish. "It's not like I need it. But I don't have it."

The hedgehog narrowed its eyes again. From the village, a few thin screams and the soft crackle of flames. It smelled like autumn, and butchering hogs.

"It's true," said Marish. "The priest of Ilmak Dale took all our souls and put them in little stones, and hid them. He didn't want us making bargains like these."

"Wise man," said the hedgehog. "But I'll have to have something. What have you got in you, besides a soul?"

"What do you mean, like, my wits? But I'll need those."

"Yes, you will," said the hedgehog.

"Hope? Not much of that left, though."

"Not to my taste anyway," said the hedgehog. *"Hope is foolish, doubts are wise."*

"Doubts?" said Marish.

"That'll do," said the hedgehog. "But I want them all."

"All . . . all right," said Marish. "And now you're going to help me against the White Witch?"

"I already have," said the hedgehog.

"You have? Have I got some magic power or other now?" asked Marish. He sat up. The screaming was over: he heard nothing but the fire, and the crunching and squelching and slithering and grinding of the chariot.

"Certainly not," said the hedgehog. "I haven't done anything you didn't see or didn't hear. But perhaps you weren't listening." And it waddled off into the green blades of the grass.

Marish stood and looked after it. He picked at his teeth with a thumbnail, and thought, but he had no idea what the hedgehog meant. But he had no doubts, either, so he started toward the village.

Halfway there, he noticed the dead baby in his pack wriggling, so he took it out and held it in his arms.

As he came into the burning village, he found himself just behind the great fire-spouting lizard-skinned headless thing. It turned and took a breath to burn him alive, and he tossed the baby down its throat. There was a choking sound, and the huge thing shuddered and twitched, and Marish walked on by it.

The great chariot saw him and it swung toward him, a vast mountain of writhing, humming, stinking flesh, a hundred arms reaching. Fists grabbed his shirt, his hair, his trousers, and they lifted him into the air.

He looked at the hand closed around his collar. It was a woman's hand, fine and fair, and it was wearing the copper ring he'd bought at Halde.

"Temur!" he said in shock.

The arm twitched and slackened; it went white. It reached out, the fingers spread wide; it caressed his cheek gently. And then it dropped from the chariot and lay on the ground beneath.

He knew the hands pulling him aloft. "Lezur the baker!" he whispered, and a pair of doughy hands dropped from the chariot. "Silbon and Felbon!" he cried. "Ter the blind! Sela the blue-eyed!" Marish's lips trembled to say the names, and the hands slackened and fell to the ground, and away on other parts of the chariot the other parts fell off too; he saw a blue eye roll down from above him and fall to the ground.

"Perdan! Mardid! Pilg and his old mother! Fazt—oh Fazt, you'll tell no more jokes! Chibar and his wife, the pretty foreign one!" His face was wet; with every name, a bubble popped open in Marish's chest, and his throat was thick with some strange feeling. "Pizdar the priest! Fat Deri, far from your smithy! Thin Deri!" When all the hands and arms of Ilmak Dale had fallen off, he was left standing free. He looked at the strange hands coming toward him. "You were a potter," he said to hands with clay under the nails, and they fell off the chariot. "And you were a butcher," he said to bloody ones, and they fell too. "A fat farmer, a beautiful young girl, a grandmother, a harlot, a brawler," he said, and enough hands and feet and heads and organs had slid off the chariot now that it sagged in the middle and pieces of it strove with each other blindly. "Men and women of Eckdale," Marish said, "men and women of Halde, of Gravenge, of the fields and the swamps and the rocky plains."

The chariot fell to pieces; some lay silent and still, others which Marish had not named had lost their purchase and thrashed on the ground.

The skin of the great chamber atop the chariot peeled away and the White Witch leapt into the sky. She was three times as tall as any woman; her skin was bone white; one eye was blood red and the other emerald green; her mouth was full of black fangs, and her hair of snakes and lizards. Her hands were full of lightning, and she sailed onto Marish with her fangs wide open.

And around her neck, on a leather thong, she wore a little doll of rags, the size of a child's hand.

"Maghd of Ilmak Dale," Marish said, and she was also a young woman with muddy hair and an uncertain smile, and that's how she landed before Marish.

"Well done, Marish," said Maghd, and pulled at a muddy lock of her hair, and laughed, and looked at the ground. "Well done! Oh, I'm glad. I'm glad you've come."

"Why did you do it, Maghd?" Marish said. "Oh, why?"

She looked up and her lips twitched and her jaw set. "Can you ask me that? You, Marish?"

She reached across, slowly, and took his hand. She pulled him, and he took a step towards her. She put the back of his hand against her cheek.

"You'd gone out hunting," she said. "And that Temur of yours"—she said the name as if it tasted of vinegar—"she seen me back of Lezur's, and for one time I didn't look down. I looked at her eyes, and she named me a foul witch. And then they were all crowding round—" She shrugged. "And I don't like that. Fussing and crowding and one against the other." She let go his hand and stooped to pick up a clot of earth, and she crumbled it in her hands. "So I knit them all together. All one thing. They did like it. And they were so fine and great and happy, I forgave them. Even Temur."

The limbs lay unmoving on the ground; the guts were piled in soft unbreathing hills, like drifts of snow. Maghd's hands were coated with black crumbs of dust.

"I reckon they're done of playing now," Maghd said, and sighed.

"How?" Marish said. "How'd you do it? Maghd, what *are* you?"

"Don't fool so! I'm Maghd, same as ever. I found the souls, that's all. Dug them up from Pizdar's garden, sold them to the Spirit of Unwinding Things." She brushed the dirt from her hands.

"And . . . the children, then? Maghd, the babes?"

She took his hand again, but she didn't look at him. She laid her cheek against her shoulder and watched the ground. "Babes shouldn't grow," she said. "No call to be big and hateful." She swallowed. "I made them perfect. That's all."

Marish's chest tightened. "And what now?"

She looked at him, and a slow grin crept across her face. "Well now," she said. "That's on you, ain't it, Marish? I got plenty of tricks yet, if you want to keep fighting." She stepped close to him, and rested her cheek on his chest. Her hair smelled like home: rushes and fire smoke, cold mornings and sheep's milk. "Or we can gather close. No one to shame us now." She wrapped her arms around his waist. "It's all new, Marish, but it ain't all bad."

A shadow drifted over them, and Marish looked up to see the djinn on his carpet, peering down. Marish cleared his throat. "Well . . . I suppose we're all we have left, aren't we?"

"That's so," Maghd breathed softly.

He took her hands in his, and drew back to look at her. "Will you be mine, Maghd?" he said.

"Oh yes," said Maghd, and smiled the biggest smile of her life.

"Very good," Marish said, and looked up. "You can take her now."

The djinn opened the little bottle that was in his hand and Maghd the White Witch flew into it, and he put the cap on. He bowed to Marish, and then he flew away.

Behind Marish the fire beast exploded with a dull boom.

Marish walked out of the village a little ways and sat, and after sitting a while he slept. And then he woke and sat, and then he slept some more. Perhaps he ate as well; he wasn't sure what. Mostly he looked at his hands; they were rough and callused, with dirt under the nails. He watched the wind painting waves in the short grass, around the rocks and bodies lying there.

One morning he woke, and the ruined village was full of jackal-headed men in armor made of discs who were mounted on great red cats with pointed ears, and jackal-headed men in black robes who were measuring for monuments, and jackal-headed men dressed only in loincloths who were digging in the ground.

Marish went to the ones in loincloths and said, "I want to help bury them," and they gave him a shovel. ✪

EPIC, THE

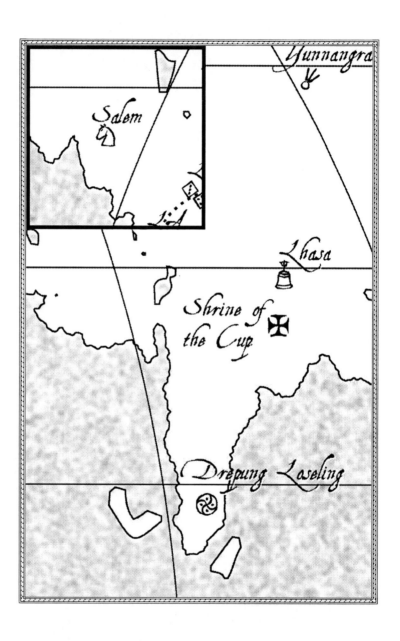

EPIC, THE
BY SCOTT WILLIAM CARTER

MARCH 15, 2005

Dear Mr. Moles and Ms. Groppi,

I am writing to ask you if it would be possible to get an extension on your deadline of March 21.

When I heard about your *Twenty Epics* anthology, I have to admit that I found the idea of writing an epic in under ten thousand words a bit daunting. I mean, brevity has never been my strong suit! So I decided to pass on the project and work on something more fitting my particular talents, some erotic hard science fiction, perhaps. At least, that was my original intention before I met the man in the white suit.

I am in the middle of a feverish work session right now, but I wanted to at least whip out this letter to plead with you for a short extension. A few weeks, at most. I guarantee you it will be worth it. I'll give you more details when I get a chance, but for now, please consider this letter a placeholder in your slush pile. The real manuscript, which I am now writing under the working title of "The Epic" (or "Epic, The" if you want to file your titles alphabetically), will be on your desk as soon as humanly possible. Perhaps even faster.

My stories have appeared or will shortly appear in *Analog, Weird Tales, Crimewave,* and *Cicada,* among other places.

Sincerely, Scott William Carter

☀

April 2, 2005

Dear Mr. Moles and Ms. Groppi,

Though I haven't heard back from you on my first letter, I'm operating
under the assumption that my request for an extension has been granted.
I certainly hope so, because the story is coming along nicely.

You deserve a better explanation of why I wasn't more on the ball
with getting you the story by your deadline, and I finally have a moment
(while my co-writer is out on the back porch, taking a "brandy break" as
he calls them) to explain.

On the day I wrote you the last letter, I went for a noon walk here
at the university where I work. We've had some unseasonably warm
weather here in the Willamette Valley and the sun was shining brightly
in a perfect blue sky. The scent of freshly mowed grass was strong in the
air. As I wandered the neighborhoods behind the school, I passed the
Woodland Park that was just on this side of the highway. The park was
empty except for an old man in a white suit and fedora who sat on the
bench near the swings. He had a belly that hung out over his belt, a full
white beard, and a face weathered and pock-marked as if he had lived a
hard life. He looked like a mix between Jerry Garcia and Santa Claus.

As I walked past, I nodded to him. He said something back to me,
but there was an eighteen-wheeler rumbling past on the highway on the
other side of the pine trees.

"What was that?" I asked. I expected him to tell me it was a nice day
or something similar.

"Have a nice day or something similar," he said.

I gaped at him. "Sorry?"

He laughed. It was a high-pitched pig squeal, not at all what I expected
from such a large man.

"You're a writer, aren't you?"

"Ah . . . yes." I was beginning to wonder what institution had allowed him to escape. The State Mental Hospital in Salem had closed years ago. I have a website, and my picture is on it, so it was possible he had looked me up and placed himself here because he guessed I would be walking by. Though I was a new writer with only a few credits, I knew it was possible I already had my first crazy fan.

I kept my distance.

"And," he said, "there's an anthology called *Twenty Epics* you were considering writing for but ultimately decided against?"

"How did you know that? What kind of game is this?"

"No game. I'm offering you the chance of a lifetime."

Then he went on to tell me that he had an idea for an epic short story so revolutionary and so groundbreaking that it would forever change the face of literature. He said he wasn't a writer, however, and he needed a capable young talent to partner with him to get the story onto the page. Would I like to help? Well, I figured I'd humor him for a few minutes, since he had been kind enough to flatter me (although I still kept my distance). He smiled and tipped his hat back on his head.

Then, his breath smelling of some sweet alcohol, he told me the story idea.

And he was right. Just the essence of it, a few sentences told in the jumbled fashion of a man who had no idea how to construct a story, moved me more than any piece of writing since *Flowers for Algernon*. And this, if it was handled right, would be even greater. It would be an epic of astonishing grace and beauty, adventure and heartache, romance and bravery—all in a mere five thousand words.

When he was finished, there was a long moment of silence. The world seemed different to me, clearer somehow. I took a deep breath, then told him I would use every ounce of my ability to make sure the story was told right. I knew that if I handled it correctly, both of our names would be linked with greatness no matter what we did the rest of our lives.

So he told me he would meet me at my house later in the day and we would begin. That's where we have been ever since. I have been burning up my sick leave (under the pretense of having a bad case of the flu) to work on this day and night. My wife has not been happy, but I told her it's all for art.

Whitey and I (Whitey being what I have taken to calling my Idea Man in the White Suit, since he still refuses to give me a name) are making good progress. Please, please be patient with us. Greatness, as Whitey has said to me more than once, can't be rushed.

My stories have appeared or will shortly appear in a number of magazines and anthologies. Though I haven't yet sold to the *New Yorker, Playboy, Esquire,* or *GQ,* I plan to appear in those prestigious markets in the near future.

Sincerely, Scott William Carter

☉

May 15, 2005

Dear David and Susan,

I hope you don't mind me calling you by your first names. I've spent so much time working on this project I almost feel like I know you by now.

Alas, it is my unfortunate duty to inform you that I have hit an impasse. I'm afraid all our hard work was for naught, and there's a good chance the story won't be finished.

Both my sick leave and my vacation have been completely exhausted, my boss has been leaving messages on my machine telling me I need to report to work or there will be consequences, and my wife and daughter are now staying at my mother-in-law's house. Whitey and I finished the first draft of The Epic two days ago. It clocked in at 1,567,986 words. My fingertips have been bleeding from the constant, round-the-clock typing, I have blisters on my bottom, and I've been averaging only three hours of sleep a night, but yes, the draft is done. I was a bit concerned at the word count, but Whitey assured me that this was part of the process to get to the true greatness of the story. Look at most of the multi-volume epics being published today, he insisted. Aren't they far too long? Couldn't they be pared down? Well, the five thousand word work of genius was now waiting for us in that million and a half words. We just had to find it.

There is only one problem. It's Whitey. I was napping on the couch at three in the morning three days ago when I heard a door slam. Whitey never sleeps himself, instead waits impatiently for me by the computer when my body demands a rest, so I was surprised not to see him when I woke. I looked everywhere in the house, but he wasn't there. It's been three days. Where is he? He needs to come back. He has to come back. If he doesn't come back, it won't be finished.

Scott William Carter, who has been working on a yet-to-be-pub-lished epic of staggering scope and depth, makes his home in Oregon. He has a two cats. More about his work can be found by doing a Web search under his name. His website currently has a Google ranking of 3.

Yours Truly, Scott

✪

May 15, 2005

Dear Dave and Susie,

All hope is not lost! Immediately after dropping my last letter into the blue mailbox on my corner, I discovered a clue to Whitey's whereabouts. Frustrated at the thought of not finishing The Epic, and the terrible loss this would be to the future of literature, I picked up my monitor to hurl it across the room. There, in an inch of dust and cobwebs, was an empty bottle of Alizé Red Passion. There was a crumpled piece of white paper inside.

I put down the monitor and retrieved the bottle. Using a pencil, I fished out the paper, which now smelled of cranberries and was red-stained at the edges. Smoothing it out, I saw that there were magazine pictures of various celebrities that had been pasted to it. There was Richard Gere, Brad Pitt, Harrison Ford, Adam Yauch, Steven Segal, Martin Scorsese, and Cindy Crawford, among other faces I didn't recognize. Dozens of them, wrinkled and bent, one overlapping the other.

I had no idea how these ideas people were related, so I punched all of their names into a few Web searches to see what came up. It took a bit of surfing, but it soon became very clear what linked them. They had all, at one time or another, supported a free Tibet. Nothing else made sense!

So I now believe that Whitey wants me to follow him to Tibet. For some reason he must believe that only there can The Epic be finished. I am going to dig out my passport, then arrange a flight. I'll be taking my laptop computer, plenty of spare batteries, and the entire manuscript in printed form. I will not stop until we have finished this story once and for all.

I don't even have to worry about my job anymore. I was informed in a letter yesterday that I no longer have it.

All my best, Scotty

✪

August 19, 2005

Dear David Groppi and Susan Moles

I have heard some disturbing rumors that you have already chosen your stories for *XX Epix*. I hope this is not true. I believe I have located Whitey, and soon we will once again be hard at worke.

It wasn't until last month that I finally found him. Months searching. Was growing desperte. No one in Tibet had heard of him. Finally I bumped into a spindly old man in the lobby of the Da Ji Jinjiang Hotel in Lhasa, the captiol of Tibet. He had thick glasses and gray sideburns as big and furry as mice. He said his name was Isaac and he had been in China since 1992. He had just gotten back from a tour of the Jokaang Temple. He talked and talked and I must be honest I thought he was a blowhard. Finally, when I was about to tell him I kneaded to get back to my room, he asked me why I was there. too tired to lie, I told him the truth. And then he said something amazeing. He told me knew the man I was talking about.

I told him to help me, but I must have seem too exited. He says to calm down and then asked me todinner, and we ate there in the restarnat. He tolde me he was once a writer of some stature himself, tho he never wrote any of that fantasy crap, and he had used the man I called Whitey (he had his own name for him) many, many times in his career. Muchof his success was based on Whitey's help, in fact.

But where could he be found, I said asked.

And thats when he tolde me the long and boring history of the Drepung Loseling monastery. Started in Lhasa in 1416 or something. The second Dalai Lama lived there. The Chinise in 1959 invated and burned all the monk places, and then a bunch of monks from Loseling escaped all the buchering and started over again in Karnataka State. Thats in South India. And over time it became real poplar and lots of new monks lerned there. Isaac said go there. Thats where Whitey will be waiting.

So thats what Im doing. I will will write again when I find Whiteyy.
[put impressive cretits here]

Sin seerly, Scott Robert Jordan

P.S. Something strage is happning to me.

☻

September 2 , 2005

Dear Gardner Moles and Ellen Groppi

I right to you frum India. I found Whitey. Isaac was rite. He was in the
[do research make sure names splet right] new Drepung Loseling monastery.
He was medatating outside the main shrine, on his knees, still in his
white suite, sipping from a bottle French Cognac. he had been waiting
for me and was very angry that it took me so longe to find him. He said
to meet him the nex morning outin the quart yard.

So I did as he says but he doesn't show. Come to find out he dies in his
sleep that night. They had a very big thing here for him. Lots of chanting
and wearing fancy clotheing with feathers and brite colours. But now I
have to finish The Epic on my own. I dont know if I can do it but the
monks here says I shud try. The say it is the jurney of my life to do this.
so I am going to. I am going to stay and finish.

It is very hot here. I wish I had better clotheses. My wife, tho, won't
send any and says only on the phone that I neede to call her lawer.

Trulee, Scott Wm. Carter, Esq.

☻

Knowvember 31, 2005

Dear Etitors,

It has now become a parent to Scott Robert Jordan Tolkien Wm. Carter, Esp. (who shall be refered to thenseforth as The Writer) that the manuscript in question (Epic, The) shall not be finished buy designaded time. The Writer wants the esteemed etitors of the soon to be published anthalogee to know that The Writer shall continue to worke on the story until it is finished, breaking only briefly to eat, sleep, meditate, or performe the chores required of all Monks here in XXX. This may take the reste of his life, since he has only the guide dance that the Budda chooses to inlighten him with, and his Mentor, Whitey, the Idea Man in the White Suite, is gone forever. the Writer is alone. afraid. but bravely he goes on.

The Writer's worke has been collected in such things as the *Bible*, *The Best of Elvis Presley*, and the *Kama Sutra*. U can find out more about Him by burnin cinnamon in sense.

Currrently makeing a mandala to cree ate
world harmonee, The Wrider

✪

At the time of publication, the editors had not received any further communication from Mr. Carter. Anyone with knowledge of his whereabouts, or of the whereabouts of his manuscript, is urged to contact us at editor@allstarstories.com. ✪

INDEX

INDEX

wizards
   cryptic xii
wolves 29
   breath of 31
   craftiness of 30
   defense against 33
   feeding habits of 32
   shepherds' hatred of 27
   war with 28
Wonder, Stevie 127
world
   end of 7, 197, 207
wounds 4

Y

Yggdrasil 202
youth
   everlasting 14
Yunnangrad 242

Z

Zen 230, 231, 232, 233, 234. *See also* Buddhism
Zimzarkanthitrugenia-fenstok 336

Printed in the United Kingdom
by Lightning Source UK Ltd.
121172UK00001B/157